The Princes of Xaviera

Two princes, conveniently wed!

You are cordially invited to celebrate the weddings of Xaviera's most eligible princes…

When Prince Dominic spends one night with Ginny Jones it comes at a price… a marriage of convenience in order to claim his heir!

Pregnant with a Royal Baby!

Prince Alex has always believed royal rules were made to be broken, but when his royal duty comes calling it's time for Alex to meet his Princess—and wife-to-be!

Available February 2016

Wedded for His Royal Duty

For better or for worse, these gorgeous princes are about to claim their brides!

Available July 2016

D1471889

WEDDED FOR HIS
ROYAL DUTY

BY
SUSAN MEIER

First Published in Great Britain 2016
By Mills & Boon, an imprint of HarperCollins*Publishers*
1 London Bridge Street, London, SE1 9GF

© 2016 Linda Susan Meier

ISBN: 978-0-263-92002-4

23-0716

Our policy is to use papers that are natural, renewable and recyclable products and made from wood grown in sustainable forests. The logging and manufacturing processes conform to the legal environmental regulations of the country of origin.

Printed and bound in Spain
by CPI, Barcelona

Susan Meier is the author of over fifty books for Mills & Boon. *The Tycoon's Secret Daughter* was a Romance Writers of America RITA® Award finalist, and *Nanny for the Millionaire's Twins* won the Book Buyers' Best award and was a finalist in the National Readers' Choice awards. She is married and has three children. One of eleven children, she loves to write about the complexity of families and totally believes in the power of love.

To my readers…
You inspire me to always write
the best stories for you!

CHAPTER ONE

PRINCE ALEXANDROS SANCHO drove his horse up a thin path that wound through the woods behind the palace grounds of his family's estate. Thor moved with the speed and agility of a true champion, creating a tunnel of wind that swirled around them.

Normally, Alex would be on the beach right now. Enjoying the bikini-clad beauties showing off their toned and tan bodies, pretending they were oblivious to the attention they drew.

With his ever-present bodyguards dressed as tourists, standing strategically around him, and a steady stream of friends at the ready, he'd swim a bit, have lunch, gamble, take a nap and then shower to start all over again.

First, he'd hit the casinos to see if he could find a woman who suited his mood as a companion for the evening, then they'd have dinner, maybe gamble some more and let the night take them where it would.

He nudged Thor to go faster. Today, he couldn't do any of the things he loved to do. Least of all find a willing female. No. Today was the day he would officially meet the woman he would marry.

The *princess*.

He all but spat the word in his mind as the wind caressed him, trying to soothe him and failing. He'd seen pictures of her, of course. Through the years, they'd also unofficially run into each other at boarding school. But she was several years younger, and he'd met her believing she'd be marrying his older brother Dominic as part of a treaty. So their greetings had been stilted, though polite. After boarding school, their paths never crossed again. She'd attended university in the United States where she'd taken up causes—everything from starving children to stray cats.

He struggled not to squeeze his eyes shut in frustration. Dominic had gotten a one-night stand pregnant, and he'd married Ginny because their son was the next heir to Xaviera's throne, which made Alex the only prince available to fulfill the terms of the treaty with Grennady. Princess Eva had turned twenty-five a few months before. She was officially marriage age, and his time of doing what he wanted, when he wanted, was up.

Even worse, she would be Grennady's queen one day. Marrying a crusader who would be queen seemed apt punishment for a prince who'd spent his life avoiding responsibility.

With another nudge to Thor, he sent the horse galloping toward the stable, only slowing the pace when they got close to the wide wooden barn door. He jumped off and tossed his riding crop to a servant girl milling about the building. Her faded blue jeans and T-shirt showed off a fantastic figure, but it was her dark hair and pale blue-gray eyes that made his hormones sit up and take notice.

Any other day, he'd flirt, itching to run his hands through the shiny black locks that probably reached her bottom when they weren't hiked up in a ponytail. But, today, he was about to meet his future bride.

"Thor gets the star treatment," he said, taking off the black helmet that matched his black leather boots and gloves. "Don't think you can scrimp with brushing. I'll be back this evening after tonight's dinner party to make sure he's been properly cared for."

The woman looked at him in bewilderment.

He sighed. "I know. He's an Arabian with four white boots. Bad luck if you want to breed him."

"But I'm—"

"New. I get it." And he didn't want to stand around chatting. Especially not with a beautiful woman, who only reminded him of everything he was tossing away because of his family's misplaced sense of duty. "Off with you, now. I have business."

Princess Eva Latvaia looked at the riding crop in her hands, then Prince Alex Sancho's back as he walked away from her. Sweat caused his white-and-tan polo shirt to stick to his skin, displaying unexpectedly toned muscles. He ran his fingers through his gorgeous, thick curly black hair.

At least their children would be getting good genes.

She shook her head and took Thor's reins. "A fine name for you, sir. A child of the gods."

The great horse whinnied.

Eva laughed. She said, "You're a misfit," but she stroked his nose to take the sting out of it. "So am I."

Thor shook his head.

"How'd you end up in a palace?"

One of the stable employees raced out of the open double doors. He grabbed the reins in Eva's hands. "I'm so sorry, Princess." He bowed.

She straightened regally, aware of her position, but

she also smiled. "This is what I get for taking a stroll when I should be getting ready for a party."

The older gentleman chuckled and turned to walk Thor into the stable.

Eva had heard the Sancho household was different. She supposed having a new baby around was part of it. But she'd also heard that the woman who'd married Dominic, the prince Eva had been dreaming of since she was four, had brought a more relaxed attitude to the royal family.

And now Eva had to face Dom tonight—and his princess—the woman who'd basically stolen him from Eva. In a way, his marrying someone else was good. She was next in line for her throne. So was he. Theirs would have been a difficult life and a difficult marriage. Still, she'd been dreaming of Dom since she was old enough to watch *Cinderella*, in love with the idea of marrying a handsome prince and ruling their countries together. Her whole world had worked itself out in her head. And now—

Now, add losing Dom to what her father had done, and everything was off. Wrong. Almost unbearable.

Head high, she walked back to the palace. She rode the elevator to the fourth floor and the guest apartment she'd been given for her stay. She opened just one door of the elegant double-door entrance, and strode through the high-ceilinged foyer to the sitting room, where her mother picked a chocolate from the tray provided as a welcome gift from the king. It seemed she'd replaced crying with eating.

"You're not going to fit into your mother-of-the-bride dress for the wedding if you keep eating those."

Her mom, a short thin woman with hair as black as

Eva's, offered the candy to her. "They're divine. You should try them."

"Then both of us will need a bigger size dress."

Eva's mother dropped the chocolate back to the tray. "You're right. I want to look nice. I want your derelict of a father to feel bad for leaving me. And I want to prove at least some of us take our royal duties to heart."

Eva sat on the sofa. "I'm glad to see you're feeling better, Mom."

"Running away with an aide." She shook her head. "Seriously. Could he be any more cliché?"

"It's not exactly cliché to give up your throne." He hadn't officially put down his crown, but a royal divorce came with consequences. Running away with another woman meant a divorce would soon follow, and her dad would no longer be king. Then she would be queen. At twenty-five years old, she'd have the weight of a country on her shoulders. She couldn't believe her father had done this to her—and for a mistress.

She thanked God that the Sancho family had insisted they fulfill the terms of the treaty that promised her in marriage to one of King Ronaldo's sons. At least she had this way of bringing herself into the good graces of their subjects before she took the crown. Even if she wasn't getting the prized prince, the son who would be king, she would prove she would do her duty to her country even when things were crumbling around her, by upholding the terms of a treaty that ensured oil and safe passage for Grennady's tankers.

"I wonder if he's coming to the wedding."

"Your dad?" Her mom winced. "Great. Thanks for reminding me that he might. Now I really do have to give up chocolates." She tossed the candy tray to the coffee table. "While you were out, did you hear any palace gossip about when the wedding will occur?"

"Xaviera's servants are a happy, obviously well-cared-for staff, and they are incredibly closemouthed."

Her mom rose from the sofa. "I guess we'll find out tonight."

"I guess we will."

As her mother turned and walked to her bedroom, Eva headed in the opposite direction to the second bedroom.

Having lived in America for seven years, she no longer had a maid draw her bath. She relished the simple pleasure of running water, adding scented oils and luxuriating—alone—for twenty minutes.

But remembering the way Alexandros had thought her a servant girl, she called for the palace hairdresser. She had housekeeping steam her gown to make sure there wasn't a hint of a wrinkle.

That evening, when she stepped out of her room and into the apartment's sitting area, her mom gasped. "Oh, Eva! Are you sure red is a good idea? And strapless? Showing your shoulders when you meet a king and your future husband? They could think you a tart."

With a quick nod of approval for her mom's sedate blue gown that showed off her thin figure and suited her black hair, she said, "Alexandros already mistook me for a servant girl."

"What?"

"I ran into Alex when I took a walk to the stables. He handed me his riding crop, told me to take care of his horse."

Her mom gaped in horror.

"I want to see the look on his face when he realizes who I am."

"Is it that or are you trying to make Prince Dominic jealous?"

Eva stopped halfway to the sofa, her heart rattling around in her chest. She'd loved Prince Dominic from the day she'd found his picture in the newspaper and her mom had told her he was the boy she would be marrying. While other girls crushed on rock stars and soccer players, she'd happily shown everyone the picture of her handsome prince. She never had to feel bad if she didn't get invited to a dance or if boys ignored her at a party. She had her prince.

And he'd married someone else.

She swallowed hard, as humiliation bubbled through her, but when she faced her mother she wore a happy smile. Her mom had enough misery of her own. She didn't need to be further upset over how uncomfortable this situation was for Eva.

"Now, wouldn't I be silly to be pining over a man I didn't even know?"

Her mother eyed her shrewdly. "You're sure?"

"I'm positive."

She seemed to buy that, but Eva's breath gave a funny catch. What was it going to feel like not just meeting Dominic, but meeting the woman who had stolen him right out from under her?

A member of the palace guard arrived and escorted them to the king's private quarters. The king himself and his new wife, Queen Rose, greeted them.

King Ronaldo took Eva's hand and kissed it. "It is such a pleasure to meet you as an adult, Princess."

Eva smiled graciously and curtsied. "The honor is mine, Your Majesty."

"This is my new wife, Rose. She's Princess Ginny's mom. She and Dominic aren't here yet, but you know how new babies are. They don't always adhere to schedules." He laughed. "Anyway, Queen Rose, may I present Princess Eva Latavia of Grennady."

Eva curtsied again. "A pleasure to meet you."

Queen Rose, a tall blonde with just a hint of pink in her hair and a very obvious Texas twang, waved her hand in dismissal. "Oh, none of that for me." She suddenly enveloped Eva in a hug. "This is the way we welcome people into the family in Texas." She pulled back and looked Eva in the eye. "You're familiar, right? You were educated in the US?"

"Yes, ma'am," Eva said, mimicking the Southern drawl she'd heard the entire time she was at Florida State.

Rose laughed. "That's my girl!"

King Ronaldo turned to Eva's mother. "And this is your mom? Queen Karen, correct?"

Eva's heart swelled with gratitude when the king mentioned nothing of her father's potential abdication of the throne and still gave her mom the respect of the title Queen.

Her mother curtsied. "Your Majesty."

He bowed. "It's my honor to meet you." He motioned to Rose. "And this is Queen Rose."

Karen curtsied again. "A pleasure to meet you."

Rose chuckled. "I know you people like your official greetings, but I'm just a hugger." She gave Karen a big squeeze.

The king directed everyone into a drawing room with a bar.

Eva looked around in unabashed curiosity. She knew some royals were wealthier than others. Xaviera's location alone gave them access to oil money. But this palace was amazing. The art so casually displayed on the walls was probably worth the gross national product of Grennady.

Her mom leaned in and whispered to her daughter, "So, the mom of the last princess ended up married to the king. Maybe this won't be such a bad deal after all?"

Eva couldn't stop a giggle that escaped. "Behave."

"Rose doesn't."

"She's the queen. That gives her license to be eccentric."

"Right."

The king motioned to the bar. "Can I get anyone anything?"

Karen said, "I'd love a wine spritzer."

"Princess Eva?"

"I'd like—"

But before she could name her wine choice, Alexandros rose from behind the bar. Dressed in the royal uniform of their country, black trousers with a red jacket filled with medals, he looked totally different than the guy in the riding breeches, white-and-tan shirt and scuffed helmet.

His dark eyes met hers, and the bottle of wine he held fell to the bar top.

She smiled.

King Ronaldo said, "I understand you've met Alex in school."

Holding the gaze of his dark eyes, she said, "And we met this afternoon. Accidentally. At the stables."

Rose said, "Oh! You ride." She winced. "Of course you do. It was probably part of your training. I'd love to go out with you one of these mornings."

Polite and proper, Eva faced Rose. "I'd like that too."

King Ronaldo said, "Funny. Alex didn't mention seeing you this afternoon."

Feeling her pride return, Eva spared Alex a glance before returning her gaze to the king. "I don't think he knew who I was."

Alex felt his face redden like a teenager's.

"He handed me his riding crop and told me to make sure his horse got the star treatment."

The king gasped. "Alexi!"

"Well, she didn't look like this," Alex said, pointing at her red gown and dark hair pinned up just enough to get it off her face while the rest spilled over her shoulders and fell in thick curls down her bare back. He thought of all that black hair fanned out on a white pillow and almost dropped the wine again.

Eva casually said, "Perhaps he was just preoccupied."

The king said, "Perhaps," but Alex stared at her red dress. The strapless top hugged her breasts and cruised to her tiny waist, before it flared out in a skirt made up of yards and yards of some kind of filmy material. It didn't bell out. It just flowed smoothly, effortlessly with every one of her graceful movements.

He didn't know what he'd expected from this woman he'd met when she was little more than a child, but it wasn't this grace. Or this sensuality. It was as if she was telling the world that she might someday be a queen, but she was also a sexy woman.

Her lips lifted into a knowing smile.

She had him stumbling all over himself, and she liked it.

No. She reveled in it. And he supposed he couldn't blame her. His family had yanked the good prince away from her and forced her to take him or nothing. Only a week after her own father had disgraced their crown, the Sancho family had decided it was time to make good on the terms of their treaty, forcing her to marry a lesser prince, then he hadn't recognized her at the stable that afternoon. She wasn't insulting him by telling everybody he'd thought her a stable girl. She was repairing her royal pride.

The door of the drawing room opened and Alex's gaze shifted as his brother and his wife arrived, and for the second time that evening he was struck speechless. Princess Ginny walked in on Dominic's arm, wearing the same gown as Eva, except Ginny's was a soft, romantic gray.

Dominic said, "Sorry we're late."

King Ronaldo and Queen Rose immediately shifted in their direction.

Rose said, "Is something wrong with Jimmy? Is he sick?"

Ginny laughed. "No, Mom. Your grandson is fine."

Princess Eva stood in front of the bar, motionless, as if stunned into silence, watching the happy couple.

Alex leaned forward, across the gleaming wooden surface. "Well, now. What have we here? You and Ginny in the same gown. Except yours is red and hers is a pretty gray. Very innocent and sweet. While yours is…well, on the trashy side. It's kind of like looking at those devil and angel pictures."

He saw her back stiffen and knew he'd struck a nerve. Good. She hadn't even tried to tell him who she was at the stable that afternoon. She'd taken his crop. Led him to believe she'd be caring for Thor. Let him walk away. And then embarrassed him in front of his father.

"Shut up."

He watched the muscles of her bare back shift as she straightened, composing herself. But he still saw the tension and knew his golden opportunity for getting even wasn't over yet.

"Oh, don't get me wrong. I don't mind one bit being the brother to marry the devilish princess. I'm just not exactly sure this was the first impression you wanted to make on the guy who dumped you."

"He didn't dump me."

"He isn't exactly marrying you."

"He's already married."

"And to somebody who looks like your polar opposite. Isn't that interesting?"

He saw vulnerability flicker in her gray-blue eyes as Dominic and Ginny approached her. He didn't really know Eva, but he did know what it was like to be second best. To be the one not chosen. To be the one who stood behind his brother and dad, a king and a man who would be king.

His chest clenched. She might be educated. She might be a tough crusader who could speak up for those who didn't have a voice, but nothing could have prepared her for meeting the woman who'd stolen her fiancé from her.

She was too damned pretty to be Dominic's second. Alex wasn't anybody's knight in shining armor, but he

did know a thing or two about fooling people into believing he was fine. Happy. That his life was perfect.
And that was what Eva needed right now. To be rescued
from an embarrassing situation that befuddled her so
much that even the royal pride she'd just gathered was
sinking fast.

He raced around the bar. Sliding his arm along her
waist, he whispered, "Here's the story…when we met
at the stables this afternoon there was an instant attraction."

She met his gaze. "Really?"

"Would you rather be somebody who unexpectedly
found herself crazy about me, or the woman left behind
by my big brother?"

Her head tilted in confusion.

"Don't be the one left behind in the dust. Leave *him*
behind."

"*Oh.*"

"You don't have a lot of experience with men, do
you?"

"I've been engaged since I was four."

"And I guess now you're going to tell me you're a
virgin."

She said nothing, just held his gaze.

"Well, I'll be damned."

"You'll absolutely be damned," Dom said as he
reached them. He held out his hand and Princess Eva
presented her hand to him. He kissed the knuckles.
"Princess Eva. It's nice to see you. I'm so sorry we're
meeting again under awkward circumstance."

Like a champ, she slid her arm beneath Alex's and
stepped closer to him. "There's no reason to be concerned. We've barely spoken to each other. Besides, I

was lucky enough to meet Alex this afternoon at the stables."

Alex winked at her. "Love at first sight."

Dom said, "Really?"

Alex laughed. "All right. Maybe lust at first sight."

Eva shifted her attention to Ginny. "And you must be the woman who stole Dom's heart." She smiled. "You have lovely taste in clothes."

Alex had trouble stifling a laugh. Still, from the way she'd put him in his place for not recognizing her, he should have expected she could hold her own. She'd simply needed help getting over the awkwardness of seeing Dom.

Ginny laughed and glanced down at her gown. "You have good taste too. Maybe better. That red is divine."

"Alex told me I looked like a devil in this dress."

"And that you looked like an angel," Alex said to Ginny. He kissed Eva's cheek. "But you know I'd always rather have the devil."

"So," Dom said, looking from Alex to Eva, appearing not quite convinced. "Things worked out for the best?"

Alex tightened his arm around her waist. "We think so."

A servant quietly shuffled into the room and whispered something in King Ronaldo's ear. He nodded once. When the servant was gone, the king faced the two couples at the bar.

"Dinner is served. If you'll all follow me to the dining room."

Dom and Ginny immediately got in line behind his father, but Eva caught Alex's arm to hold him back. When the room was empty she said, "I owe you."

He couldn't help it. He grinned. She might be able to

hold her own, but she'd needed him to get over that awkward introduction. "Yes, you do. I just saved you months of embarrassment—maybe years if the press decided to make an issue of Dom marrying someone else—and I have the perfect way for you to pay me back."

CHAPTER TWO

EVA'S HEART CHUGGED in her chest. After Alex's good guess about her virginity, she couldn't imagine what he had in mind as payback, but she did know she owed him. So when he asked her to meet him at the stables at midnight, she hadn't argued. She'd simply enjoyed the dinner, keeping up Alex's pretense that their chance meeting that afternoon had sparked an instant attraction. Then she'd said polite goodbyes to the king and his new wife and Dom and his wife, before she walked her mom back to their quarters, changed into jeans and a lightweight sweater and headed for the stable.

The moon rose high in the sky. A faint ocean breeze lured her down the cobblestone path. An island in the Mediterranean, Xaviera had January temps that were much warmer than the climate of her country, which was nestled between Finland and Russia. If she were home right now, she'd be wearing boots and a parka and battling a winter wind to get to her stables.

She reached the big stone-and-wood building and entered through a door on the side. Though the stable was the cleanest she'd ever seen, the earthy scents of horse, hay and leather hit her. She glanced down the long row of stalls and saw Alex standing in front of the last one, petting the nose of his Arabian, Thor.

She strode down the aisle.

Alex heard her and smiled. "So you've come to dicker."

"I didn't come to negotiate anything. I came to see what my payback will be for you saving me tonight."

He laughed. "It's odd to hear somebody say that. Usually I'm the one who has to make amends."

"Quite a reputation my future husband has."

"Actually, that's the point. The best way you can pay me back is to not marry me."

She gasped. "I have to marry you!"

He bobbed his head, as if thinking through her comment, then said, "Not really."

"We have a treaty!"

"Made decades ago." He caught her gaze. "Were you mature enough at age four to commit to someone?"

He knew the answer to that so she said nothing.

"Of course, you weren't. And then we pulled the rug out from under you. The prince you were supposed to marry is now married to someone else. You're not getting the prince who was promised to you. You're not even getting the good prince, the one who will someday be king. You're getting second-best."

She looked at him, wearing a T-shirt with the front tucked into nice-fitting jeans, with his dark curly hair casually messed, and those intriguing brown eyes. For a beat of time, she wondered if she really was getting second-best. Dominic was handsome in the perfect, straitlaced way. This guy? Alex? He was rough-around-the-edges gorgeous. A sexy bad boy. And all hers in a few months—

She swallowed hard as strange tingling sensations cruised through her.

She ignored them. When all was said and done, this was about duty. Oil and safe passage for their tankers trumped which prince she would actually marry. And needing to make herself look strong and loyal to her country trumped both of those.

"I don't have a choice."

He walked toward her. "Actually, I read the agreement and the treaty. *You* might not have a choice. *I* might not have a choice. But *we* have a choice. If both of us decide not to marry, we can nullify it."

She gaped at him. "Nullify a treaty? Just because you don't want to marry me?"

"I don't want to get married at all. And we wouldn't be nullifying the whole treaty, just that one clause." He sighed. "Look, I rescued you tonight because it's not right that somebody as pretty as you are should be perceived as an also-ran, the woman who didn't make the cut."

Her pulse slowed, then speeded up again. Forget all about Dominic dumping her. Forget about the treaty. Alex thought she was pretty? He was one of the most eligible bachelors in the world and she was a woman whose dad had tossed their family into an unfathomable scandal. Alex should be running from her as fast as his feet would take him. Instead, he thought she was pretty? Too pretty to be known as the princess who didn't make the cut.

"But I'm not anybody's knight in shining armor."

He hadn't mentioned her father's betrayal, or the fact that she'd soon become a queen, but she was well aware of both and the consequences. Alex might not want to rescue her, but he was her only option to show her subjects that her family still remembered their call to service.

She lifted her chin. "Like it or not, you have to be mine. Or your country is in violation of our treaty."

"I told you we can—"

"No! My father disgraced us enough! I have to prove I will do my duties!"

His eyes narrowed. His full lips pursed. "You're refusing my plan."

"Yes."

He stepped closer. Instinct told her to step back. Common sense told her he'd see that as a sign of weakness. So she held her ground, looked him in the eyes, as he circled her, inspecting her as if she were his next purchase. Waves and waves of chill bumps trickled down her spine.

"Why would a girl as pretty as you are want to marry someone she doesn't really know?"

"I told you I have to—"

"Prove you'll do your duty," he interrupted her. "Got it. And I believe that's part of it." He stopped at her side and slid his hand under the thick lock of hair that fell over her shoulder to her breast. Running the silken strands through his fingers, he said, "I would think you'd be eager to find somebody your own age. Maybe somebody who shared your interest in land mines and whatnot."

"First, I'm not part of the land mine fight. Second, you are my age. Five years isn't that much of a difference."

He flipped the strand of hair over her shoulder, and

the tingles that rained down on her when his fingers brushed her skin nearly made her shiver.

"So you like me?"

"I didn't say that."

He smiled knowingly, stepped close. "Just attracted then."

"To you?" She'd meant for it to sound like a scoff. It came out as a squeak.

"Or maybe you're simply not clear about what attraction is. Being a virgin and all."

If the feelings tumbling around her right now were attraction, then he was correct. This crazy combination of fear that he'd touch her again and longing to feel his fingers graze her skin totally confused her. Her chest was tight. Her body wanted to shiver. Even her lips tingled.

"I've had boyfriends."

"So you wouldn't mind if I kissed you."

"As a way to get me to drop the idea of marrying you? How badly do you kiss?"

She'd barely gotten the word *kiss* out of her mouth before he grabbed her by the shoulders, drew her to him and planted his lips on hers. The shock of it buckled her knees. His arm fell to her waist, anchoring her against him as wave after wave of warmth flowed through her. But as quickly as he'd yanked her to him, he released her.

She stared at him. Her nerve endings glowed like the sparks from a Roman candle. She couldn't quite get air into her lungs.

He grinned.

Not sure what to say, what to do, she fell back on dignity. As haughtily as possible, she said, "I'm still marrying you," before she turned on her heel and walked out of the stable.

Head high, she marched up the cobblestone path so afraid he was following her that her neck hurt from fighting the urge to look behind her.

When she reached her quarters, she breathed a sigh of relief, though her hands shook and her knees still wobbled.

Her mother awaited her on the sofa. "So how did it go?"

How did it go? In twenty seconds, he'd reduced her limbs to jelly, and no matter how hard she tried she couldn't get her heart to stop thumping.

"He doesn't want to marry me. He says if we both say we want to step away from the marriage, that section of the treaty will be nullified."

Her mother gasped. "Oh, no! Our family has disgraced our country enough! You have to do something to prove you're still loyal enough to the crown to do your duty!"

She fell to the sofa beside her mom. "I know. I told him that."

But convincing him of her duty was only part of her problem. One twenty-second kiss had thrown her for a loop. Made her feel hot and cold. Changed her breathing. Given her chill bumps. When she'd pictured marrying Dominic, the images were warm and sweet. When she thought of marrying Alex, the images became hot and steamy.

And, oh, dear God, she was *not* a hot and steamy girl.

"Our family has been respected as leaders of Grennady for centuries. But your father has put us in a precarious position. You cannot look weak or wishy-washy. You cannot walk away from a treaty mere weeks before you become queen. The press will crucify you. Your entire reign will be tainted."

Eva's brain tried to pay attention to her mom but couldn't. She couldn't stop thinking about how experienced Alex was and how little she knew. How did a virgin please a playboy?

Her mother grabbed her hands. "You've got to marry Alex."

Her chest filled with anxiety. There was no good option here. If she returned to her country without marrying Alex, it would appear she had no respect for treaties. If she married Alex, she was so far out of her depth she'd most likely make both of them miserable.

"I don't think he's going to give up on trying to get me to bow out."

"Then you have to make him like you."

Right. Leave it to her mom to reduce this to something that sounded simple but really wasn't.

She took a breath. "How exactly do I do that?"

"Flirt. Compliment him. Women have been doing it for centuries."

Every woman but Eva. In high school, she'd only dated boys who were friends. As an adult, she gone out with men who knew she was promised to a prince and would have thought it odd if she flirted. Worse, Alex had probably been flirted with by the best. If she got it wrong, or was clumsy, she'd make a fool of herself.

Still, she didn't have options. She *had to* go through with this marriage. Plus, it would be months before the actual wedding. There was time to fix this. Time for him to get to know her. Time for her to learn to flirt.

She just had to stop being smart with him and treat him with respect—

And Google flirting.

* * *

The next morning at six, Alex's phone rang. He groaned and rolled over, but when it rang again he recognized the ringtone as his father's. He sat up, ran his hand down his face and snatched his cell from the bedside table.

"Yes, Father."

"It's me, sweet pea," his stepmother Rose said cheerfully. "Your dad just realized that we never actually talked about the date for the wedding last night, and I thought it would be a good idea for all of us to have breakfast while we chat. So we can keep it light and friendly."

"Great."

"Great as in you will be there?" Without giving him a chance to reply, she said, "Thanks. You're a love."

She hung up the phone and Alex groaned again. The last thing he wanted to do was set a wedding date when he didn't want to get married. But marrying a woman who would be a queen? Somebody who'd keep him in the papers for real reasons, not just his winning streaks at the casinos or his escapades with women? Oh, man. That sucked.

Marrying somebody he didn't know because of a treaty was antiquated. Stupid. And he wouldn't do it. It was crazy to even consider marrying Eva. No matter how pretty she was.

He rose from the bed trying not to think about how her cheeks turned pink when he teased her or how hot that one quick kiss had been.

Because it had been hot. Ridiculously hot. Kissing someone who clearly hadn't been expecting to be kissed had been exciting. Challenging—

Hot. The hottest kiss he'd had in forever.

How long had it been since he'd had to woo a woman—

Damn it! He was thinking about her again. And he wasn't supposed to be thinking about her. He was supposed to be hatching a plan to get her to ditch this wedding.

He headed for the shower determined to get Eva out of his head, but what replaced her almost stopped his heart. The shadowy memory of his mom's death. His father falling apart. An entire palace full of servants weeping silently as they went about their duties.

He sucked in a breath, banishing the images, but in their place came other, more difficult visions. Memories of being told that his girlfriend, the first woman he'd really loved, had been killed in a boating accident. Vivid recollections of the soul-crushing grief that consumed him for nearly two years.

The loss had been so difficult that as the memories hit, he rubbed his chest to salve the ache always came when he thought of Nina.

Five years had passed, and he had gotten beyond Nina's death, so he told the images to go away. If his subconscious was reminding him of his mom and his first love because it was worried he could get feelings for Eva, it needn't have bothered. There was no way in hell he'd fall for a woman just because a treaty said he should. His subconscious could rest easy.

But he knew a royal summons when he got one. He couldn't refuse his father about this marriage. As a prince who'd very publicly enjoyed his royal lifestyle, he did not have the option of refusing. *Eva* had to refuse. Then he could tell his dad she was a virgin, and say he didn't want to force an innocent young woman to marry him. He'd look like the good guy. And his dad would agree.

That was the plan that would work, and that was the plan he was sticking to.

He dressed in lightweight slacks, a pale blue dress shirt—no tie—and navy sport coat, and headed for his father's elaborate quarters. He entered through the gold-trimmed doors into a foyer with high ceilings and Monet on the wall, and walked to the smaller dining room, the one his father used for informal breakfasts and lunches.

Rose immediately stood, raced to him and hugged him. After being without a mom since he was a boy, having her around was equal parts sweet and disruptive. Up until Ginny had gotten pregnant, this palace had been the home of men. Gold-trimmed and filled with precious art, but still a home of men. No women. No talk of babies or fashions—

"You look very dashing."

And no one commenting on his clothes unless he was inappropriately attired.

Luckily, he liked Rose. He was just grouchy because of this whole marriage mess. "Thanks."

"You and Eva will be seated there," his father said, pointing to the two chairs to his right. "We'll put your fiancée's mom on my left and Rose, of course, will sit across from me."

"No Dom and Ginny?"

"No need for Dom and Ginny to be here," his father said in his most kingly voice. "You're the one getting married."

He felt the noose tightening around his neck.

Escorted by his father's butler, Eva and her mom entered. Alex's mouth fell open. If he'd thought Eva a knockout in the red dress, the little white dress she wore tied his tongue. Simple and sweet, with some sort of short pink sweater thing, the dress shouldn't have made her look sexy. But there was something about the way the pink made her dark hair look even darker—or maybe the way the color set off her pale gray-blue eyes—

Damn it! What the hell was wrong with him? If he was noticing colors, it was definitely time to get out of this thing.

The butler bowed, announced Karen and Eva, and left the room.

Alex automatically pulled out the chair beside his for Eva. His father directed Karen to sit to his left.

As the king's attention was on offering the seat to his guest, Eva whispered, "Well, don't you look like the proper man about town?"

"Would you rather I came to breakfast in my robe and slippers?"

She laughed.

He frowned. "Where's the smart remark?"

She fiddled with her napkin. "No smart remarks today."

"Oh, come on. We both have reason to be unhappy about this wedding. Don't start playing Good Princess now."

"I am the good princess."

He didn't want to bring up her dad. Having a father abdicate his throne wasn't just embarrassing for a royal. It was humiliating. Still, he could use it without out-and-out saying it.

"You're about to become a queen. That's two huge life changes in the span of a couple of months. Too much for one person. Think this through."

"I don't have to think it through. Queens don't ignore treaties."

"Yeah, well, I don't want to get married."

She said nothing.

"And I'm going to do everything in my power to get you to agree."

She faced him, her eyes narrowed, as if accepting his challenge. "Great. Give it your best shot. Because I intend to convince you to marry me."

Alexi's tongue tied again. Her anger brightened her blue-gray eyes until they were almost silver, and sent a shiver down his spine. He skimmed his gaze over her hair, the pink tint in her cheeks, her lush mouth, and realized there absolutely were worse fates than being assigned to marry this woman.

Except she was a virgin, who was about to become a queen, and he didn't want to get married. He'd seen what happened to his father when his mom died. The king had crumbled from grief. And then there was his own loss. His first love—

Pain squeezed his heart. A wave of sorrow enveloped him.

That was why he'd thought of them this morning. Not to warn him that he could get feelings for Eva, but to remind him of why he didn't want to get close to *anyone*. The pain of loss was just too great to risk.

His father picked up his juice glass. "We should have toasted this wedding last night, but we got a little preoccupied with baby talk."

Rose and Karen laughed.

The king raised his glass. "To the wedding that unites our two countries."

Everyone lifted his or her juice glass. "To the wedding that unites our two countries."

Alex said the words and drank his juice, but Eva could see his heart wasn't in it. A flame of anger licked at her soul. She was the virgin facing sleeping with a man she didn't know, a man experienced enough to have a harem, and *he* was unhappy?

She did not give a damn. She was going through with this wedding. Just as her mother said, she had to get him to like her.

He reached for a tray of fruit, and presented it to her. "Melon?"

"Yes."

Their eyes met, and thoughts of the kiss from the night before flooded her. The solidness of his body against hers when he yanked her to him, the press of his lips.

Though her breath hitched, she held his gaze. Intuition told her this was the time she should begin flirting, but not one cute or flirty thing came to mind. Her chest was so tight it was a wonder she could draw in air. She barely managed to say, "Thank you."

She scooped up a serving of the honeydew. When she handed the spoon to him, their fingers brushed and the memory of how he'd brushed her shoulder when he'd flipped her hair out of the way sent a shower of tingles down her spine.

He smiled. "Happy to see you're more nervous about our wedding today than you were yesterday."

"I'm not nervous about our wedding."

"Then what made your hand shake?"

There was absolutely no way in hell she'd tell him that

remembering their ten minutes together the night before filled her with warmth. So she said nothing.

He looked away to serve himself some fruit. The sounds of good silver and elegant china filled the air. With the exception of her mom and Queen Rose discussing gardening, the room was quiet.

Alex said, "So how are your stray cats doing without you?"

Her chest loosened. Finally, something they could talk about. "They're fine." She risked a glance at him. "Thank you for asking."

"Don't they miss you when you're gone?"

"I started a few shelters that care for them. I don't need to be there twenty-four-seven...or even once a month. Every shelter is fully staffed, mostly with volunteers."

"That makes sense. Always good to have a staff in place."

"Yes. Especially when they are a competent staff. A staff that shares my vision." Eva relaxed a bit more. "I—" She caught the gaze of his dark eyes and almost lost her train of thought. It was no wonder he had the reputation with women that he had. He was gorgeous. His dark eyes had a lost, soulful quality that touched her heart in the weirdest way. And if they went through with this wedding, he would be hers. She would be married to one of the most gorgeous, richest men in the world. He could have his pick of women, but *she'd* be in his bed.

She sucked in a breath to banish those thoughts. If she let her brain leap ahead to their wedding night, she'd hyperventilate.

"I intend to start this kind of shelter in as many cities as I can."

"In the United States?"

She had his full attention. He was curious. And she was floundering because being near him was overwhelming. While he was cool and confident, she almost shook with emotions she didn't understand.

What she wouldn't give for the ability to flirt.

Maybe if she batted her eyelashes? Or smiled?

That was it. Maybe she should just smile? Instead of a big flirty move, she should just break the ice with a smile.

She raised her lips, let the corners tip upward. "Yes. The problem doesn't seem to be as bad in my own country."

He tilted his head and studied her. "Interesting."

She hoped he was still talking about the cats. Because if he was making fun of her smiling at him, she would die. On the spot die. But not before she killed her mother for telling her to flirt with him.

"Being a rural country, Grennady has more barns and stables, places cats and dogs can find shelter in the winter."

"I see—" He held her gaze. The look in his eyes was so confusingly intense that she couldn't take another second. She let her gaze fall but when it did, it landed on his mouth—the mouth that had kissed her and changed her whole perspective about this arranged marriage.

Okay. Now she really was nervous. And felt hot and cold.

She yanked her gaze away from him and tried to focus on the main conversation at the table. King Ronaldo was discussing the latest thriller novel he was reading. She hoped to insert herself into that discussion, but no such luck. As her mother and Alex's father and stepmother found common ground in a book they'd all read, she and Alex were left behind like outsiders.

"So who's funding your shelter?"

"I am. I—"

She stopped. Her dad had been gone a little over a week. Her mother had only stopped crying the day before. She had gotten her monthly stipend the week before her dad left, but until her dad returned or made a decision there was no one to authorize the checks.

Good God. She might not be broke, but without her dad to approve her stipend, she had access to nothing.

She drew in a long, life-sustaining breath. She might not be penniless, but she might as well be.

"I *was* funding my shelter. With my allowance." She swallowed hard. "But, with my dad gone, there's no one to authorize my stipend." She caught his gaze. "At least four shelters will have to close."

"That must have been some allowance."

Damn him for being such a twit! Her life was a mess and he was making jokes! "Thank you for making fun of me."

"I'm teasing you to lessen the awkwardness for you. I'm sorry about your dad."

She straightened her shoulders, sat up taller in her chair. She'd rather have him be a twit than feel sorry for her. "Nothing's official yet. He could take months before he actually divorces my mom…" And she'd be penniless until then.

The dining room doors opened again and a short, dark-haired woman entered. Dressed in a green business suit and simple taupe pumps, she carried a huge black book and a smaller one that could have been a calendar.

The king tapped his water glass to get everyone's attention. "Princess Eva, Queen Karen," he said, "This is Sally Peterson, our minister of protocol. She's here to officially set the date for the wedding."

Alex leaned in and whispered, "This date means nothing to me. All I'm finding out right now is how much time I have to try to convince you not to marry me."

Eva fumed. Her entire life had been turned upside down and he couldn't for two seconds pretend to do his royal duty. No. He had to keep rubbing it in that he wanted her gone.

Sally bowed and faced Eva. "Actually, Princess, your country gave us three dates. The second weekend in April."

Alex choked. Eva blanched. Even for someone willing to go through with this marriage, that wasn't very much time, not quite three months away. She had to convince Alex to marry her and get accustomed to the fact that she was getting married in three short months?

"The first week in March."

Alex picked up his water glass. Eva gaped at Sally Peterson. That was worse! Why were the dates so soon? So close?

"Or the second week in February, to coincide with Valentine's Day."

Four flipping weeks?

Eva coughed to cover her gasp of disbelief.

King Ronaldo said, "I like the February date. So that's our date." He rose from his seat. "Sally, perhaps you and the ladies would like to use this morning to talk about dresses and designers."

Rose rubbed her hands together with glee. "I'd love

to! What do you say we take a pot of coffee into the living room and look at swatches and Google designers?"

Karen grinned. "That sounds like fun." She faced her daughter. "Eva?"

Eva's throat had closed. She swore she couldn't breathe. She had four weeks to persuade Alex to like her and to figure out what the hell she'd do on their wedding night.

Before she could answer, Sally said, "I'm sorry, Your Majesty, but as minister of protocol I'm in charge of the budget, so I'll need particulars on who's paying for what."

All eyes went to Karen, who looked at Eva.

Eva's heart stopped. All the blood drained from her body. "I—I mean, my mother and I—"

Alex glanced at Eva, who had gone white, and he almost cursed. She'd just told him she and her mom had no money. Her country probably had an obligation to pony up at least part of the millions it would take for a royal wedding. But with her father gone there was no one to ask. If Xaviera's legal counsel had to force Grennady to pay, the story would hit every newspaper in the world. The embarrassment of it would be horrendous for Eva.

Before he realized it, he was on his feet. "Actually, I think we should pay for the wedding. We're the ones who called in the terms of the treaty, and said it was time for the marriage to occur." He licked his suddenly dry lips. His voice slowed as he added, "I'm just saying paying for the wedding seems like our responsibility."

Karen visibly relaxed. Eva gave him a curious look. And no wonder. He hadn't exactly ruined a way to stop this wedding, but he was participating when he should just keep his mouth shut and let it all apart.

Time slowed to a crawl.

His father cocked his head, but after only a few seconds he smiled. "You know what? He's right. We are the ones who said it was time for the marriage to take place. We'll pay for the wedding."

Sally gasped. "But, Your Majesty—"

"No buts, Sally. Alex is right."

Sally wrote something in one of her big black books. "Fine." She turned to Rose. "I'll have coffee sent to the living room where we can discuss designers."

Rose said, "Great!"

Rose and Karen began chattering about dresses, but Eva turned to Alex as he sat again.

"Thanks."

He felt color rise to his cheeks. Confusion and anger with himself met and merged into an emotion that made him want to kick his own butt.

"It means nothing. The way I see it, our kingdom can absorb whatever loss results when we cancel this thing."

"Because you know my mom and I have no money."

He shrugged. "That's temporary."

She put her hand on the back of his. "Yes, but you saved us from being embarrassed."

"Is that enough to earn the payback of you backing out of the wedding?"

She laughed lightly, obviously relieved, but also the way someone would laugh with a friend. "No."

Damn her for being so cute. His mouth tugged upward until he couldn't stop a smile. "Don't make me like you."

She peeked up at him from beneath lush black eyelashes. "You'd rather hate me?"

The heat that roared through him nearly stopped his heart. Her magnetic blue-gray eyes held his. Her pretty hair rippled around an even prettier face. Everything inside of him chanted that he should lean forward and kiss her.

Kiss her.

Kiss her.

Kiss her.

But that was the real problem, wasn't it? She was pretty enough, tempting enough, that maybe she *should* be the woman he married.

And then what?

Fall in love for real?

The very thought tightened his throat. He'd loved two women in his life and lost both. Only a crazy man set himself up for that kind of pain.

"I will talk you out of this."

CHAPTER THREE

ALEX WATCHED EVA leave the dining room with her mom and Queen Rose, then exited through the hidden door in the back. Ready to change out of these stuffy clothes and put on riding breeches, he strode through the echoing maze of tall-ceilinged halls, but at his private elevator, one of his father's secretaries caught him.

The older man bowed slightly. "Your Majesty, your dad sent me to find you. He wants you in his office now."

"Now?"

The old man's eyebrows rose, an indicator Alex shouldn't argue, and that usually meant he'd done something wrong.

Alex winced. Best-case scenario was that the king wanted to chastise him for suggesting they pay for the wedding. Worst-case, he'd overheard Alex telling Eva he'd talk her out of the wedding.

Damn.

Without a word, he motioned for the man to lead him back to his father's office.

When they arrived, he entered, but the secretary reached inside to grab the doorknob, and walked out, closing the door behind him.

His father didn't look up from the letter he was signing. "You cannot talk Eva out of this wedding."

Okay. It was worst-case.

He fell to one of the velvet chairs in front of his dad's desk. "I can't believe you're forcing either of us to marry when Eva was barely out of diapers and I was pulling a wagon with my bike when that damned agreement was signed. It's ridiculous. Antiquated. And you know it."

His dad studied him for a few seconds, then he sighed heavily. "All right. You're right. And this situation is too important to leave to chance. You were smart enough to pick up on the money problem that I'd somehow missed, so I need you in the loop."

Alex sat up. "The loop?"

"Eva's dad didn't leave her mom."

"What?"

"King Mason got wind of the fact that his brother was about to stage a coup."

"So he ran?"

"For his life. His brother's coup didn't involve taking over parliament. He intended to have King Mason assassinated so he could look like a grieving brother, reluctantly filling his murdered king's shoes."

Alex sat back. "Oh, my God." He thought for a second, then said, "But if Mason dies, his brother wouldn't become king. His daughter would."

His father locked his eyes with Alex's. "Exactly."

Alex's heart thundered in his chest. "He was planning to kill Eva?"

"Gerard couldn't just murder Mason. He had to kill Eva too. The plan was to stage an accident or an attack on the palace, and have both killed at the same time, so he would be the next in line to rule. That's why we separated them. Now, the two of them dying at the same time will look like the assassination that it is."

"Oh, my God."

"This marriage isn't about a treaty. We brought Eva and her mother here on the pretense of a wedding to get them out of their palace and keep them safe."

Alex gaped in disbelief. "And you don't think putting Eva in the public eye is dangerous?"

"Exactly the opposite. As long as she's in the press, her murder would be too public. Gerard can't even do something like kidnap Eva and her mother to use as leverage to bring Mason out of hiding. It would simply call too much attention to him when he wanted all this to look like an accident."

Eva's image popped into his head. Her waist-length hair, her shy smiles, her fearless personality. The thought that someone wanted to kill her infuriated him.

"And you think a wedding keeps her safe?"

"As long as this wedding's on a fast track, Eva and her mother are protected."

Though he was angry that his father hadn't told him this in the beginning, he understood the principle behind the plan. "You're right."

The king held his gaze. "For the next four weeks, you have to cooperate. This plan only works if we can keep everybody's attention focused on a happy wedding. And that means you've got to make this look real."

Alex didn't even hesitate. "You have my word."

King Ronaldo leaned forward, laying his arms on his desk. "Once we get your wedding date announced to the press, we're off and running. That's actually why we set the date so soon. All the royal events will happen too fast and too close together for the spotlight to leave Eva. Plus, Mason doesn't believe he'll need more than four weeks to sort this out."

"What's he doing?"

"Going through back channels to figure out who he can trust, so he can get the proof he needs that his brother wanted to assassinate him. Once he gets it, he can have his brother arrested."

"He thinks his own staff is in on it?"

"Only some. But we both know it only takes trusting one wrong person to risk everything. And in this case what he risks is his life and his daughter's."

Merely thinking that someone wanted to kill Eva sent anger careening through Alex again. But he understood palace intrigue. Though there had been no siblings who wanted his father's throne, there had been other challenges. Some subtle. Some obvious. All dangerous.

"We'll do the press conference announcing your wedding tomorrow. Which means you and Eva need to be seen together this afternoon, looking like a couple getting married."

"You want us to look like we're in love?"

"No. Everybody knows you barely know each other. So I want you to look like a man and woman getting acquainted in a positive way. Then after the press conference tomorrow, you can take Eva to the country house to show her where you would live as a married couple. The press will love that. It will also keep you and Eva in the papers. And even if anyone notices the extra bodyguards, they'll just think it's because there are two of you, not you alone."

He rose. "Okay."

His father rose too. "And Alex, if Mason can't get this done in four weeks, you will be marrying her."

A wedding for a treaty was ridiculous. Marrying Eva to keep her safe gave him a weird feeling. His muscles hardened, his brain sharpened. He hardly knew the woman, but no one would hurt her on his watch.

"Absolutely."

Eva, her mom, and Queen Rose walked to the formal living room with Sally from the protocol office. Once seated on the velvet sofas, Sally ordered coffee while Eva and the dynamic mother duo got down to the business of discussing designers and considering various styles of wedding dress.

The coffee hadn't even been delivered before a member of the palace staff arrived, whispered something to Sally and left.

Sally turned to Eva. "It seems, Princess, that Alex has arranged a date for the two of you this afternoon."

Working to keep the surprise out of her voice, she said, "He has?"

"You'll be lunching at a seaside restaurant. It will be the first time the press sees you as a couple. They won't get to ask questions, but they could shoot them at you from behind their cameras." She smiled briefly, obviously still miffed over the fact that her crown was paying for the wedding. "But you've handled this kind of thing before."

"Yes." Since she was old enough to stand behind a microphone, her dad had let her have her own voice.

She had to fight not to squeeze her eyes shut in misery. It was the first time in a week she'd had a good memory of her dad. He'd been the best supportive, funny, loving dad, and she suddenly missed him with a fierceness that brought tears to her eyes.

She blinked them away as she rose from the sofa. She refused to get maudlin over a man who had left her and her mom in such a precarious position.

"Thank you, Sally." She faced her mom and Queen Rose. "I'll need to leave to get ready."

Rose jumped up to hug her. "Enjoy the afternoon."

Karen kissed her cheek. "Yes. Enjoy yourself. Remember, brides are happy."

Rose laughed and batted her hand in dismissal. "We went through this with Ginny. Got pregnant in a one-night stand, barely knew Dom and suddenly had to marry a man she didn't know because her baby would be a king." She hugged Eva again. "It worked out for Ginny and Dom. It'll work out for you too, sugar."

"It will," Karen agreed sagely.

Eva only smiled. Obviously, they hadn't overheard any of Alex's comments about convincing her to call off the wedding.

She turned to leave, but Sally stopped her and handed her a computer tablet.

"All the links to the websites of the approved designers are in here. I'll need a name very soon so I can have him or her here ASAP to take measurements." She tapped her watch. "We don't have weeks for you to mull this over. We have, at best, a few days for you to choose a designer."

Her nerve endings popped with apprehension. Everything would be happening so fast, she had to get with the program. This afternoon's date with Alex had to be step one in her plan to get him to like her.

Three hours later, she stood in front of the mirror in her dressing room, inspecting herself. After watching several video demonstrations on flirting, she'd received

a call from Alex's staff with the time and location she
was to meet her betrothed.

Deciding she had a good variety of flirting tech-
niques, she'd showered and dressed in black pants and
a white top, with her long hair pinned up on her head
in a tight bun.

She sighed. She looked like a librarian. Casual Prince
Alex would most likely wear something übercomfort-
able. This outfit only highlighted their differences, all
but shouting that they didn't belong together—

Oh, darn him! Now she got it. The prince who kept
saying he would talk her out of this marriage hadn't
scheduled this lunch as a date. He'd set it up to get them
out of the palace and in front of the press, as a way to
publicly demonstrate that they didn't belong together.

She fumed as the truth settled in. What better way to
get her to back out of this wedding than by proving they
were different? Really different. So awkward as a couple
that the media might make an issue of it and make her
life too miserable to endure.

Furious, she yanked the pins out of her hair and let
it fall around her. She turned right, then left. The effect
was better but still not good enough for the woman marrying Xaviera's casual playboy prince.

Rummaging in her drawers, she found denim capris
and a flirty blue top. Sleeveless and low-cut, made of
airy material that billowed out when she moved, the
blouse was one of her favorites. Not only was she comfortable in it, but she was pretty. She *felt* flirty. And the
videos she'd watched on YouTube said feeling flirty was
half the battle. He might be on a mission to get her to
dump him, but she was on the opposite mission. If it

killed her, she would get him to like her enough he'd go through with this wedding.

No! By God, she would get him to fall in love with her!

After filling her black clutch bag with her phone and other necessities, she headed out.

When she saw Alex at the small side entryway where he'd indicated he would meet her, she watched his expression falter. Wearing worn boat shoes and scruffy jeans, with a white Oxford cloth shirt that tried unsuccessfully to make him respectable, he looked like a commoner. A dirt-poor, derelict commoner.

She didn't quite look that bad, but she hadn't dressed like a proper princess either, and from the quick once-over he gave her, it surprised him.

He shook his head as she approached.

She smiled. "You wanted to point out our differences by looking scruffy. But I figured out your game. So I scruffed down my outfit and, guess what? Here we are. A match."

"I did not set this up to point out our differences." He smiled engagingly. "And you'd look great no matter what you wore."

She'd look great no matter what she wore?

Eva stepped back. "What?"

"You look great. But, more important, we need to be out in public today because we'll be announcing our wedding tomorrow at a press conference."

Her eyes narrowed. "I thought you were going to talk me out of it?"

He laughed lightly. "Let's just take this one day at a time."

Her eyes narrowed even more as she studied him. He

might be a nice enough guy to save her from embarrassment twice, but he did not want this wedding. He should not be acting as if everything was fine.

"All right. What's up?"

He pointed at a black Mercedes. "Nothing."

As he helped her into the car, she analyzed their situation one more time, and realized that maybe there *was* nothing wrong. He had to look attentive and proper in public or his dad would know he wasn't taking this seriously. But that really worked in her favor. She could use the four or five hours they'd spend together getting him to like her.

To her surprise, he drove, with bodyguards following them in a big black SUV. Being accustomed to security details in her own country, she didn't even blink. Instead, she glanced out the window at the scenery. Though she'd viewed most of the island from the air as her royal family's jet touched down, being close to the thick green foliage and the rocky coastline took her breath away.

She sighed.

He eyed her curiously. "What's up?"

"Your country is beautiful."

"It is."

Okay. Even though it worked in her favor, his being nice to her was getting weird.

She stole a glance at him, running the situation through her brain again. He was so sexy in his scruffy jeans and white shirt that she had to admit she sort of liked the idea of marrying him. Even if his being nice to her was an act for the press, this was her shot. Her chance. She should not be overanalyzing this. She should be using it, engaging him in normal conversation to soften him up for when she experimented with flirting.

"What was it like growing up in such a warm climate?"

He took another quick look at her. "You mean as opposed to being required to wear a parka ninety percent of the year?"

She laughed at his perceptiveness. "Yes."

"Nice." He thought for a second. "I loved the beach, but I didn't like the private area behind the palace. I wanted to be on the real beach, the public beach, with kids my own age. It wasn't easy, and my bodyguards would groan when I was home from boarding school, but they generally found a way for me to be a normal kid."

"That's why I fell in love with America. Most Europeans knew who I was. And if they didn't, they knew I was 'famous' for some reason, so they'd Google me and that would be the end of any casual relationships. But in America, even knowing I was a princess, they'd shrug and say, 'that's cool,' but otherwise, I was just a person to them."

"Interesting."

"I'm surprised you never encountered that."

He sneaked another peek at her. His brown eyes softened when he thought. His lips tilted up just slightly, as if something he remembered made him want to smile.

Tingly warmth filled her. Oh, boy. It would be so flipping easy to fall for that smile. But it wasn't real. And even though his behavior could only be an act for the press, something felt wrong. Off. Really, really off.

"Stop the car."

"What?"

She huffed out a breath. "Stop the car. Go back to the palace."

"We can't. We're supposed to be seen in public."

"I can't behave normally at a restaurant or anywhere with you acting like this. It'll make me a nervous wreck. I'll look like an idiot."

"You're fine."

"No. I'm not. And neither are you. What the hell happened to you while I was getting ready for this lunch?"

"Nothing." He laughed. "Just chill. Okay?"

"Chill?"

He shifted on his seat. "Yeah, just relax."

Her eyes narrowed. "Relax?"

"My dad wants us out there looking like people preparing to get married. So we're going out. It's nothing sinister."

"So you talked to your dad?"

He drew in a long breath as if holding back his anger—or maybe holding back a smart-assed comment, the kind of thing he would have said to her at breakfast. And her suspicions quadrupled.

"Tell me what your dad said or turn the car around. I'm not going anywhere with you until you explain yourself."

Alex realized his mistake a little too late. Of course, she was questioning his behavior. That morning he'd pushed her at breakfast then vowed to get out of marrying her. This afternoon, he was being nice to her. She was too clever not to realize something was up.

"I'm just working to keep up the pretenses for the press."

"We're in a car. No one can hear you. There's no one to be keeping up the pretense for."

"The press has extremely good long-range camera lenses. They can pick up expressions in a car. Even a moving car."

Her eyes narrowed and she gave him that fierce silver stare of hers again.

"Which is exactly why the Alex I talked to this morning would be taking this opportunity to make us look unsuitable."

He squirmed on his seat. Damn. She was bright.

She shook her head. "Okay. Fine. You don't want to talk? Turn the car around. Take me back to the palace."

Her tirade would have been cute, except she was ruining an illusion that she desperately needed in place. He stole a peek at her with his peripheral vision. He'd never fool her for four weeks. No one would. But there was more to this than just how smart she was. This charade was life and death for her. She deserved to know the truth.

"You can't go back to the palace."

"The hell I can't!"

He sucked in a breath. "No. Really. This little tantrum you're having right now actually ruins *your* father's plan."

Her forehead wrinkled. "*My* father's plan? What does my father have to do with you suddenly being nice to me?"

"Your dad didn't leave your mom."

"Right."

"You are here, in Xaviera, because you are under my dad's protection. Your dad discovered a plot to kill him and you. The wedding is to keep you in the public eye

so your uncle doesn't try to kill you or use you as leverage to bring your dad out of hiding."

She gaped at him as if only a third of what he'd said
had sunk in. "What?"

"Your uncle wants to be king. But he's not getting
your country's throne unless both you and your dad are
out of the picture. Your dad discovered he'd hatched
a plot to have both of you killed in what would look
like a terrorist attack on your palace, so he left Grennady, using a cover story that seemed believable. But
he's working back channels to get proof so he can have
your uncle arrested."

Eva just gaped at Alex as he pulled the car into an alley
and virtually hid it between two tall stucco buildings.

Killing the engine, he said, "You and I are now officially co-conspirators."

She shook her head. "This has to be a mistake."

"No. My father doesn't move on something unless
he's positive it's real." He paused, giving her a curious
look. "You've never had trouble, dissension among the
ranks before?"

"No." She squeezed her eyes shut.

"Xaviera's had weird things like this happen at least
eight times. Last year we had a pirate who invaded our
island. Dom was the one who got rid of him."

"We've never been invaded, but there's always been
bad blood between my dad and his brother. They're
twins. My dad was born first. Uncle Gerard has always
felt two minutes cheated him out of his destiny."

"There you go."

Understanding seeped in by degrees. Her dad hadn't

deserted them. But this was worse. She and her dad were in danger.

"You've got to take me back to the palace. I have to tell my mom."

"Oh, no! No. No. No. My dad took me into his confidence because he trusts me. Now I'm taking you into my confidence because this is your life we're protecting. Plus, you're too smart. At some point, maybe the wrong point, you'd have figured out something was going on behind the scenes, and if you said something, asked the wrong question at the wrong time, it would ruin everything. You need to be a part of this. Your mom doesn't."

"But she's so upset!"

"And that's what makes this plan work. As long as she's sad about your dad leaving her, but happy for you, trying to make this the best wedding ever, everybody will believe your dad left her. Besides, Rose is taking care of her."

"Does Rose know?"

He shook his head. "You, me, my dad and a very few select members of his royal guard, people who are protecting your dad and helping with his investigation."

She sank back into the comfortable leather seat.

He took her hand, kissed the knuckles. "My dad assured me your dad is safe, and that they will get to the bottom of this."

The warmth of his kiss lingered on her skin. But something more important made her smile. "You trust me."

"I guess I do. Especially since this is the first official thing my father has ever asked of me. You could make me look really, really bad if you blow this."

She glanced down at the console between them,

where their joined hands sat. She'd never, ever had feelings like this before. She wasn't just making friends with this gorgeous guy. They had become partners.

"I don't want to make you look bad."

"So we've got a deal?"

She stared at their hands. His were strong and hers were tiny compared to his. They looked right together. But they weren't. This was all a ruse. A ruse to protect her life, but still a ruse.

In spite of the confusion and fear, disappointment fluttered through her. The marriage to a prince from Xaviera that she'd been dreaming about her whole life wasn't going to happen.

"Or do we not have a deal?"

Her head snapped up. She caught his gaze. She hid her disappointment that she and Alex wouldn't marry because it wasn't his fault, and he was protecting her. Her father wouldn't abdicate and she wasn't about to become a queen. She didn't have to rescue the reputation of her royal family, as she'd thought. Instead, she was protecting herself and her dad, as Alex mended his reputation with his dad—

And she could help him. She wouldn't marry him. She'd never have his children. But this fake, probably-won't-take-place marriage was more important than their real one would have ever been.

"Of course, we have a deal."

He released her hand and turned to open his car door. "Good. Let's go get some lunch and pretend we're the happiest two people in the world."

CHAPTER FOUR

"I'D LIKE TO hear how the princess feels about her dad running away with his mistress. It's only a matter of time before he abdicates his throne and then she'll be—what? The queen? Will she and Alex be moving to Grennady?"

After five minutes of talking about his engagement and taking a ribbing about finally settling down, Prince Alex wasn't surprised by the question. He also wasn't surprised when his father nudged him and Eva away from the podium and took the mic.

"You received the rules for this press conference yesterday and you know questions about the embarrassing situation with King Mason are off-limits."

Alex suppressed a smile. Leave it to his dad to tell the press what they could and couldn't ask.

"But for the record, let me state that Princess Eva should be allowed to enjoy her engagement and wedding without being reminded that she has a father who embarrassed her family, her *country* by quite openly taking a mistress on vacation—"

"It's our understanding this woman is more than a mistress, and that King Mason left a note for his wife saying their marriage was over. If he abdicates, which a divorce will force him to do, Eva will be Grennady's new queen," a member of the press shouted from the sea of reporters below them.

Alex stole a quick glance at Karen, who straightened regally, as if to agree with his father. The actions of her husband would not put a damper on her daughter's wedding.

King Ronaldo's eyebrows rose. "I said no questions or comments about this and I meant that. This wedding is a happy occasion and I intend to keep it that way."

"But he's—"

That was all Alex heard before being whisked out of the press room, Eva at his side.

In the hall outside the press room, his father straightened regally. "All things considered, I'd say that went very well."

Eva nodded. "Yes. Thank you."

Her congenial reply made the king's expression go from proud to confused. Alex could almost see the wheels turning in his head as he realized she knew enough about the situation to thank him. And there was only one way she could know.

The king snapped his gaze to Alex's.

Alex inclined his head toward Eva, a silent indicator that he'd told her. His father hadn't said he couldn't, though it was clear he'd counted on Alex's discretion. But, in his opinion, Eva didn't just have a right to know; Alex had had a responsibility to tell her.

Getting the message, his father sighed. "Okay, then. I hope you two know what you're doing."

Alex said, "We do," at the same time that Eva said, "We do."

Alex stole a glance at her. He wouldn't exactly call her stubborn but she was her own woman. A woman, the comment from the press had reminded all of them, who would someday be a queen.

Still, she was in line for the throne of a rather young king. Her dad wasn't even fifty yet. Plus, most kings didn't retire. Mason could rule until the day he died. But if Eva's dad died unexpectedly or decided to retire, she would be queen of her own country.

After only a few days with her, he could see it. He could envision her overseeing a parliament, directing the affairs of a country.

Obviously not pleased, but resigned to their situation, King Ronaldo sighed and walked away.

Chatting about the imminent arrival of the designer who had been chosen for Eva's dress, Queen Rose and Karen also walked away.

With a quick kiss on Ginny's cheek, Dom headed for his office, and Ginny excused herself to go to her apartment to check on the baby.

Alex directed Eva to the right, toward the elevator that would take them to the floor for her apartment.

Eva quietly said, "Your dad is very clever."

He laughed. "No kidding. It's one of the reasons Dom works so hard. He's got very big shoes to fill." He stopped talking, waiting for the elevator to reach them. When they were inside, behind the closed door where no one could overhear, he stole a glance at her.

"I know your dad isn't abdicating and you're not going to be taking your throne in the immediate future, but that doesn't change the fact that you'll someday be a queen."

She straightened, the same way his father did, and Alex laughed again. "Oh, yeah. You've thought about it."

"Actually, my father and I have discussed it. When

Dom married Ginny my dad told me it was a blessing because my entire focus was needed to be Queen of Grennady. And I probably will be for a while. But, honestly, I don't think I'm made to rule."

"Oh, trust me. You are."

"I hope to be in my sixties before my father dies. Which could make my oldest son close to forty. And ready to reign. I see myself more in the role of placeholder for a few years to soften the blow of my father's death, then I'll turn everything over to him."

He tilted his head and studied her. "You really have thought it all through."

"Of course I have. Ruling lines don't think in terms of decades. We think in terms of generations. But you know that."

He shrugged. "Sort of."

"Which was why I didn't argue this marriage. I know your bloodline. I know you and I would have produced a wonderful king."

He shook his head. "My son would have been a king."

She stepped close, straightened the collar of his shirt and then his tie. "Does it make you sorry you're not marrying me?"

He looked down, into her pretty gray-blue eyes and at her smiling face. He let his gaze skim her soft black hair. When his gaze fell to her lips, the one kiss they'd shared jumped into his brain. That one really hot, really great kiss.

For a second he almost was sorry he wasn't marrying her, but not for the reasons she thought.

The elevator door opened. He ignored it. "If your dad doesn't straighten things out before our wedding date, we may still be getting married."

"Let's hope it doesn't come to that. But even if it does, we can get an annulment. Far different than a divorce. It won't preclude me from taking the throne."

She took a step to walk out of the elevator, but he caught her hand, stopping her and letting the door close behind her. Trapped in the gaze of her magnetic blue eyes, he saw some problems she didn't. She talked about this wedding as if it were nothing but a business deal, but he could see a million reasons she could get sucked into it.

"I just don't want you to get any ideas while we spend four weeks together."

She laughed. "I liked it better when you kissed me to warn me off."

More memories of the kiss flooded him. And here she was again, within reach, working her smart mouth against him, filling him with challenge.

She smiled, put her small white hand on his chest. "Maybe you're warning me because you need the warning yourself."

The elevator door opened again. This time, he let her walk out, but he called after her, "Be ready at four. I'm to take you to the country house to show you where we'll be living."

She turned, smiled and nodded, then walked away.

Alex sucked in a steadying breath. Her behavior should infuriate him. Instead, it constantly challenged him. What would it be like to be the guy who tamed a future queen? She might be the woman who ruled their country, but he would be the guy who ruled their bed.

He shook his head to dislodge that thought before it took root. He wasn't marrying anyone ever. Let alone someone who would be his ruler.

* * *

Eva managed to remain perfectly cool until she was behind the door of her apartment. Then she leaned against
it and squeezed her eyes shut.

Why in the hell had she just flirted with him?

She shook her head on the way to her bedroom. Of all
the times for those stupid flirting videos she'd watched
on YouTube to pop into her head, the day after he'd told
her the truth about their marriage was the worst.

Still, he'd presented her with eight or ten really good
jumping-off points, and in the end she couldn't fight her
brain from using the knowledge it now had—

Oh, please. If there was one thing Eva didn't do it
was kid herself, and she wouldn't let herself start now.
She'd flirted because she'd wanted to. The Alex she'd
met at the stables had been angry. The Alex she'd dealt
with at her arrival dinner and breakfast the morning
they'd chosen the wedding date had been determined
to talk her out of it. The Alex who'd been released from
his commitment was fun. Happy-go-lucky. Yet fiercely
determined to protect her and her dad. His brown eyes
sparked with the challenge of their situation. He clearly
liked having a role, a part to play, and he was a natural.

Plus, he looked great in a suit. Really handsome.

Put all that together and the man was just sexy.

Tempting.

And oh, so easy to tease.

She told herself to stop thinking like that. Not because
she was worried for her life. She wasn't. She trusted
King Ronaldo and Xaviera's royal guard to keep her
safe. And she trusted her dad to find the proof, arrest
his brother and right their world.

The problem was, at any time before the wedding

her dad could call and say he had everything in hand and she and her mom could go home. This might go the whole way to the day before the wedding or it could end tomorrow, but no matter how long the ruse lasted, she would be going home. Without Alex.

Getting involved with him was pointless. Except—

As Alex had reminded her, she was also a woman who would be a queen, who had to produce a royal heir, who had no skills with men.

She might not be marrying Prince Alex Sancho, but her four weeks with him could help her figure out how she could find the husband she'd need to do her duty and create an heir.

Alex had just reached his apartment door when his cell phone buzzed with a text. He pulled his phone from his pocket and saw the message from Dom.

Meet me in your office.

He almost laughed. He hadn't been in his own office in months. Meetings were typically held in the king's office or Dom's. He didn't exactly have a lot of official business.

Still…

It felt right. Maybe because his father had taken him into his confidence about Eva's situation, but he suddenly didn't mind being called to his office.

He typed, On my way... turned around and took his elevator back to the first floor.

Dom awaited him in the empty secretary's space that fronted his furnished, but never used office. "Hey, kid."

"Hey, older brother." He led Dom into the room,

walked behind his desk and fell to the chair that was slightly uncomfortable, given that no one had worn it in. The walls were paneled with rich wood. Thick Persian rugs covered the floors. Velvet drapes framed the huge window that overlooked the courtyard. And no one ever saw any of it.

Dom sat on one of the chairs in front of his desk. "Dad told me about King Mason."

"He did?"

"Yes. After your talk with him, he realized it wasn't right that he was doing an end run around me with the royal guard I supervise."

"Wow. He's really loosening up."

Dominic chuckled. "Dad's not the hard case you think he is. In the past months, he's been handing over a lot of his responsibilities to me." He caught Alex's gaze. "And he sees you as the one running point on this situation with Eva and her mom."

"Running point?" He sniffed, not quite sure how to handle the fact that his father trusted him. "For the next four weeks I'm going to be dating a really pretty girl."

Dom laughed. "That's one way to look at it. Or you could say that for the next four weeks you're protecting the daughter of one of Dad's closest political allies. It's a big deal."

Alex rolled his eyes. "I was making a joke."

"Right. You love being funny. But you're ready for this. As much as you like pretending that you aren't." He shifted on his seat. "I took a few minutes to go over everything that happened at the press conference and you and Eva were great."

Alex laughed. "We're both born to this life. We know how to keep up appearances."

"And you did. But here's the thing. The two of you stood close together at the podium. You smiled at each other at just the right times. But when we left the press room and gathered in the hall, your demeanors changed. There was a visible distance between you."

"So? The press couldn't see."

"I know, but the biggest group of people you have to fool wasn't in that press room. They were in the corridor outside the press room."

Alex frowned.

"It's our staff. It took only two phone calls for my secretary to get the scoop that you've never been to Eva's apartment and she's never been to yours."

Alex's face scrunched in disbelief. "What?"

"The staff knows you've basically just met, so it's not like they expect you to be sleeping together, but they're gossiping about the fact that the only times you're seen together are when you're expected to be."

"Really?"

"There's a betting pool. All the stable boys believe you'll never actually marry. The maids are divided. And even though Chef's a romantic she's betting against the marriage too. That's not good for your charade."

He sat up, totally confused by the fact that he hadn't thought of this. "I guess not."

Dom rose. "Convincing the staff here at the palace should be your first priority. In fact, if I were you, I'd put on such a show that the stable boys start changing their bets and the maids can't resist gossiping to their neighbors."

Alex leaned back in his chair. He appreciated the heads-up. He would have figured it out for himself in another day or two, but he was glad he hadn't had to.

He pulled his phone out of his pocket and brought his schedule onto the screen. He cancelled every event he had arranged for the next week.

He glanced up at Dom. "If you don't mind, I'd like to see any plans the guard put in place for Eva's protection, and the names of the men in her security details."

"I'll tell the lieutenant."

Alex rose. "Great."

As Dom turned to the door, he said, "And don't forget what I told you about the staff."

"I won't."

After Dom left, Alex thought for another second, then strode out of the office.

The staff hadn't seen him in Eva's apartment? Well, there was no better time than the present. He took the elevator to the guest floor, walked down the massive hall to her rooms and lifted his hand to knock—

A fiancé wouldn't knock.

He opened the door and ambled through the tall-ceilinged foyer to the living room.

"Alex!" his stepmother yelped as she tossed a white robe to Eva who stood on a platform similar to the one his tailor used. She hugged the robe to her bosom, but it was too late. He'd seen the yellow bra and panties. He'd seen the creamy white arc of her breasts. He'd seen the curve of her hip.

He stopped dead in his tracks.

Rose about had a coronary. "What are you doing here? And why didn't you knock?"

"A fiancé doesn't knock." He tried not to watch as Eva turned her back to him and slipped into the robe. But the vision from the back was as awe-inspiring as the front. For a short woman, she had a long, sloping back that ended in perfect round hips and a round butt.

Eva slid into the robe, yanked the belt at her waist and turned to the sixty-something man who stood with a tape measure in hand, gaping at Alex.

"Could you give us a minute?"

The older man said, "Of course, but only a minute. Considering time for fittings, I've got about two weeks to make a gown the whole world is going to see. Everybody's got to be on board with the timing or I swear I will fold like a house of cards."

Composed now, Rose took his arm. "Of course, we'll cooperate with your timing." She tossed Alex a pointed look. "This will not happen again."

"At least not without a phone call to warn us you're coming," Eva's mom said haughtily. "You might be engaged, but a gentleman caller is still a gentleman caller."

The three trooped out of the room and Alex laughed. "Have a lot of gentleman callers, do you?"

"My mom is struggling to find any sense of normalcy in this situation. She thinks her husband left her. And she's in the public eye. If she wants to ban you from the room, I say we let her."

"We can't. Dom reminded me this morning that the most important group we have to fool is the servants."

She frowned.

"The palace staff. There's a betting pool. Apparently no one believes I'll actually marry you."

Her delicate eyebrows rose. "And who do we have to thank for that, Mr. Date-Every-Woman-in-the-Known-Universe?"

"You're a woman in the known universe and I never dated you."

She held up one finger to stop him. "No, you haven't. And maybe that's the problem. Just jumping into this wedding the way we have, everybody sees it as nothing but a royal responsibility." She tapped her finger against her lips, thinking. "So maybe what we need to do is have a date. A real date. Not lunch, but something smashing."

"In front of the staff," Alex reminded her, letting his gaze roam along her fluffy white robe, knowing the pretty bra and panties were beneath, and that they covered a gorgeous butt and breasts just the right size for his hands. "That means the trip to the country home is cancelled. It smacks of PR."

"So what can we do here? In the palace?"

He knew one very important thing they could do. In his apartment. In his bedroom. Too bad the staff couldn't see that. But they would see the seduction leading up to it—

"Have dinner at my apartment."

She laughed. "Oh, how many times have you used that line?"

The way she said it cut through him like a knife. His success with women was legendary. But in a good way. She didn't have to sound so snooty about it. "I wasn't that bad."

She stepped down from the platform, tightened the belt with a quick yank. "Oh, please."

"You know, maybe we're looking at this all wrong. Maybe the reason the staff doesn't think the wedding will come off is you?"

She gasped. "Me?"

"You have an attitude about me."

She gaped at him.

"Maybe what you need to do is start being nicer to me."

"Okay. Fine. I'll be nicer to you. But I need specifics so I can do some prep work. What's your plan for tonight?"

"If this was a normal date, I'd call the kitchen staff and tell them to set up a romantic dinner around eight. You'd arrive in something pretty and I'd be spellbindingly witty while they served dinner. We'd dismiss them after they served the main course. Then you'd still be at my apartment tomorrow when they bring up breakfast, and it would look like things got so cozy that you didn't leave."

Eva swallowed. She could picture it. She'd be wearing a pretty gown; he'd be in a tux. She'd be shy. He'd be… well, himself. Playful. Sexy. Seductive.

She swallowed again. "It works." She cleared her throat. It really, really worked. She got breathless just imagining it. Plus, four hours of a dinner with him, while he was being himself? Just think of the flirting practice she'd get.

Queen Rose walked into the living room again. "We have a designer who's about to melt into a puddle of despair if we don't get your measurements today. Can we speed this up?"

Eva said, "Yes, of course. Give us one more minute." She faced Alex. "I'll be there at eight."

Alex smiled. "And take a nap. I don't want the serving staff telling the press you yawned all night. I want them thinking all kinds of naughty thoughts when they find your gown on the floor."

"My gown on the floor?" Her face turned red, but she understood what he was saying. There was no better way to perpetuate a story than to physically stage it. "Okay."

"Maybe we'll make a whole trail. Gown. Bra. Panties…" He caught her gaze. "My shirt."

Picturing undressing in front of him and having him take his shirt off in front of her sent her hormones scrambling.

He leaned toward her and kissed her cheek. "This'll be fun."

CHAPTER FIVE

WHEN HIS DOORBELL rang at eight, Alex walked through the foyer entryway to answer it. He straightened the bow tie of his tux, before reaching down for the knob to open the door for her.

"Good—"

His voice faltered when he saw her in a yellow gown, the same color as the bra and panties she'd been wearing when he accidentally walked in on her fitting. For a good twenty seconds, he was struck dumb. Then common sense filtered through the image of her standing on the tailor's platform. Yes, he'd seen her in a bra and panties, but he'd seen women dressed in far less at the beach.

"—evening."

He sucked in a breath. He might have seen women dressed in less, but that didn't take away from the fact that she was beautiful. Her dark hair had been pulled up in a style that reminded him of a Greek goddess. Her dress clung to her curves, but just at the bottom of her hip it flared into tons of material that frothed out like a bell. "You look amazing."

She smiled. "Thanks."

Her humble acceptance of his compliment did crazy things to his pulse, but he didn't try to pretend he didn't know why. Her innocence struck a funny chord with him. And why not? Her naiveté made her sweet. It had been a long time since he'd met, let alone spent time with, a woman who was sweet.

But she was also strong. Pretty much his smart-ass equal when he pushed her, which made her kind of fun to be with. He'd have to be deaf, dumb and blind not to be attracted to her.

But that might be good. What better way to get the tongues of the staff wagging than to let himself act naturally, the way he would with any beautiful woman?

He reached down, took her hand and kissed the palm. "I hope you like Italian."

He saw the little pulse point at her throat jump. Too bad the servants hadn't seen that.

She laughed nervously. "Something rich and fattening?"

"Of course. I'm sure we can find a way to work off the calories."

He'd said that for the benefit of the young man who'd walked to the table set up by the large window to light the candles, but Eva's nervous laugh returned.

He smiled. After his thirty-second lapse of sanity after seeing her in the dress the same color as her panties and bra that afternoon, it was good to knock her off balance, too. They had to appear to be attracted to each other. Not just him to be tongue-tied over her. They also needed for her to be smitten around him.

Still holding her hand, he led her into the living room where two glasses of wine sat on the low table in front of the sofa.

"I took the liberty of choosing a wine."

She smiled and accepted the glass from him. This smile wasn't nervous, but pretty. Soft. Sensual.

His attraction returned—expanded—became more of an urge for action than a feeling. He pictured himself running his hands along her curved torso, and the lines between reality and pretense blurred a bit. If he'd met her in a casino he would have pursued an evening like this for real. She was pretty. Her innocence was endearing. And she made him work for her affection. If nothing else, the challenge of it appealed to him.

But this wasn't real. It was a fiction for the benefit of the press. He was supposed to be acting. Playing a part. He shouldn't be having real urges.

He directed her to the sofa. They sat together, side by side, and the soft material of her gown billowed around her as if she were buried in fabric. But, really, no matter how huge the skirt, a strapless gown was only held together by a hook-and-eye catch and a very long zipper. He could probably have that gown undone in twenty seconds, and then he'd get to touch all that soft-looking skin.

Damn it! What the hell was wrong with him? This was supposed to be acting, not fantasizing.

He stretched out the collar beneath his bow tie. "Is it warm in here?"

She fanned herself. "A little."

"Maybe we should just get right to dinner?"

She rose. "I am hungry."

"Good." He set his hand on the small of her back, directing her to the table set up by a wall of windows that displayed the sea behind the palace.

After he pulled out her chair, she sat and looked up at him with a smile. "What an amazing view! This is lovely."

He stared down at her. When she was relaxed, her eyes were a soft, pretty blue. He liked it almost as much as the sharp color they turned when she was angry or determined.

Realizing he was doing it again—behaving as if this was real—he jumped away from her, tugged the vest of his tux into place and walked to his seat across from her.

"Thank you. Our legend is that it took three years to build our palace."

She opened her napkin and set it on her lap as servants began bringing salads. "I'd love to hear about it."

He shrugged, feeling awkward. This scene should have been a piece of cake for him. But once again urges and possibilities flashed through his mind. Things he could do. Things he'd like to do. Things he knew he wasn't supposed to do. Because this was a charade.

It was crazy. Odd. Confusing.

"There's not much to tell. It took my ancestors three years to build this back in the Middle Ages. End of story."

"But it's so modern."

He cautiously met her gaze. "We've added on."

"And done a lovely job."

The servants stepped back, but they didn't leave. He and Eva began eating their salads. The room was quiet, as if populated by two people with nothing to say. Which was ridiculous. He was a pro. He'd had a thousand first dates. Hundreds of dates in this apartment. And he knew the goal. It wasn't to take her to bed or even kiss her. This was all about fooling the servants. They had to jump to conclusions when they found her dress on the floor the next morning. And they wouldn't, if he couldn't even talk to her.

He cleared his throat. "And what about your palace?"

"It's a little cozier."

"You mean smaller."

"No. I mean cozier. There's a fireplace in every room. There are only a few months in the year when we don't need a fire. We wear warm pajamas and do a lot of snuggling."

He laughed, but he suddenly pictured her in flannel PJs, sitting under a warm blanket, in front of a fire. She was curvy and soft. Made for snuggling. Made for fires and cognac.

Damn it. Why was he doing this?

"Tell me about your education." The sentence wasn't fully out of his mouth before he winced. He wanted the servers to run to the press with stories of red-hot kisses, not two people reading their biographies.

He had to get his head in the game. He was sharper than this.

"Are you okay?"

He laughed and combed his fingers through his hair. "I'm fine."

But they ate most of the dinner in silence because he couldn't think of anything to say. Every time he came up with something suitable, something intimate, it wouldn't feel like part of a ruse. It would feel real, so real, his nerves tingled with an anticipation he wasn't allowed to feel.

When the meal was eaten, he escorted her to the sofa, and walked to the bar. "What can I get you?"

"Why don't we just stick with wine?"

"Great idea."

"Good."

She smiled the soft smile and he fought an avalanche

of urges. The urge to tease her. The urge to tell her just how great she looked in yellow. The urge to make short order of her gown and slide his hands along the curve of her waist...

But every time he decided it was okay to make an urge a reality, as part of the ruse, his stomach tumbled. Kisses that were meant to be seen by the staff weren't supposed to have actual meaning. Even she'd believe they were fake. But he really wanted this.

Which was wrong for so many different reasons he couldn't even count them.

He poured more wine and sat beside her on the sofa.

"I don't think it's inappropriate for us to talk about our pasts."

He glanced around, saw no one was listening and said, "Except we're getting married. We should already know each other's pasts."

"Not really. It's an arranged marriage. Besides, I once heard that the best way to get people to believe a lie is to stick with the truth as much as possible."

He laughed at the wonderfully naive way she said that. "Who told you that?"

"A vet who came to the shelter. She was one of those people who talked all the time." She laughed. "Knew a little something about everything." She tilted her head. "Not sure why I suddenly remembered that."

"Because we need it?"

"Maybe. But I think the real problem is you know a great deal about me, but I know very little about you beyond the stuff everybody sees: the fact that you date a lot, love casinos and in general goof off."

"Because that's about all there is."

"Really? That's it? You've never been in love?"

The question hit him like a sucker punch. He should have expected it, but hadn't, and when Nina's face popped into his head, it threw him for a loop.

He pulled in a quiet breath.

She leaned in. "It would make the charade so much more believable if the staff heard you telling me the truth."

Realizing his reaction had given him away, he raised his gaze, met her pretty blue eyes. "Yes. I was in love. Once."

"What happened?"

He said, "She left me," because that was the easy, no-explanation-necessary way of telling the story. But when he said it, his chest tightened and his brain froze.

"Why did she leave you?"

He swallowed.

Her gaze swept his face. "She must have broken your heart."

The vise grip on his chest tightened another notch. His brain jumped in revolt at the way he was fooling her, even though this wasn't the first time he'd used this loophole in his explanation. He'd never really admitted the truth in his Nina story to anyone. Yet, he knew if he wasn't totally honest, Eva's questions would continue. The conclusions she'd draw would be wrong.

"She died."

Eva pressed her hand to her chest. "Oh. I'm so sorry."

His mouth felt dry. Dusty. He took a sip of wine.

She said, "I'm sorry," again. "Really, we can talk about something else."

But he pictured Nina, always in a bikini, always on a boat or a Jet Ski or water skis.

He swiped his hand across his mouth. "Yeah, we should probably talk about something else."

"Sure."

The room got quiet. Except for the sounds of the staff gathering dishes and silverware from the table by the window, his entire apartment was silent.

"Was she pretty?"

He blew out his breath. "That's not talking about something else."

"I know."

She smiled, and for the second time in only a few minutes he got the sucker punch. Resisting that smile would be harder than telling a few simple, unemotional facts.

"She was very pretty. Tall, blonde, and only twenty-two." He shrugged. "Of course, I wasn't much older."

"So it was a long time ago?"

"Five years."

"You're past it, then?"

He should be. Most days he thought he was.

"Did your father like her?"

That made him laugh. "We spent most of our time on the water. Jet Skis. Water skiing. Diving. Because all that kept me out of the casinos, my father thought she was good for me."

Eva eased back on the sofa, getting comfortable. Alex leaned back too. They sat side by side. With only a slight tilt of their heads, they could look at the ceiling.

"*Was* she good for you?"

Alex shrugged. "We were daredevils." And things he hadn't thought about in those five years began tiptoe-ing into his brain. "There was no official investigation into her accident, or if there had been her father kept it hushed up. But I heard from the people with her that day that she'd been driving too fast, pushing boundaries."

"I'm sorry."

He sniffed. "It's not your fault. If anything, it was hers." Saying the words out loud hurt his chest. Crumbled his heart into a thousand pieces. Until this very moment, he hadn't realized how angry he was with Nina. "And now it's officially time to talk about something else."

"Want to hear about the guy who almost had me calling my parents to see if I could get out of my marriage to Dominic?"

He laughed with relief. "Absolutely."

"It was my first year at university. He was a tremendous geek."

He laughed again, thinking it remarkable that he could talk so openly about Nina, then two seconds later laugh.

"A geek?"

"Oh, I thought he was so brilliant. I hung on his every word."

"I'm not exactly brilliant."

She turned her head on the sofa and waited until he turned his, and their eyes met. "I'm not exactly the water skiing type. I've never water skied. I'm not fond of boats. *Daredevil* is the last word anyone would use to describe me."

Yet right at that moment he wanted to kiss her more than he wanted his next breath of air. His body tingled when she was around. She made him laugh. Protecting her gave him a great sense of responsibility that didn't annoy him, it pleased him. And he'd told her about Nina.

Oh, no.

He was beginning to like her. For real. That's why seeing her in the bra and panties had switched him into genuine seduction mode. Getting feelings for her brought reality into their fantasy.

He bounced up on the sofa, noticed the last servant leaving the dining area by the window, and reached down for her hand to help her stand. "Well, that was certainly an interesting conversation, but all the servants are in the kitchen now. In five minutes everybody will be out of here."

She glanced at his hand. Her head tilted in confusion.

"You can take off your dress—" in the bathroom, behind closed doors so he didn't see "—and be on your way."

She frowned. "That's it?"

"What did you think? This is a charade." Stronger now that he'd figured out why he felt so different around her tonight, he caught her gaze. "We're not really going to sleep together."

But his heart felt funny as the words slid out of his mouth.

When she finally took his hand and said, "No. I'm sorry. I just somehow thought I'd be staying longer," his heart squeezed.

He stepped back. He wasn't letting one slip-up cloud his brain. So he liked her? He liked a lot of women. This was a charade. To protect her. He couldn't—wouldn't—let these feelings for her grow.

He shifted another step away from her. "No point in going overboard."

Especially since these feelings were amazingly different. Warm. Happy. The kind of feelings he'd run from his entire life.

CHAPTER SIX

ALEX DIRECTED HER to a powder room, where she removed her gown and slipped into the sundress she'd squished into her little clutch purse. She walked out, handed her gown to him and watched him drop it to the floor about halfway down a discreet hallway. Then he walked her to a back door.

He motioned for her to go before him into a thin, quiet hall. "This corridor is private. Even servants aren't allowed to use it."

They reached the elevator and he pressed the button. The doors opened.

She waited a beat. Not quite sure what she wanted until she realized she was waiting for him to kiss her good-night—though she wasn't quite sure why. This was a ruse with a purpose. Not real. The only time they had to pretend they liked each other was when someone was watching. And no one was watching—

Hadn't he reminded her of that?

He stepped back. His hand on the elevator door, holding it open, but now a good two feet away from her, he said, "Good night."

Disappointment fluttered through her. "Good night."

She stepped into the elevator, believing herself certifiable. Why the hell would she possibly have stood there like a ninny expecting him to kiss her...?

Because she'd seen the odd looks he'd given her, caught him staring at her face and gazing into her eyes, and knew he was beginning to like her.

Still, only an idiot would have missed how he'd changed when he started talking about the woman he'd loved. The one who had died.

As the elevator rose to her floor, her heart caught a bit at the thought of his loss. She'd never lost anyone. Never really had her heart broken, but he had. He hadn't just lost his first love. His mother had died. He'd been through things she'd never even considered. It was no wonder he lived a surface life. Hid his feelings. Tried to pretend he didn't have feelings. He was protecting himself.

She couldn't fault him for that, even if it did disappoint her that he'd rushed her out, and hadn't made good on the promise that they'd make a trail of clothes.

She almost giggled at the devilishness of that, but caught herself. He wouldn't have swooned at the sight of her stripping. Though she couldn't say the same for watching him take off his shirt—

The elevator arrived at her floor and she sighed. Why was she thinking like this?

Because he was good-looking.

Because he was smart.

Because he trusted her enough to tell her about her dad, to make her a co-conspirator.

And tonight he'd told her about his lost love.

The few days they'd spent together they'd been forced to be brutally honest. She hadn't just been honest with him; he'd been honest with her. And, God help her, she'd liked it.

Like it? Or liked him?

She squeezed her eyes shut. She didn't know. But the evening had been different than she'd expected. Very different. Instead of struggling to keep her dignity while he tried to impress the servants with his sexual prowess, they'd talked.

And it had been nice.

No, better than nice. It had been one of the best nights of her life.

She shook her head as a crazy thought filled it.

What if pretending to be involved, being co-conspirators, put them in each other's company enough that they actually grew to like each other?

He was confiding in her. She was relaxing with him. Was it so far-fetched to think that a charade actually set them up to fall in love?

It might not be far-fetched but it did sound a hell of a lot like wishful thinking. Especially since a few short days before they'd been at odds.

Still, when she went to bed that night, she thought of telling him that her palace was cozy and she smiled. She wouldn't mind sitting in front of a fire with him.

The next day Eva had breakfast with her mom, and spent the morning with her and Queen Rose, looking at table arrangements for the engagement party to be held in less than two weeks and the wedding two weeks after that. When Alex called and told her they would be going to dinner that night, both mothers made kissing noises.

Remembering that they believed this wedding was real, she blushed. They thought it was cute, but actually it was lying to her mom that embarrassed her. Still, it was for a good cause. And any day now her mom would know that.

And any day now, she and Alex wouldn't be in this game they were playing out to help her dad. That was probably the best reason to keep her wits about her. They didn't have the four weeks everybody thought they did. Her dad could call tomorrow, and they'd never see each other again.

When Alex came to her apartment to pick her up, he immediately glanced around to see if anyone was there.

"Mom is having dinner with your dad and stepmom."

He visibly relaxed. "Good. Because I wanted to apologize for being abrupt last night."

She said, "That's okay." Then after a slight pause, she carefully added, "I was kind of glad you shared." She didn't want to make a big deal out of it. She especially didn't want to say so much that he'd realize she was getting feelings for him. The man was a playboy. And she was someday going to be a queen. She couldn't be falling for a guy who would very publicly break her heart. But she did need to acknowledge the obvious. They'd shared some secrets.

"Nina died five years ago. I'm over it."

"I get that. I still appreciate that you told me."

He mumbled something under his breath, walked over to the door and opened it for her.

"I'll tell you what. We'll put the top down on the Mercedes." He dangled his car keys. "And I'll even let you drive, if you promise to forget I told you any of that."

Walking to the door, she snatched the keys out of his hand. This was what they did best. Argue. Playfully, of course. She finally figured out that was the way he liked life, conversations, maybe even relationships. Easy. Silly. Meaningless.

"Oops. Looks like you just lost your leverage."

He laughed but didn't try to take the keys back. Once she settled in behind the steering wheel of his car, she started the engine and Alex pressed the button that folded the roof down.

She breathed in the warm Xaviera air. "I'm gonna miss this."

He laughed. "I thought you liked being snuggled in front of fireplaces."

She waved to the bodyguards, put the gearshift into Drive and drove to the gate which opened in front of her, then off palace grounds. The air was warm and sweet, and the way Alex remembered that detail of her life made her feel soft and squishy inside.

But she didn't say anything.

"No comment on the fact that I remembered your palace is cozy?"

"No." She stole a peek at him. "That would sort of be like flirting." And what a hell of a time for her to finally catch on. "If we were in public where the press could overhear, I might have said how nice it was you remembered, and maybe tease you into admitting you'd like to sit with me under a blanket in front of the fire. Where we could, you know, snuggle up and *accidentally* rub up against each other. But since we're alone there's no point."

She glanced over at him again. His eyes were wide. His mouth was sort of open.

"What?" She shook her head. "The whole flirting thing is new to me. I got that wrong, didn't I?"

"No. No. You were fine."

"The part about rubbing up against each other under the blanket... That was too much?"

"Nope. That was pretty much spot-on. Class-A flirting."

She cast a quick look at him, knowing she was grinning like an idiot. "So I'm getting it?"

"You never tried to flirt with the geek?" Before she could answer, he shook his head. "No. Of course, you didn't. You probably were like a deer in the headlights around him."

She laughed and attraction sharpened all of Alex's senses, but he ignored it. He'd sorted all this out the night before. He could not fall for her. He was not the kind of guy who had relationships. It was best to just do what he needed to do, but otherwise maintain his distance.

The best way to do that would be to keep them both busy. So he took her to a casino after dinner, and showed her how to play blackjack. She wore a pale pink gown that made her look sweet and innocent. Her long black ponytail heightened the effect, and he was glad. She was tempting, but also innocent, and the visual reminder that he could hurt her if he acted on his impulses got his head in the game.

The dealer dealt her an ace, then gave a card to the other four players at their half circle table. When he came back to Eva, Alex said, "Take a card."

She sat and he stood behind her. He'd had to lean down to look at her card. But that was okay. He could smell her perfume, feel the smoothness of her shoulder as he brushed it, but he was in control now.

She peeked up at him. "Take a card?"

"Say hit me."

She laughed. "I've never before asked to be hit."

In the few days he'd spent in her company, he knew there were a million things she'd never done. A million things he'd love to show her.

He kept all that to himself. "So, go ahead. Say it."

With a giggle, she faced the dealer. "Hit me."

The dealer laughed too as he pulled a card from the dispenser. "Ten." He met Eva's gaze. "Twenty-one."

She peeked back at Alex.

"You win."

She jumped off her seat. "I win!" She spun to face Alex. "I win!" Like Rose on steroids, she enveloped him in a fast hug. But when she pulled away, their gazes caught, and he could see in her shiny silver-blue orbs the very second she realized she had her hands wrapped around his biceps.

Time stopped.

They stared into each other's eyes, both of them silently acknowledging that having her hands on him felt good.

But she didn't step back, didn't pull away. She just kept gazing into his eyes, as if spellbound.

And he wanted to curse. The innocence that was so tempting was the very thing that would keep her safe from him. Yet tonight he wanted to be with her. To just let his guard down and see where the night would take them.

But he wouldn't do that. No matter how much he thought he wanted her tonight, they potentially had weeks of being together. He would not make this into something it wasn't supposed to be. Something that might hurt her.

He plucked her hands off his arms and directed her

back to her seat. "All right, Cinderella. That was just your first hand. You've got a whole night ahead of you."

She laughed but there was a hesitancy to it. What passed between them had been a powerful, but normal, male/female thing, yet it had thrown her for a loop.

The odd protective feeling he felt around her grew, swelling into something that had him looking around. There were three bodyguards playing blackjack at the surrounding tables. He knew there were another six or so at the casino entrances and stationed strategically nearby. But anxiety caused his nerve endings to jump.

He pulled back from Eva and casually motioned to his lead guard. When he came over, Alex whispered, "Do we have a female guard?"

"No, Your Majesty."

"It's something we might want to consider for to-morrow."

When the guard frowned, he whispered, "For the ladies' room and other places she goes that we can't go."

He looked around the casino floor and saw more flaws in the security. Not because his team was inept but because he'd decided on a whim to teach her how to play blackjack, and his people weren't as prepared as they normally would have been.

"We'll need a meeting tomorrow morning."

The guard bowed. "Yes, Your Majesty."

A few days later, the rumor finally got out that house-keeping had found Eva's gown on the floor of the hall-way leading to Alex's bedroom. A firestorm erupted in the tabloids. Alex couldn't take Eva to lunch without re-porters shouting questions at them. From that day for-ward, they never went anywhere without a plan.

After every outing Alex held a debriefing. His father and Dom attended the first meeting. Dom was still in attendance after the third. But four days in, Alex was handling Eva's security on his own.

And rightly so. Because he was with Eva everywhere she went, he considered himself to be her number one bodyguard. Her first line of defense. No one questioned why he stood so close or held her hand every time they walked. He was her fiancé. But really, he was watching, waiting, ready to stand in front of her or pull her out of the way if anything happened.

Two days before their engagement party, he automatically caught her hand as they walked out of the casino at the end of their evening together. Night air warmed them as his limo driver strode around the hood of the vehicle to open the door for them.

Before they could get into the car, a guy in jeans and a big T-shirt with a camera strapped around his neck ambled up to them. "You know it's funny. I've never seen you steal a kiss."

Alex's bodyguards instantly tensed. But Alex smiled. He'd seen this kid in press conferences and knew he was credentialed, not a threat.

"Did you ever stop to think that there's a reason for that."

The guy laughed. "Yeah. You've never kissed her."

"He's kissed me," Eva said, then she blushed, and Alex felt his own color rise. Not because he was embarrassed but because that kiss had been such a scorcher. With his mind wrapped up in her security, he'd forgotten that kiss. But the reminder brought all his feelings back to life. The innocent way she'd responded. The challenge she'd be if he really wanted to woo her. It was all so fresh in his head, as if it were yesterday, not almost two weeks ago.

"Come on," the guy wheedled. "One kiss."

Eva glanced up at Alex expectantly.

And his hormones sat up. Eager. Ready to pop.

"Let me get *the* picture. There's a bounty on this. Quarter of a million dollars."

He gaped at the kid. *"Quarter of a million dollars for one kiss?"*

"Yep. And it would go a long way to pay off my student loans."

Eva smiled encouragingly, as Alex's blood bubbled with enthusiasm. But that was the point. He wasn't supposed to want to kiss her. Yet he did.

Which was why he couldn't.

He turned to the photographer and said, "Sorry, bud. You're going to have to work for that shot."

His driver pointedly opened the limo door.

The photographer cursed, but Alex didn't care. He handed Eva into the car and followed her into the backseat.

But he chastised himself as he walked her to her apartment. One simple kiss would have put an end to the bounty and the speculation. And it wasn't like he would have gotten carried away. Not in public. Not in front of a member of the press.

So why hadn't he just kissed her?

She stopped at her door. "Tonight was fun."

"You're a natural at blackjack." Plus, it wasn't as if he wasn't ever going to kiss her. He had to kiss her at the engagement party, after their first dance. It was tradition. And, now that he'd made an issue of it, it could be awkward.

He should kiss her right now, a quick, chaste kiss so he'd get used to the feel of her mouth. Then at the engagement party, he could kiss her with ease, some photographer would catch it, the bounty would be lifted and that would be the end of that.

"My family has a high math aptitude."

Her answer drifted away into thin air and the hall in front of her door grew quiet.

His chest tightened. This was it. The moment. He could swoop in, give her the quick kiss that would get him accustomed to her, and swoop back out. No big deal. No problem.

But she looked up at him with her pretty blue eyes and his breath froze.

She ran her finger down his tie. "Want to come in for a minute?"

And there it was. The reason he couldn't let himself kiss her. She might be getting better at flirting, but all he saw was innocence. Sweet, wonderful innocence that she deserved to keep, to save, for the right guy.

He took a second to take in her pretty face. Her full lips. Her pert nose. Those striking eyes. He didn't exactly want to commit them to memory, but he might want to remember this, to remember that there were good people in the world who definitely deserved protecting. Even from him.

He turned and walked away, calling, "Good night," after him.

But the truth followed him down the hall to the elevator, nagging him.

He refused to acknowledge it.

So it forced its way into his brain one more time. She really was the kind of woman a man fell in love with. But he was not the kind of guy to fall in love. Love hurt, so he'd never be that vulnerable, that honest again.

And even if he tried, at some point he'd pull back, pull away, maybe even sabotage a charade she needed.

Eva watched him go, disappointment like a vise around her chest. She turned, opened her door and walked into the echoing foyer of her apartment.

So he wouldn't kiss her? It was no big deal.

Except that she wanted him to. She was getting in all kinds of flirting practice, and that was good. But this longing whooshing through her when she was around him wasn't about the practice she needed for when she actually had to find a husband. She just wanted him to kiss her.

He'd kissed every woman within kissing age in his country, and he wouldn't kiss her. It was embarrassing. Demoralizing.

It made her look at her wardrobe the next morning, toss anything that her mom might borrow and order seven really sexy blouses from a local shop, including an especially pretty one for their date that night.

But he broke their date, reminding her that this was a ruse.

"I got to thinking that maybe we've been out a little too much if photographers are so bold with us."

"We're engaged," Eva said. "We're supposed to be together all the time."

"Not really. Everybody knows this is an arranged marriage. I think we might be taking it one step too far. In fact, it might be good if the press saw me out alone."

"Alone?"

"I used to go out all the time. Now it probably looks

odd that I'm always with you. This will make it look like you're not going to change me."

"That's stupid." But she felt a ring of truth to it. As if he'd said it as a message to her. Which made no sense. They hadn't even kissed for real. What would make him think she needed even more confirmation that he didn't like her?

"I think it will be very good for me to be seen at the casino, gambling with friends, but not flirting. Then the press can talk about how I only have eyes for you, instead of speculating on why I haven't kissed you in public."

Eva said, "Sounds great," but pulled in a slow breath as she disconnected the call.

Alex Sancho was the first man in her life to make her laugh and make her long to be kissed.

And he didn't want her.

He didn't have to spell it out. Didn't have to say the words. He didn't want time apart to give the press something new to speculate about. What he wanted was not to have to kiss her...or to be bored with a woman not up to his usual standards.

She set her cell phone on the dresser, sat on the edge of her bed and put her elbows on her knees and her head in her hands.

She had to get hold of herself and force herself to remember this was just a ruse, or she was going to end up getting the heartbreak she'd managed to avoid for the first twenty-five years of her life.

CHAPTER SEVEN

THE NIGHT OF the engagement party, Alex walked to her apartment to retrieve her and her mother, feeling more confident than he had since this whole business started. Now that he'd reminded himself that he wasn't the kind of guy to fall in love, and she deserved the chance to save herself for the right guy, he'd also realized he'd probably made too much of their kiss in the stable.

So it was hot? He'd had hot kisses before. He was fine. He'd very easily be able to kiss her after their first dance tonight. Not just because it was tradition. But because they'd be on the dance floor, surrounded by hundreds of guests. He could give her a nice, chaste kiss and no one would care because that was what was expected. And that would be the end of it.

Including that stupid-assed bounty.

He walked up to her apartment door. Though she was expecting him, he remembered the last time he'd entered her apartment without knocking, and he tapped twice before he stepped inside.

When he saw Eva in another yellow gown, he had to clear his throat. Visions of her in the yellow lingerie filled his head, but he told himself she was just a woman, like every other woman. Nothing special.

"You look lovely."

"Thanks." She did a quick, flirtatious turn. "You like the gown?"

"It's—" sexy, tempting "—exquisite."

He could actually see himself loosening the laces in the back of the dress. He could see himself kissing her senseless. Taking what he wanted.

His breath stuttered in then wobbled out.

He had to stop this. He was ruined for love, a man who lived behind walls and didn't want emotions, and she'd saved herself for a prince. A real prince. His brother might not have married her, but some decent guy would. Somebody would love her beyond reason. Somebody would love her the way she deserved to be loved.

And he would act accordingly.

He escorted Eva and her mom to the assembly area outside the back door of the ballroom. Rose raced over and straightened the white flowers in Eva's hair. "Oh, my, my, sugar. You give new meaning to the word beautiful."

Karen puffed up. "My daughter is going to be the perfect bride."

Alex watched his dad's eyes soften and knew exactly what the king felt. Eva was regal, yet sweet.

King Ronaldo took her hands. "You would be a welcome addition to any family."

Alex's heart bumped against his ribs. His father knew Eva was in on their ruse. She was being protected, not getting married; and he was subtly telling her that her day would come and that some family would be lucky to get her.

Just not the Sancho family. Not Alex.

His chest tightened. His stomach hollowed out. He'd

already worked his way through this. So why did hearing his dad say it make him want to punch something?

They entered the ballroom in a grand procession that became a receiving line for guests.

When her uncle—a short, thin man with a manicured beard and beady brown eyes—walked up to Alex's father, the king was gracious and polite. "Prince Gerard."

Gerard bowed. "King Ronaldo." He looked past Rose to Eva and Alex. "And who have we here?" In an unprecedented display of disrespect, he stepped around Rose, took Eva's hand and kissed her knuckles. "You will be a beautiful bride."

Beside Alex, Eva stiffened. Alex joined her in her feelings of distaste. He'd rather be exchanging fists than pleasantries with this pasty little man, who looked like King Mason but certainly didn't have his class.

Eva bowed. "Prince Gerard."

He glanced around. "This is a spectacular place for a wedding."

"The entire kingdom is spectacular," Eva said, smiling when Alex wanted to choke the little man.

Gerard laughed. "More beautiful than Grennady?"

"Nothing is more beautiful than Grennady," she replied, still smiling. "But you should stay in Xaviera a few weeks and enjoy the sun."

"With your father gone and you getting married, there's no one else to head parliament."

Keeping her smile in place, she cocked her head. "My father isn't gone. As far as I know, he's on vacation."

"With a mistress."

"Whom he has not married because he's still married to my mother. With no divorce, he's still king. It's my understanding he receives his daily updates the way he always has, and he's ruling as he's always ruled."

Alex swallowed a laugh.

"Well, it's assumed that with such a public display he'll be getting divorced—"

"You know the saying about what you do when you assume," Alex said, surprised his answer was so civil, but desperate to get the evil little man away from Eva.

As if reading his mind, Dom was suddenly at his side. "Luckily, your kingdom is wonderfully peaceful, and it's easy for a king to take a few weeks' vacation," Dominic said, drawing Gerard away from Eva and Alex. "I don't believe you've met my wife, Prince." He pointed at Ginny. "This is my beautiful bride, Princess Ginny."

Alex breathed a sigh of relief. Eva glanced down, straightening the full satin skirt of her gown, but he felt tension pour from her in a dark wave. Normally, he hated politics, but he'd take on the devil to protect Eva.

The receiving line lasted an hour. Standing behind the podium at the main table, Alex's father made introductions and a few comments about the engagement and wedding, and dinner was served.

The evening went well, smoothly, until it was time to dance their first dance as a couple.

Still brooding for her over the audacity of her uncle, Alex took her into his arms, and caught her gaze. Everything she'd felt as her uncle had greeted her was there in her sad blue orbs. Yet she'd kept her cool. Done her duty. Not let on that she knew Prince Gerard had put a price on her head.

She was a strong, wonderful woman. Like no one he'd ever met. And maybe that was the problem. She wasn't just another woman. She was Eva, a princess, someday a queen. But very much a woman.

He took a step, then another, then another, gliding them into the waltz he'd chosen, their eyes locked, his entire body vibrating.

She glanced around nervously. "You look like you swallowed a lemon. Please, try to at least *look* happy, even if you aren't."

He forced his lips upward, but only with great difficulty. "You should want to punch your uncle."

She laughed. "You think I don't?" She paused to smile at the crowd as he twirled her around. Then caught his gaze again. "There are times to act on feelings and times to pull back. This is a time to pull back."

"You're right."

There was so much more going on in this situation than just how he felt. He might be her protector, but she was correct. There were times to back off. To be wise.

Wasn't that what he was doing with her? Being wise. Not letting himself get involved with her personally—to protect her?

Of course he was. It was why he would give her a soft, chaste kiss at the end of their dance. He was strong enough, smart enough, to protect her from him.

The last note sounded and faded away. He raised their clasped hands, presenting her to the crowd. Then he stepped forward and delicately took her chin in his thumb and forefinger, tilting up her face and letting his mouth fall to hers.

When his lips met the softness of hers, she hesitated before lifting them to answer his kiss. The one-second pause spoke of her innocence and reminded him of every

good and pure thing about her, every reason he had to
want her.

But he knew he couldn't have her.

Just when he began to pull away, her lips brushed his,
eagerly as if she were starting some kind of romantic
overture, but she didn't finish the kiss. She pulled away.

His breath caught at the mere thought of her trying
to seduce him.

Their gazes held.

Warmth and confusion coursed through him.

Then she smiled and presented her hand to him again.
He took it and bowed as she curtsied.

They left the floor amid a round of applause. Guests
spilled onto the space in front of the band for dancing
as Eva's mom hugged her fiercely. Then Rose hugged
her. Then Ginny. Then Dom. Then the king himself
embraced her.

Pulling away, he took her hand. He kissed it. "I have
never seen a more beautiful first dance."

Feeling oddly left out, Alex said, "I was there too."

Rose caught him in one of her Texas-sized hugs. "Oh,
sugar, you were divine, too."

But he wasn't. *She* was. *Eva* was. She was small and
beautiful and cultured—a future queen.

Who turned him on like no one ever had before.

Something totally foreign rumbled through him. A
need so strong, so powerful, the fight he waged to stop
it went beyond anything he'd ever had to do around her.

It was ridiculous. They'd had two stupid kisses. One
he instigated to prove a point. And the engagement dance
tradition kiss that he'd started and she tried to finish but
she'd stopped too soon.

He'd recognized days ago that he'd made too much of

that first kiss, and maybe that was the problem? Maybe if they had one normal kiss, he'd see there was nothing different about her.

The small crowd of family had swallowed her up, as if protecting her, and perhaps they were. At least Alex knew Dom and his father were.

He managed to wiggle his way through the crowd and tap her shoulder. She turned, her face flushed. Her smile radiant.

"I think you and I need a minute together."

"Sure."

Preventing her from getting away from him or getting sucked into another vortex of well-wishers, he grabbed her fingers, and wove through the happy dancers with her. He walked her down one corridor, turned left and walked her down another. At the end of that hall, he opened the French doors and led her into a private garden.

Before she could say a word, he caught her by the shoulders and pressed his mouth to hers. This time there was no hesitation. No innocent pause. This time, her lips lifted to meet his.

Good. This was what they needed. A real, honest-to-God kiss that would prove to them both they were nothing special.

He deepened the kiss, nudging her mouth open with his tongue, and she responded. He pulled her closer. She slid her arms up his shoulders and looped them around his neck. Her breasts nestled against his chest. Their tongues twined—

Need exploded through him. His heart rate tripled. He ran his hands down her bare back and luxuriated in the silkiness of her skin before he realized he was in deep, dark trouble. Her kisses weren't innocent. They were greedy. And made him hungry for everything he knew she wanted to offer.

Kissing her hadn't accomplished what he'd set out to prove. He might have even made things worse.

He broke the kiss and bumped his forehead against hers. "Sorry."

"No woman wants a man to say he's sorry he kissed her, Alex."

The way she said his name caused a jolt in his stomach. Brought a fresh avalanche of desire. They'd shared so many secrets, spoken so honestly because of the ruse, that there was an intimacy between them now that made him feel he had a right to her.

"But I am sorry."

"Because you don't like me."

He pulled away, looked into her eyes. "Because I do like you. I like everything about you. Including the fact that I can be me with you. There's never been any pretense between us."

Her eyes studied his. "That's good then."

"No. It isn't. You're someday going to find the right guy. I don't want to screw that up for you." He tried to step away, but she caught his hand, stopping him.

"I know all this confuses you, but I sort of like *you*." She shook her head fiercely. "No. I don't sort of like you. I really like you. A lot. Including the fact that I can be *myself* with you."

"Don't say that."

Exasperation trembled through her voice. "*Why not?*"

"Because I'm not the kind of guy who's going to fall in love. And if you're as smart as I think you are, you know that."

To his chagrin, she laughed. "How do you know you can't fall in love?"

"If you have to ask, you don't know much about me or falling in love."

"Alex, every day I like you a little bit more. Even when you make it clear you want nothing to do with me, I have no control over this feeling that just keeps growing no matter how much I tell it to stop."

He shook his head. "And there it is. The difference between us. You're new. Innocent. The very fact that you can't stop those feelings shows how different we are. I know how to put the brakes on those feelings. Love's hurt me a time or two."

"And you don't want to get beyond your hurts?"

"It isn't a matter of *wanting* to get beyond the hurts. It's a matter of having almost twenty years after my mom's death to become cool, pragmatic. I learned a lot of tricks to make it look like I'm having fun and in the game, when really I'm not."

"But you fell in love with Nina."

"And got hurt again. All falling in love with her did was prove to me that I didn't dare let my guard down. I don't share secrets. I don't tell anybody my dreams. Somewhere in here…" He rubbed his chest. "There's a ping that happens that warns me when I'm getting too close. And it stops me." He caught her gaze. "It's stopped me with you a million times. You've noticed some of them. Some of them have hurt you. This isn't something I'm going to grow out of or change. I'm a lot harder, a lot colder, than even my dad."

"You talk like a guy who thinks he knows everything, but maybe you don't."

"And you talk like a woman with stars in her eyes.

A woman who is going to get hurt. And I won't let it be me who hurts you."

"I see."

"Look, we have another few weeks of this, then you're going to go back to Grennady, and I'm going to go back to who I was. You'll get so busy you'll forget me as much as I'll forget you. Unless we do something stupid."

Her face scrunched in confusion. "Something stupid?"

"Like get carried away. I'd say make love, but for me it would be just sex and for you it would be more. And you'd be devastated when I walk away at the end of this thing. So let's just keep things the way they should be. Light. Fun. Nothing serious so we can both get out of this with our sanity."

"Alex? Eva?"

The sound of Sally Peterson's voice echoed around the dark outdoor space. Alex stepped even farther away from Eva.

"Here you are!"

"Yes. We're here." He pushed back his shoulders and gave Sally his full prince stare. "May I ask what you're doing, following me?"

"Your father noticed you were missing. I volunteered to look for you."

Eva sneaked another peek at him. In all the confusion of wanting to kiss her for real to straighten all this out in his head, he'd forgotten there was a potential threat against her life.

No wonder his father had sent someone to look for them.

He caught Eva's hand, said, "We're fine," and headed through the garden, into the palace and down the hall toward the engagement party again, glad they'd had the honest talk.

Unless they did something stupid, they could both walk away from this. But if they followed through on these unwanted feelings that he knew were more physical than emotional, they'd both be sorry.

And part of him absolutely revolted at the thought she'd be sorry she met him. If he couldn't love her, if nothing else, he wanted to be the guy she remembered and smiled.

CHAPTER EIGHT

EVA MANAGED TO make it through the engagement party with her head high and a smile on her face. The next day, she happily accepted congratulations from her mom on the success of the event.

But when there was a quick knock on their door and Alex walked in, her stomach plummeted.

He didn't want her. Not because he didn't like her, but because he did. But the boy who'd lost his mom and a man who'd lost his first love had built walls. Even if they did fall in love, there would always be walls, a distance between them.

She saw it all the time in the way he related to her. The way he could walk away from kisses. The way he used protecting her as a convenient distraction so he didn't have to talk to her.

He walked into their living room, caught her shoulders and put a soft kiss on her cheek. She suspected he'd done it for the benefit of her mother, but the unexpectedness of it stole her breath, made her heart ache all over again.

"Sally has informed me that gifts have begun arriving."

Her eyebrows rose, but her mother clapped her hands

together with glee. "Oh, that's marvelous." She faced Eva. "This is the most fun part of getting married."

Alex laughed. "Really? Getting gifts is the best part of a wedding?"

"It's not about being materialistic." Her mom sniffed. "Gifts are kind of like a way to see what people really think of you." She tapped Alex's arm. "Trust me. You'll know who your friends are by what they get you."

Eva shook her head in shame at her mom's one true vice. She liked presents. "Sorry, Alex."

Alex shrugged. "Maybe she has a point. Maybe it will be fun."

"It'll be a blast," Karen assured him. "Are you going down now to start weeding through?"

"We could." Alex caught her gaze. "Or we could get some lunch. I'm kind of hungry."

Realizing he wanted time alone for a private discussion, maybe even to explain his staff's plan to return the gifts since there really wasn't going to be a wedding, Eva said, "Great. I'm hungry too."

"There's a wonderful little bistro that serves the best salads."

She glanced down at her jeans and top. "Is this okay?"

He smiled. "You're with me, remember? The Prince of Scruffiness."

She laughed. "That's not exactly what I called you."

"But it's close," he said, directing her to the door.

They said goodbye to her mom, then walked in silence through the echoing corridor to the elevator.

When the door closed behind them, she said, "So what's up?"

"Up?"

"What do you need to talk about?"

He frowned. "Nothing."

"You didn't ask me to lunch to talk?"

"No. I asked you to lunch because I'm hungry."

"At the engagement party, you said—" She stopped herself. "Never mind." He might have said they were seeing too much of each other two days ago, and he might have warned her off at the engagement party, but today, the day after a real kiss and their honest conversation, he'd asked her to lunch for no reason except that he was hungry. And she was not questioning it.

He drove the Mercedes to a bistro so far out of the way she knew it wasn't a haunt for tourists but somewhere locals ate, drank and had fun together. Bodyguards escorted them to the restaurant, but instead of Alex opening the door, he pointed at a cluster of tables on the sidewalk bathed in hot sun and the breeze coming off the ocean.

She frowned. "Outside?"

"Among friends," he said, guiding her to a table in the corner. The wall of the restaurant was at their back. A clear view of the ocean was on their left. The other diners were to the right and in front of them.

"Prince Alex!" A tall man wearing a white apron scurried out to greet them.

Alex rose to shake his hand. He faced Eva. "This is Angelo. He owns the place. And this is—"

"Your beautiful bride," Angelo said before Alex could finish.

She smiled at him. "Thank you."

"Lunch is on me!" Angelo said effusively.

Alex laughed. "No. You cook. I pay." He took his seat again. "Amaze us with a salad that will fill us up, but not make us fat."

Angelo happily raced away, and Eva sucked in a long drink of the sea air.

Alex laughed. "You're getting a tad too comfortable with our weather."

"I know." She shook her head. "I'm in for so much culture shock when I get home."

Alex glanced around. "You mean when *we* get home."

She nodded, realizing she'd forgotten the charade, but ready to pick up the ball and do her part. "You know we'll live in a wing of Grennady's palace the way Dom and Ginny do."

A waiter arrived with a plate of appetizers and Alex plucked a piece of cheese and popped it into his mouth. "I suspected as much."

He ate another piece of cheese then said, "As heir, do you have duties?"

She shrugged. "Not really. About once a month I'm briefed on what's going on in the country. Four or five times a year I'm needed for photo ops."

He considered that. "That's very different from what Dom does. He's actually in on the politics. He has jobs."

"Your country's very different than ours. We don't have access to a cash cow like oil. We also aren't open to attack from enemies as you seem to be. We're rural. Our subjects mostly make their livings from farms."

"So you've said."

She stiffened. "What's wrong with that?"

"Nothing."

But she'd heard something in his voice. Something condescending. "Oh, so the playboy prince suddenly knows government?"

"I've heard about government around our dinner table since I was in diapers. I've picked up a thing or two."

"Such as?"

"Such as, it's a big booming world out there. With the internet, everybody can be educated. Your father hasn't considered that the generation coming up might want more from their lives than what their parents had?"

She took her napkin from the table, opened it and set it on her lap, busying herself so she didn't have to look at him. "Our country's claim to fame is that we are small and comfortable."

He leaned back, settling on his chair, as Angelo rushed out with two heaping plates of salad.

Alex complimented the owner, who blushed with pleasure at the praise, and they began eating.

But though the conversation had ended, Eva had a weird feeling in the pit of her stomach. A feeling that wouldn't let him get away with saying part of something and not finishing it.

Finally she said, "So what would you do?"

With a forkful of salad halfway to his mouth, Alex said, "Do?"

"About the next generation in my country?"

He drew in a breath, thought for a second, then said, "If I were in charge of a country like yours, a place that's quiet and peaceful, I'd probably try to lure an internet company into making its home there. You could provide hundreds if not thousands of jobs when you consider that ancillary businesses would shoot up. Not to mention extra jobs from the restaurants, shops and auto mechanics needed to support the population that would migrate to wherever the company settled."

"Most corporations want a warmer climate."

"Internet companies don't necessarily want a warmer climate. They want ambiance. Your country has it in abundance. Skiing. Snowmobiles. Snowboarding. Sleigh riding. And in the summer, hiking and horseback riding. Rock climbing. Your country has enough ways to commune with nature, which internet companies believe inspires creativity, to entice just about anybody you want."

She drew in a breath. "Impressive."

He laughed. "Impressive that I can't help overhearing conversations at dinner?"

"You make light, Alexandros Sancho, but you're not the player you try to make everyone believe."

He smiled. "There are already plenty of rulers in my family. We don't need another."

But the next day after a meeting with the royal guard, Dom asked Alex to come to parliament, and he went. Not because he someday wanted to be a ruler. But because he enjoyed the feeling of being productive.

His mornings soon filled with meetings over Eva's protection because designers and florists and all sorts of wedding prep people began trooping to her apartment almost nonstop for consultations.

Every day he'd take her to lunch, then he'd return to find Dom and walk with him to parliament, to the section of their government that connected them to their people.

And the whole time he wondered about Eva's country, about Grennady. How could her father let them get so far behind the times?

He wouldn't let himself think about it while eating dinner with her. He was a prince supposedly marrying a beautiful princess. It wouldn't do to have anyone overhear them talk about politics.

But one day, when he walked in on a conference call

his father was having with King Mason and Dom, it all poured into his head again. He didn't argue when his dad motioned for him to sit in.

He also sat in the next day and the next. He didn't say much. He didn't think it was his place to give advice, though it was clear King Mason needed it. He offered the idea of enticing an internet company to Grennady, then he sat and listened without comment for the next two days' calls, until the fate of his "wedding" to Eva came up for discussion.

When the phone in the apartment buzzed, Eva jumped. So did her mom. The phone never rang, except to announce a wedding vendor, and they had no one scheduled for that day. Eva looked at her mom. Her mom looked back.

"I'm guessing we should answer it."

Eva carefully made her way to the discreet beige phone that sat inconspicuously on a table by the sofa.

"Hello?"

"Good afternoon, Princess. This is Maria Gable, King Ronaldo's personal assistant. He requests your presence in his office. A member of his guard should be arriving for you shortly."

"Oh." Confusion rumbled through her, but one didn't say no to a king, not when she was at his palace, and not when he was protecting her. Especially since he could have news about her dad.

Three weeks had passed since her father had stashed her and her mom in Xaviera. Her father had had plenty of time to get the proof that his brother had conspired to have him killed. Plenty of time to arrest Prince Gerard. The day she'd been simultaneously praying for and dreading might be here.

"Thank you."

She hung up the phone, glancing at her blue jeans and white tank top. She and Alex had decided to spend the afternoon poking around the shops in the village. Very visible again. They'd hold hands. They'd smile, and they'd talk.

Her nerves jumped at the thought of it. She loved talking to him. She loved that he saw things, knew things, that she didn't. And even though he might have all kinds of strategies in place to resist her, she wasn't so experienced, so lucky. Every day she liked him a little more.

But it might all be over. She might have been summoned to the king's office because her dad was back. Safe. Maybe even already in Grennady.

An odd queasiness filled her.

After today, she might never again see Alex.

A knock at the door announced the royal guard member who led her to the king's office. She hadn't been in the administrative offices of the palace, but she was so nervous that the art on the walls barely caught her attention.

She walked into a sitting room, then a huge space full of secretaries and assistants, then an office with one woman, who rose.

In her forties, with reddish-blond hair and brown eyes, she bowed. "Princess." She walked to the door of the office behind hers, and the guard with Eva stepped back, as if handing her off. "I'm Maria."

"A pleasure to meet you."

"You too, Princess." She opened the door. "This way."

They walked through another room to a gilded door in the back, which Maria opened.

Eva walked into an office so grand, she blinked. The king, Dominic and Alex all rose from the seats around a huge mahogany desk.

Alex walked over and took her hands. Catching her gaze, he said, "Your father is on the phone."

Her heart lurched. "He is?"

"Yes."

Her dad being back in Grennady was good news, but Alex's expression was serious, concerned, as if he was afraid she might shatter into a million pieces.

Confusion pummeled her as King Ronaldo rounded his desk. "You take my seat and we'll give you some privacy. Just press the blinking button on the phone. That's the line he's on."

Eva's stomach fell. Something was dreadfully wrong. Nonetheless, she held her head high. "Thank you."

As she walked behind the desk, the Sancho men left the office.

She sat. Took a breath. Pushed the blinking light on the phone.

"Dad?"

"Hey, sweetie. How are the cats?"

Her eyes filled with tears. "I haven't seen my cats in weeks." She gulped a breath, so scared and so confused she didn't know what to say, what to ask. A million possibilities loomed in her mind. None of them good.

"How are you? *Where* are you?"

"I'm fine. But I'm still in hiding. Investigating everything that's going on, I realized that my brother being a traitor is only part of the problem. But I don't want to clean house in parliament, or reorganize the government. I want to show my detractors that I'm willing to work with them. There's been dissension growing for years. I've seen it, of course, but I didn't realize it had hit a crisis point."

"What kind of dissension?"

"Our country is horribly behind the times."

Hadn't Alex told her that? "And we have a generation coming up that wants something more."

He laughed. "When did you get so smart?"

"I'm not. Alex mentioned it. He suggested luring an internet company to Grennady, convincing them to put their corporate headquarters there."

Her dad laughed again. "He suggested it to me too. I'm in negotiations with a company right now. But I can't go back until I have a solid plan, proof that when I return things will be different."

Her entire body froze. "Oh."

"But the danger has passed, sweetie."

"It has?" She sat back in the chair. She should have been relieved, but the feeling that Alex had been in on all of this sent little lightning bolts of anger through her. She was to be the queen of her country someday, yet everyone knew this plan but her. "Really?"

"Yes, your uncle is under secret house arrest, until I come home. But I still need time to create a new vision for the country."

She sat up. "How can I help?"

"By doing what you're doing. I don't want word of this to get out. I don't want to give my dissenters a chance to find a voice before I can come home strong, with a plan. That's why I'm calling. You and Alex are going to have to go through with the wedding."

She took a few seconds to let that sink in. Three

weeks ago she could have married him in an award-winning performance. Now? He'd protected her. Kissed her. Told her he didn't want her. And gone behind her back to help her dad, when she should have been the one in on the discussions.

Her dad drew in a breath. "Sweetie, I had no idea things were so bad. We're a small, quiet country. I thought we could go on the way we were, the way we have been for generations. But there's dissension that runs deep enough that my own brother wanted to kill me." He took another breath. "I should have known how bad it had gotten. But I didn't. And now I have to fix it."

"Wouldn't it be better for you to go home now?"

"I can't go home until I have a solid plan. If I go home, admitting that we have things to fix, but without a way to fix them, the rebels will see we're shaky and take advantage."

She got what he was saying. He just seemed to be taking the long way around. Still, a princess didn't question her king.

"We've always been so small that we haven't really had a plan. We simply solved problems as they arose. Now, we know we need to think of all of the needs of the people and meet them. Ronaldo has sent financial advisors. Prince Dominic is flying here to help us tomorrow. We have the information. We just have to sort through it and figure out what works for us."

And now he'd called *Dominic* for help. Not just Alex but Dominic? Her nerve endings fluffed out like porcupine quills. But she said, "Okay."

"I'm sorry I won't be at the wedding."

"It's not a real wedding." But that thought depressed her even more. She'd be standing up in front of a mountain of press, her friends, her family, Alex's family, saying vows that weren't real. To a guy she was growing to like, but who didn't like or trust her enough to tell her he'd been helping her dad for God only knew how long.

"What happens if you can't do this? Three weeks have gone by. How do you know your detractors aren't already planning to take over?"

"Oh, I'm pretty sure they are. That's why this wedding is so important. You're distracting everybody. Buying time. And I swear, I won't need more than another few weeks."

A few weeks of being married to Alex? She squeezed her eyes shut. If he were a mean, ugly man, none of this would matter. She could do this with her eyes closed. But he was good-looking, kind, smart. A born leader who, quite obviously, her father trusted.

And maybe the real reason he didn't want her was bigger than she'd suspected. Maybe he saw her as her dad did. A figurehead? Not a real person, not someone who could give or take love. Someone who simply held a place and did what she was told.

She swallowed hard, but said what her dad needed to hear. "I'm fine. I serve at the pleasure of my king."

"That's my girl. And when everything's straightened out, I'll come to America and visit your cats."

Pain skittered through her. The very thing she'd done to keep herself busy, to make a mark while she bided time, made her look foolish.

She swallowed again, played her role with a dad who was too busy to see how he was hurting her. "So you've said a million times."

"This time I mean it. We'll attach the trip to a formal, official visit to the United States."

She took a slow, necessary breath, as the truth of her life made a ring of sadness around her heart. She was nothing. "Okay."

"Great. I'll talk to your mom this afternoon."

"I think she's going to skin you alive."

"No. She'll understand."

Eva hung up the phone a few minutes later knowing that her mom *would* understand. Her mom would do her duty. So would Eva.

But her hands shook and her heart hurt. In four weeks, her entire life had changed. She'd believed it was because her dad had gone through a midlife crisis, but it was so much more serious than that. And the Sancho family had stepped in to help them. But she'd been tucked away like a porcelain doll.

A few seconds after she'd hung up the phone, Alex and his father returned to his office.

Alex said, "Are you okay?"

She nodded. "He says he's going to talk to my mom this afternoon."

The king reached for his phone. "I'll tell my secretary to arrange that. You two do whatever it is you had planned for today."

She nodded again and Alex took her elbow to guide her out of the office.

In the corridor leading away from the administrative offices, Alex glanced at her jeans and tank top and said, "So I see you're ready to go into the village."

She forced a smile. "Sure."

He stopped. "You're not ready?"

She shook her head as the implications of everything her dad had said rained down on her. What did she expect? Her father had no intention of retiring. She was a well-loved only child…only *daughter.* She busied herself with charities, but essentially lived in America. Even *she* didn't see herself as a ruler.

"No. No. I'm fine."

He studied her face. "You're not fine."

"Does it matter? There are so much bigger things at stake here."

"True, but you're not going to convince a block of reporters that you're a happy bride if your smile falters."

"I can pull it off."

He glanced down the empty corridor. "You know what? Maybe you can, but this has been a long, weird bunch of weeks for you. You're accustomed to low-key. I've dragged you around town. Maybe today would be a good day to take a break."

She hated to say it. Hated to think she was this weak. Except she wasn't weak. She was worn down by the truth. Her father didn't trust her. She'd thought he did because he let her live her own life, but if he really trusted her, she'd be preparing to be queen. To be a ruler. But she wasn't. Her dad had said she'd rule only long enough until her son—a son who wasn't even yet born—could take over.

"No. I need to go somewhere. I can't sit around the palace all day. That would just make things worse."

He smiled. "I think I have an idea." He glanced at her outfit again and confusing longings rolled through her. This man pampered her, protected her, and kept her out of the loop even more than her father did. Why should she want him to look at her with interest in his eyes?

"You'll do."

Thank God that made her laugh. "I'll do?"

He took her hand. "Yes. I have an idea."

He rushed her out of the corridor to a slim hall that led to another slim hall.

"What are we doing?"

"Escaping."

Shades of the real Alex returned, the simple guy she really liked. Not the one who apparently went to secret meetings with her dad. "Escaping?"

"Yes. There are times when I can't stand the body-guards, hate the media...don't even want my dad to know where I am."

Her eyebrows rose. This truly was the Alex she liked.

"So—" He opened a small, inconspicuous door onto a huge garage. "I go here."

She glanced around in awe at the sheer number of vehicles. Everything from limos to tiny sports cars and bikes. "To a garage?"

"Nope," he said, grabbing a motorcycle helmet from a shelf.

Realizing what was happening, she skittered back. "Oh, no..."

He plopped the helmet on her head. "You don't ride?"

"No."

"Then this is the perfect day for you to start." He put a helmet on his head. When he spoke his voice came to her through a speaker by her ear. "You'll love this."

She had the horrible feeling of going from the frying pan into the fire, but if anything would make her forget that her dad didn't need her help—didn't want her help—fear for her life would probably accomplish it.

He climbed on a small, rather simple bike.

She looked at him. "*This* is the royal motorcycle?"

"This is a bike no one looks at twice. In jeans and a

T-shirt, with a helmet on my head, I'm just another guy out for a ride on a bike."

She climbed on behind him. "Good point."

He was right. Maybe what she needed was even for *her* to forget she was a princess.

CHAPTER NINE

ALEX REVVED THE engine and headed for a garage door that automatically opened when they got close. A warm sun beat down on them, but as soon as he turned them onto the road that wove through the trees, the air cooled.

Eva clung to him, obviously a first-time rider. But the farther they got into the woods, the more her grip loosened.

He missed it. As happy as he was that she'd relaxed, he missed having her arms wrapped tightly around him for support. He knew something was wrong. He'd expected her to be thrilled her dad was safe, and had a plan in process. Instead, she seemed confused, disoriented. So he vowed that no matter what it took today, he would distract her.

They drove and drove. Up a mountain, through another patch of trees. The feeling of the wind swirling around him always calmed him, and he could feel her relaxing behind him.

Finally, the house came into view. A nine-bedroom, two-story stone monstrosity with brown shutters and a wide wooden porch that ran across the entire front and curved around the right side, the house had been designed as a retreat, a place for the Sancho family to be a family. Not royalty. Not rulers. Just people.

He heard her small gasp through the system of mics in their helmets.

"It's gorgeous."

"It's old," he said flatly. "And in general need of repairs."

He drove the bike down the winding road that took them to the aging country house. He punched the alarm code into the box by the gate. It swung open, and they rode through, then the gate automatically closed behind them.

Standing on the front porch, he used another code for the house alarm.

As he reached for the knob to open the door, she glanced around nervously. "You're not worried about security?"

"We're fine here. I'll bet nobody even realizes we're gone. I told my guards we'd ring when we were ready to head for town. If I don't ring, they'll just think we decided not to go out."

He opened the door revealing a dusty foyer. Furniture was covered with cloths. Cobwebs danced like streamers from the chandelier to all four corners.

He batted them away so Eva wouldn't have to walk through them. "Just FYI, the press knows this is the house we would be living in if we got married."

"Really?"

"Yes. It's already crowded in the palace. It's a gift to be given a real home."

She stepped around a chair that had been placed haphazardly in the foyer, as if someone had been moving it to storage and forgotten it.

"How long has it been since anyone's been here?"

He didn't even have to think about it. "Since my mom's death."

She faced him. Her eyes filled with apology, the first real emotion he'd seen from her since her call with her dad. "Sorry."

"Don't be. Some things are just facts."

Her eyes softened. "Facts to me. Sorrow for you."

He sniffed a laugh. "At one time. But I'm accustomed to it, remember? I'm the guy with the walls." He led her out of the foyer to the huge room beside it. The dusty fireplace was the only thing not covered by cloths.

"You have a fireplace!"

"We only used it to hang stockings at Christmas."

She walked over, ran her hand along the rich wood of the mantel, sending dust flying. "So you had Christmases here?"

"Actually we came here a lot. My mother believed that living where he worked kept my dad from relaxing. So most weekends she'd bring him here."

But Christmas memories were the strongest and they floated to him. Trays of cookies and tea. Mountains of presents wrapped in shiny foil. His mother laughing.

They walked through a sitting room and formal dining room, an office, and a craft room that had been his mother's, down a long corridor to a ballroom.

"You have a ballroom in a country house?"

"My father always hosted a grand party."

She walked inside. Her voice echoed around her when she said, "Wow."

But he suddenly pictured the room clean, decorated for the holidays as it had been when his mom was alive. He could see Eva in her red gown, greeting guests at the door because parties here had been formal, but comfortable…wonderful.

He shook his head to clear the haze. "Let me show you the kitchen."

Rather than a huge restaurant kitchen designed for a staff, the room was small, intimate. His mother had created it that way. After the big party, she would dismiss the servants—let them have their holiday. Then she would make Christmas or Easter breakfast and dinner. He and Dom would stay in their PJs and lean against the center island as she cooked.

"Oh, I could see myself making pizza on that island."

"You make pizza?"

She laughed. "I love to cook."

"My mom did too."

"Let me guess. That was part of your holiday tradition. That she cooked."

He walked around the room slowly, memories tripping over themselves in his head. He might have only been eight when his mom died, but he remembered enough to fill a lifetime.

"When we were here we were normal."

"You're not now?"

He caught her gaze. "My father's a king. My brother will be a king. And I'm the extra guy who hangs around in case my brother dies." He shook his head. "We're kind of creepy."

"It's only creepy if you focus on it."

"Which is why I lived the kind of life I did before this mess with your dad started. I didn't want to think about it, let alone focus on it."

"You still fit. If you've felt left out before this, it was by your own choosing."

"Says the woman who went to America to be herself and have a good time before she becomes a queen."

She stiffened. "Is that how you see me?"

He shrugged. "It appears, Princess, to be how you want to be seen. You're the woman who doesn't want to be queen, remember? You just want to rule long enough for your oldest son to be groomed for the top spot."

She stiffened again. And he had absolutely no idea why. She'd told him that herself.

But rather than admit it or tell him to shut up, she looked around the kitchen. "I know how I'd remodel this room."

He laughed at her quick change of subject. "Really?"

"White cabinets. Probably a marble countertop. Updated appliances. And a long oak table over there." She pointed at a space by French doors that looked out over a garden. "With four chairs and a bench for kids, so they could nudge each other and misbehave."

He laughed. "You can tell you haven't been around kids much. Misbehaving children aren't fun."

"For adults. But I'll bet it's fun to be one."

He remembered himself and Dom wrestling like two bear cubs and couldn't lie. "It is."

And suddenly he saw the room the way she saw it. White cabinets. Marble countertops. Chairs filled with kids. Laughter mixing with the scent of burning toast.

"You want a family, don't you?"

She glanced around again at the cobweb-filled room, smiling, obviously not seeing the dust. "Being an only child is miserable." She motioned around the kitchen. "For decades I thought this was what I wanted. A real house. A place for memories and kids. Lot of kids. Breakfast, lunch, dinner." She sighed. "Birthday parties and horseback riding lessons. Managing schedules and dance classes."

"You wanted to be a mom."

She squeezed her eyes shut, as if furious. "I'm a queen."

He frowned, confused. "But not forever. You said you only want to rule in the space between your dad and your future son."

Her gaze met his. "You knew my dad intended to coax an internet company to Grennady."

Another change of subject. Still, he kept up. "I gave him the idea."

Her face whitened. "In secret meetings with him?"

"Not meetings. Conference calls. One every day for the past few days."

When her mouth fell open in what looked to be disbelief, he defensively said, "I am in charge of your protection."

She whirled away from him. "I'm the next ruler of my country! I should have been in on those calls!"

And suddenly it all made sense to Alex. Not only was she out of the loop, but also their positions had reversed. When they met, he was a happy-go-lucky prince with no ambition and she was a princess devoted to duty. Now, he had jobs and her dad had hidden her away.

"Hey, look, I'm sorry." He raised his hands in apology. "If it's any consolation, I liked you enough to want to protect you."

She sniffed a laugh. "Yeah. Sure. That makes it all better."

"And my dad's not the only one thrilled that I've gotten off my duff and found a place in our kingdom. Dom is also thrilled. I am thrilled. And we owe it all to you.

You motivated me to do things I would have never believed possible."

He watched the truth of that settle in on her, and pushed when another man might have let her wallow in her deserved misery. "You redeemed me. You probably had the biggest role of all of us."

"Yeah. It's pretty great."

He laughed. "Don't try to kid a kidder. It's no fun being the one in the background. I've lived that life. But though you're in the background, you still played a part. Everything you've done has served a purpose. Plus, your dad brought you into the big picture situation during that telephone conversation this afternoon. And he still needs time, which you are buying by going through with a wedding to me."

She sort of laughed, so he walked over, put a finger under her chin and lifted her face until their eyes met.

"So what? You don't want to marry me now?"

Eva's heart skipped a beat. He seemed to realize how different he was, how strong. Not that he hadn't been attractive before. But this smart, committed version of the sexy guy she'd been seeing was nearly irresistible.

"I'll do whatever my king needs me to do."

"I also think it's time you and your dad had a chat about your job."

She laughed. "Two weeks as a working member of your palace staff and suddenly you think everybody needs a job?"

"I don't think everybody needs a job. I think your years in America were the whim of a young princess finding her feet. I think this crisis showed you who you want to be."

Oh, lord. He was right. And she didn't have a clue what to do about it. "It has."

"So now you have to make sure the talk you have with your dad sinks in. Make sure he understands you're not a pampered daughter holding a place until a new man comes along to take over. You're a smart woman, more than capable of ruling."

And when he talked like that, she wanted to melt at his feet.

He grinned at her. "Need help talking to your dad?"

She laughed again, but this time she also swatted him. "Stop."

"What? I can be very helpful."

She knew he meant it jokingly but the truth was this Alex, this smart Alex, could be very helpful. She could see him heading up her palace's royal guard. See him being a trusted husband, advisor.

And she found herself at the place where the charade became scary. These weeks had grown him enough, changed him enough that he would be the perfect husband for her.

Now she had nothing to battle with. Nothing to help her resist the feelings she was getting for him. Three weeks ago he might have been the absolute worst choice for a queen to take as a mate. Right now? He was perfect.

Not to mention gorgeous. Sexy. Fun. He'd known she'd needed time away and he'd given it to her.

How was she supposed to resist this guy?

"Come on," he said. "What would you cook if you were mum here?"

She shook her head, hoping to shake off her ridiculously sober mood. They'd use this time to make a plan about talking to her dad, about her place in her kingdom, which she would implement when they returned to Grennady. But he didn't want to be her husband and she had to respect that. She needed to show him she was fine.

She walked to the big center island, pictured it white with a big marble countertop. "I'd make pancakes."

"I love pancakes."

"How about apple?"

"I could be persuaded to try one."

She laughed, but her heart shattered. She could see them in this kitchen. Before she became queen there'd be plenty of time to be a real family, to teach their kids the things she and Alex hadn't learned because their parents didn't know to teach them. She could see the dark-eyed, dark-haired little boy who would take the throne after her. She could see the dark-haired, blue-eyed little girl who'd be Daddy's favorite. She could see Alex as a daddy, know he'd love the role.

But he couldn't see it. Because he didn't want it.

It was one thing to grow enough that he could take his place in his country's royal family. Quite another to take down those walls around his heart.

CHAPTER TEN

ALEX EXPECTED HIMSELF to be nervous the day of his fake wedding. What he hadn't expected was the weirdness that accompanied it. When the royal photographers snapped pictures of him, his father and Dom, he decided he got an odd shiver because it was all so real. Everything might be fake, but it needed to appear real, so they'd spared no expense. Left no tradition unturned. Including the exchange of personal gifts. Because it all had to be documented to look real.

His father went first. Handing him the keys to the country house, which were largely symbolic since the retreat now had key pads, he said, "This house gave your mother and me great pleasure." The photographers snapped nonstop. "It's my hope it will give you and Eva many years of happiness too."

Flash. Flash. Flash.

He took the keys, hugged his dad, and suddenly felt something he'd never felt before. Overwhelming respect for the king, followed by blind sorrow for the man who'd lost his wife and been forced to raise two sons alone. He squeezed his eyes shut, wrapped his arms around his dad more tightly.

It was the first real hug he'd given his dad since his mom passed.

When his dad pulled back, his eyes were filled with tears. Rose stepped forward. Wearing a very simple pale blue gown, she looked elegant and regal. She handed his dad a handkerchief. "Here, sweetie."

The king took it and waved off the photographers. "Don't get pictures of that. No one wants to see me maudlin."

"Then you're not going to want to watch him open this," Dom said, taking the small rectangular box from Ginny, who had her lips pressed together as if forcing herself not to cry. Eva's maid of honor, she wore a pale green dress with her hair pulled off her face and cascading down her back, a vision of yellow curls.

Dom handed the box to Alex. He removed the lid and there was an eight-by-ten picture of their family, a candid shot at one of their Christmas parties. Their mother beaming. Dom trying to look kingly. And Alex sticking out his tongue.

The room grew silent.

It seemed the photographers held their collective breaths.

"It's—"

"It's so very you," Ginny said with a sniff that was half laugh, half sob. "Sticking out your tongue. Being a pain in the butt."

Emotion tightened his chest. He remembered the day as one of the happiest of his life. But when he pictured the ballroom in the house, he didn't see himself, his mom or even guests. He saw Eva standing in the cobwebs.

He hugged Dom, then Ginny, thanking them.

His father's manservant, Henry, who'd been at the

palace for as long as Alex could remember, took the gifts with the promise that they would be in Alex's apartment when he returned from his honeymoon.

Alex nodded. The photographers left. The little family dispersed. His father needed to be in the church's front row with Rose when Alex and Dom walked onto the altar, but first they had to retrieve Jimmy from the nanny because Ginny was maid of honor but Rose wanted the baby at the wedding.

When the bells chimed out four o'clock, Dom and Alex walked onto the altar. Rose and the king were in their seats, Rose holding Jimmy who patted her cheeks. The organist began a processional and Eva's two university friends walked in followed by Ginny.

Then the music changed and Eva was at the door of the church. With no father to walk her down the aisle, she'd decided to walk in unescorted.

At the time it had seemed like the bad choice, but after their discussion at the country house, when he'd seen just how strong and smart she was, it no longer seemed wrong.

In her long white dress, with her black hair pulled into a tight knot with a ring of pearls around the knot, connected to a veil that fell from the pearls to the long, long train of her dress, Eva was the epitome of quiet elegance. Perfection. Strength.

Yet somehow she managed to look innocent and beautiful.

His breath fluttered in and stuttered out. Longings filled him.

She walked up to him. The minister said, "Who gives this woman in matrimony?"

She held Alex's gaze. "I give myself."

Emotion trembled through him. Because he finally saw. For as much as he'd believed he didn't have a place in his family, she'd felt worse. She had no siblings. And all her country seemed to want her to do was produce the next heir.

But she was a queen.

He took her hand, kissed her knuckles. Then turned her to face the altar.

After a long ceremony and hours of pictures, they wound their way down the palace halls and corridors to the back door of the ballroom for a receiving line and reception.

This time there was no Uncle Gerard. Alex was sure his absence would be reported in the papers tomorrow, and wondered how the world would react when King Mason finally announced his brother hadn't attended Eva's wedding because he was under house arrest for treason.

What a world his wife would be returning to.

When it came time for their first dance as a couple, he led her to the dance floor. When their gazes met, he saw her fatigue.

As he swung her around to the tune of the waltz, he said, "It's been a long day."

She forced a smile. "Yes, it has."

"Where's the woman who wanted to make apple pancakes?"

She laughed. "I think I left her back at the country house."

"Maybe we should go get her?"

She laughed again.

His spirits lifted. He twirled her around. "It is a little nerve-racking to be guest of honor in front of eight hundred people."

She met his gaze again. "And sitting for hours for a bunch of pictures no one will see."

He danced her in a big looping circle around the floor, twirled her out, then pulled her back in, making her giggle.

"Stop! That's not a waltz."

"And we care because?"

She giggled again. "I don't know. Honestly. I just don't know anything anymore."

"Sure you do. You have tons of stuff you have to face when you go back home. But that could be days away. Weeks away." He dipped his head to catch her gaze again. "Why don't we have some fun?"

Why not?

She could think of a million reasons, but most of them revolved around keeping her heart when she desperately wanted to lose it to him.

Still, when he twirled her around again, she laughed. When the dance ended and he gave an exaggerated bow, she laughed again. The wedding guests loved him.

She loved him.

And there it was. The truth that stood on the edge of her mind every day, but which she wouldn't let manifest because it was too frightening. How could she love a man who didn't love her?

When the dance was over, her mother met her on the edge of the dance circle and led her to the private table set up for Alex and Eva. She handed her a glass of water.

"Drink this."

Eva shook her head. "I'm not thirsty."

"You need to stay hydrated," her mom insisted.

Alex took the glass from her. He cast a funny glance at Eva's mom. "We'll both take regular breaks and have *sips* of water. Not glasses or gulps."

Karen sighed, but Eva nodded, as the photographer came over to take a candid shot of them in a down minute. She smiled, but inside her heart broke a little. There would be thousands of pictures of a fake wedding.

Alex pulled her out to the dance floor again. "What are you doing?"

He drew her into his arms. "You think too much. And tonight we're not thinking. We're dancing."

She recognized his point immediately. Her face probably showed her unhappiness. He didn't know it was over the fact that she loved him. He thought she was upset about documenting an event that was essentially fake. But that was good. It gave her breathing room. And maybe even a chance to let herself feel the love she couldn't deny—if only for a minute or two.

He tightened his arms around her, and she realized the music had shifted and they were dancing a slow song.

Even considering all the times they'd kissed, she hadn't ever had the presence of mind to appreciate being close to him. The first time he'd kissed her to persuade her not to marry him, he'd yanked her against him. They'd been pressed together from chest to knees and she'd felt the strength and power in his tense body.

Then he'd sneaked the kiss at the engagement party. The real kiss. And the press of their bodies had nothing to do with strength or power. That had been a kiss of real emotion. And she'd felt it in every place their bodies brushed.

But now they were dancing. Her brain was clear

enough to take in the breadth of his shoulders, the solidness of his chest, the leanness of his torso. She let the hand she had at his shoulder drift down and come up again.

His head tilted as he caught her gaze.

What would he do if he knew she was nearly overwhelmed by love for him?

What would he do if he knew curiosity about how he felt beneath all these clothes raced through her?

What would he think if she told him she was tired of being a woman one step behind everybody else her own age because she'd been sheltered, protected by an arranged marriage?

What if she told him she wanted to make love with him once, just once, for the pleasure of being with the first man she truly loved? So that she could move into the rest of her life a whole person, a real woman, the woman she was meant to be?

If she promised him no emotion, no attempt to break down his walls, and asked for just one night of everything…

Would he be able to say no?

CHAPTER ELEVEN

THEY WERE SCHEDULED to spend the night at the palace and leave for their honeymoon the day after the wedding, but for security purposes Alex had changed that, deciding they should leave immediately after the wedding.

The royal guard whisked them to the family helicopter which took them to the yacht. Alex led Eva to the king's suite of rooms, and at the door, lifted her into his arms.

She laughed. "Isn't carrying me over the threshold an American custom?"

He shrugged, deftly turned the doorknob with one hand and used his foot to nudge the door open. "Who cares?" He said it light and breezily, knowing he didn't have to remind her he was doing it for the staff, but feeling the odd sense of longing that had followed him around all day.

She laughed again, and the sound reverberated through him. It reminded him of sunny days and happiness, so he put her down quickly, in front of the sofa of the sitting room.

She turned to him with a smile, but he walked to the bar. She knew the drill as well as he did. Theirs was a fake marriage. The dancing and flirting they'd done at the wedding had been wrong. Dangerous to her future and his sanity. Now that there were no crowds to please or fool, he had to step away from her.

A bottle of his father's best champagne lay in a bucket of ice on the bar. He sniffed a laugh. His father certainly knew how to carry a charade to its full conclusion.

He lifted the bottle. "Champagne?"

Her satin gown swished and swirled as she made her way to the bar. "Yes. Thank you."

He popped the cork, found two glasses and poured.

He handed her a glass and she saluted him. "To us?"

"Sure, why not?" He said it swiftly, easily, but seeing her so casually sitting on one of the seats of his royal family's yacht, looking like she belonged there, sent a ping of that yearning through him again.

He ignored it.

"There are two bedrooms in this suite."

She raised her eyes, caught his gaze. "I figured."

Her eyes were filled with the emotion that always stopped his heart. Hopeful, yet somehow resigned. She was a woman so married to duty that she rarely got what she wanted, but a part of her still hungered for it.

She took a sip of her champagne, then another, her full lips barely touching the flute. The delicateness of her face was at odds with the strength of her character, which somehow managed to mask a very feminine, very sexy woman. And right at that moment he'd give anything to run his hands down her arms, along her torso, while he kissed her, if only to show her that she was worthy—worth it. That she was beautiful and powerful and perfect.

He took a step back. Dom had said there had been a moment on his wedding night when he'd looked at

Ginny and simply hadn't been able to resist her. At the time, Alex had thought his brother a besotted fool, or a man who simply hadn't been with enough women. But tonight, looking at Eva, knowing her the way he did, he wondered how much willpower he'd have to muster to walk away from what he so desperately wanted.

She finished her champagne and slid off the stool, her gown a glorious complement of silks and satins that rustled around her. She pointed to the right. "I imagine my bedroom is that way."

"Yes."

"I'm pretty good at this guessing stuff."

"You had a fifty-fifty chance of being right."

She smiled. "Better odds than blackjack."

"Much better odds."

She waited just the tiniest bit, while he waged a battle in his head. Not because he wanted her so much… though he did. But because she wanted him. It was there in her eyes. And it was easier to deny his own need than hers. The moment was fraught with possibilities. Glorious, wonderful things.

With slow, deliberate movements she walked over to him. He took a breath, held it.

But she didn't rise to her tiptoes to press her lips to his. Didn't touch him. Instead, she pulled the long, looping net veil to the side as she presented her back to him.

"Can you undo this for me?"

He swallowed. His fingers went to the small hook-and-eye closure above the long zipper of her strapless gown. "You know the night we left your dress in my hallway?"

She hesitated. "Yes."

"I told myself I could have had that little yellow gown off you in about twenty seconds."

The hook and eye disengaged. She turned and met his gaze. "Sure of yourself?"

"Experienced."

Their eyes held. If there was one strike that counted against him with her, it was his experience. He'd slept with everyone from starlets to vacationing waifs. She'd given herself to no one.

"Sometimes experience is a good thing."

"You didn't think so when you first met me."

"I was wrong."

He held her gaze. "No. You weren't."

She turned, presenting her back to him again so he could get the zipper. "I've been wrong about a lot of things, remember? I thought I didn't want to be a queen. Thought I'd be content being a placeholder. Turns out I'm not."

He glanced down at the zipper for her gown. Once he began pulling it down, he'd be seeing her back, the slope of her torso that led to her perfect bottom.

He stalled. "And you've got something of a fight ahead of you when you go home."

"I'm ready."

He wasn't. He thought no woman could tempt him beyond his power to resist. But as his fingers itched to pull down the zipper of her dress, his libido sat on the bleachers of his brain, munching popcorn, waiting for the show to begin.

His brain screamed that he should turn her around, send her to her room and dispatch a maid to help her with her dress.

His libido groaned, told him that was a damned fool idea. He'd seen her back before. One more peek wouldn't hurt.

He took the zipper in his tingling fingers.

She looked over her shoulder at him. "Do you want me to call a maid?"

Yes. "No." This was stupid. He had seen her back before and for the love of all that was holy, it was only a back.

He pulled the zipper down past her strapless bra and when he saw the yellow lace, he laughed. "Yellow undies for your wedding?"

"With all the white that was floating around, I wanted a little bit of color. I love yellow."

He was beginning to love yellow too.

He pulled the zipper to her waist, thinking that would be the end of it, but to his surprise it ran the whole way to her bottom. The whole way to yellow satin panties, trimmed in lace, looking so sexily feminine, his gut tensed.

The room suddenly got hot.

The top of her strapless dress collapsed into her hands and she brought her arms up to catch it. When she turned to face him, the bodice was a crumbled heap against the pretty yellow bra and bare shoulders that were creamy white as if they'd never seen the sun.

The temptation that had been hovering on the edge of everything they'd done the past four weeks overwhelmed him. All he wanted was a simple touch.

He put his hands on her shoulders, onto skin that felt like new velvet.

And maybe a taste.

He leaned down, his gaze trapped with her expectant one, and knew this was absolutely wrong, but telling himself he could handle it.

When his lips met hers, she lifted her arms to his shoulders and the dress fell, puddling on the floor between them. The lace of her bra crushed against the silk of his shirt but he swore he didn't feel the barrier between them. He felt that lace brushing his chest—

He pulled back, sucked in a breath of air. As much as he wanted this, he couldn't have her.

Bending down, he picked up her gown, pressing it against her chest until she took it.

"This is wrong."

She leaped to her tiptoes and brushed her lips across his. "No, it's not."

"I think you're forgetting something very important. You told me you wanted to become queen."

She held his gaze, waiting for his explanation.

"I want you to fulfill your destiny."

"And you don't want to be a husband to a queen? Don't worry. I don't expect you to stay married to me. I just want this. Want you. Just once."

He laughed, shook his head. "That's actually the point. Our annulment will be predicated on the fact that we never consummated the marriage. If we do this now, you can't get an annulment. You'll be forced to get a divorce. And you, with a divorce in your past, won't be allowed to reign."

She stared at him, as if she'd actually forgotten. Then she stepped away. "Oh."

Disappointment swelled inside him. For some damned reason or another he thought she'd say, "So what?"

"You never thought of that?"

She shook her head, then smoothed an errant strand

of black hair off her face. "I'm kind of making a fool of myself, aren't I?"

He reached out, took her elbows and pulled her close again. "I'm the one in the wrong. I want you enough that I almost slipped." He admitted it because he couldn't stand to have her think that any of this was because she wasn't beautiful, sexy, special. She was. And he wanted her so much his whole body ached. He almost didn't know where he got the courage, the honor to say, "But I also like you too much to deny you of your destiny. I don't know what you're going to do as queen, but I know you well enough to realize that whatever you do it will be special, wonderful. Your country probably needs that."

Her eyes saddened into the soft blue that made his chest hurt. But he held his ground, and his breath.

Eva stared into his eyes, a million confusing truths racing through her brain. This was the unspoken reality of what happened to people with destinies. Alex hadn't said it. He didn't need to. It was all there in his eyes. People with destinies rarely got what they wanted. Duty, responsibility came first.

She cursed it, then reminded herself of all the feelings she'd had the day her dad had called. The horrible knowledge that she'd been overlooked. The intense desire to be part of the team that put her beloved country back together again.

Would she throw it all away for one night with a man she longed for? The first man she'd ever really wanted?

She swallowed. She'd thought the answer would be easy. Instead she stood frozen. How could she decide without a kiss? Without a touch?

Her lips tingled at the thought of another kiss. Her entire body exploded at the thought more of his touch.

Something must have changed in her expression because he pulled back. "Oh, you are temptation. But, no. I can't be the person who steals your destiny from you."

Her eyes clung to his. "There is one way."

His eyebrows rose.

"I know I told you I wouldn't force you to stay married…but what if we wanted to?"

"Stay married?"

She nodded.

He squeezed his eyes shut. "You have known me four weeks. I can't ask for a life commitment after four weeks."

"But you were willing to marry a princess you didn't know."

"And now I know her and now I know she deserves more. Real love. Trust. A man who doesn't have walls."

He turned her in the direction of her room. "Go before I can't be noble anymore."

The next morning, she met Alex in the sitting room of their yacht suite for breakfast, pretending nothing had happened. He'd said that she hadn't made a fool of herself, that he wanted her, and if the intense expression in his eyes had been anything to judge by, he had wanted her.

In some ways that made her happy. In others, it turned her heart inside out. The very fact that he couldn't consummate their marriage once again said he might like her, he might be attracted to her, but he didn't want her forever.

Still, what did she expect? Everlasting love after four

weeks? That was silly. And if there was one thing she'd realized she wasn't, it was silly.

So she put on shorts and a T-shirt, combed her hair but really didn't fix it. It might not be a real honeymoon, but it was a vacation. Then she sat at the small table with Alex.

Without looking up from the newspaper he was reading, he said, "I didn't know what you'd want so I asked the staff to bring a bit of everything."

She laughed and the paper fell. Obviously, he'd been waiting for a sign that she didn't hate him.

How could she hate him for sticking to a deal she'd agreed to?

So she smiled.

He carefully returned her smile. "What do we want to do today?"

"I got word two days ago that my stipend was in my bank account. I need to get money to my shelters. But I was also hoping to have time to make phone calls to all the managers."

"That's what you want to do when you have an entire yacht at your disposal?"

"I haven't spoken to them in weeks. I need to catch up."

"All business on our honeymoon?"

"I'm sorry."

He folded the paper. "No. No. Don't be sorry. The staff assigned to our suite is made up of our most loyal personnel. They won't breathe a word of the fact that we don't sleep together. So, they won't bat an eye if you spend our first day on the phone handling business."

"It's okay then?"

"Yes, but tomorrow we should do something together."

"I don't water ski or do any of the daredevil sports you like."

He laughed. "That might be a good thing. The whole purpose of all this is to keep you alive."

She smiled. "Okay. So tomorrow we'll sit on deck chairs and read."

"Sounds good."

It really didn't sound good to Eva. It sounded like another chance in her life passing her by. She'd never make love to her first love.

It was the price she'd pay to be a queen. The price he'd pay to protect her.

And for the hundredth time, she wished the old Alex, the Alex who didn't care about royalty and responsibility, would swoop in and save her. Sweep her off her feet, make her glad to give up the crown.

But that was stupid…wasn't it?

CHAPTER TWELVE

THE MOOD IN the palace was celebratory when Alex and Eva arrived home two weeks later. Everyone had gathered in the king's quarters to greet them, so they headed there first.

Her mom enveloped her in a huge hug, a hug to rival one of Rose's hugs, and Eva laughed. "I see the Sancho family is rubbing off on you."

Karen took a glass of wine from King Ronaldo who was enjoying an afternoon of playing bartender.

Eva turned to Alex and whispered, "Your dad's in a weird mood."

Alex watched him mixing a martini for Rose. "I have a vague memory of him liking the job of bartender." He frowned. "If I'm remembering correctly, I think that's how he played host—"

He stopped abruptly. Eva wound her hand around his upper arm. She waited until he looked at her before she said, "Before your mom died."

His face shifted as if something had clicked into place for him. "It's so amazing to see him becoming himself again."

Just as it was probably amazing for the king to watch Alex become the prince he was always meant to be. Eva didn't say it, but pride for Alex surged through her, along with the abysmal realization that this family she was becoming a part of, this man she was so in love with, would soon be gone.

She pulled in a breath. "You know what? I'm a little bit tired. Do you mind if I go back to my quarters."

Alex whispered, "You can't go back to your quarters. We're married now. Staff will have already moved your things to mine."

"Oh." And the break she was hoping for flitted away.

"It's no big deal. We'll figure out how to handle it."

"Yes." She straightened her shoulders. "I'm sure we will."

"I can walk you back now."

She looked away. "I can find my own way, remember? I've been there for plenty of pretend lunches and suppers."

She knew that sounded bitter, so she faced him and said, "Sorry. I'm just very tired and getting a headache. Let me go get settled. You enjoy your time with family."

He nodded but walked her to the door of his father's quarters. He said, "Maybe you should take a nap."

She said, "Sure. That's probably what I'll do."

As she turned to walk away, she noticed Alex motioning to one of the guards to follow her to the apartment, and suddenly she was very, very tired.

She entered Alex's apartment, working not to remember the casual dinners they'd shared where she'd slowly but surely fallen in love with him.

Given that the staff believed they were married for real, she knew that her things were in Alex's closet, so she walked to her room deciding she could take a nap in her camisole and panties. She wouldn't be so bold as to walk into the man's closet when he wasn't there. Worse, his bedroom. She didn't want to see if he was tidy or messy. She didn't want to see his toothbrush and shaving creams. They'd already done too many personal, intimate things. Too many things she'd have to forget when they parted. She didn't need more reminders of everything she was losing. She just wanted all of this to be over.

On the way to her bedroom, she kicked off her sandals. She yanked her sweater over her head and it fell from her tired fingers. She stopped long enough to slide her jeans to the floor and step out of them. Some little voice in the back of her head told her to pick up the jeans, pick up the trail of clothes she was leaving, but a heaviness consumed her. She barely got to the bed before she crumbled, luckily landing face-first on the mattress.

From the way his dad and Rose, and Ginny and Dom behaved, Alex would have thought they believed he and Eva were actually married. He knew part of this was for the benefit of the charade. But, really? Sometimes his dad and Rose just got carried away. They loved family.

Twenty minutes later, with Rose still regaling them with stories from her days as a public school teacher in Texas, Alex looked at his watch. He'd known Eva had needed some space. He didn't blame her. Though they'd spent their days on the yacht resting, reading, watching glorious sunsets, it was wearing to pretend to be honeymooning when they would go back to their suite and sleep in separate rooms.

But this afternoon there'd been something a little different in her eyes. Something more than exhaustion. So he gave Rose's hilarious stories another ten minutes, then excused himself and headed for his quarters.

He saw the trail of clothes to her room and burst out laughing.

"Very funny, Eva."

He picked up the first shoe, then the second. Took a few steps and grabbed her sweater. Another few steps and he could scoop up her jeans. He turned to open the door of her bedroom but it was already open, and Eva lay, face-first, on the soft comforter of the queen-sized bed.

He laughed. "That's a weird way to take a nap." But as he walked into the room darkened by thick drapes, he realized she was in nothing but panties and a camisole. Silky white with a wide lace border.

He stopped. Cleared his throat. Obviously she was sleeping, so he'd just drop her jeans, sweater and shoes on a chair in the back. He walked past the bed, dumped the clothes, and turned to leave the room, but as he approached the bed, he noticed her breathing was labored, difficult.

He walked over. "Eva?"

She didn't move.

He bent and nudged her shoulder. "Eva?"

She still didn't move.

He grabbed the receiver from the palace phone by her bed. "This is Alex. Send a doctor to my quarters immediately."

It seemed to take forever for the doctor to arrive with a nurse, but the second they rang the bell, he opened the door.

Alex had turned on the overhead light, pulled back

the covers and shifted her on the bed so that she was lying on her back.

When he took the doctor to her room, it was easy to see the bright red splotches on her cheeks. Her head shifted on the pillow. She moaned as if in pain.

Dr. Martin looped his stethoscope around his neck. "I can see from here that she's got a fever." He walked over to the bed, took a look at her face and turned to Alex. "I'm going to have Sarah take her vitals." He motioned Alex to the door and walked him out of the room and up the hall.

"After Sarah gets the vitals, I'll have a look at her. We'll also need to draw some blood for tests."

Alex said, "Okay."

"Do you want me to call Dom to come and sit with you?"

"No. I'm fine."

The doctor smiled. "Okay. Great." He headed down the hall, but faced Alex again. "You know I have to report this visit to your dad, right?"

Alex nodded. Didn't every flipping thing they did have to be reported?

"Great. Blood tests will take a few hours. Are you sure you don't want somebody called?"

He nodded, realizing that the person he'd want called to help him through an afternoon of waiting was Eva. But she was the one who was sick.

When Dr. Martin and Sarah came out of her room after the exam, he asked, "Can I go in and sit with her?"

Dr. Martin winced. "Actually, Alex, you risk catching the flu. I can't be certain, but it looks like that's what she picked up. Maybe from someone on the yacht."

"Which means I've already been exposed."

The doctor shrugged. "I'd prefer you stay away. If you want someone with her, I can send up nurses who will do twenty-four-hour shifts."

A sudden memory of his mom being sick sprang into his head. He remembered his dad by her side twenty-four hours a day and suddenly understood why.

"I'll take the risk."

"I have to report this to your father."

"So you said."

The doctor sighed and left with Sarah the nurse and Alex walked back to her room.

She was under the covers, dressed in a pair of pajamas. Alex had no idea where they'd come from, but all Doc had to do was get on the phone and tell someone in housekeeping to send pajamas and they'd probably be delivered through the back door.

He walked to the bed, not liking Eva's labored breathing, but knowing she was being cared for by one of the best. Crouching at the side of the bed, he pushed her hair off her forehead and wished that they'd met under different circumstances.

Because wishing accomplished nothing, he forced himself to his feet, but didn't leave her room. He pulled a Queen Anne chair from a corner of the room to the side of the bed. When he fell asleep, it was only for a few minutes at a time. So he crawled onto her bed. He stretched out beside her and fell asleep for a few hours, but when he woke up she was thrashing. The second he touched her hand, she stopped. So he stayed, right where he was, not under the covers, on top. Sometimes he'd smooth her hair from her face. For the most part he just held her hand. Until she scooted closer and snuggled against him. He wrapped his arms around her and slept. Not for long stretches, but longer than he might have slept on that uncomfortable chair.

In the morning, the doctor ordered him to go to bed and he told the old grouch that he'd go as soon as the doctor's visit was over.

But he didn't leave. He stayed in the chair, watching her. Though the temptation was strong to lie on the bed with her, he resisted it. He watched nurses take her temperature, wake her up enough to give her meds and even cool her head with a wet cloth.

When the doctor returned that evening it was to announce that her fever had broken.

"Now, there's no reason to sit by her bed. You can get some sleep."

He walked the old man to the door, and hesitated at the place where he'd go left to his own room, or right to Eva's.

But staying in her room was silly. She was over the worst of it now. And he needed some sleep.

He turned left, got a shower and shrugged into a T-shirt and a pair of pajama pants. But when he lifted the cover off his bed, he couldn't slide inside.

For some reason or another, he simply could not leave her alone. He knew she only had the flu. He knew her fever had broken. But he just couldn't leave her by herself in a room that was unfamiliar to her.

Still, he was tired. Exhausted. So he walked to the empty side of her bed, lifted the cover and slid inside. When she turned to him, he wrapped his arms around her. The second he closed his eyes, he fell asleep.

When Eva awakened she had no idea what time it was... or what day. Vague images passed through her brain but nothing stuck. She was also comfortably tucked against someone. Not the way a mother or father cradles a child, but closer.

Alex.

Some of the images gelled in her mind. Him ordering around a man in a gray suit. Him giving uniformed nurses instructions.

She smiled.

"Go back to sleep. You might have slept away the past thirty-six hours. But I've slept in fits and starts."

On this bed. With her. Flashes of him lying beside her, stroking her hair, flitted to her. That's why his arms around her hadn't awakened her. He'd done this before. Maybe even the entire night before.

She stilled her hands at her sides and felt silky material.

"The nurses did that. Changed your PJs twice. They also gave you two sponge baths. Though I volunteered, they shot me down."

She laughed.

"There you go. Now I know you're not just awake, you're feeling better."

"I am."

"Well, go back to sleep. It's still night. And I'm tired."

He was staying? Was he going to hold her the entire time he slept?

Happiness overwhelmed her and suddenly she felt every inch of him that touched her. Not just his warmth, but the softness of a T-shirt and cotton sleep pants. His bicep was her pillow. Her cheek rested against his chest. It was the most intimate, most wonderful feeling.

"Don't ever do that again."

His voice filtered to her softly, filled with a casual

intimacy that caused joy to radiate to every nook and cranny of her body.

"Do what?"

"Get so sick that half the palace worried you were going to die, or that we'd put so much stress on you we'd killed you."

She carefully, slowly raised her hand until she could lay it against his chest. Not so much out of curiosity about what he felt like, but more out of a longing to know what it felt like to be allowed to touch him.

"All I remember is a headache."

"You had a virus."

Here they were, apparently in the middle of the night, having a conversation while wrapped in each other's arms. She flattened her palm against his chest, reveled in the steady rhythm of his breathing, knew this was what being married felt like: a quiet, unspoken connection.

"A weak virus if I've only been sleeping thirty-six hours."

"Strong enough that your mother almost sent for clergy."

She laughed and snuggled against him. His arms tightened around her. "I seem to remember you bossing around the nurses."

"I have a marriage license that says I can."

She suppressed a smile. "So you're one of those types who throw their weight around."

"I haven't spent six weeks protecting you only to have a virus kill you."

He said it so easily, as if that was all it was, but his muscles tightened.

She suddenly wished she could see his face, see the naked emotion in his dark, dark eyes. But then she'd have to pull away. It wasn't often he let her be so close, let her touch him, let himself touch her.

"You like me."

He laughed. "Of course, I like you."

"No. You *like* me."

He stilled. The room got very quiet.

"Does it matter?"

It mattered to her. A great deal. If only because her heart needed to know. Needed to hear him say that something had blossomed between them, because she couldn't take another day of being so close to him, yet being emotionally separated.

"It matters."

"Then, yes. I have feelings for you that I shouldn't have."

"I have feelings for you too." Such an inadequate description of the emotions that squeezed her heart and captured her soul. Made her hot and cold. Made her long to be with him as he distanced herself from her. Made her understand the bond between her parents that was strong enough that her dad could pretend to leave with a mistress and trust her mother would collapse into his arms when the truth was revealed. She almost couldn't bear the strength of it… Yet it slipped out as one tiny sentence.

His voice was slow, hesitant as he said, "I know."

Her heart tripped over itself in her chest. It wasn't the first time they'd talked about this. But it was the first time she believed they could both be honest. "I—"

"Go to sleep, Princess."

She heard the tiredness in his voice. Felt his muscles relaxing as if he were drifting off and wanted to shout, "No! I need this." But she didn't. She didn't say anything else and soon she knew from his relaxed body that he was asleep.

She awakened the next morning to find him gone. She slid her hand along the space where he'd slept. It was cold.

Hopelessness billowed through her. She'd had her moment, but it was gone.

She showered and dressed in jeans and a top, not quite sure what her mother would have planned for the day, but knowing she needed to spend time with her mom to make up for their fourteen-day separation.

Expecting to find Alex's quarters empty, she stopped short when she walked in on him in his small dining room, eating breakfast. He rose when he saw her and came over to pull her chair away from the table. But before he let her sit, he took her shoulders and looked into her eyes.

"Don't ever scare me like that again."

The crazy feeling of intimacy from the night before trembled through her. "I won't."

He kissed her cheek then sniffed a laugh as he returned to his own seat. "You just promised you'll never get the flu?"

His words slid through her, as she sat. He said it as if they would be together forever. The hope that had died tried to flicker to life. She swallowed.

"I should have gotten the vaccination."

"You should have." He frowned when she reached for a platter of eggs. "You might want to go easy on food today, give your body a chance to recover."

"I'm ravenous. Besides, the flu is gone. I was better last night when we—"

She couldn't say snuggled. She wanted to. But she

couldn't even say slept together, even though sleep was all they did. Silly superstition filled her. Almost as if she was afraid that if she said any of it out loud, she'd jinx it.

He caught her gaze. "Had our chat?"

"Yes."

He rose from his seat. Tossing his napkin to the table, he walked over to her, bent down and kissed her cheek. "I have things to do this morning, but don't make plans for lunch. If your stomach really is up to it, we'll go see Angelo."

Her body went soft, almost boneless, over the wonderful intimacy that hadn't disappeared as she'd believed it would.

On the way to the door, he stopped a maid. "My wife is better this morning. But I don't want to take any chances with germs. Clean her room as if the royal health inspectors will be visiting."

Eva laughed. He spun to face her. "You laugh. But you don't know what a scare you gave me."

"Over the flu?"

He said, "Over something," then left the apartment.

Eva sat very still. The only other "something" in that equation had been the possibility that he'd lose her.

The hope flickering in her roared into a flame of possibility. Would he eventually realize that he'd lose her when her father returned? Would he stop her?

After a morning spent with his brother and father, catching up on everything that had happened while he was gone, Alex was glad he'd made lunch plans with Eva. The two weeks they'd been away had been quiet. Dom was even shaving back the amount of time he spent helping Eva's dad. Soon, King Mason would be returning to rule. He'd upend his country; that was for sure. But the changes would be for the better.

Everybody was happy. Especially Alex. Eva had scared him beyond belief with a simple case of the flu. But she was well now. And he couldn't shake the out-of-proportion happiness that brought. She'd had the flu, not the plague. Yet every time he looked at her and saw the light in her eyes, the color in her cheeks, crazy pleasure flooded him.

It was weird.

He hoped lunch with her would get him beyond it. Except she wore a pretty blue top that made her eyes look even bluer and Angelo didn't just make lunch. He sat with them, telling Eva stories of when Alex was at university and he'd sneak the private plane to come home and have dinner at Angelo's.

"Just because I could," Alex said, shaking his head.

Angelo tapped Eva's hand. "He was drunk with power."

Eva laughed but Alex straightened. "I wasn't drunk with power as much as I was experimenting with my power."

Catching his gaze, Eva said, "Ah. I get it now."

And he felt it again. That fluttery happiness that was more than relief that she was well. It was as if somebody turned on a light in a very dark room.

He got up from his chair. "Angelo, the next time we come here, I want to vet the stories you decide to tell."

The old chef laughed merrily. "What fun would that be?"

"Are you trying to get my wife to run for the hills?"

"No. I'm telling her the stories before she hears them from strangers." Angelo rose as Alex helped Eva stand.

"Look at it this way, if I tell them in front of you, then you have a chance to defend yourself."

"Good point."

He took Eva's hand. She smiled at him. As they made their way to his Mercedes, bodyguards shifted and scrambled. They all seemed a little too alert, more alert than they had just two hours ago when they'd driven to the restaurant.

He told himself he was imagining it.

"Can I drive?"

He glanced at Eva as he reached into his pocket for the keys, but Jeffrey, today's team leader, walked over.

He bowed. "Prince, allow me the honor of driving."

Alex handed him the keys. He knew better than to argue. Something had happened.

But he didn't get an inkling of a word about it when he left Eva in their apartment and went to his father's office and Dom's. Both were out at meetings and no one on either staff seemed to know what was going on.

When he asked Jeffrey, all he said was, "Your father implemented a secondary protocol which we followed. I assumed it was a test or a dry run since we've had no threats."

"A dry run?"

"We do them all the time."

And wouldn't it make sense that his father would want his bodyguards preparing for the day when Eva's father returned.

His gut tightened. Though he tried to tell himself it was out of fear, he realized it was because he would miss her.

When he finally returned to the apartment, Eva stood in the sitting room wearing a slim red dress.

His eyebrows rose. "Going somewhere?"

"We're all having dinner." She pointed to her dress. "Semiformal, with your dad and Rose, Dom and Ginny and my mom."

"So no tux?"

She shrugged. "I'm not entirely sure. You never know with Rose."

"Maybe I can get away with nice trousers and a dinner jacket."

"Do you feel lucky?"

He laughed. "Are you quoting American movies to me?"

"An old one. Go. You have about ten minutes before we have to leave."

He showered quickly and though he looked at a tux, he decided on a simple jacket and trousers. His day might have been calm and casual by Dom's standards, but it wasn't easy to get back into the swing of working. Especially not when he'd spent the afternoon thinking something was up, only to discover his cause for alarm had only been something like a fire drill.

When he met Eva in the sitting room, she walked over and straightened his collar. "There. Now you're perfect."

The strange sensation he kept getting around her filled him, then grew.

He shook his head to clear it of the feeling and motioned her to the door. "We have about a minute and a half left then we're late and Rose hates it when anybody's late."

"My mom does too."

He stopped her at the door, before they would have been in public space where someone could have overheard. "How's she holding up, by the way?"

"Now that she knows the truth, she's like a kid at Christmas. She's proud that she did her job and eager to see her husband again."

He said, "That's good." But a weird empathy rippled along the edges of his skin. He'd decided it was because they'd all had a part to play. So of course, he understood Karen's feelings.

But after a long elaborate dinner that seemed more like a celebration, Alex walked Eva to their apartment in silence.

He didn't even want to think that the so-called fire drill this morning had been practice for possible trouble when her dad made his announcements about the plot to oust him. He didn't want to think tonight's dinner had been a goodbye dinner for Eva and her mom.

That would mean she was leaving the next day, and he just didn't want to think about it.

He opened the apartment door and directed Eva to walk in before him. She stepped into the sitting room, removing her earrings.

"That was unexpectedly nice."

"Yes. It was."

She faced him with a smile. "Your father found a real gem when he found Rose."

"Technically, Dad didn't find Rose. Dom brought her here to help Ginny adjust."

She walked over to him, her head angled to the right, a silly smile on her full lips. "I'm guessing that was a great story."

"It was. What I know of it, at least. I'm not privy to all the private stuff, but Dom very honestly admits he simply couldn't resist Ginny."

"The power of love."

Gazing into Eva's silvery blue eyes, he almost believed it. But it didn't matter. She had a destiny and he wasn't ruining that for her. She, at least, needed the chance to decide who she was. To go home, as herself, to figure out what role she wanted to fill in her kingdom.

But what he wouldn't give for one night.

She bounced her earrings in her hand. "I guess I'll go to bed."

He stepped back. "Yeah. Me too."

But she didn't move. And the temptation that rocked him almost pushed him over the edge. She was beautiful, soft, smart, elegant and poised, yet delightfully normal. And the law said she was his.

But she wasn't a private jet that he could commandeer, use and return. And he wasn't a kid anymore, who took what he wanted without consideration for the consequences.

Though it felt like an actual, physical pain when he forced his legs to move, to walk away from her, he did.

CHAPTER THIRTEEN

ALEX WAS IN parliament the next day when one of his secretaries stealthily entered and slid a note into his hands.

The news has broken that Prince Gerard of Grennady has been arrested. King Mason is in your father's office. Your presence is requested.

He bounced out of his seat, caught Dom's gaze, then nudged his head in the direction of the door. Dom gave a quick, curt nod.

Alex exited calmly, but once in the high-ceilinged foyer, he began to run. He wasn't sure why. He had no idea where the sense of urgency came from. But he had a picture in his head of King Mason loading his wife and daughter into a helicopter or plane and Eva waving goodbye from a window—

And he'd never see her again.

Wouldn't even get a proper goodbye.

He ran faster. His heart was pounding, his breaths shallow and uneven until he reached the secretary's office outside his father's door.

He stopped, leveled his breathing and, without asking permission from the secretary, opened his father's office door and stepped inside.

"Here's the man of the hour now," his father boomed. He, King Mason, Rose, Karen and Eva stood in a cluster in front of his desk. There was no silver tea service with coffee and scones on the low table in front of the sofa in the conversation area in the corner. There was no sigh of relief, no relaxing on the overstuffed chairs. No one sat. Everyone stood, as if the King of Grennady was eager to be off.

"I've never seen anyone step up the way Alex did." When Alex reached his father, he clapped Alex on the back. "The wedding was perfect. No one would have ever believed the two of them weren't in love."

Alex's gaze snapped to Eva's. Her eyes were red-rimmed as if she'd had a tearful reunion with her dad. When she smiled at Alex, her lips wobbled.

He held her gaze. He knew the past six weeks had been difficult for her. But there had been joy in there too. A wedding. Stolen kisses. Confidences that had rocked his soul. "It's Eva who deserves the credit."

He wasn't the screw-up he had been when she arrived. The guy who lived for himself. He'd more than done his duty. He'd become the prince his father had always wished he would be.

Knowing her had made him who he was.

And now…

Right now…

His whole life was in her hands.

Except he didn't think he had the right to ask her to stay. She couldn't rule from Xaviera.

King Mason slid his arm around his daughter's shoulders. "I watched your news every day. She was magnificent. But I had no doubt that she would be." He smiled at her. "She'll be a queen one day." He looked over at Alex. "And you'd have made her a fine husband for real. I'm sorry we had to screw that up."

Alex glanced at Eva. No one, it seemed, realized something had happened between him and Eva.

He waited a heartbeat for her to say something. Anything. To ask him to come with her. Because that was their only option.

But King Mason said, "We really need to be going. This hit the press two hours ago and I need to get in front of my parliament."

Alex's dad shook Mason's hand. "You have your speech."

"I'll be refining it on the flight home."

Karen hugged Rose. "This might have been nothing but a charade but I think you're the best friend I've ever had. I hope we can get together."

Rose winked. "I think we need to do a little shopping in Paris."

Karen laughed. "I would love that."

Alex waited. Eva had missed the opportunity to tell her family that what she felt for Alex had been real. Hell, he'd let it go by too. Because it wasn't really his choice. It was hers. She'd asked him once to stay married to her, but he'd said no. He wouldn't steal her destiny. He couldn't change his mind now. Could he?

Eva hugged his dad. "Thank you."

"Princess, you were a delight. Anytime you feel like a beach vacation, you just fly down."

"I will."

Then she turned to him. Her eyes were bright, not filled with the hopeful, wistful look that had made him feel he could see the whole way to her soul. She was happy.

"Thank you, Prince Alex."

He sniffed a laugh. "I think that's the first time you've given me a title."

She held his gaze. "You earned it."

And he couldn't think of anything to say. He couldn't say, "Please stay." He couldn't pull her away from a country where she would be queen. He couldn't say, "I love you," because he wasn't sure he did. So he couldn't ask her for a little time to get to know each other—or date—because that seemed ridiculous.

But she could ask him.

Just ask.

Just say the word.

One word.

Any word.

She stepped forward and put her arms around him, hugging him awkwardly. He smelled her scented hair. Breathed in the scent, as his heart realized she wasn't going to say anything.

She pulled away.

And his heart did something he'd never felt before. Not even when Nina died.

It shattered.

"Goodbye, Alex."

"Goodbye, Eva." He meant for that to sound strong. Instead, his voice was hoarse, scratchy.

She turned to her parents, who gathered her up and walked through the door where members of the royal guard awaited them.

"They have to go five floors to the roof and run a good distance to their helicopter," Dominic said.

Alex whipped around to face him.

"You can catch her."

He blinked. He *could* catch her. He could stop her.

And tell her what?

Promise her what?

She would someday be a queen. She was strong. Smart. Capable.

What the hell would she want him around for?

But his father made a sound of distaste and said, "Never belabor goodbyes. Leave Eva with the memory of you strong. I'm sure you'll meet again, and you'll laugh about this. But right now I'm releasing you for a much deserved holiday."

The helicopter flight to the royal airstrip and Grennady's private jet was too noisy to talk and Eva was glad. She'd never felt this odd feeling. Almost as if she were outside her body, watching this happen to someone else.

She knew her dad coming home would be disruptive. Surprising. Totally out of the blue. Especially for her mom, who was so desperate to see him, to know that he really was still hers. But it wasn't seeing her dad that left Eva feeling as if she were vibrating with confusion.

It was leaving Alex.

It was being there in that room, almost begging him with her eyes to admit to their families that they'd become close for real, and having him step back, away from her, that caused her stomach to fall and her nerve endings to shimmy.

She'd thought he was beginning to see that they belonged together but apparently she'd been wrong.

The helicopter landed and they ran to the plane. As

soon as they were inside the main cabin, her mom put her hands on both of Eva's cheeks and kissed her soundly.

"You have definitely proven yourself. You are Grennady's next queen."

She tried to smile.

"Yes. Your mother is right. I realized while watching you every day that you weren't just the woman who'd bear our next heir," her dad said, hugging her one more time. "You were made to rule."

She sniffed a laugh. "I realized it too. Actually, Alex realized it first." Saying the sentence out loud, picturing the times and the ways he'd said it, slowed her heartbeat. Their relationship had always seemed so real to her because some of it was. He'd been her friend. Her partner in their charade. And eventually he'd grown to like her.

How could something that real be over in the space of what seemed like seconds?

She almost said something, but her mom began talking about her having a real reign and her dad began enumerating things she'd have to do, like get daily briefings and attend parliament when it was in session, maybe take over a committee or two.

She nodded and smiled, thrilled for the opportunity, but she couldn't stop thinking about Alex.

Actually, what she probably needed was time alone.

But her parents went on discussing her reign through the plane ride with Eva participating as much as she could. Her dad wanted her on the dais with him at the press conference the following day. But he wanted her to wait to actually introduce herself into parliament until after he'd totally settled things. This was a point in his reign when he needed to look strong and though having her at his side was good, a king had to be autonomous.

When she was queen, there'd probably come a time when she'd have to do the same thing. Stand alone, as a leader. Someone their subjects could trust.

When they arrived in Grennady, their airstrip was quiet, deserted. The drive to their palace was still, though the air hummed with the realization that her dad had a lot of work to do. As soon as they arrived, he walked directly to parliament.

Her mom went to her quarters to lie down and Eva spent some time on her bed too. But she couldn't sleep. She couldn't anything. Her mind was numb. She was so filled with sorrow and confusion that she couldn't even close her eyes.

Engaged in the duty of pulling his country together again, her dad didn't come home for dinner. Eva met her mom in the private dining room in her parents' quarters. But she didn't eat. She stared at the food as if it was a foreign object.

"Sweetie?"

Her head snapped up. "What?"

"I was just about to ask you the same thing. What's wrong?"

"I think I'm just having a little trouble adjusting. This time yesterday I was married—" She stopped herself. "Pretending to be married. Then suddenly Dad was in King Ronaldo's office and we were on a helicopter."

Her mom's eyes narrowed as she studied Eva's face. "It did all happen fast."

"No warning," Eva agreed. "No time to prepare."

"What would you have had to prepare? You were in on the plan. You knew that at any moment your dad would come to Xaviera to get us and take us home."

Eva cleared her throat. "That's the way it was in the

beginning. But the pretending went on so long." She sucked in a breath. Closed her eyes. "I got married, Mom."

"As part of a charade," her mom reminded her. Then her face changed. "Wait." She gasped. "You didn't—"

"No. We *didn't*."

"Well, thank God for that because if I'm reading this right that's your basis for an annulment."

"Yes."

"And you need an annulment, not a divorce if you want to be queen."

The dining room got quiet. Karen ate a few bites, but glanced at Eva again. "Are you sure you're okay?"

Eva nodded.

Her mom sighed. "Tomorrow, you will have to go in front of the press to answer questions and with the knowledge that you won't just be a placeholder. Your father saw your strength. He knows you can rule and he will be telling the country that tomorrow. You can't be this—" She fumbled for a word and finally settled on, "Quiet."

"I'll be fine tomorrow."

Her mother studied Eva's face again. "You're sure?"

"Yes."

"And there's nothing you want to talk about?"

She would have loved to have talked. But as her mother said, she was a woman who would someday be a queen. Anytime she fell apart, had doubts, was human, she would be perceived as weak. And she'd seen first-hand that her uncle's family, the ones next in line for the throne, would exploit that.

So she couldn't talk. Except to a confidant...like a husband who understood. Like Alex.

She licked her suddenly dry lips. He hadn't asked her to stay, hadn't told their families that the charade had turned to real love—probably because for him, it hadn't. And he had a real life to get back to. Their charade had changed him. He had duties, responsibilities now.

Truth wore away some of her shock and created a struggle inside of her. The woman who loved him wanted to weep. The woman who would be queen put her shoulders back and recognized her duty.

But in bed that night, the tears came and she realized she'd finally had her heart broken. And if this pain, this sorrow, this anguish, was anything to go by, Alex must have suffered a thousand times over when he lost his first love, the woman who kept him from wanting to love again.

The next day, she and her father were in front of the press, explaining the entire charade.

At the end, when a cheeky reporter asked her if she hadn't, even once, wished her marriage to Xaviera's handsome Playboy Prince was real, she'd shaken her head with a laugh and said, "Absolutely not. I was doing my duty."

Alex stared at the TV in his father's office, watching the closed circuit TV feed that Grennady had provided the rulers of Xaviera who would most assuredly be contacted for comments.

Eva wore a red suit—the color recommended to all leaders when they wanted to show their power. Her soft blue eyes were sharp today. Her gaze was clear, direct. Her chin was high. Her shoulders were back. Her comments were short, emotionless. Even as she demonstrated she would not steal her father's thunder, she wore all the marks of a queen.

When she said, "Absolutely not. I was doing my duty," his muscles froze. He told them not to. He reminded them he should have expected this.

But he pictured her on the yacht, eating dinner with him in the moonlight.

He saw her in the wedding dress.

He remembered holding her the night she was sick, when he all but admitted he had feelings for her.

And he saw past the future queen to the woman she'd buried somewhere inside her.

He knew that woman was weeping.

But he also knew he was out. She didn't need him.

His chest hurt and he rubbed it, the way he used to when he thought of Nina. Funny, he hadn't even had an inkling of a memory of her in weeks. Not once.

Rose peered over at him from the leather couch in the corner. "You okay, sweet pea?"

He grabbed a breath of air, giving himself a second to make sure he looked and sounded normal. "Yes. I'm fine."

The king rose from the oversized chair in front of the TV. "Of course he's fine. He's better than fine. He should be proud of himself. His changes to security details and eye for finding the loopholes might have saved Eva's life." He glanced at his watch. "Aren't you scheduled to be on the jet in a few minutes?"

"Yes." He was. Though his father had told him he could leave yesterday he hadn't been able to figure out where to go. This morning, he'd booked the royal family's jet to take him to the United States. He loved New York, but he wasn't going there for the restaurants or the shows. He wanted to see Eva's shelters. It filled him with pain to admit it. But he just couldn't take the sudden goodbye. Yet he also knew he couldn't just fly to her country and expect her to see him. He just wanted another day or two to get adjusted to the fact that she was out of his life, and her cats were about as close to her as he would get.

Then he'd be fine. He'd force himself to be fine.

He tried a smile, reached way down in his soul until he found the frivolous personality that had served him so well for decades.

"I haven't been to the US in a long time. I'm sure Vegas has missed me."

Dom slapped his back. "You enjoy yourself."

The king snorted. "If you hadn't earned this, I'd be a bit angry that you booked four weeks. You have duties now. When I told you that you could go I was thinking more like a week."

And Alex laughed. Because he knew he was supposed to. "Right. But I'm thinking I earned a little longer. I'll see you all next month."

He headed for the door, but Rose suddenly popped up from the sofa. "I'll walk you to your apartment."

He frowned. He hadn't needed someone to walk him anywhere in decades. But he didn't argue. Frivolous Alex rarely argued. "Sure. Great."

Their heels clicked on the marble floor of the corridors that took them to the elevator to his wing.

When the doors closed, Rose faced him. She didn't say a word. She just stared into his eyes.

"What?"

"You miss her."

"Of course, I miss her. She's a good person. She was

a good sport about the charade. We spent a lot of time together. And I thought we'd become friends."

"Did it irritate you that she didn't even blink when they asked her if she'd gotten feelings for you?"

He picked imaginary lint off his jacket sleeve. "No."

She caught his hand to stop it. "Oh, sweetie. It's worse than I thought. You love her."

"I loved two women in my life. They both died." He faked a smile but thinking about them no longer hurt. His mom and Nina felt like part of his distant past with no place in his future except for memories of happy times. But Eva had been in his present for weeks. She had given him more happy times, more fun, more of a sense of purpose than he'd ever had, but he'd known she was going. Hell, he wanted her to go. He wanted her to fulfill her destiny. Yes, he was a bit sad, but he'd visit her shelters, suck it up and move on. Because that's what he did.

"Wouldn't I be a fool to fall for someone I *knew* would be taken away?"

To his chagrin, Rose laughed. "Seriously? You think I'm going to buy that. I did not fall off a turnip truck yesterday."

"Turnip truck?"

She batted a hand. "Never mind. It's a saying we have in Texas. It sort of means I'm too smart to believe what you're saying. My point is you can kid your dad and maybe even Dom for a while, but I see all the signs."

"You see nothing."

"Exactly. A guy who'd only been in the charade to do his duty would be preening about his success. You're too damned quiet."

"That doesn't mean I love her." He tossed Rose his

most charming smile. "I'm not the kind of guy to settle down, remember?"

She shook her head. "I'm not buying that stupid smile either."

"Oh, chill. Being the happy-go-lucky prince is my place."

She shook her head. "That's baloney."

"Baloney? A luncheon meat?"

"Sorry. It's another thing we say in the US." She stopped, took his hands and looked into his eyes. "When the chips were down, you stepped in. And for the six weeks Eva was under intense pressure, you supported her."

"So?"

"So you're different. Very different. You took charge of her protection. Scrutinized her security details. Had a say in every route she took."

He said nothing. He knew he was different. They all knew he was different. But he could be responsible Alex in four weeks. Right now, he wanted his time off.

"You didn't just love her enough to take care of her; you loved her."

When he didn't reply, she sighed.

"You can't tell me you don't see it."

Anger whooshed through him. "All right. I see it! Damn it. But everybody I've ever loved has been taken from me. Why in the hell would I deliberately connect with or commit to someone whose very title makes her a target?"

Rose's features softened. "You're afraid."

"It doesn't matter."

"Of course, it does when your fear is unfounded. Your father told me Lieutenant Carver told him you were the most naturally gifted strategist he'd ever seen. You could spot a hole in a security detail that looked airtight. You came up with some of their best strategies." She nudged his arm. "Did you ever stop to think that makes you perfect for her? She's a tiny woman with a big future, and she leaned on you and you were there for her. Now she's a tiny woman with a big future who has no one."

He sucked in a long breath. "All of this is pointless. While she was here, she thought she loved me. Now that she's home, I'm barely a footnote in a press conference."

To his surprise, Rose laughed. "She's a future queen. She will never let herself look weak in public. But don't forget, you let her walk away."

He drew in a breath as an avalanche of thoughts tumbled down on him. She didn't wear her heart on her sleeve. She would be a strong ruler. And she did love him. "She does love me."

Rose smiled. "Yeah. She does. And she needs you."

He pulled his fingers through his hair. "I should have admitted my feelings when her dad returned."

Rose batted a hand. "No. You shouldn't have. You needed to think it through. Plus, you don't want your declaration of love to be public. You want this to be private. This time, you're not two royals fulfilling the terms of a treaty. She is a woman and you are the man who loves her. This needs to be done privately. It has to be done correctly."

CHAPTER FOURTEEN

IT TOOK TWO weeks for the furor over the assassination plot to die down. Another week for Grennady's royal family to be seen in public, proving the threat had been neutralized and they were back in control. Week four, Eva's dad sent her to the US, to her projects—as he called them. She might be next in line to the throne but he was king now. He wanted it to look like things were back to normal.

So she left. Though she would be briefed every morning, via video call, so she could take over in a moment's notice if need be, she would essentially be going back to living her life the way she had pre-threat. Pre-Alex.

She could think about him now without getting tears in her eyes. She hadn't told her mom. She hadn't told her friends. She hadn't told anyone that she loved him, that she'd fallen for a charade because that wasn't what future queens did.

Future queens were always strong.

But in America, where everyone knew who she was, but no one cared, she could be whatever she wanted. She could have a few glasses of wine with friends who let her be her. She could go to nightclubs. She could browse bookstores. She could stay in her apartment twenty-four-seven. Whatever she needed, she could do. Even if she wanted to sit in Central Park and cry, the new bodyguards assigned to her were sworn to secrecy.

She drove her nondescript little car up to a shelter she'd created in a New York City borough and parked. Her bodyguards in the SUV parked across the street. She'd decided to live her life exactly as she always had pre-threat. Instead of her new detail of bodyguards driving her, she'd taken a page from Alex's book and had them drive behind her. Always there but out of the way.

Thinking of Alex made her close her eyes and draw a long, deep breath. Her six weeks with him had been the most intense, yet somehow fun weeks of her life. Of course, he'd impacted her. Of course, she'd remember things.

But eventually the memories would fade. That's what she had to cling to.

She stepped out of the car and walked to the old building that had once been a florist shop. When she opened the door, two tabbies and a tortoiseshell cat raced over. They wrapped around her ankles, not trying to get out, but looking for love.

She picked up the tortoiseshell. "Hey, Sophie. Still here I see." The cat nuzzled her face. Basking in the warmth of the cat's affection, the first hint of normalcy returned.

Angela, the shelter manager, raced out from the back room and over to Eva. "Oh, my God! I thought that was your voice." She hugged her fiercely, squishing the tortie between them, then she pulled back and looked Eva in the eye. "Someone tried to kill you?"

Eva laughed. After four weeks, it was possible to laugh about a plot that had been foiled. She scratched behind Sophia's ears. "There was a plot but we stopped it."

"With the help of another royal family. And a fake wedding where you looked gorgeous, by the way." She sighed eloquently. "So dreamy."

She wasn't surprised the entire story had reached the US. Royal gossip was royal gossip. Everybody loved it. But she couldn't think of the Sancho family or the wedding without getting a ping of pain in her heart. And it was time to move on.

"Dreamy is in the eye of the beholder."

"So what was he like? The prince?"

"He was doing his duty." And she wasn't quite as ready to talk about this as she had thought. She smiled. "So what's going on here?"

Angela walked behind the counter. "I'd rather hear about the prince, but if you insist on talking shop, you're the boss." She lifted some papers from beside the cash register. "We were able to stave off creditors until you got some money to us."

"I'm so sorry that I forgot you."

"If my calculations are correct, the slip was right before your wedding." She laughed gaily. "I still can't believe you got married."

"Fake married," she reminded Angela. "What else?"

"Same old. Same old," Angela said, then she brightened. "But we did get a new volunteer."

"Really?"

Angela leaned across the counter and whispered, "He's gorgeous."

"Gorgeous doesn't matter. Ability with cats does. And why are you whispering?"

"He's here. In the back. Doing chores."

"Oh."

Angela bounced from behind the counter. "Wanna meet him?"

"Sure. Why not?" There was no time like the present to get herself back into the swing of things. And the biggest part of her job was making sure every volunteer knew exactly what they were doing. And loved cats.

She set Sophie on the floor and motioned for Angela to lead the way to the curtain that separated the storeroom floor from the back room.

As they walked the twenty feet, she said, "There is one thing I need to tell you before we meet this guy."

Angela nodded.

"The threat on my life, the palace intrigue, the fake marriage, all the drama, sort of reminded everybody that I'm the heir to our throne." She didn't tell Angela the part about her father seeing her only as a placeholder. No need for that to be public. "So I'll be attending more functions in Grennady than I used to be. I won't be spending as much time in America as I have in the past."

Angela stopped walking. "Really?"

"Yeah. But it's okay. Until I'm actually crowned queen, I'll be learning the ropes, spending time with my dad, going to parliament. I can still visit."

Angela laughed. "Okay."

"But my stays will be more like visits than me being manager. That means you'll be handling things now. Maybe even coordinating between shelters. I'm not quite sure how I'm going to handle it all yet."

Angela laughed. "Is there a raise with this promotion?"

Eva smiled. "Yes. I really appreciate you."

They reached the curtain, which Angela whipped to the side so they could enter. Cat beds lined the floors, along with climbing poles. And cats. At least thirty of them sat, stood or slept somewhere.

And in the center was the new guy, sweeping up.

She couldn't tell if he was gorgeous from the back, but he certainly was tall and built...

Her heart thumped. All the blood seemed to drain from her body. *OMG.*

"What are *you* doing here?"

Broom in hand, Alex turned. "I'm sweeping up."

She wanted to kill him and hug him simultaneously. In his jeans and long-sleeve T-shirt he looked more like a biker than a prince. But he was a prince. A playboy. Somebody who did his duty then disappeared.

"Don't you have a blackjack game somewhere?"

He leaned the broom against the wall. "It's not as much fun as it used to be. You ruined it."

She gaped at him as he walked closer. "*I* ruined it?"

"Yes. I used to be able to play for hours. Now it seems boring without your silly comments."

She laughed. This was her Alex. Her chest loosened. But that only made seeing him all the more difficult. If he expected her to be his friend, she didn't know what she'd do, how she'd handle it. She was barely getting over him as it was. Seeing him every day? It would kill her. "Seriously. What are you doing here?"

"Helping you."

She frowned as he took the final two steps that put him directly in front of her.

"I was also waiting for you to be done with your official business so we could have a proper romance."

Angie leaned toward Eva and whispered, "You know this guy?"

"He's the prince I fake married."

Angie's eyes widened.

"Well, not really," Alex said. "The marriage was very real. Millions watched it on TV."

Wide-eyed, Angie nodded. "I got up at four so I could see it." Her gaze drifted to Alex. "But you look really different without the red jacket and all those medals."

Alex paid no attention to Angie. "We can't divorce. You'll lose your crown. And you haven't filed for an annulment."

Eva stared at him. "I thought you were filing."

"I'm not the one who needs an annulment."

Her heart thumped again. What did that mean? "So we're still married?"

"Exactly."

Alex faced Angie. "Would you give us a minute?"

Shaking with awe, Angela said, "Sure." But she backed out of the room as if she didn't want to take her eyes off Alex.

And who could blame her. He was every inch a rebel prince.

But that was the problem, wasn't it?

She stepped back, away from him. "Did you come here to tell me you wanted me to file for the annulment?"

"I told you. I'm here to help you."

She sniffed and looked away. He'd hurt her once because she hadn't guarded her heart. She wouldn't be so foolish again.

"Well, sweep up cat fur to your heart's delight. We certainly need the assistance."

She turned away, but he caught her wrist, spun her around and planted his lips on hers.

The kiss was warm and sweet with just a hint of desperation and for a second her heart opened up to the possibility that he didn't just love her, too, he was willing to admit it.

She pulled back, studied his dark wonderful eyes. Her heart actually hurt when she whispered, "What are you doing?"

"Showing you that I'm willing to do whatever needs to be done for you."

"Because?"

"Because I love you."

Her heart stuttered. "And?"

He frowned. "And? You didn't used to be this slow. I don't want the annulment. I want you."

Her heart about melted at that, but there was so much more to this than just not getting a divorce. "My life is constantly in danger, remember? You've lost enough people. You weren't going to be so foolish as to fall in love again."

"About that. Rose reminded me that I've said one or two really stupid things in our time together." He slid his arms around her waist, tugged her to him and kissed her again. One of those soul-melting kisses that weakened her knees and made her want to curl against him and purr.

But she couldn't. She wouldn't. She had to get what she needed from him.

She straightened. "I don't want your fun and games. I want to know this is real. I want somebody to love me."

"I want days like the one we spent at the country house. I want to do things like make pancakes, and just be normal. Add a few kids in there and I think it could be downright wonderful."

She held his gaze. "So do I."

"You know, we could raise an entire family before your dad decides to retire."

She laughed. "Yes. We could."

"We will raise your country's next king, but you'll spend years grooming him because you'll be the best ruler your country has ever seen."

Her heart speeded up, expanded in her chest, blossomed with life it had never had before. "God knows I'll try."

He held out his hand to her. "Do you have an apartment in the city?"

"I do."

"Too bad because my dad booked me an entire floor in a lavish hotel on Fifth Avenue. Right by the theatre district. Or if you feel like flying, my family owns a casino in Vegas."

She couldn't quite take the hand he offered. She wanted to believe it was real. Did believe in some ways. But it all felt too wonderful. Too perfect. So she laughed. "We can play blackjack."

"We could, but there are other more important things I think we need to do first. Like the one thing we know makes this marriage real. Permanent."

He wanted to make love. Her body shimmied with need. Her heart wanted to burst with anticipation.

But this was huge. Her destiny if he decided it was a mistake or couldn't handle the craziness of her life.

He smiled. "Take my hand. We'll make it. I swear."

She glanced at his hand and back to his face. He was serious.

Everything inside her stilled. She'd been waiting for her prince since she was four, and now here he was, promising what she really wanted. Love. Real love. Total love.

She placed her hand in his. He closed his fingers around it and squeezed. "We're going to have such fun."

"I know."

She felt a shift. A knowing. The years of being a sheltered princess ended and in their place came a real life, a life where she had someone with whom she could be totally honest and somebody who could be honest with her.

He led her to a coatrack where he grabbed a black wool coat and hat. After he slipped into the coat, he kissed her again. "I say we go back to my floor of the hotel, make this a real marriage and then spend our real honeymoon in Vegas."

She nodded.

"After that, it's six months of the year in the country house in Xaviera and six months in your cold but snuggly country."

"What about the cats?"

"We'll keep Angela on staff. Put her in charge of everything."

She tilted her head in amazement. "I sort of already did."

"Then we're set to visit a few times a year. Maybe do a fund-raiser."

As they walked from the back room to the shop floor, she laughed and waved goodbye to Angela, who stared after them as Alex led her out into the world, out into the real life that could be anything they wanted.

Because he had a crown and she had a crown, but right now they had each other and that was all they needed.

* * * * *

He just wanted things the way they'd been.

When they'd been as comfortable and familiar as a pair of old, beloved boots.

He dropped his hand and looked at Tabby from the corner of his eye. "If I let you punch me in the nose, would you finally get over your anger?"

She stabbed her fork into her pie, seeming to focus fiercely on it. "We're not five."

"We were nine." He rubbed the bridge of his nose. "I remember it vividly, since you managed to break it."

"I never intended to break your nose," she muttered.

"I know." He waited a beat. "We survived that. So can't we survive another kiss, even one—I hate to admit—as badly executed as the last one was?" It had been a helluva lot more than a kiss, but he didn't figure she wanted to get into that territory any more than he did.

"It doesn't matter. It was years ago."

He leaned over the arm of his chair toward her. His gaze caught on the wedge of creamy skin showing between the unbuttoned edges of her shirt. Stupid, because there wasn't anything like that between him and Tabby.

Except that one time they were both trying not to think about.

THE BFF BRIDE

BY
ALLISON LEIGH

MILLS &
BOON

First Published in Great Britain 2016
By Mills & Boon, an imprint of HarperCollins*Publishers*
1 London Bridge Street, London, SE1 9GF

© 2016 Allison Lee Johnson

ISBN: 978-0-263-92002-4

23-0716

A frequent name on bestseller lists, **Allison Leigh**'s high point as a writer is hearing from readers that they laughed, cried or lost sleep while reading her books. She credits her family with great patience for the time she's parked at her computer, and for blessing her with the kind of love she wants her readers to share with the characters living in the pages of her books. Contact her at www.allisonleigh.com.

For my daughters
and the fine young men who love them.

Prologue

Nineteen years ago

"Come on, Tabbers." The boy holding the chains of the swing leaned closer to her and grinned. His weird bluish-purple eyes were full of mischief. And goading.

But that was something Justin Clay had always been good at.

Goading. And a whole lot of it.

Usually, it led to her getting her rear end in trouble with her mom and daddy.

"I told you. I go by *Tabitha* now," she said firmly. She'd just turned nine. Tabitha seemed more fitting than Tabby, much less *Tabbers*.

Justin's eyebrows skyrocketed, and he hooted with laughter, giving the swing's chains a shove so that she shot backward then forward again so unevenly that her bare toes dug into the sand beneath the school's swing set.

"That's bat-crap crazy. You're Tabbers," he said with the annoying superiority he'd developed lately. Catching her chains again, he stopped her forward progress with such a jolt that her chin snapped against her chest. "And you might as well just kiss me. It's gonna happen, one way or another."

She glared at him. "You made me bite my tongue."

If anything, he looked even more devilish. "You going to cry about it?"

She curled her lip. "Not 'cause of you, that's for sure. And I'm *not* gonna kiss you just so you can make Sierra Rasmussen jealous!"

His eyebrows drew together. "You're my best friend," he complained. "We're supposed to help each other out."

Now it was her turn to snort. "Good thing your best friend isn't a boy, then. And I'm still not kissing you!"

"One day you're gonna wanna kiss me," he warned.

Annoyed at the absurdity, she shoved her hand against his chest and pushed him away far enough that she could jump off the swing. Even though his daddy was the tallest person Tabby had ever met, for now, she and Justin were exactly the same height. She looked him straight in the face. "Try it and I'll punch you in the nose," she warned. "I'd sooner kiss a toad than you."

His skinny chest puffed out. "Lotsa toads down at the swimmin' hole, Tabbers."

She puffed out her own chest. It was just as skinny as his. And as flat. Which was fine with her, since boys seemed to have more fun than girls did. At least all the ones she knew around Weaver, anyway. Who wanted to be all prissy and perfect when there were baseball games to play and cow chips to throw and worms to be threaded onto fish hooks? Summer was short enough in Weaver without spending half your time playing indoors with dolls and dress-up. And Justin's granddaddy had the best swimming hole around, out on his Double-C Ranch. She and Justin, along with his cousin Caleb, spent half their summer vacation out there. "I can make you kiss a toad just as easy, Justin Clay, and you know it." She scuffed her bare toes through the sand. The sun was hot as Hades, and now that he'd brought up the topic of swimming, that's all she wanted to do. "I dunno why y'all are so gaga over Sierra, anyway," she groused. The other girl was a year ahead of them in school and the biggest snot around.

"'Cause she's got boobs," he said, as if the answer were obvious. "And Joey Rasmussen says his cousin won't kiss no boy who ain't already kissed someone."

"So? Since when're you interested in kissing girls?"

"Erik's already kissed three girls!"

She rolled her eyes. "Who cares if your brother's kissing girls?"

"I do. So now I gotta kiss someone, and I ain't gonna kiss Caleb!"

She leaned over, pretending to gag. "That's just gross."

"That's just 'cause you don't got any boobs."

She rolled her eyes and shoved his shoulder hard enough to tip him over in the sand.

He laughed, squinting up at her in the sunlight as he stuck out his suntanned hand. "Help me up."

Sighing mightily, she grabbed his hand and yanked.

He sprang easily to his own bare feet and pecked his thin lips against hers before she had a chance to evade him.

Then he danced around her, cackling like a madman, waving his arms over his head in victory. "Told you!"

She made a face. "You are disgusting."

He laughed even harder. "You're just mad 'cause I got my way."

"And *it* was disgusting, too. Still don't know why you gotta keep up with your big brother. I don't gotta keep up with mine."

His smile didn't die, but he stopped his victory dance and dropped his arm over her shoulders, like the best buddies they were. "Come on." He started walking away from the swings. "Let's find Caleb and go out to the swimming hole to catch some toads."

She shrugged. Because she did want to go swimming. "Sure. But first—" She hesitated when they left the sand for the closely shorn green grass covering the rest of the playground.

He hesitated, too, his eyebrows lifting again over his weird bluish-purple eyes. "What?"

She smiled.

Balled her fist.

And punched him in the nose.

Chapter One

"Hey there, Tabby! Happy Thanksgiving." Hope Clay reached for the covered dish in Tabby's gloved hands. "Every year we keep telling you all you need to bring is yourself," she chided with a smile.

"And every year, you know I'm going to bring something to share," Tabby countered easily as she followed the older woman out of the cold November air into the warm, soaring foyer. This year, the rotating Thanksgiving feast was being held at Hope and Tristan Clay's home. The smells of Thanksgiving dinner filled the air, along with the sounds of music and laughter as Tabby pushed the heavy wooden door closed behind her. "I can't take credit for the casserole, though. That's Bubba's doing." Robert "Bubba" Bumble was the cook down at Ruby's Café, which Tabby managed for Hope's two sons, who owned the place.

"How *is* Bubba?" Hope asked over her shoulder as she turned left and sailed into the dining room, where an enormous table was set with white china and sparkling glasses. Next to it—jutting out into the wide hallway—

was a slightly smaller portable table set with disposable plates and cups.

The kids' table, Tabby knew, though the kids generally ranged from her generation down to any child old enough to hold her own spoon. "Bubba's fine," she said wryly. "He's been cooking once a week for Vivian Templeton when her usual chef has the day off."

Hope glanced toward the great room across the wide hallway, as if she were afraid Tabby's words might be overheard. She even put a finger in front of her lips in a silent shush, and her "that's nice" was barely audible.

Tabby had spent as much of her childhood roaming around Hope and Tristan Clay's home as she had around her own. She raised her eyebrows pointedly but lowered her own voice to a whisper while she pulled off her gloves and her coat. "What'd I say?"

"That subject is still a little…sore…with some," Hope replied.

Tabby started to glance toward the great room but managed to stop herself. She'd have to encounter Justin sooner or later. And later was better. "Squire?" she mouthed, more to keep her mind off Hope's youngest son than anything.

Hope nodded, adjusting a few dishes in the middle of the table to make room for Tabby's casserole dish. She looked over her shoulder toward the sound of the crowd in the other room getting all riled up again. "Ever since I married Tristan," she said in a more normal tone, "he's told me how stubborn his father could be. But I've never seen Squire be truly cantankerous until Vivian moved to Weaver. He's downright ornery when it comes to the subject of her." She straightened, her violet eyes studying the table through her stylish glasses.

Tabby knew there was bad blood between Justin's grandfather and Vivian Templeton dating from way back, though. The elderly woman had only arrived in town a little more than a year ago.

"Guess it's good that she's not going to be here for Thanksgiving dinner, then," she said drily. "And I assume there aren't going to be any other Templetons at the table today?"

Hope shook her head, making a face. "That would have been nice, but everyone is still feeling their way after learning they're all related through Tristan's mama."

"Understandable." Tabby's hearing was acutely attuned to the voices coming from the great room, but she kept her gaze strictly on the table. She didn't need to listen too closely to be able to pick Justin's voice out from the others.

He never missed spending Thanksgiving with his parents. He'd never once failed to come home from Boston for the holiday, even if it meant flying in one day and right back out the next—which was what he'd done for the past four years.

"Anything I can do to help get the meal on?" she asked, trying to drown out her memories.

"Bless your heart, honey. You're not on the job here. But I'd be lying if I said I wasn't grateful for your help."

Tabby grinned. "You know me. Always happier being useful and busy than sitting around on my thumbs." And it kept her from having to go into the great room just yet.

She couldn't imagine spending Thanksgiving anywhere else—particularly when her own parents were away—but being with the Clays on the holiday came with a price.

Thankfully, her hostess was unaware of Tabby's thoughts. "You're just like your mama." She tossed Tabby's coat onto the pile in the study, then drew her into the kitchen, where nearly every inch of counter space was covered with one dish or another. "Even though she and your dad are off visiting your grandma this year, I'm pleased you still came."

Hope and Jolie Taggart had been best friends for Tabby's entire life. "You're my second family. Where else would I be? So put me to work."

Hope gestured at an enormous pot steaming on top of the stove. "I just need to get the potatoes finished. Selfishly, I was hoping you'd get here in time to do the honors. Nobody makes mashed potatoes like you do."

Tabby immediately rolled up the sleeves of her white blouse and plucked a clean white flour-sack towel out of a cupboard. "Flattery'll get you everywhere."

Hope laughed. "I'd hoped. I should have everything you need all set, but if I don't, you know where everything is, anyway."

Smiling, Tabby tied the towel around her waist like an apron before turning off the flame under the potatoes and hefting the pot over to the sink to drain it. From the great room came a loud burst of laughter and hooting catcalls. "Football game must be a close one." She was recording it at home to watch later.

"Sounds like." The older woman glanced over her shoulder when her sister-in-law Jaimie entered carrying an empty oversize bowl. "More tortilla chips?"

"And salsa." Jaimie smiled at Tabby and bussed her cheek on her way to the far counter where a variety of bags were stacked. She deftly tore open a large one and dumped the entire contents into the wooden bowl. "You'd think the hordes hadn't eaten in a week."

"Or that they weren't going to sit down to turkey and ham in only a few minutes." Hope grimaced but handed Jaimie the near-industrial-size container of salsa she pulled from the refrigerator. "I know better than to warn any of them."

Tabby didn't bother hiding her smile as she began scooping the steaming potatoes into the ricer, which Hope had left on the counter next to the sink along with two large crockery bowls. At the diner, she made mashed potatoes by the ton, so the work was simple and easy. But unfortunately, it also allowed her mind to wander down the hallway to the great room and the people there.

Her parents traditionally spent every other Thanksgiving with her grandmother. Tabby's brother, Evan, and his family had gone this year, too. Tabby could have accompanied them. She still wasn't sure why she hadn't.

She grimaced at her own thoughts and scooped more potatoes into the ricer. Steam continued rising up into her face, but she barely noticed as she squeezed out the fluffy fronds, filling the first bowl, then the second.

Who was she kidding?

There were only a few times every year when she was guaranteed to see him. Thanksgiving and Easter. He'd missed Christmas for years. Birthdays? Forget about it.

Seeing him was like picking at a wound that wouldn't heal. She couldn't stop herself, to her own detriment.

She huffed a strand of hair out of her eyes and re-filled the ricer yet again. Fortunately, the contraption was just as large and sturdy as the ones she had at the diner, so the work went quickly.

"Don't you agree?"

She realized the question had been directed at her, and she looked over her shoulder at Hope, only to realize Jaimie had left the kitchen with her chips and salsa and she'd been replaced with another one of her sisters-in-law, Emily. Tabby racked her brains, trying—and failing—to recall their conversation. "Sorry?"

"Thanksgiving is an easier holiday than Christmas," Hope repeated.

"Oh. Sure." It was a lie, and she looked back down at the potatoes. "None of the Christmas gift shopping stress." Just *all* the stress of knowing Justin would be back in town.

She huffed at her hair again and scooped the last of the potatoes into the container, making quick work of them before running the ricer under the faucet.

"Frankly, I don't know what to get *anyone* this year for Christmas," Emily was saying. She moved next to Tabby, holding a saucepan filled with steaming cream and melted butter. "I don't suppose you have any ideas for my son-in-law, do you?"

Tabby made a face and left the ricer to drain while she grabbed a long-handled spoon from the drawer. "*I* don't have any ideas for him, and Evan's my brother." She gestured for Emily to begin pouring the liquid into one of the bowls while she gently stirred the riced potatoes.

Hope stepped up behind Tabby, watching over their shoulders. "I swear, honey, watching you work is like watching a cooking show on television."

At that, Tabby snorted outright. "Only doing the

same thing *your* grandmother taught me to do when I started working at her diner."

"Hope's grandma was quite a cook." Emily drizzled more hot cream into the second bowl at Tabby's prompting. "But I'm just thankful Ruby taught you how to make her cinnamon rolls."

"My hips aren't that happy," Hope said drily. "I can't tell you how many times Gram tried to teach me how to make her rolls." She shook her head. "I can make them, but not like she could. Or you." She patted Tabby's shoulder. "She would roll over in her grave hearing me say so, but I think yours have got hers beat."

"Good grief, don't say that." Tabby looked up at the ceiling, as though she was waiting for lightning to strike. "I loved Ruby Leoni, too, but oh, man, did she have a temper."

Hope laughed. "You nearly finished there, honey?"

Tabby focused on her work again, giving the creamy potatoes a final stir. "All set." She picked up both bowls, cradling them against her hips. "You want them on the table now?"

"That was twenty pounds of Yukon Golds. I should get one of the boys—"

"No worries. I've got them." Tabby quickly cut her off and carried the bowls out to the dining room, placing one at one end of the main table and the other on the kids' table. Hope and Emily followed along, bearing platters of freshly carved roast turkey and glazed ham.

"I have a good mind to let them all watch football while we feast on our own," Hope said when a caterwaul of cheers and jeers burst out from the other room. She adjusted one of the platters just so and stood back to admire the display.

Emily, meanwhile, was counting off chairs and place settings. "I think we're a few short," she warned.

"We're always a few short," Hope returned. "That's what happens these days when nearly the whole family turns out." She stepped to the archway opening onto the wide hallway. "Food's on," she called briskly. Her one-time schoolteacher's voice cut across the racket of televised sports and thirtysome family members debating the latest call. Considering they weren't all rooting for the same team, it was chaotic, to say the least.

Nevertheless, at Hope's announcement, the television volume immediately went mute and those thirtysome individuals turned en masse toward the dining room.

She didn't rush.

For as long as she could remember, she'd sat at the kids' table.

"Tabby! I didn't even hear you come in." Hope's husband, Tristan, grabbed her up in a bear hug that lifted her right off her toes. "Thank God we'll have decent mashed potatoes." He kissed her forehead and dropped her back down. "When Tag said he and your ma were visiting Helen this year, I was afraid it was gonna be boxed potatoes."

Hope gave him a pinch. "Since when have I *ever* made you mashed potatoes from a box?"

The tall man, still blond in his sixties, grinned and gave Tabby a quick wink before he made his way toward the head of the big table, jostling his relations while Hope directed butts to seats and ultimately determined that Emily had been right. They were short of chairs. Erik—Hope and Tristan's eldest—immediately pigeonholed his adopted son, Murphy, to help him search down more.

Tabby, long used to the process, just moved out of

the way as far as possible and bit back a chuckle when Squire brushed past everyone to take the first seat—which happened to be Tristan's at the head of the table. "All that fancy money you earn, boy, seems you ought to have a bigger table 'n' chairs."

"That's my chair, old man," Tristan said mildly. But Tabby could see by the humor in his blue eyes that he wasn't offended. Or surprised. "And the way this family keeps growing, we'd need a reception hall to seat everyone at one table."

Erik and Murphy returned with two more chairs and a piano bench, and the shuffling began again.

"Same thing happens every year."

Tabby stiffened inwardly at the deep voice. She didn't look at the tall man who'd stopped next to her, bumping his elbow companionably against hers. She didn't need to.

There'd been a time when she knew everything there was to know about Justin Clay. And he'd known everything about her. They'd been best friends.

Now…they weren't.

"Yes, it does. Some people like that," she answered smoothly and moved toward the kids' table. She sat down in the only spare seat, next to fourteen-year-old Murphy, who was eyeing her from the corner of his eye the way he had been for at least a year now. On her other side was April Reed—one of Squire's grandchildren courtesy of his long-ago marriage to Gloria Day.

"Haven't seen you since last summer." She greeted April with a smile, all the while painfully aware of Justin trading barbs with Caleb Buchanan behind her. "You cut your hair. I like it."

The young woman flushed and looked pleased that

Tabby had noticed. She toyed with the shoulder-length auburn bob. "Job hunting," she said. "Thought it looked more in keeping with a suit."

"Looks great." Tabby tugged the ends of her own hair. It was riddled with wayward waves. "I've been thinking of cutting mine, too."

"Why?" Justin nudged Murphy's shoulder. "Scoot your chair over, kid."

Murphy made a face, but he moved over enough to accommodate Justin, who pushed a backless stool into the space and straddled it. "Your hair's been like that as long as I can remember."

Tabby knew he wasn't trying to get cozy with her. There was simply a finite amount of space available for chairs and bodies. She looked away from the jeans-clad thigh nudging against her. "All the more reason it's time for a change, then, right, April?"

"I suppose. But I've always thought you had gorgeous hair. Such a dark brown and so glossy."

Tabby couldn't help but laugh a little at that. "Grass is always greener, my friend with the smooth red hair." She leaned over the table a little, mostly so she could shift away from that damned masculine thigh. "So, how *is* the job hunt going out in Arizona? It's advertising, right?"

"Dad wants me to work for him at Huffington," she said, referring to the network of sports clinics he operated around the United States. "The Phoenix location is getting huge. But I want to make my mark on my own."

"Makes sense."

Justin jostled Tabby's arm. "Remember when you wanted to go to Europe to make your mark on the great art world?"

"Lofty dreams of a teenaged girl," she said dismissively. She wasn't going to let him bait her. "*I* learned I was perfectly happy right here in Weaver," she told April, though the words were aimed at Justin. "This is my home. I can't imagine living anywhere else."

"Ruby's would have to shut right down," someone interjected from the other table. "Weaver would never be the same."

Tabby rolled her eyes. "Erik and Justin own the place." She still didn't look at the man beside her. "They'd hire someone else to manage it."

"There's a nasty thought," Erik said. He was sitting at the main table next to his wife, Isabella, and didn't look unduly concerned.

The same couldn't be said of their son. "You're *not* gonna leave, are you?" Murphy gave her a horrified look.

She lifted her hands peaceably. "I'm not going anywhere!"

Justin jostled her again. "Do you even still paint?"

If she'd have been five—or maybe even twenty-five—she would have just elbowed him right back. Preferably in the ribs, hard enough to leave a mark. Because the Justin she'd grown up with could take as well as he could give. "Yes, I still paint." Her voice was even.

"Absolutely, she still paints!" Sydney, who was married to Derek—yet another one of Justin's plentiful cousins—called from the far end of the other table. Their toddler son was sitting in a high chair between them. "An old friend of mine who owns a gallery in New York has sold a couple dozen of her pieces! He wants her to give up working at Ruby's and focus only on painting."

Tabby shifted, uncomfortable with the weight of everyone's eyes turning toward her. "I'm not quitting Ruby's," she assured them, wondering how on earth the conversation had gotten so off track.

"We know that, Tab," Erik assured her calmly. Of the two brothers, he was the active partner in the diner, though he pretty much left the day-to-day stuff to her.

Squire cleared his throat loudly. Tabby was quite sure if he'd had his walking stick handy, he'd have thumped it on the floor for emphasis the way he tended to do. "We gonna sit here and jabber all the livelong day, or get to eating?"

Tristan chuckled. "Eat."

"Not before we say grace," Gloria said mildly. And inflexibly. So they all bowed their heads while Gloria said the blessing.

Justin leaned close to her again. "Nothing changes," he murmured almost soundlessly.

Tabby's jaw tightened. She looked from her clasped hands to the insanely handsome, violet-eyed man sitting only inches away from her.

"You changed," she whispered back.

Then she looked back at her hands and closed her eyes. Gloria was still saying grace.

Tabby just prayed that Justin would go away again, and the sooner the better.

He'd been her best friend.

But he was still her worst heartbreak.

Chapter Two

His mother might have put the meal on the table, but it was up to her husband and sons to cart everything back to the kitchen when the meal was done.

Not even the Thanksgiving holiday—or televised football games—got them out of that particular task.

So even though Justin generally would rather poke sharp sticks into his eyes than load a dishwasher, he did his fair share, carting stacks of plates and glasses from the dining room to the kitchen, following on Erik's heels.

And while the rest of the women in the family had pitched in to help Hope, the three men were brutally left on their own by their fellows.

"Typical," Justin muttered, dumping the plates on the counter next to the sink his dad was filling with soap and water. "Couldn't even get Caleb to help."

Erik chuckled. He was five years older than Justin and he good-naturedly threw a clean dish towel at him. "You ever help clean up when we have a meal at his folks' place?" The question was rhetorical. "Be glad that half the crowd today used disposable plates."

Justin had personally filled a big bag with the trash.

He would have been happy to fill a half dozen of them if it meant not having to load a dishwasher.

"Stop grousing and get it done," their father ordered. "Dessert's waiting on us, and Squire never likes waiting for his dessert."

"The old man looks good," Justin said. He left the dish towel on the counter and pulled open the dishwasher. He began to load it methodically, mechanically transferring the items his dad rinsed into the racks.

"He's gonna run for city council," Tristan said, shaking his head as if he still couldn't believe it. "There's a special election coming up in February."

"Squire?" Justin couldn't help but laugh at the notion of his ninetysome-year-old grandfather sitting at a council meeting. "That ought to shake things up around Weaver. He's always hated politicians."

"Which is the reason why he figures an old rancher ought to try his hand at it." Erik started filling containers with the leftover food. They heard a cheer from the great room and he groaned a little.

"Shouldn't have bet against Casey on the game," Justin said knowingly. Their cousin had an uncanny gift for picking winners. "What're you gonna lose to him this time?"

"Week out at the fishing cabin. And I haven't lost yet."

"When's the last time you won a bet against him?" Tristan stacked more rinsed plates on the counter. "What's going on with that promotion of yours, Jus?"

Justin added the dishes to the rack with a little more force than necessary. "Not a damn thing."

"You crack those plates, son, you'll be the one to face up to your mother."

Justin straightened again and met his father's gaze. "It's gotten…complicated."

Erik blew out a soft whistle. "Probably happens when you're dating the boss's daughter. Warned you."

"I didn't get the job at CNJ Pharmaceuticals nine years ago because of Gillian. I won't lose it because of her, either." He was trusting that his relationship with Charles Jennings, her father and the owner of the company, was on firmer ground than that, at least. He swiped his damp hands down his jeans and retrieved a cold bottle of beer from the refrigerator. "And we stopped seeing each other almost half a year ago."

"Thank God," Erik muttered. "Woman was a nose-bleed."

Justin grimaced. "I don't sneer at your choice of women."

Erik grinned. "How could you? Izzy is the perfect girl."

Justin couldn't deny the truth of that, though he liked arguing with his brother merely for the sake of it. And he didn't really want to think about Gillian, anyway. Because she *was* a nosebleed, even though his brother shouldn't rub it in. And even though it had taken Justin several long years to face it.

He toyed with the beer cap but didn't actually twist it open. "The complication isn't because of Charles's daughter. He's put me on a special project we've had some problems with. If I can bring it in on time, the VP position should be mine." Making him the youngest vice president in the company's century-long history.

"Give me cows over pharmaceuticals," Erik said, hanging his arm over Justin's shoulder. "But I suppose if anyone can do it, it's my genius little brother, Dr. Justin Clay."

Justin shrugged off the arm. He had a PhD in microbiology and immunology, and dual master's degrees in computer science and chemistry. But he rarely used the title that went with the PhD. The fact was, he'd often felt a little out of step among his extended ranching family, even though his computer-geek father had bucked that trend, too.

"I want to work on the project from Weaver," he announced, and saw the look his brother and dad exchanged. "I'll be able to concentrate on it better here. I figure Aunt Bec might clear the way for me to work at the hospital, since she runs the place."

"Rebecca probably can, though that's—"

"Rebecca probably can what?" Justin's eldest uncle, Sawyer, entered the kitchen carrying several empty beer bottles.

"Approve space in the new lab they're building for a project I'm working on for CNJ. The company will cover all the costs, of course."

"Sell that to my wife," Sawyer advised wryly. "Every day for the past two years I've been hearing about problems with that lab she's trying to get built. Construction delays. Cost overruns. Losing the lab director didn't help, and now it's that fund-raiser event they're having in a few weeks." He dumped the bottles in the recycling basket and pulled open the refrigerator to retrieve several more beers. "You gonna be done in here soon? The old man's getting impatient for dessert. He's been debating pumpkin pie versus pecan versus chocolate cream for the past half hour."

"We'd be done sooner if we had some help," Tristan told his brother in a pointed tone.

Sawyer just laughed, snatched the unopened bottle out of Justin's hands to add to his collection and left the kitchen again.

When Justin went to the refrigerator, he found the shelf empty of beer.

"Snooze you lose, son," Tristan said. "Just because you choose to live in Boston doesn't mean you're excluded from that basic fact." He pointed a thumb at the stack of rinsed dishes still waiting to be loaded.

Sawyer's intrusion was followed almost immediately by the rest of his brothers—first Jefferson, ostensibly to make sure there was still hot coffee on the stove, then Matthew and Daniel together, who made no bones that they were wanting their dessert, too.

"Nothing changes," Justin repeated when the kitchen eventually cleared.

"Ever consider that there are times that's a comfort?" Tristan finally turned off the faucet and dried his hands on a towel.

"Never thought so before, particularly."

His father's gaze wasn't unsympathetic. But then, back in his day, Tristan had left Weaver for a good long while, too. Until he'd married Hope Leoni and they'd settled in Weaver permanently. He'd established a little company called Cee-Vid that became a huge player in consumer electronics, and Hope had taught at the elementary school and then ended up the head of the school board.

"Someday—" Tristan's voice was unusually reflective "—you might sit up and realize one of the most disturbing things in life is finding out that something you'd counted on never changing has already done so, without you ever having noticed." Then he tossed the towel on the counter and left the kitchen, too.

Frowning, Justin turned toward Erik. "What's with him?"

"Nothing that's new. You're just not usually around to see it."

"What's *that* supposed to mean?"

"Just a fact," Erik said mildly. "You're in Boston. You don't see the day-to-day effects of the crap he deals with. And I'm not talking about Cee-Vid."

No. Erik was talking about the real work their father did. The secretive, frequently dangerous world of Hollins-Winword's black operations, where their father was second in command. Cee-Vid was the legitimate front that hid the covert work, which Justin and Erik knew about but rarely discussed.

"It's been a hard year," Erik said.

"Isn't it always hard?"

"Harder than most," his brother amended. "I think he's getting tired of it."

"Then he should quit."

"Who should quit what?" Izzy entered the kitchen, her brownish-black gaze bouncing from her husband's face to Justin's and back again.

Erik just looped his hands around her waist and tugged her close. "Are you hungry again?"

She smiled impishly. "For pecan pie. I came to help with the dishes in order to get at dessert more quickly."

"Too late." Justin stuffed the last glass in the dishwasher and closed the door. He'd arrived barely an hour before they'd sat down for dinner, so he hadn't had an opportunity to catch up very much with anyone, including his sister-in-law. "You're looking better than ever, Iz."

She turned in the circle of his brother's arms and beamed at him.

It took a few seconds for Justin to notice the way their linked hands were clasped over her belly. But when he did, it took less than a second for him to realize why. "Holy—" He broke off. "You're pregnant?"

Izzy glanced up into Erik's eyes. "Looks like we're announcing it today whether we planned to or not."

Erik smiled slowly and Justin felt an unfamiliar— and unwanted—jolt of envy. His brother looked so damn happy. So content. And Justin felt so…not.

Still, his brother *was* happy. And Justin was genuinely glad for that. And Isabella…well, she'd always been a looker with her white-blond hair and dark eyes. And now she had an extra shine around her.

He blew out a breath because his throat actually felt tight. "Damn. Congratulations." He wrapped them both in a big hug, which made Izzy laugh and complain, because she was a good foot shorter and couldn't breathe while stuck between two big men. When Justin finally stepped back, envious or not, he knew he had a big, stupid grin on his face. Probably one that matched Erik's. "So when's he—"

"She," Erik corrected.

"Due?"

"The *baby*," Isabella said with a soft laugh, "is due the end of April. We're not going to find out early what we're having."

"Murphy knows there's a baby, though?"

Isabella nodded. "We told him yesterday."

"He figures it's his right to make the announcement today," Erik said wryly. "Being the big brother and all."

"Sounds like he's got the Clay tendencies down, born into them or not." He leaned over and kissed Isabella's cheek. "You're going to be a great mom, all over again." The circumstances leading to her becoming Murphy's mom had been tragic. But they'd ultimately prompted their move to Weaver, where they'd found Erik and become a family.

She blinked, looking teary through her smile. "Thanks." She sniffed quickly. "We'll all learn together, anyway."

"So...pretty much status quo," Erik said wryly.

Isabella chuckled and swiped her cheek. "Pretty much." They all looked back at the sound of footsteps as Tabby entered the kitchen.

The easy smile on Tabby's face faded a bit as she hesitated. She didn't look at Justin. "Um... I just came to help get the pies—"

Isabella quickly moved out of Erik's arms. "Squire's probably getting testy," she said with a knowing laugh. She picked up two of the pies sitting on one counter and handed them to Erik before she grabbed two more. "Bring the plates," she said as she and Erik left the kitchen.

Tabby quickly snatched up a stack of pie plates and started to follow, but Justin grabbed her arm. "Wait a sec."

"They can't eat pie without plates."

"My family? You're kidding, right? They could eat without hands. You've been giving me the cold shoulder since I got here. Don't you think it's time we got past that?"

Her brown eyes—usually warm and shiny as melted chocolate—were unreadable. "I don't know what you're talking about."

"Your lying's on par with your French. You remember French, right? I had to help you pass it in high school."

Her lips tightened. She pulled free and opened a drawer to extract a cake server. "If you want a slice of Gloria's chocolate cream, you'd better get out there quick."

He was tired of the chasm that had developed between them, even though he knew he was the cause of it in the first place. "Come on, Tabbers. We were friends long before—"

She lifted her eyebrows and gave him a look that stopped any further discussion. "Pie's a big deal in this house at Thanksgiving. Or have you forgotten that, living the fancy life in Boston?"

She turned on her heel, and her glossy hair flipped around her shoulders as she left the kitchen.

He exhaled, pinching the bridge of his nose.

There were a few things he'd always counted on. The love and support of his big, crazy family. His own ability to figure out a convoluted puzzle. And the easygoing friendship of one Tabitha Taggart.

Yeah, he knew he'd messed up with her pretty good, but that had been four years ago. Stacked up against the rest of their lifelong friendship, couldn't one monumentally stupid move on his part be forgotten?

Or at least forgiven?

He blew out another breath and grabbed the last two pies that were sitting on the counter and carried them out to the dining room.

"Oh, good. Set them there, honey." His mom pointed with the long knife she was using to cut the pies, and he set them on the table. She'd already divvied out two pumpkin pies onto plates. "There's a gallon of home-made vanilla ice cream in the freezer. Would you mind getting that, too? Oh, and the glass bowl in the fridge with the whipped cream."

He turned around and retrieved the items. When he got back to the dining room, she'd finished plating the chocolate cream. He grabbed a slice while the grabbing was good and went back into the living room. It was a huge space. Always had been, with three couches long enough that even his dad—nearly six and a half feet tall—could stretch out, and an eclectic collection of side chairs and recliners. With all the family around—or close to it, anyway—there still weren't enough seats. So folding chairs had been dragged in. And cushions to lean against on the floor.

He took the same corner he'd been in before dinner. Since he'd forgotten a fork, he picked up the wedge of pie in his fingers and took a bite.

"Neanderthal." His cousin JD dropped a plastic fork onto his plate as she carried two plates to the couch closest to him. She handed one to her husband, Jake, then sat down on the floor in front of him, her legs stretched out. Justin knew she'd have sat on Jake's knee if it hadn't already been occupied by their sleeping little boy, Tucker.

Justin jerked his chin toward her. "When does Tuck start kindergarten?"

"Next fall." She looked over her shoulder at the little boy and gently swiped his messy brown hair off his forehead. "He was upset that he didn't get to go this year."

"Gonna have any more?"

She and Jake shared a look.

"Yes," she said.

"No," he said.

Justin hid his smile around a bite of his grandma's delicious pie. Tucker had been born very prematurely. Though it looked like JD had gotten over it and was ready to go again, her husband had not.

"When're you gonna get yourself a wife?" Squire's voice carried across the room, and there was no question he'd directed his words to Justin. The old man was looking straight at him.

For some reason, Justin found himself glancing toward Tabby across the room.

"Justin's never gonna get married," Axel—yet another cousin—drawled before he could answer. "He told us all that when he graduated from high school. He was gonna go off and cure disease and save the world. Remember?"

Justin grimaced.

"He'd just had his heart broken by—what was her name?" His dad's eyes narrowed as he thought back. "Pretty girl. Short blond hair."

"Colleen," his mother called out from the dining room.

"Collette," Tabby corrected. "Summers. Her dad worked for the electric company."

"Collette Summers," Caleb repeated. "She was so hot."

"What do you know about hot? You were dating Kelly Rasmussen," Justin reminded.

"Whatever happened to Kelly," someone asked.

"Can I tell 'em *now*?"

Everyone looked toward Murphy, who'd loudly interrupted the conversation.

Erik grinned. "Go for it, Murph."

The boy uncoiled from his seat on the floor, standing up to his full height. "We're getting a baby," he announced, his cheeks red, his eyes beaming.

Isabella laughed and reached out to squeeze his hand. "I don't know about *getting*," she said humorously. "But we're definitely having one. Should be making his or her arrival sometime next April."

Justin's mother had finally finished cutting pies. She stared at them slack jawed for a moment before virtually vaulting over people and furniture to grab Izzy in a hug. "Another grandbaby." She looped her other arm around Murphy and kissed his forehead. "A grandson has been wonderful, and this baby is going to be fabulous!"

Hope had about a half second before the rest of the crew started climbing around them to give their own hugs.

When Justin got the third elbow in the head during the process, he gave up his corner spot and found refuge across the room in one of the vacated chairs.

Which happened to be next to Tabby's spot on the floor. "If you get up and move now, someone's gonna notice," he told her under his breath.

Her lips tightened, but she stayed where she was, recrossing her denim-covered legs again just as she'd done when they were little kids. Only difference now was that the legs those jeans covered were long and shapely, instead of skinny with scrapes all over 'em.

At least, he was assuming they weren't all scraped

up anymore. He hoped not, anyway. Because her skin was smooth and creamy—

He pinched the bridge of his nose, cutting off the memory. It was as unwanted as the envy he'd felt at his own brother's happiness.

He just wanted things the way they used to be.

Easy. Comfortable and familiar as a pair of old, beloved boots.

He dropped his hand and looked at her from the corner of his eyes. "If I let you punch me in the nose, would you finally get over your mad?"

She stabbed her fork into her pie, seeming to focus fiercely on it. "We're not five."

"We were nine." He rubbed the bridge of his nose. "I remember it vividly, since you managed to break it."

She huffed out a breath. "I never intended to break your nose," she muttered.

"I know." He waited a beat. "We survived that. So can't we survive another kiss, even one—I hate to admit—as badly executed as it was?" It had been a helluva lot more than a kiss, but he didn't figure she wanted to get into that territory any more than he did.

He was right. "It doesn't matter. It was years ago."

He leaned over the arm of his chair toward her. His gaze caught on the wedge of creamy skin showing between the unbuttoned edges of her shirt. And he couldn't look away. Which was stupid, because there wasn't anything like that between him and Tabby.

Except that one time they were both trying not to think about.

"And things haven't been right between us since," he said.

She slowly sucked a smear of chocolate from her

thumb, taking long enough for him to get his eyes off her chest and onto her lips.

Now he was focused on her soft pink lips pursed around her thumb. How freaking stupid was that.

She finally lowered her hand, wiping it on her crumpled paper napkin. Then she rose to her feet with as much agility as she'd had when they were nine. "You're gonna leave again before any of us can blink, so why does it even matter?"

Slipping his empty plate out of his fingers, she worked her way around the horde of people blocking the way and left the room.

Chapter Three

"Stupid. Stupid, stupid, *freaking* stupid." Tabby was still kicking herself an hour later when she got home to the triplex she'd bought the previous year.

If she'd wanted to prove that she wasn't affected by Justin Clay, she'd failed.

Monumentally.

Running out the way she had while everyone was still congratulating Izzy and Erik over the baby?

"Stupid," she muttered for the fiftieth time while she made way through the apartment, flipping on lights as she went until she reached her bedroom at the back.

She tugged the tails of her white shirt free from her jeans and yanked it over her head, not bothering with the buttons. Her bra—a glorified name for the hank of lace and elastic that was all her meager bust had ever required—followed. She'd ditched her cowboy boots at the front door already; now she kicked off her jeans, pitching all of the clothing in the general direction of her closet before pulling a football jersey over her head.

"Stupid," she said again. Just for good measure and because she evidently liked punishing herself.

In stocking feet, she went back to the living room and flipped on the television to watch the football game she'd recorded.

"He'll be gone tomorrow," she said to herself. "You won't have to think about him for another six months." The sounds of the football game followed her into her kitchen, but it didn't drown out the cackle of laughter inside her head.

Since when had Justin's absence ever stopped her from thinking about him?

She shoved a glass under the refrigerator's ice dispenser, but not even that racket outdid the cackle.

Which just annoyed her all the more.

She thought she'd prepared herself for seeing him.

Every year, she thought she'd prepared herself for seeing him.

And every year, she failed.

The phone hanging on the wall next to the fridge suddenly rang, and she snatched up the receiver. "What?"

A brief hesitation, then female laughter greeted her. "Criminy, Tab. Happy Thanksgiving to you, too."

Tabby forced her shoulders to relax. "Sam," she greeted. "Aren't you still on duty?" Samantha Dawson was the only female officer with the local sheriff's department.

"Taking my supper break."

"Too bad you have to work on a holiday."

"Not for my bank account. Double-time pay. How was the big get-together over at the Clays'?"

Even though Tabby had gotten pretty friendly with Sam over the past few years, the other woman wasn't privy to the history between Tabby and Justin.

Nobody was.

"It was fine." She shook herself. "A lot of fun. Always is. Have you heard how Hayley's day went?"

Hayley Banyon was a good friend of Sam's. She was also a Templeton, and as such, would have had as much reason or more to be at the Clay family fete as Tabby, since she was one of the relations the Clays had recently learned about.

"I saw her, actually," Sam said. "Needed her professional help on a family dispute call that came in. She said she was grateful for the call, if that gives you any hint."

It did. "That's too bad." If there was dissension between Vivian Templeton and Squire, according to Hayley there was even more between Vivian and her own sons. One of whom was Hayley's father. "So did you call to shoot the breeze, or what's up?"

"Just checking whether you're opening the diner tomorrow."

"Yup." She'd be there before 4:00 a.m. as usual to get the cinnamon rolls going. "Pool tournament at Colbys kicks off tomorrow and I'm figuring I'll get overflow business from it like I did last year. Why?"

"Promised a dozen to Dave Ruiz if he covers a shift for me next week."

"They'll be hot and fresh by six, same as always."

"Good enough. See you then."

Tabby was still smiling when she hung up. The phone rang again before she had a chance to take her hand off the receiver, and she picked it up again. "Let me guess," she said on a laugh. "Two dozen?"

"Two dozen what?"

Her nerves tightened right back up at the sound of

Justin's voice. "I thought you were somebody else. What do you want?"

"I want you to get over the damn stick you got up your—"

She hung up on him.

It took only a second before the phone rang again.

She disconnected the phone line, and it went silent.

Then she turned back to the refrigerator and poured cold tea over the ice in her glass, flicked off the light in the kitchen and went back to the living room to watch her recorded football game.

She fell asleep on the couch before halftime and woke up around 3:00 a.m. to the fuzzy, bluish-white light from the blank television screen.

There was no point in going to bed when she needed to be at the diner soon, anyway.

Rubbing the sleep from her face, she went to shower and got dressed for the day.

Thirty minutes later, with her damp hair hidden beneath a bright blue knit cap and her gloved hands shoved deep in the pockets of her wool coat, she walked the three blocks from her triplex to the restaurant and let herself in the rear door. She didn't need to turn on any lights to make her way through the back of the diner, because aside from updating an appliance here and there over the years, nothing significant had changed since she'd started working there as a teenager.

She went out to the front of the restaurant, where the glass windows overlooked Main Street, and started fresh coffee brewing. With that delicious aroma following her, she went back into the kitchen, turned on the lights and got down to work.

By the time she heard the back door open again,

she had three baking sheets of cinnamon rolls cooling on the racks and was sliding two more into the oven. "Grab that third sheet from the counter, would you?"

She looked over her shoulder, expecting Bubba.

But it was Justin who picked up the large metal pan. "This one?"

Her lips tightened, and she took the sheet pan from him, sliding it into the oven along with the others and closing the door. "Come to check on your investment?"

She didn't wait for an answer and went back out through the swinging door to the front, where she poured herself a cup of coffee. It wasn't quite 6:00 a.m. yet, but she unlocked the door and flipped the Closed sign to Open, anyway.

When she turned back, Justin was sitting on one of the red vinyl–upholstered stools at the counter. He was wearing dark gray running pants and a zippered jacket with *CNJ* printed on the stand-up collar.

His clothes looked expensive. And darn it all, they fit his tall, exceptional physique as if they'd been tailored for him. Which, for all she knew, they had been. He'd admitted quite a few years ago that he not only had his suits tailored, but his shirts, as well. His precious Gillian had seen to that.

Since Tabby didn't want to think about that, she focused on everything above his neck. His thick, short hair was damp, making the blond strands look brown. He'd obviously showered. Her nose was even prickling from the vaguely spicy scent of his soap. Or…whatever.

"You need a shave." She flipped over a thick white mug, filled it with coffee and pushed it in front of him.

His long fingers circled the mug. "You should keep the door locked when you're here by yourself."

"Please. Be mighty hard for customers to come in to Ruby's if I kept the doors locked whenever I happen to be alone." Hard for customers. Hard for intruders.

She pushed aside the thought and went back through the swinging door, pulled on clean plastic gloves and turned out the first batch of rolls, deftly packing several up individually, then punched down the dough that was rising in an enormous steel bowl.

He hadn't budged when she went back out to the front.

She deposited the pastry boxes next to the register, threw away the gloves, refilled her coffee and leaned back against the rear counter, studying him over the brim of her cup. His eyes were bloodshot. Which, annoyingly, just seemed to make the violet color stand out that much more. "Tie one on last night?"

His jaw canted to one side. He shook his head and squinted as he sipped the steaming-hot coffee. "Should have. Couldn't sleep, anyway. At least then it would've been worthwhile."

She smiled sweetly. "I slept like a baby." On the couch. Plagued by dreams about him, only to wake with a crick in her neck that still made it hurt to turn her head too far to the left.

"Were you always this much of a witch, Tab?"

Despite everything, she felt a stab of some unidentified emotion. "Isn't that how spinsters are supposed to act?"

He leaned on his elbows and looked at her through his lashes. "Twenty-eight is spinsterhood now?"

She sipped her coffee. It was to some old-fashioned folks around Weaver. But truthfully?

She felt that stab again. Regret, perhaps. Maybe loss.

It was hard to tell. When it came to Justin, things had started getting complicated long before they'd become adults. "Close enough to be a regular at Dee Crowder's spinster poker night."

"'Spinster' sounds like you're seventy-five and still pining for your first kiss." He gave her that through-the-lashes look again. "And I know you don't qualify there. Hell." His lips twitched suddenly. "I remember when Caleb kissed you when we were freshmen in high school."

About the time when she'd wished Justin would have been interested in kissing her. But he'd never been interesting in kissing her for *her*. She'd always been a substitute on that score. A substitute he'd left behind the same way he'd left behind Weaver.

"Doesn't count," she said promptly. "It was a practice kiss. He was afraid he'd mess up when he planted his first one on Kelly Rasmussen."

Justin's head came up, his expression genuinely surprised. "I always figured you gave him the same response you gave me when we were nine. Without the broken nose."

It was nearly six. She figured Sloan McCray, one of the deputy sheriffs, would be showing his face soon before he went on duty. And frankly, she would be grateful for the interruption.

She flipped on the radio and glanced over the stack of to-go cups she kept near the big brewer. "If he'd done it without permission in order to make Kelly jealous, I probably would have given him the same response." She lifted her shoulder. "Apples and oranges, though."

"I didn't kiss you to make Sierra jealous."

"And you didn't sleep with me four years ago to

make—what's her name? Oh, right. Gillian." The name was seared on her brain. "That wasn't an attempt to get her to sit up and take notice of you?"

"How many times do you want me to apologize for that?"

"I don't know. Maybe a few million." She looked past him when the front door opened, making the little bell on top jingle softly. "Good morning, Deputy. Get you the usual?"

"Yeah. Thanks, Tabby." Sloan stepped up to the counter and handed her his insulated travel mug for the coffee. She turned and filled it while he greeted Justin. "How's life in Boston?"

"Cold," Justin admitted. "Not as cold as here—" he glanced at Tabby "—but still cold. How's your wife?"

"Keeping me warm," Sloan drawled. "Very warm."

"And the boy—Dillon, right?"

"Growing like a weed," Tabby said, turning to hand the deputy his coffee mug, along with one of the pastry boxes. "He and Abby came by last week. Dillon's going to be a heartbreaker one of these days."

"Fortunately, I think we've got a few years yet before we have to worry about that." He pulled out his wallet.

She waggled her finger at him. "You know your money is no good here, Deputy."

"And you know I'm gonna argue."

"Justin's half owner of this place. Tell him, Justin."

"What Tabby said," Justin said obediently, without moving a muscle. "Easier to go along with her than argue, because you'll never win. Trust me."

Sloan stuffed a few dollars in the empty tip jar by the register. "You won't give that back, because I know it gets split among your crew." He took a sip from his mug, turning his gaze to Justin again. "You in town for the long weekend? Going to play in Colbys' pool tournament?"

Tabby busied herself restacking the pastry boxes. Justin would be gone by nightfall just like always. He never stayed the entire Thanksgiving weekend. At least on that score, she could relax a little.

"I'm here until January. But no, I leave the pool games to my brother."

She accidentally dropped the boxes and they scattered. "January!"

As Sloan leaned over and picked up the boxes that had landed on the floor, the radio attached to his belt crackled. He adjusted the sound and set the boxes on the counter. "Sure I'll be seeing more of you then," he said. He gestured with his mug and picked up his own pastry box. "Thanks, Tabby."

"You bet." She waited until the deputy departed before she focused on Justin again. *"January?"*

"I know the thought's horrifying to you, but try to dial it down a little." He came around the counter and refilled his coffee mug.

And even though she wanted to tell him to get back on his own side of the counter, she couldn't very well do so.

Like it or not, he *was* her boss. It didn't matter that he'd always left the decision making to his brother when it came to Ruby's. But Justin was still half owner. It wasn't something she dwelled on, but when they were standing right there in Ruby's, it was kind of hard to forget.

She mentally counted to ten and tried again. "You're here until January?" Calmer or not, her voice had still gone a little hoarse at the end. But she held up her chin as if it hadn't. "Why is that?"

"I'll be working on a project here for CNJ. At the hospital, mostly. My aunt cleared it last night, though she's going to have me jumping through a few more hoops than I expected because of it."

Tabby let his answer roll around in her head a few times. "Why can't you work on it in Boston at that big state-of-the-art laboratory you love?"

"Too many distractions there."

"Gillian being one of them?"

"Yes, but not the way you th—" He went silent when the bell over the door jingled again, and Sam strolled in.

She hadn't yet changed from her jogging gear into her uniform. Tabby waited for the usual male reaction to register in Justin's expression as he took in the sight of Sam's figure lovingly outlined from neck to ankle in vibrant, clinging purple fabric.

But he didn't do the typical double take like all the other guys.

Instead, he nodded politely at Sam and turned back to stare into his coffee mug while Tabby rang up a dozen rolls.

If he was so crazy about Gillian that a beautiful woman like Samantha didn't even merit a glance, what was he doing making Tabby's life harder by sticking around Weaver for the next few months?

The thought was more than a little irritating. "Sam, you haven't met Justin Clay yet, have you? He's Erik's brother."

Sam turned her bright eyes back to Justin. "No kidding? You're the genius scientist who works back East." She stuck out her hand, cocking her blond head a little to one side. "I guess I see the resemblance to Erik," she said with a smile. "Except you're prettier."

Tabby nearly choked on her amusement when Justin flushed.

"He'd argue that," he said and nearly yanked back his hand from Sam's.

"Sam's one of Max's deputies," Tabby told him. "Like Sloan."

"Well, I wear a badge like Sloan," Sam allowed wryly. "But nobody calls me their boss like they do Sloan." She picked up the box of rolls. "Still warm. Wonder if Ruiz will mind if one is missing before I get them to him?"

"I'd like to see the day when you actually indulge yourself for once," Tabby challenged.

"Oh, I indulge." Sam's gaze sparkled as she glanced at Justin on her way toward the door.

"With a *sweet roll*," Tabby called after her.

Sam just laughed and sketched a wave as she left.

"Heard there was a lady deputy now," Justin said when the sound of the bell over the door faded. "She still the only one?"

"Max has been trying to recruit more women." Tabby picked up a rag and started needlessly polishing the counter. "It's hard. Small-town USA is bad enough. Small town in the middle of Wyoming—where the tumbleweeds often outnumber the residents—isn't the life for everyone." Her fingers clenched around the rag as she rubbed harder. "Not even when you're born and raised in it. You ought to know that better than anyone." He was the perfect example of getting out, after all. "So what's this big project you're doing? Curing the common cold?"

"Nothing that profitable. Just an R&D project that should've been wrapped up already, but—"

There was a loud bang from the back of the diner, followed by, "Yo, yo, yo!"

Justin shoved his fingers through his hair, looking impatient. "Now what?"

"Bubba," Tabby said evenly. "If you want peace and quiet, Ruby's Café isn't the place to find it. Why do you think those profit checks you get have a decent number of zeros at the end? Not that you probably notice them much, anyway, with your gigantic pharmaceutical salary." She pushed through the swinging door to greet her cook. "Morning, Bubba."

"Hey, girl." Bubba Bumble had a gentle soul that he hid behind a lumbering, rough-looking, hard-talking exterior. "Figured you'd have the hash browns going already." He was wrapping a white apron over his white T-shirt and slouchy, black-and-white-striped pants. Next came a pristine red-and-black bandanna that he wrapped over his forehead and tied in the back over his neatly shaved salt-and-pepper hair.

"Sorry. I got—" *Distracted by Justin.* "Busy," she said instead.

Bubba grunted and grabbed a knife to start peeling potatoes. Leaving him to it, she went back out front. The regular waitresses would begin arriving any minute, but until they did, she was on deck. Once they were there, though, she'd spend most of her morning in the kitchen with Bubba. She could man the grill when she had to, but he was the cook. She took care of the baking—he didn't like the ancient oven Tabby still used—and did the books and serving or kitchen prep when the load was heavy. And considering the pool tournament being held down the street, she was crossing her fingers for a heavy day.

She topped up Justin's coffee again without waiting for him to ask and began restocking the rack that held individual boxes of cold cereal.

"Does anyone still order those things?"

"Absolutely." She gave the rack a whirl. "Or did you think these were the same boxes of Fruity Twirls that were here when your great-grandma ran the place?"

He ignored her sarcasm.

"Since you're here, you might as well eat. Biscuits and gravy? Pancakes? Or have your tastes gotten fancier along with your running clothes?"

"If they had, I wouldn't be sitting on this stool," he replied with such an even tone that she felt guilty. "What's the special?"

She kept a small chalkboard propped on a shelf behind the counter where she listed the daily specials. But she hadn't gotten to writing them out yet today, and the board was still wiped clean, the way she'd left it two days earlier.

"Bubba," she called without looking behind her toward the pass-through window to the kitchen. "What's the special this morning?"

"Turkey hash," he yelled back. "Turkey noodle soup and salad this afternoon."

She retrieved the board and chalk and wrote everything out. She'd just set the board back in place when the front door opened and a couple she didn't know came in. They were both carrying long, distinctive cases. "Good morning," she greeted. "Looks like you're in town for the tournament. Sit anywhere you like. I'll be right over with menus." Without waiting a beat, she looked at Justin again. "So? What'll you have?"

"Scrambled eggs and wheat toast."

He liked eggs now? Withholding comment, she turned and leaned closer to the pass-through. "Scrambled eggs and wheat for Justin, Bubba."

Her cook looked up from the growing mountain of potatoes he'd shredded. "Justin's here?" He immediately set down his knife and crossed the kitchen to look through the pass-through. "Justin! How's life treating you, man?"

"It's good, Bubba. You?"

Ignoring their conversation, Tabby carried two waters and menus over to the couple, who'd chosen a booth in the corner. "I'm Tabby. Can I get you coffee or anything else besides water while you have a chance to look over the menu?"

"Bloody Mary?" The young woman looked hopeful.

Tabby smiled and shook her head. "Sorry. No alcohol here. Colbys will be able to accommodate you on that, though, if you have your heart set. You'll get a good breakfast there, too. Not as good as here—" she gave a quick wink "—but good all the same."

"I suppose I can live without one." The girl propped her chin on her hand. "What about you, honey?"

"Coffee's good for me. And one of those pecan cinnamon rolls that I keep hearing about." The man flipped open the menu.

"Oh, me, too." The girl's expression brightened. "And cream for my coffee if you've got it. It's a holiday weekend. If I can't splurge on a Bloody Mary just yet, I'll splurge on that."

Tabby's smile turned into a grin. "Coming right up."

Infinitely comfortable with this particular role, she returned to the counter area, prepared a little white jug of cold cream, plated up two warm rolls and returned with them, along with the coffeepot, to the table. While she was serving the couple, the door jingled again, and two more parties of two came in. Everyone had pool cue cases.

She hid her delight and called out another cheerful "Good morning."

She'd just gotten them situated with menus and drinks when Bubba called out that an order was up, and she went back to grab Justin's plate. Which also had a side of biscuits and gravy.

Bubba figured he knew Justin pretty well, too, obviously.

Tabby set his plate in front of him, and Justin eyed the fat, fluffy biscuit that was mounded over with golden-brown gravy studded with chunks of sausage. She reached below the counter and came up with a bottle of hot sauce. She was tempted to hold it out of his reach, but she set it in front of him. "Anything else I can get for you?" She lifted her eyebrows, waiting. "More coffee?"

"No coffee. But there is something else." He hesitated a moment, then suddenly dumped the biscuit and gravy on top of the eggs, completely hiding them, and grabbed the hot sauce.

She hid a smile as she pivoted on her heel to grab an order that Bubba set on the pass-through. "More gravy?"

"The key to the empty unit you've still got at the triplex," he said. "I want to rent it."

Chapter Four

Tabby turned and was staring at him as if he'd started speaking Swahili. "What's that?"

"You still have an empty unit at your triplex, don't you? Erik told me last night—"

"Yes," she said, looking consternated. "I haven't managed to rent out the third unit yet, but—"

"Well, now you have," he said, content to do his own share of interrupting. "At least for six weeks or so."

Her lips parted, and he knew she wanted to tell him no. He knew it. Just as he knew there was no way that she could. Their families were too close. Their moms were best friends. Her brother was married to one of his cousins.

She managed the diner he and his brother owned.

"I'll pay twice what you were planning to charge," he said in a low tone. "Just say okay, Tab, and neither one of us'll have to go around explaining why we're the only ones who don't think it's such a great idea. My family suggested it last night after you cut and ran."

"I didn't cut and run." Her lips twisted, and she looked away. The bell over the door jingled twice more in rapid succession. "Fine," she said abruptly. "Meet me over there at two this afternoon. I'll give you the key." Then she snatched two slick, laminated menus out of the slot next to the cash register and smiled almost maniacally at the newcomers. "Good morning!"

Justin wondered if he was the only one who heard the wealth of false cheer that had entered her voice.

He wished to hell he'd never admitted to Erik the night before that he wasn't exactly anxious to move back home for the next several weeks.

Not because he didn't love his folks. He did. But he'd been out on his own for a long time, and he was used to having his own space. One where his mother didn't figure she ought to make up his bed every morning.

If he hadn't made that admission to Erik, then Izzy wouldn't have overheard, and then his mom wouldn't have come in on the conversation. Hope hadn't been insulted at all, either. In fact, she'd been the one to toss out ideas for places he might rent temporarily. Erik, though, had been the one to remember Tabby's place.

And wasn't that just the perfect solution?

Everyone knew Justin and Tabby were friends. Always had been. *Thick as thieves*. That's how his mom had put it as she'd reminisced.

He wasn't about to tell them those days were over. That Tabby would just as soon kick him to the edge of town than agree to rent one of her triplex units to him. And he definitely wasn't about to tell them the reason why.

He dumped more hot sauce on the sausage gravy.

And when he was finished, it was one of the waitresses—a girl he didn't know named Paulette—who took away his half-empty plate.

* * *

Tabby spotted the dusty black pickup truck parked in front of her triplex the second she rounded the corner of her street.

She wanted to turn on her heel and go back to the safety of the diner. Justin might be half owner, but at least there she figured she was safe from him showing up again that day.

Huffing out a breath, she tucked her chin inside the turned-up collar of her coat and trudged forward. When she got closer, she saw that he was sitting on her front porch. He'd changed into jeans and a light gray hoodie.

The cigarette dangling between his fingers wasn't such a welcome sight. He stubbed it out when he spotted her and rubbed his hands down his thighs as he stood, waiting for her to walk closer. But the faint smell of smoke lingered.

"When'd you start smoking again?" He'd smoked for a few years in grad school. Never around his folks. And rarely around her. And she knew he'd worked like a dog to give up the habit. Because what good was a guy researching cancer cures who died of it himself?

He frowned. "I haven't started up again."

She pointedly pushed the toe of her boot against the cigarette butt sitting on the edge of her cement porch.

"I've been working on the same pack for weeks."

She looked at him from the corner of her eye as she passed him to unlock the front door of her unit. "Question is why you have a pack of cigarettes at all."

"I know. Disgusting habit. Unhealthy as hell."

All of which was true.

So why, darn it, had there been something so stupidly sexy about him sitting there with one?

It was insane.

Maybe it went along with that whole bad-boy appeal thing.

Not that Justin had ever been a bad boy.

He'd just been the boy who got away.

She pushed open the door. "You coming in or going to stand there and wait while I find the key for the empty unit?" It was pretty much an excuse. She knew where the key was. She just wasn't all that anxious to hand it over to him.

But then, she wasn't all that anxious to have him inside her home, either. As it was, she thought about him often enough without him ever having stepped foot inside.

He bent over and retrieved the crumpled cigarette butt and stepped through her doorway, pushing the door closed behind him. "Trash?"

She gestured to the kitchen, which was separated from the living room by only a bat-wing-shaped breakfast bar. "Under the sink." She chewed the inside of her cheek, watching him cross the room. "The empty unit is on the other end. Floor plan's just like mine. Two bedrooms. Fireplace. One bath. Furnished, which I assume you heard. Minimally, though, so don't expect all the comforts you're used to. You've got a utility room, but no washer and dryer." And she'd be hanged if she would offer the use of hers. He had plenty of family around Weaver he could ask, and if not them, then there was a brand-new Laundromat out on the other side of town by Shop-World.

"I don't care what the floor plan is or whether there's a washer and dryer. I don't know what luxuries you figure I've got in Boston. I don't have a washer and dryer there, either. Long as it has running water and electricity, I'm good. What prompted you to buy this place?"

She raised her shoulders, a little thrown by the abrupt question. "I don't know."

He gave her a look.

She pressed her lips together. "Fine. With all the new building going on at the other end of town, some of these old places are starting to go vacant. The original owner—do you remember Mr. Samuelson? He had that bait-and-tackle shack—" She made herself stop rambling. "Anyway, he died. Had no family. There was talk about an investor who wanted to buy this lot and the house next door, but only to raze them and put up a convenience store."

He grimaced.

"Right. That was my reaction, too. Plenty of new building going on at the other end of town. But downtown here? It's charming just the way it is. Anyway," she hurried on, skipping the rest of her reasons, "it's close enough to work that I can usually walk."

"Like you did today."

"Obviously."

"Even though when you walk *to* work, it's early. And pitch-dark."

"So?"

He sighed. "Christ, Tabby. That's practically the middle of the night. You shouldn't be out walking—"

"—the three very short blocks in this town where nothing ever happens?"

"Why didn't you charge Sloan McCray this morning for his coffee and roll? It's not because he works for the sheriff's department. You charged that blonde lady deputy for hers."

Tabby clamped her lips shut. The fact that he'd asked told her that he already knew.

"He busted a guy who was trying to rob the diner, that's why." Justin pressed his hands flat on the granite-topped breakfast bar and stared at her. "Yeah, I asked and heard all about it. He busted in. While you were there. Alone before hours. With the damned door unlocked."

"And for a year after it happened, I *kept* the door locked," she snapped. "Until I got tired of having to stop what I was doing and go unlock it every time I turned around, because half this town knows I'm there long before six when the place officially opens and stops by, anyway!"

"You need to be more careful."

"I locked my house door, didn't I?" She realized she was yelling and let out a long breath. "I'll get your key," she muttered and hurried down the hall.

She used the spare room as a studio and office. She found the key in the bottom of an empty coffee can that also held her clean paintbrushes and returned to the living room.

He was still standing in the kitchen, and she set the key on the granite. "There you go. Rent's due in advance." She blamed the devil for prompting her to make that up right then and there.

He spread his hands. "Not exactly packing a checkbook here, Tab."

"The bank's open until five. But you'll have to park a few blocks away because of the traffic in town for the pool tournament."

He sighed a little and pocketed the key. "Who lives in the middle unit?"

"Mrs. Wachowski. She used to teach history at the high school—"

"I remember her. She was ancient when we were in school. Surprised she's still around. She must be a hundred and twenty by now."

Tabby didn't want to feel amusement over anything he said, but the retired teacher *had* seemed ancient when they were teenagers. And she would have been totally displaced, just like Mr. Rowe, who was seventy and lived in the house next door, if someone hadn't purchased the triplex. "She's eighty-five. And she's very nice, but she's a light sleeper. So if you're still prone to blasting old Van Halen when you can't sleep, be aware."

"I played it when I studied," he corrected her. "And it was AC/DC. Not Van Halen."

"Whatever." She was blithely dismissive. As if she didn't remember very well what it had actually been. She went to the door and opened it. "Don't forget the bank."

He crossed the room and stopped in front of her, so close she could see the faint lines radiating from his violet eyes. "I don't forget anything."

Her palm felt slippery clenched around the doorknob. "You forgot we were friends," she said huskily.

"I didn't forget that, either."

Her throat went tight, and she damned the sudden burning she could feel behind her eyes. "Fine. Whatever." She just wanted him to go.

"Tabby—"

She clenched her jaw.

He sighed. Shook his head slightly. "I'll bring you the rent money later."

She nodded stoically.

He sighed again and stepped through the door. She barely waited for him to get through before she pushed it closed after him.

Then she leaned back against it and let out a shaking breath.

He remembered her name now.

Maybe if he'd remembered it that night they'd slept together, she wouldn't feel the way she did now.

But no. That night four years ago, after he'd peeled off her clothing as if he'd been unwrapping something exquisitely precious and pulled her into his arms, taking her virginity and her heart in one fell swoop, he hadn't remembered her name at all.

It hadn't been Tabby's name he'd whispered against her skin.

It had been Gillian's.

That night, Justin stuck the rent check in an envelope and shoved it through the mail slot in Tabby's front door.

Call him a coward, but he didn't think he had the stomach to go another round with her.

Instead, he'd killed the evening at Colbys, the bar and grill owned by his cousin Casey's new wife, Jane. It had been crowded as hell there, what with the tournament going strong. But since several of the participants were relatives of his, he'd managed to slide his way in. During a break in the play, he'd thrown darts with Caleb and April. He'd tilted beers with JD and argued politics with Jake.

He'd also spent nearly an hour on the phone with Charles, convincing his boss that helping to fill the hospital's shortfall in funds for their lab expansion was an investment worth making if CNJ wanted Justin to successfully bring the results of their latest research project in on time.

It hadn't been Justin's project in the first place. It wasn't even in his usual area of research, which was cancer treatments. Though even before this latest issue, Justin seemed to keep getting pulled farther and farther from the lab.

But Charles had dumped the matter in his lap only a week ago, when the guy who *had* been in charge of it had been arrested on drug charges. Not only was Charles trying to minimize the scandal of that, but he needed the final report on the project to be ready for presentation at a conference in Europe right after New Year's. CNJ was small potatoes in the pharma world. But with this report, Justin's boss expected major results.

If the report was completed on time.

If the results of the project were even accurate. Which was what Justin had yet to prove, considering the situation.

Five weeks to accomplish something that usually took five months. Sometimes five years.

Was it any wonder he'd wanted to get away from Boston and the pressure of his own responsibilities in the lab there? Much less the pain in the butt Gillian had been making of herself.

Key in hand, he walked along the sidewalk fronting all three of the connected units to the door at the opposite end. It was dark, but there was a porch light on, so he had no trouble fitting the key in the lock, and the door swung open with only a slight creak of the hinges.

He stepped inside and felt around for a light switch on the wall but couldn't find one. Swearing under his breath, he pushed the door wider so that the light from the porch could extend inside and felt his way into the pitch-dark interior.

His knee connected with something hard and solid, and he swore loudly, reaching out to feel his way around it.

A couch. Which hopefully led to a side table and a lamp.

Why the *hell* hadn't he checked the place out while it was still daylight?

Tabby was why.

He reached the end of the couch and cautiously felt around for a side table. He nearly knocked the lamp over when he found it, but finally, he felt the switch and turned it.

The resulting light nearly scorched his eyeballs.

He blinked and looked away, going back to the door to close it. It was cold outside and nearly as cold inside the apartment. He looked over the living area. It was definitely a twin to Tabby's place. At least in layout.

The furnishings were a lot sparer. The couch looked like standard-issue hotel stuff, making him wonder where she'd gotten it. The simple side table and the lamp were straight out of the '80s. Not that he cared. He didn't plan to spend a lot of time here, anyway.

He just hoped the bed was big enough to stretch out on and comfortable enough to allow him a night's sleep.

He found the thermostat on the wall in the hallway and turned on the heat, then checked out the two bedrooms. They were identical except one was outfitted with twin beds—which was never gonna work, since he was six foot four—and the other had a queen-size bed. Not perfect, but doable.

Only thing it was missing was the bed linens.

He looked in the closets, which were all empty except for little cedar blocks that hung from hanger poles. He found nothing in the dresser drawers, either.

Evidently, the term *furnished* only went so far.

He went out to the truck he'd borrowed from the Double-C for the duration of his stay and retrieved the suitcase holding his clothes. He left the other two suitcases containing the research materials locked inside the cab of the truck. Tomorrow he'd take them to the hospital, where his aunt had promised him some dedicated lab and office space that, truthfully, she hadn't had to agree to. He was glad that she had, though, even though it would cost CNJ a nice chunk of change.

Maybe he was glad *because* it would cost CNJ a nice chunk of change. It made up, just a little, for the chaos his life had become there.

CNJ had millions to throw around. The Weaver Hospital—which served this entire region of Wyoming—didn't.

It didn't take him long to unpack. There wasn't any need here for the suits and ties he typically wore to work in Boston on those days he wasn't suited up in scrubs. He also hadn't bothered bringing his heavy coat, just a few sweatshirts and his leather jacket. He figured if he needed something heavier, he'd borrow it from Erik or his dad.

And if he was honest with himself, it had felt good leaving that stuff behind. Stuff that Gillian had always had a hand in choosing, only because he'd never been interested in it himself.

The contents of his suitcase took up a third of the

bedroom closet and one of the dresser drawers. He dumped his shaving kit on the bathroom counter.

The heater was running steadily, filling the cold air with a faint, burning odor that he figured would dissipate after an hour or two. From the smell, he doubted that the heater had been used in months.

He went out to the kitchen to verify he had running water. He did. Hot and cold, even. He pulled open a few drawers and cabinet doors. He hadn't been able to find any bed linens. But there were dishes. A few pots and pans. Silverware. All clean and neatly stacked in their various spots. Next, he checked the refrigerator. It was cold inside, with only an opened box of baking soda occupying space on one of the shelves.

With a mental list forming of the basics he could pick up out at Shop-World, he left the apartment again and headed out to the truck. He couldn't help looking toward Tabby's place at the other end.

Despite the late hour, light was shining through the closed curtains over her front window.

He wondered if she was really awake this late when he knew she'd have been at the restaurant since around 4:00 a.m.

Even as he was looking, he saw the curtains twitch. A moment later, her front door opened, and for a moment she stood there, silhouetted by the light.

Then the door closed, and she was heading toward him, little more than a dark shadow against the darker night.

"Here," she said, stopping a few feet away. She extended her hand. She was holding a square, plastic-covered package. "I meant to put them in your place earlier, but I fell asleep on the couch. It's a new set of bedsheets."

He took the package. "Thanks. One less thing to pick up at Shop-World."

"That's where you're heading?"

"Somewhere else to go at eleven o'clock at night?" It was also the only place close by where a person could pick up bedsheets, a set of mattresses to put them on, pajamas to wear when you lay down on them and food to cook when you got up again. There was nothing fancy about the big store, but it did have its purpose around these parts.

She was shifting from one foot to the other and back again. Her hair was darker than dark, but he still imagined he could see the gleam of her eyes in the thin moonlight. He thought he caught a whisper of a smile on her lips. "Colbys, particularly when there's a pool tournament going on."

"Already spent enough time there for one day." He was surprised she'd given him the sheets, much less remained there, voluntarily speaking with him about anything at all. "Look, Tabby." He gestured with the package. "I appreciate the place. I know you'd have rather—"

She cut her hand through the space between them. "Let's just not talk about it. For everyone's sake, we can pretend everything's hunky-dory. Same way we've done when you've been in town before."

Pretending for several weeks would be harder than pretending for a few hours. But he wasn't going to look a gift horse in the mouth. "So. Truce?"

She laughed. The sound was soft. And entirely unamused. "Pretense doesn't mean truce, Justin. But I love

your family as much as I love my own. Just because
you and I—" She moistened her lips and shifted restlessly. "They all think we're still the same kids who
played together in the sandbox. That belief makes them
happy, and I see no reason to rock that boat. Particularly when there's enough of that going on with your
family already."

"What's *that* supposed to mean?"

She exhaled. "Your grandfather's reaction to Vivian
Templeton moving to town."

"Oh. That." He raked his fingers through his hair.
"Erik mentioned it." Frankly, he failed to see what the
fuss was about. There'd always been a lot of Clays on
the family tree. Now there was just another branch
they'd never known about before. It was hardly the end
of the world.

"Anyway, it's not like we have to sit down to a holiday meal with everyone every day. So—" she crossed
her arms and shrugged "—you'll go your way and I'll
go mine. We'll hardly see each other. And before we
know it, this'll all be over. You'll go back to Boston and
Gillian." She started to turn away.

"Not Gillian."

Tabby looked back at him. Her skin was as creamy
as the cameo his mother had let him play with during
church when he was a kid so he'd sit still in the pew.

"She's not part of my life anymore," he said bluntly.
"We broke up. For good this time." He wasn't sure what
reaction he expected. But he did know it wasn't the mus-
ing little "hmm" he got. "Six months ago," he added
for good measure.

"She's still your boss's daughter?"

He didn't answer. Obviously, Gillian was still Charles's daughter.

Tabby wasn't done, though. "You're still both working at CNJ?" She started walking toward her doorway. "Then she's not out of your life," she said without looking back.

Justin opened his mouth to argue, but he didn't.

Tabby reached her door. Opened it and disappeared inside. A moment later, the light shining through her curtains was extinguished.

He stood there in the dark for a long while, listening to the silence.

In Boston, where he had a dinky apartment with an exorbitant rent in the South End, there was never such a wealth of silence.

He'd always thought that was a good thing. Everything about Boston had energized him. The city. Grad school. His work. His tumultuous relationship with Gillian.

He looked up at the sky. It was mostly cloudy, allowing only a stingy stream of moonlight. But on a clear night, he knew the stars would be laid out like a thick, sparkling carpet.

When they'd been young, he, Tabby and Caleb had often camped out behind her parents' house. They'd pitch a tent and everything, though they usually ended up pulling their sleeping bags out of the tent. They'd fall asleep under the stars, amid ghost stories and trying to figure out the constellations.

Caleb had been the best at identifying them. Tabby's artistic eye had usually seen something else in the stars—a bunch of dancing fairies and such.

Justin had seen cities. And skyscrapers.

Even then, he'd been thinking about someplace else. A place where everyone in town didn't know the name of everyone else in town. And certainly didn't know their business. Where a person could walk down the street in complete anonymity if he wanted. Where tumbleweeds didn't travel down the center of Main Street more frequently than cars.

He shook the thoughts out of his head.

Then he unlocked his truck, tossed the bedsheets onto the bench seat beside him and drove out to Shop-World.

He could have survived a night without sheets. But in the morning, he was gonna need coffee. And even though he had ample justification to stop by the café to get a cup on his way to the hospital—they were spitting distance from one another, practically—he figured he and Tabby both would be better off if he gave Ruby's a wide berth.

At least for a while.

Chapter Five

On Monday, Tabby dragged the box of Christmas decorations out of storage and turned the radio station to one that played only holiday music.

It would drive some of her customers a little bananas at first. But after a week or so, they'd be humming along with the music, too.

She was hoping that the decorations and the music would immediately put her in a more cheerful state of mind. Ordinarily, once she got past the hurdle of Justin's brief Thanksgiving visit, she would throw herself into the Christmas spirit. She was determined that this year was going to be no different.

Even if the hurdle happened to be a living, breathing obstacle temporarily residing all but next door to her.

So what if her humming along with "White Christmas" sounded a little manic? She was the only one who knew the reason why.

By the time Bubba arrived and fired up the grill, she had green garland strung around all of the windows. By noon, she'd rearranged a few of the tables to accommodate the Christmas tree. It wasn't a live tree; she didn't want to have to deal with needles dropping on the floor in the restaurant. But it was a nice artificial one all the same. And by the time she closed up again at two, everyone had had a hand in decorating it. Even some of her customers had pitched in.

And the Christmas tunes she was humming had become a little less frantic sounding, even to her own critical ears.

It probably helped that Justin hadn't shown his face at the diner. Not that she'd expected him to, but still.

She left the locking-up duties to Bubba and walked the till from that day and the weekend over to the bank to deposit.

Then, considering it *was* officially the Christmas shopping season, she stopped in one of her favorite shops, Classic Charms, to see if anything struck her fancy. She figured she'd run into either Sydney or Tara, who owned the eclectic shop. But neither one was there. The cash register was being manned by a teenage girl Tabby didn't know.

Tabby's mother, Jolie, however, was browsing the racks.

"Honey!" Jolie smiled broadly and hastily tucked a hanger back on the circular rack of clothes. "I didn't expect to see you here."

"Same goes." Tabby gave her mom a quick hug and tried to spy what she'd been looking at. "Thought I'd get a start on Christmas gifts. What was that you were looking at? Anything good?"

Jolie gave the rack a whirl. "This place is full of many good things," she said, smiling serenely and almost evasively. "I just came from lunch with Hope. Why didn't you tell me Justin was staying at your place?"

Tabby's smile felt suddenly wooden. "He's renting the empty unit." *Staying at her place* had an entirely different connotation, as far as she was concerned. "Just wants somewhere to crash while he works on some project. Haven't seen much of him, actually."

"Well, that won't last," Jolie said with certainty. "Bring him by for dinner this week. Your dad and I would love to see him."

"I think he's got a lot of work—" The words died when her mom gave her a curious look. Tabby knew the more she made excuses, the more curious Jolie Taggart would likely become. "But I'm sure he'd take a break for you guys," she finished.

"Wonderful." Jolie glanced around the shop. "Now, we could both save a lot of time and effort if we just told each other what in here we've had our eye on."

Tabby couldn't help but chuckle. "Yes. But where would be the fun in that?"

Her mother sighed dramatically. "You are your father's daughter." She glanced at her watch and made a face. "I'd stay and pump you for gift ideas, but I'm meeting a new client this afternoon."

"Designing another wedding dress?" Her mother was a seamstress, and in the last several years, wedding dresses had seemed to be one of her most frequent requests.

Jolie shook her head. "A ball gown, actually." She glanced around the shop that sold bits of everything from clothing to furniture. "She doesn't want it getting around before she sends out invitations, but Vivian Templeton is planning a Christmas party. It's a little short notice, but she asked me to make her gown."

"Flattering."

"I thought so. Heaven knows the woman could hire any designer in the world if she felt like it. I was surprised she didn't request Izzy, though. When it comes to doing the fancy stuff, she's a lot better at it."

Before moving with Murphy to Weaver, Izzy had been the costume designer for a ballet company based in New York. She'd waited tables for Tabby for a while, and she'd been a good worker. But designing clothing was clearly more up her alley, and since she'd helped Jolie out with one particularly difficult bride, the two of them had done several more jobs together.

"Izzy's married to Erik, though," Tabby reasoned. "Maybe Vivian was trying to be sensitive to the fact that she's part of the Clay family."

Jolie tucked a runaway curl of blond hair behind her ear and pursed her lips. "Possibly. Hope and I were talking about all that over lunch. She says Squire's more adamant than ever about having nothing to do with Vivian.

"Obviously I never knew Squire's first wife, Sarah, since she died before I was even born. But Vivian was Sarah's sister-in-law. I know she interfered somehow and prevented her husband from having any sort of relationship with Sarah, but that was years ago. You know that old man is all about family. And learning now that there's a passel of them living practically under his nose ought to count for something."

Tabby frowned. "I hadn't heard that Squire wasn't willing to acknowledge the family connection at all."

Jolie waved her hand dismissively. "I wouldn't go that far. But he's sure got a grudge, and is dead set against meeting Vivian face-to-face. Evidently, she's asked him several times, but he flatly refuses."

"They all seemed okay when I was over there for

Thanksgiving dinner. Of course, nobody mentioned Vivian's name within his earshot, either. At least not while I was there." A customer came in, and Tabby slowly twirled the display rack. There was a goldish-brown blouse she spotted that exactly matched the color of her mom's eyes, and as soon as her mother left, she planned to get a closer look at it.

"Well, the only thing I know directly from Vivian herself is that she's planning a formal party the weekend before Christmas," Jolie said in a low voice. "And now I'm going to have to hurry, or I'm going to be late." She bussed Tabby's cheek and headed for the front door. "Let me know what night you're bringing Justin by," she said as she left.

Tabby's shoulders sank. She'd *almost* managed to forget that particular request.

She pulled the hanger off the rack and looked at the pretty blouse. It would suit her mother very well.

But Tabby's spurt of holiday shopping spirit had abruptly dissipated, and she replaced the hanger.

She didn't have to examine the reason why.

Justin.

The office space his aunt was able to allot for him at the hospital lab was considerably smaller than what he was used to, but Justin didn't care. He had room for all materials he had to go through, a safe to lock them in and a lock on the door. Not that he was particularly worried about industrial espionage. Not in Weaver.

But he knew stranger things had happened.

So when he finally left the office late that Monday night, he packed up his laptop to take with him, closed the research logs in the safe and locked the door behind him.

"Finally heading out?" Scott Brown, the only lab tech on duty that night, barely glanced up from his microscope.

"Yeah." Justin slid his laptop into his messenger bag and slung the strap over his shoulder. He didn't know much else about the technician besides the guy's name. "When do you get off?"

"Two o'clock in the morning." Scott replaced the slide he was studying with another. He looked about Justin's age. Maybe a few years older. "Hate the swing shift, but I like the extra pay that comes with it." He tapped his foot on the metal rung of his high stool to the beat of the country music coming from a radio sitting on one of the steel shelves lining the walls. Walls that would be opened up soon, effectively tripling the current space.

Justin stopped at the locked door that controlled access to the lab and signed out. "You're not originally from around here, are you?"

"Braden."

Weaver's nearest neighbor. A good thirty miles away. It wasn't as if there were any handy public transportation methods around. No subway. No commuter train. And maybe the drive wouldn't be considered that much of a commute to some, but it was only a two-lane highway that got you there and back.

When the weather was good and there were no accidents or semitrucks to slow you down, the trip wasn't difficult. But when the snow and ice came?

Different story.

"Don't envy you that," Justin said and lifted his hand before leaving.

Even though his borrowed truck was in the parking lot, Justin could have walked from the hospital back to Tabby's.

It was no farther than walking to the diner from the triplex.

Knowing that she did so—regularly—annoyed the hell out of him. Weaver was still a small town, yes. But it wasn't the same small town in which they'd grown up.

The streets weren't the same streets where they'd raced around on their bicycles when they were ten. These days, you were just as likely to encounter a stranger on the street as you were a person you'd known your entire life. And a weekend pool tournament like the one his cousin-in-law had just thrown didn't have to be going on to draw strangers to town.

These days, strangers were actually *moving* to town.

He dumped his messenger bag on the passenger seat and headed home. His cell phone buzzed before he got there. Half the time, the cell service didn't work around Weaver, so he was surprised enough that he glanced at the display.

The sight of Gillian's name had him grimacing. He silenced the thing, not answering, and shoved the phone into the messenger bag. Two minutes later, he turned onto Tabby's street and parked in the driveway next to a gunboat of a vehicle left over from a dozen decades ago. Mrs. Wachowski's, no doubt.

He wasn't sure if Tabby still drove the sporty little coupe she'd had years ago. He hadn't seen it around. But he also hadn't seen any other car he could peg as hers, either.

When he got to his front door, there was a piece of paper taped to it, and he peeled it off and unfolded it.

Tabby's handwriting was as illegible as it always had been. For a girl who'd been able to draw circles around his stick figures from way back, she'd always had the most atrocious penmanship. And no amount of trying was going to help him decipher the scratchings. He was too far out of practice.

He went inside long enough to dump off the messenger bag, then walked down to her door and knocked.

And knocked.

And knocked.

He'd given up and was turning to go back to his place when the door finally squeaked open and Tabby stood there, several paintbrushes threaded through the fingers of one hand. Her hair was haphazardly pinned on top of her head in a messy knot, and she had a smear of red paint on her cheek.

"Looks like you still throw yourself entirely into your painting," he said and swiped his thumb over the dab of paint, holding it up to show her.

She tossed the rag that was hanging over the shoulder of her misshapen T-shirt at him. "If your plumbing's stopped up, call a plumber."

"Nice landlady you make."

She made a face at him and turned on her bare foot. "Come in and close the door. You're letting out the heat. I suppose you're here about the note," she said, heading out of the living room.

He wiped the paint off his thumb and pushed the door closed with his shoulder before following her. "Since I could only make out about three words of it, yeah." He stopped in the doorway of the bedroom she'd entered and stared. "Damn, Tabby." There seemed to be dozens of paintings stacked up against the walls. Large canvases. Small canvases. And every size in between. "Do you paint instead of sleep these days?"

"Sometimes," she muttered. She'd sat down on a tall wooden stool in front of her easel positioned near the window but remained facing him. She took up another rag from a stack of them and started cleaning her brushes. "Any night'll work."

He tilted the nearest stack of paintings away from the wall so he could look through them. They were all abstracts. "Looks like Jackson Pollock and Georgia O'Keeffe had a baby." He glanced at her. "Any night'll work for what?"

She turned to set aside her brushes on her worktable, and her T-shirt slipped off one shoulder. "Dinner. Did you read the note or not?"

He tossed the note next to her brushes. "It's harder to figure out than your paintings."

"My mom expects me to bring you around for dinner this week. I couldn't come up with a good reason to tell her no." She folded her arms across her chest. She was wearing narrow blue jeans with stains and rips on them that he knew came from years of use rather than some deliberate fashion style. She had one knee bent to prop her foot on the base of the revolving stool and one leg stretched out in front of her, and her toes were painted as brilliantly red as the smear he'd wiped off her cheek.

Over the years, he'd noticed lots of things about her, but he couldn't remember ever really noticing her toes. They were decidedly…cute.

Shaking off the thought, he started looking through another stack of paintings. "I don't care what night. Just pick and get it over with." He lifted the canvas closest to the wall to look more closely at it. "Reminds me of a blizzard. Remember that time we got stuck at the high school during that February blizzard?" Twenty kids and one adult, sleeping on gym mats in the auditorium with no lights or electricity.

The corners of her lips barely lifted in acknowledgment. "How about Wednesday? Six o'clock. If you can manage an hour, I'm sure they'll be satisfied. We probably won't have to play this charade again until Christmas Eve."

When his family had always gone to her folks' place after church. When they'd been kids, they'd all bedded down together in the basement, whispering about what Santa might bring, while upstairs, they could hear their parents laughing.

"Wednesday's fine." He lowered the painting back in place and carefully leaned the canvases once more against the wall. "Do you sell them all?"

"Most of them." She clasped the round seat beneath her. "Bolieux sells them, anyway."

"That the gallery Sydney got you hooked up with?"

"Mmm-hmm." She spread her fingers and looked at her fingernails. Picked at some dried paint. "Once I ship all of these to them, they'll display and catalog them. List them online, too. I've sold a lot more since they started doing that."

"You getting good money for them?"

"Not enough to buy Ruby's yet, but I'm getting there."

He stopped in his tracks.

She raised her eyebrows. "What? You find that surprising?"

"I don't know. I never thought about it. Does Erik know about this?"

"I've mentioned it a time or two in passing." She shrugged, and the shirt slipped down her shoulder another inch. It was clear that she wasn't wearing a bra. At least not one with straps.

He shook himself again. Why the *hell* was he noticing stuff like that? He'd worked damn hard over the years, training himself to overlook such things where she was concerned.

"Until I started making some money with my art," she continued, "it's just been a nice thought."

"Tabby's Café," he mused. He wasn't sure whether he liked the idea or not. It was as unsettling as thinking she had cute toes.

But she shook her head. "I wouldn't change the name. The place is Ruby's. Always has been. Always will be. At least as long as I have any input on the matter." She pushed off the stool and slipped past him through the doorway. "Wednesday at six. You s'pose they'll think it's odd when we don't drive out there together?"

Her parents lived outside town on a small spread where her dad still trained cutting horses. He found his gaze dragging over the stack of paintings containing the one with the blizzard-like blue, gray and white swirls. "Uh, yeah." He went after her. "They'd think it was odd."

She'd gone into her kitchen and pulled open the refrigerator door. Unlike the plain white model in his unit, her stainless steel one looked brand-new. So did the coordinating range and the built-in microwave.

"So what're we going to do?" She took out a diet soda

and pulled the tab. It was obvious she wasn't going to offer him one.

"Drive out there together."

She turned her head around, as though she had a pain in her neck.

Of course, he was pretty certain his presence *was* the pain.

"Tell me again why you couldn't do this oh-so-important work of yours in Boston?"

Her T-shirt had slipped off her shoulder again.

He turned away from the sight and headed for the door. "Too many distractions there. I'll drive on Wednesday." His voice was abrupt. "Like you said. We'll probably be safe after that until Christmas Eve."

They weren't safe.

Two nights later, Tabby stared out the passenger window of Justin's truck as they drove back into Weaver from her parents' place.

What was supposed to have taken only an hour or so—just long enough to politely eat and run—had ended up consuming the entire evening. Mostly because Jolie had invited Tabby's brother and his family to join them.

The only saving grace was that Evan and Leandra's three kids—Hannah, Katie and Lucas—had kept the spotlight off Tabby and Justin.

And the fact that they'd barely exchanged five words even though they'd sat next to each other at the dinner table.

"Hannah looked good." Justin's voice broke the monotonous sound of the tires on the highway. Who knew how long ago the radio in the borrowed ranch truck had stopped working.

"She's comfortable at Mom and Dad's." Her eleven-year-old niece had autism. "She would have had a harder time with the whole crew at your folks' place on Thanksgiving. That's one of the reasons why Evan and Leandra tend to go see Helen in Gillette." Helen was her dad's stepmother. She was a difficult woman, to say the least. She had always been kind enough to Tabby, but the older she'd gotten, the less she appreciated Helen's attitude toward Jolie. Even after all these years, Jolie and Helen's relationship was strained.

"Your grandmother still dote on Evan?"

"To his chagrin, yes."

"He, uh, ever see—"

She knew where he was going. "Darian?" Her father's half brother was Evan's biological father, though he'd never spent one minute of his life acting like one. That had always been the role Drew Taggart held. He'd met Tabby's mom when she'd been pregnant with Evan, and they'd been married ever since. "No. Not for years, far as I know." It wasn't the only twist in her family tree, but given what was going on with the Clays and Templetons, it seemed mild in comparison. At least to her.

To her it was easy. Jolie and Drew were her parents. Evan was her brother. End of story, as far as she was concerned.

They fell silent, and she listened to the roll of the tires for a few more minutes. But it felt as if those tires were connected to a string that kept pulling tighter and tighter until she couldn't bear the silence another second.

"I didn't know they were going to bring up the tree

lighting," she said abruptly. "It never occurred to me. You're never here for it and—"

"It's not the end of the world."

She finally turned her head and looked at him.

The only light came from the occasional headlights of an oncoming vehicle. But even though she felt that he'd become a stranger these past few years, his features were forever imprinted in her mind.

"It's just one more time when our families are going to be together and we're going to have to keep pretending everything is hunky-dory between us." The tree-lighting ceremony was a town affair, scheduled for the coming Friday, just two days away.

She'd always enjoyed the festivity.

Now, the entire idea of it made her want to climb into bed and pull the covers over her head.

Could she do that until January without anyone noticing?

Inside her brain, she let out a frantic laugh.

"Well, maybe things *would* go back to being hunky-dory if you'd just let the past go." He slowed suddenly and pulled the truck off onto the shoulder of the highway, shoved it into Park and looked at her. "It was a *mistake*, Tabby."

"You got that right," she said tightly.

He exhaled noisily and shoved his fingers through his hair. "Okay, not a mistake. An accident. Do you think I intended—" He broke off again and swore under his breath. "I never meant to hurt you. I didn't mean to—"

"Call out another woman's name while you were caught in the throes of passion?" She filled her voice with sarcasm, because it was so much more preferable than letting the pain she still felt show.

"Yes!" He slammed his hand against the steering wheel, making her jump.

Then his wide shoulders rose and fell. "Yes," he repeated quietly. "I was drunk, Tab. You and I were *both* drunk. I was home, celebrating getting my PhD. Gillian and I were on the outs. Again. And you were my best friend. I didn't plan to get you into bed. I didn't plan any of that. It just…just happened."

It felt like a noose was tightening around her throat, and her eyes stung.

And when he spoke again, his voice was as ragged as she knew her own would have been. "And I know none of it excuses anything." His long fingers closed over her arm, squeezing. "D'you think I haven't regretted everything? That I haven't kicked myself every damned time I turn around? I'm sorry. I'm sorry. A hundred million times, I'm sorry. Just—" He cleared his throat. "Just tell me what I can do to make it right again, and I'll do it."

Did he regret making love with her? Or did he regret calling her by another woman's name?

Or was it the entire humiliating fiasco that he wished away?

Her throat felt raw. "It's not something that can be made right, Justin."

He exhaled. Squeezed her arm. "You haven't done anything in your life that you wished like hell you could take back? That you could undo?"

She closed her eyes, and a hot tear escaped. "Yes."

She wished she could undo falling in love with him. But she'd done that when she was about fifteen years old, when they'd been stuck together in the high school auditorium during a blizzard.

And she'd long ago given up hoping that she'd get over it.

"Then you understand," he said huskily. "I know you can't forget it. But you're one of the best people I've ever known, Tab. Can't you find some way to forgive?"

Yes, she could forgive.

But for years now, ever since he'd gone off to college and had never really come back, she'd had to watch him leave.

Again and again and again.

And in January, she'd watch him one more time.

So after the debacle four years ago, it had just been easier to hold on to the anger that resulted. And now, she wasn't sure if she could actually let it go. Even if she tried.

His fingers were hard and hot on her arm. Insistently reminding her that right now, right *now*, he was here.

"Fine," she whispered and felt something hard inside her chest start to give. A little. "It's over. In the past."

He waited a moment. Even in the shadows, she could feel the intensity of his gaze. "You forgive me?"

She inhaled deeply. Let her breath out slowly. Her tight shoulders sank.

"Yes. I forgive you."

Chapter Six

When Justin showed up at Ruby's before she'd unlocked the door at six, she realized he was determined to make sure she'd meant her words from the night before.

He'd always been determined that way. And she'd always been one to stand by her word.

So she unlocked the front door and threw her arm wide in invitation. "Scrambled eggs?" Her tone was dulcet.

The lines beside his violet eyes crinkled. His hair was damp, and he smelled like heaven when he walked past her.

"G'morning to you, too." He crossed to the counter and dumped his messenger bag on a stool before sitting down. "And you know I hate eggs."

She chewed the inside of her cheek, trying not to laugh and failing.

And laughing, honestly laughing, with Justin felt too good to regret. Even though she knew the opportunity to do so came with an expiration date. "I knew you ordered those the other day just to be contrary." Some things about him hadn't changed.

"Fortunately, Bubba's sausage gravy helped cover the taste. Mostly." He leaned over the counter to grab the coffeepot, and she quickly looked away from the sight of his faded blue jeans hugging his very perfect rear end. He didn't have quite the brawn that his cattle-ranching brother possessed, but there wasn't a single inch of Justin Clay that wasn't lean and oh so prime.

She didn't want to get caught ogling his butt and quickly went behind the counter to finish filling the saltshakers, which she'd been doing when he'd knocked on the glass door.

"So what are you going to be doing at the hospital today?" The night before, during dinner with her parents, he'd talked briefly about the space Rebecca had situated him in at the hospital, but he hadn't said much about the project he was working on there. And when he'd talked about it the other day right here in the diner, Bubba's arrival had interrupted.

"Reviewing five years' worth of research." He got up and went into the kitchen and returned a moment later with one of her sticky cinnamon rolls on a plate. He sat back down and cut the oversize roll in half before picking it up. "They're still hot." He took a bite and blew out a breath. "Really hot," he said, chewing fast.

She poured him a glass of water, slid it in front of him and went back to filling saltshakers.

"What's the research about?"

"I could tell you." His set down the roll and gulped down half the glass of water. "But then I'd have to kill you."

She rolled her eyes. "Well, you've already said it's not a cure for the common cold, so I know it's not that.

Some newfangled weight-loss pill? The next advance in the little blue pill for men who can't—"

"No. And no. But if the research bears out, then it could be another step forward in treating infertility."

She capped the last saltshaker. "You think something's wrong with the research?"

"I didn't say that."

"Your expression did."

"It wasn't my research project. I have no idea what I'll find."

"Whose project was it?" She told herself she was prepared for him to say Gillian's name, but when he didn't, she still felt her shoulders relax.

"A guy named Harmon Wethers."

"Why isn't he handling it?"

His lips twisted. "He's got other things to take care of right now. Regardless, *my* boss—Charles—assigned it to me. I've got a lot less time than I would if the research project had been one of my own design. We're both in research, but Wethers's area of expertise was entirely separate from mine, and there's a lot of stuff to validate before I can even start writing the paper."

Tabby studied him for a moment. "You're really worried you won't finish in time." It wasn't a question. She could see it in his eyes.

"Pretty much."

"What happens if you don't?"

"CNJ loses a whole lot of money."

"It's a multimillion-dollar company."

"And they'd be losing millions." He frowned slightly. "I'd just as soon not lose my job over it."

"You've been Charles Jennings's golden boy since you identified that one cancer strand thing right out of college—" She had the clippings about it from the medical journals still tucked away in her dresser.

"I wouldn't say golden," Justin countered. "But he has invested a lot in me, and now it's time for me to keep delivering. If I succeed, there should be a good promotion in it."

"The vice president deal?" She shrugged one shoulder when he gave her a surprised look. "Erik mentioned it."

"Yeah. The vice president deal."

She leaned over, folding her arms on the counter. "You don't sound entirely thrilled."

"It's what I've worked toward since before I even finished college."

She tucked her tongue behind her teeth for a moment. But she still couldn't stop herself. "Is it what you still want, though?"

"Why wouldn't it be?"

She shrugged her shoulders and dropped it. She used to dream of him wanting to come back to Weaver to stay, but time and experience had finally killed those thoughts off for the fantasies they were. "If anybody can do it, I'm sure you can. Even if it means proving the results aren't what everyone expects, you'll finish in time to meet your deadline."

His eyes met hers, and he smiled faintly.

And for a moment, her heart stopped a little.

She didn't even realize that Sloan McCray had entered the restaurant until he cleared his throat.

"Morning," he said, setting his travel mug next to the cash register with a bit of a thunk.

Her cheeks felt hot, and she straightened, quickly

grabbing the coffee carafe to fill his mug. "Cinnamon roll this morning?"

"Now that I'm addicted to them, yes." The deputy nodded toward the nearly decimated one on Justin's plate. "That's how it starts," he said. "You think you can have just one. Run a few hundred miles to work off the calories. But you keep coming back for another. Pretty soon, you're missing work, selling your dog. Anything for another fix—"

"Please." Tabby pushed the pastry box into his hand. The deputy was in superb condition. Even before he'd married Abby Marcum, every female in town had either wanted to marry him or mother him. "You come in because you like the coffee. Pam Rasmussen told me half the time you're auctioning off your roll to the other guys in the office."

The deputy smiled slightly. "Our dispatcher does like to talk."

"Along with nearly every other person who lives in Weaver," Justin added drily.

Sloan's smile widened a little, and Tabby wanted to cringe at the speculation in his eyes as he looked from Justin back to her again.

"Well." Sloan dropped a few bills in the tip jar. "Hope you two enjoy your, ah, morning." Still smiling slightly, he ambled out of the restaurant.

"Well, *that's* great," she muttered when the door closed and the bell jingled.

"What's that?"

She propped her hands on her hips. "You didn't see that look he gave us?" She tossed up her hands at the blank response she got.

"What?" He popped the rest of his roll in his mouth.

"Nothing." At least the deputy wasn't the kind to gossip the way Pam Rasmussen was. She plunked the coffee carafe on the counter in front of him. "I've got to get started on the hash browns for Bubba." She escaped into the kitchen. "Don't choke on that roll!"

Justin smiled at the door swinging to and fro after her and swallowed down his roll. Then he filled a to-go cup with coffee, added a few bucks of his own to the tip jar and headed out, the weight of his messenger bag bumping against his hip.

Things were getting back to normal with Tabby.

The day was looking up already.

Every year, Weaver's community tree lighting was the town's official kickoff for the holiday season.

About fifty Christmas trees—fresh, unlike the one at the diner—were set up in the town park at the end of the block and strung with lights. A band was on hand to play Christmas music. There was an enormous pot-luck, with everyone who could bringing covered dishes to share. They were arranged by the tree-lighting committee on plastic-covered plywood planks propped on barrels. Kids chased each other around. Adults overate and gossiped. And when it was time for the tree lights to come on, everyone gasped a little, cheered a little and felt swept up in the holiday spirit.

At least that's how it always worked for Tabby.

She didn't bring a dish from her own kitchen, though.

Using a three-shelved rolling cart from the restaurant, she wheeled over several serving pans of barbecue that Bubba had prepared at Ruby's. Pulled pork. Brisket. Shredded chicken. She had it all, plus fat, yeasty rolls on which to pile it. There was enough food on her rolling cart to feed a small army, and that's the way she liked it.

Because there were those families around who came to the event who *couldn't* bring a dish to share.

It was up to places like Ruby's to make sure that no one went away hungry.

Pam Rasmussen—the gossipy dispatcher from the sheriff's office—had been chairperson of the tree lighting for more years than Tabby could count. Pam grabbed her in an enthusiastic choke hold the second she spotted her. "Merry Christmas!"

Tabby laughed as much as her limited breath allowed and worked some distance between them. "Everything's looking great as always, Pam."

The other woman beamed. "I've got a table reserved just for your food." She admired the pans on the cart. "Can I peek?"

"Knock yourself out. It's exactly what you asked for at the last committee meeting."

Pam peeled up the foil edge covering the topmost pan. "Smells heavenly. My husband loves Bubba's brisket." She tucked the foil back in place. Then she straightened and pulled down the hem of her brilliant red sweatshirt festooned with a glittery snowman on the front. "Okay." She was clearly back in chairperson mode. "Your table is closest to the pavilion." She waved toward the round structure situated in the middle of the park.

"You moved the food this year?"

"We'll try it. Everyone sets up their picnic chairs to face the band in the pavilion, so I'm hoping with more focus in that direction, we won't have any incidents of kids spiking the punch like we did last year. If I could get the committee to agree that serving punch in punch bowls is passé, we wouldn't have that problem."

"I like the punch bowls," Tabby admitted. "It's tradition."

Pam made a face. "So is spiking them with booze when nobody is looking," she said drily.

"It only happens later in the evening when most of the folks with children have already gone home."

Pam propped her hand on her hip. "Please tell me you're not packing a fifth of vodka somewhere under that red sweater you're wearing."

Tabby laughed and held up her palm. "On my honor," she assured Pam and wheeled her cart in the direction of the pavilion.

Residents were beginning to show up in the park. Most of the picnic tables had already been staked out. There weren't enough there to accommodate all the people who would attend, so they were prime real estate. Others brought chairs of their own and blankets to spread out on the grass that had begun browning over a month ago. Some—like the Clays and her folks—brought their own folding tables to use.

After she'd stored her cart out of the way behind the pavilion, she headed toward her family's collection of tables.

She gave a general wave to all and sat down on the blanket next to her sister-in-law, Leandra. "Where are the kids?"

"Evan's got them over on the playground." Leandra leaned back against her hands and stretched out her legs, knocking the toes of her boots together. "You decided yet what you're going to wear to the hospital fund-raiser next weekend?"

Tabby shook her head. She kept forgetting that her brother had purchased a table at the event. "Can't I just wear the usual?"

Leandra laughed slightly. "Blue jeans and boots? It's cocktail attire, sweetheart. That means a dress, typically. Or at least some sparkle on slacks that aren't made of denim."

Tabby made a face. "Do you have anything in your closet that I can borrow?"

Leandra laughed wryly. "I don't have anything in my closet for *me*. Izzy is whipping up a dress for me, though. Talk to your mom. Maybe she can do the same thing for you."

Except her mother had already admitted she'd be making a dress for Vivian Templeton's hush-hush party. Nevertheless, Tabby glanced around. "Is she even here yet?" It was obvious to her that her parents weren't. But the person she was really looking for was Justin. Who was also absent.

"I talked to your mom an hour ago. They should be pulling in any minute. I need an idea what to get her for Christmas, too."

Tabby laughed ruefully. "That is an infectious problem, girlfriend. I saw a blouse over at Classic Charms that looked nice, but when I went back to buy it, it was gone. Sydney told me that she sold out half their stock last weekend with all the people in town for the pool tournament."

"Good for business. Bad for us. And one more reason I'm glad I've already talked to Izzy." Leandra suddenly lifted her hand in a wave and pushed to her feet. "I see Squire and Gloria. Going to go give them a hand."

Tabby waved at them but stayed put because she

spotted her brother crossing the grass from the playground with his kids in tow. She greeted them with hugs. Katie and Lucas both flopped down on the blanket beside her and started begging for food. They were four and six and full of energy. Hannah sat, too, but was quieter.

"Hey, bugs." Tabby leaned close to the girl. "Did you have fun at Grandma Helen's for Thanksgiving?"

Hannah nodded.

"Look what I brought for you." Tabby pulled a coloring book out of her oversize purse. "All of the pictures are flowers, just like you like. And—" she reached in her purse again and pulled out a small box "—brand-new crayons."

Hannah's eyes lit with delight. She had a particular fondness for new crayons, loving the way they were all the same length and the tips were sharp. "Just for me?"

"Just for you, bugs."

Hannah reached out and gave one of her rare hugs. "Thank you."

"You're welcome."

"What about us?" Lucas and Katie hung over her back, and Tabby laughed and pulled out two more boxes of crayons.

"You guys, too. But I thought you were all anxious to get your food?"

They snatched their crayons and spread out on their stomachs, dumping everything out in a haphazard pile while they flipped open their coloring books.

"Hey." Evan tugged her hair as he threw himself down among them. "How's my favorite sister?"

She barely had time to respond, because it seemed as though everyone in town suddenly descended on the park all at once. Tabby got up to help her nieces and nephew get settled with their plates of food, and then she got busy helping Pam keep the tables—which were groaning under the weight of potluck dishes—somewhat organized. She passed out paper plates, helped fill plastic cups with punch and carried servings of cake and pie to the masses. And all the while, she kept her eye out for Justin.

But he never showed.

She hated the disappointment that sat like a lump in her gut. If she hadn't expected him at all, she would have enjoyed the event as much as she always did.

Still, she kept a smile pinned on her face at least until the bulk of the people had departed and the band had packed up its instruments. There were only a few diehard celebrators hanging around after that. Someone was playing a radio loudly, and when Tabby checked the dwindling contents of the last punch bowl, she caught her breath at the strong alcohol content. Once again, despite Pam moving the serving tables, someone had managed to spike the punch.

There were only adults left in the park, so she didn't dump out the bowl, but left it and moved on to loading up the cart from her restaurant with her empty trays. She had plenty of light to work by. The white lights strung on the Christmas trees were still lit. From now until New Year's Day, they'd automatically turn on at dusk and off at dawn. With the music coming from the radio and the sound of laughter from the diehards, it wasn't unpleasant work.

She even poured herself a half cup of the spiked punch and sat down on the raised platform of the pavilion to sip it.

* * *

And that's where Justin found her.

Sitting on the edge of pavilion stage, with her legs hanging down, swinging them back and forth.

He couldn't help but smile at the sight as he walked toward her. "Remember when Joey Rasmussen got caught behind the pavilion making out with—"

"Yvonne Musgraves?" Tabby tilted her head slightly, and her hair slid over her shoulder. He saw how the Christmas tree lights were reflected in her eyes when he stopped in front of her. "Lots of kids got caught making out behind the pavilion."

He sat down beside her and dumped the messenger bag with his laptop and the files he still needed to go through that night next to him on the stage. "You didn't get caught."

"Because I never made out with anyone behind the pavilion." Her voice was dry.

"Ever?"

She let out an exasperated laugh. "Don't sound so shocked. Just because the spot was a hotbed of passion with the various girls you and Joey would get back there doesn't mean every high school kid was doing the same thing."

"I only ever took Collette back there," he retorted, defending himself. "But I think Joey had a different girl every week."

"He did have variety. Whereas you simply took Collette there every chance you got."

Tabby swung her legs a few times while they fell silent. Bob Dylan was singing about "Knockin' on Heaven's Door" from someone's radio. Justin inhaled the spicy scent put off by the dozens of Douglas fir trees and wondered when the last time was that he'd just sat somewhere to *be*.

Then his stomach growled, butting in on his uncommon contentment. He wished he hadn't lost track of time while he'd been working. He'd missed all the food. There was nothing left on the picnic tables except a big old-fashioned punch bowl that was nearly empty.

"Why'd you break up with her, anyway?"

He dragged his thoughts away from his stomach. "Who? Collette? She dumped *me*. In favor of her brother's college roommate. You ought to remember that. You were there when it happened."

"Not Collette."

She was talking about Gillian, he realized.

And the last person he wanted to talk about was Gillian. She was also the last person he wanted to think about.

"She slept with someone else." He leaned forward and looked toward the bare tables set up adjacent to the pavilion. "Is the punch any good?"

In answer, she handed him her plastic cup. "Spiked."

"It's ten at night. Of course it's spiked." He took a healthy swig and nearly coughed as it burned all the way down. "That's a helluva lot heavier a dose of spiking than we used to pull when we were young."

"Speak for yourself on that *we*," she said. "I never pulled that particular stunt. You forgave her the last time she did it."

Trust Tabitha Taggart not to be diverted from the conversation. "More fool on me."

"You'll forgive her this time, too."

He sighed. In the seven years of their on-again, off-again relationship, Gillian had never come home with him to Weaver. His brother and parents had only met her one time when they'd come to Boston and toured his lab at CNJ. Her disinterest in the people who mattered to him had been only one of the problems between them.

In hindsight, now that he'd finally made the break, it was easy to see how futile it all had been.

"I don't have to forgive her," he said. "When I realized I didn't even care, I knew I was done."

Tabby made a soft little humming sound of disbelief.

He didn't want to debate the topic with Tabby. There was no point to it, because there was no way she could possibly understand the level of done that he'd reached with Gillian.

As far as he knew, Tabby had never been involved with anyone beyond a few dates. If he'd taken a leaf from her book, he'd have moved past Gillian after two dates and saved himself a helluva lot of chaos.

He finished off the contents of Tabby's plastic cup, then pushed off the stage and stood. "What kind of food did I miss out on?"

"The usual. Fried chicken. Three-bean casseroles. Seven-layer salad with peas and cheese. About twenty boxes of pepperoni pizza and more store-bought pies than Shop-World carries. Bubba's barbecue."

His ears perked. "Bubba's barbecue? Any left?" His stomach growled again, right on cue.

And loud enough for her to hear, because she made a face and rolled her eyes before standing also.

"It's only because you own the place that I'll open up Ruby's in order to raid Bubba's leftovers."

He grinned and dropped his arm over her shoulder, ignoring her quick little flinch. "Bubba will never know," he promised.

Chapter Seven

Bubba knew.

And he complained about it through the entire morning rush the next day.

Tabby didn't usually work on Saturdays. But she'd gone to the diner to take care of the books, which she did in one of the corner booths, because Ruby's diner had never possessed something as fancy as an actual office space.

She had a filing cabinet shoved into one corner of the kitchen, along with several narrow lockers that the crew could use to store their personal belongings. But an office? A space to house a computer, a desk or even the phone?

That hadn't been necessary in Ruby Leoni's day, and Tabby—who'd been managing the place longer than anyone else besides Ruby—hadn't found it necessary, either.

Even if it did take a table out of the rotation on a particularly busy Saturday morning.

"You leave setting the special to me," Bubba said, dropping a hand-scrawled sheet of paper on her table as he passed by with a loaded tray to deliver to a six top. "Can't do that when you're comin' in all hours of the night, eatin' it up."

"I think the customers will survive, Bubba." Her voice was mild. She was used to Bubba's occasional dramatic flare-ups. They'd been coming a little more frequently since he'd started cooking privately for Vivian Templeton, but Tabby blamed that on Vivian's regular chef, Montrose. According to Hayley, Montrose was pretty much a monstrosity in the personality department. The chef had been with Hayley's grandmother back in Pennsylvania, and to say he had a highfalutin attitude was putting it mildly. "Instead of the special, they'll order off the menu. No harm in that."

"Harm in not having any pulled pork when folks come wanting it," he muttered after he'd delivered his tray and was heading back to the kitchen.

"Then put it on the menu."

If the temperature hadn't taken a nosedive overnight, she'd have just worked out back, where they had a grassy, treed area with a picnic table to use during breaks. But the weather was hovering below freezing, and she wasn't a glutton for punishment. She also could have worked at home, but the sight of Justin's truck parked outside had made her too antsy to stay there.

She wrote out the last of the paychecks for the month as well as the handful of bills and logged everything into the laptop computer sitting open on the table in front of her. She'd take the checks out to the Rocking C for Erik to sign sometime that weekend if he didn't come into town before then. She looked over Bubba's scrawled list of supplies and ingredients and put together an order for the coming week. Some things—

like the strawberry jam, the dairy and the eggs—she sourced locally. Other staples—flour, sugar and the like—she got from distributors out of Casper or Cheyenne, occasionally even Denver, depending on where she could get the best deals.

For a small-town diner, the quantity of food they went through was almost shocking. But she'd long ago realized that—whatever else might be going on in the world—people still found their way to Ruby's for a cup of joe and a bite to eat.

And thank goodness for it, or she wasn't sure what she'd be doing with her life. Painting was something she enjoyed. But she'd realized a long time ago that it didn't feed her soul the way running Ruby's did.

She smiled to herself. She fed others to feed herself.

"What're you sitting there grinning about?" Justin slid into the bench opposite her.

She looked at him over the screen of the laptop and only smiled a little wider. She couldn't help it.

It was Saturday. Her bookkeeping was done, and it felt like all was right with the world. "Snow," she answered him. "Weatherman's calling for it by tonight."

He shook his head. "I talked to my uncle Matt this morning. He said it wasn't coming yet. And you know his nose for snow."

She wasn't going to let him rain on her parade. "Well, maybe the famous Matthew Clay nose will be wrong for once. It could happen."

"Anything *could* happen," he allowed. "But it won't snow yet. Not today."

She closed the laptop and tucked the checks to be signed into a folder. "Usually by the beginning of December we've had at least *one* snow. Even if it doesn't stick. But not this year. Did you come in for breakfast?"

"What else?"

She smiled through the sting. It was silliness in the extreme to entertain the idea he might have come to see *her*. Particularly when he was staying two doors away from her. "As long as you're not wanting pulled pork barbecue for breakfast, you're in the right place." She slid out of the booth. "What'll it be?"

"Pancakes and sausage."

"Turkey or regular?"

He looked surprised. "You serve turkey sausage now?"

"Gotta change with the times," she drawled. "We even have a quinoa salad and cucumber water. The mayor's wife is partial to both. So what'll it be?"

"Regular."

"Coming up." She went over to the counter to give Bubba the order. The other waitresses were all busy, so she started a fresh pot of coffee in the brewer and carried the carafe back to fill Justin's mug.

He'd flipped open her folder of checks and was fanning through them. "They're not signed."

"Erik signs them."

She moved to the next table, holding up the carafe. "Refills for you?" Both young men—she was pretty sure they worked out at Cee-Vid—pushed their empty mugs toward her. She filled them and continued around the diner, greeting and filling until the carafe was empty and she moved the freshly full one onto a warmer and started another pot. She'd barely finished that when the delivery truck came with a package. She signed for it and peeked inside, recognizing the custom-made storybook she'd ordered for Hannah for Christmas, and stored it in her locker in the kitchen. Then she delivered Justin's pancakes to him, along with a little pitcher of warm maple syrup.

"Anything else?"

"Yeah." He stuck the checks back in the folder and gestured at the empty bench across from him. "Sit. I thought you didn't work on Saturdays."

She sat. "This isn't work."

He snorted softly. "Most people would disagree. Want a pancake?" He lifted the edge of the one on top of his stack.

"Nope."

He let the edge down and dumped the entire pitcher of syrup on top. "Why don't you sign the checks?"

"Because I'm not on the bank account. No reason to be." Neither was he, but only because he hadn't been around to add his name to the account when Erik had changed banks several years ago.

"You should be." He took a mammoth-size bite of syrup-drenched pancake and gestured slightly with his fork. "You take care of everything else around here. What happens if Erik's not around to sign a check and you need money for something?"

She lifted her eyebrows. "I've got petty cash. It's a system that's been working for a lot of years. Why are you suddenly so interested?"

He shrugged and attacked his pancakes again with the enthusiasm of a man who hadn't eaten in days, much less twelve hours ago in this very restaurant. "I've always been interested."

She could have argued the point but couldn't imagine to what purpose. Interested or not in the management of the place, he was still one of the owners. "Did you get your homework done last night?" Over Bubba's purloined pulled pork, he'd told her about the work he still needed to get through.

He nodded and shoveled more pancake into his mouth.

"You're gonna choke," she said drily and got up again to make another round with the coffee. Hayley and her new husband, Seth, came in before she was finished, and she gestured toward a booth that had just been cleared. "Be right with you two."

The couple smiled and crossed toward the booth, stopping to say a few hellos on the way.

Tabby headed back toward Justin when the door jingled again, and she looked toward it, a greeting already on her lips.

She'd only ever seen Gillian Jennings in a photograph. A snapshot that Justin had pulled out of his wallet ages ago when he had started dating the woman in college.

But Tabby recognized her now. From the top of her gleaming light blond hair to the toes of her expensive, ridiculously high-heeled pumps.

Feeling something go cold inside her, she approached the newcomer, anyway. "Can I help you with something?"

The woman smiled, seeming friendly enough. "Directions, I'm hoping. All the cars on the street are parked in front of this place."

"It's a busy morning." Tabby wondered how long it would be before Justin would look up from his pancakes to see his erstwhile lover standing fifteen feet away. "Directions where?"

Gillian pulled a piece of paper from the pocket of the light brown leather jacket that fit her svelte figure like a glove and read off the address of Tabby's triplex. "I'm looking for my fiancé," she added with a smile.

Tabby went a lot colder. "Oh," she inquired with amazing mildness. "What's his name?"

Gillian tucked away the paper again. "Justin. Justin Clay. He always said Weaver was a small town, but I never imagined just how small. Do you know him?"

Tabby smiled humorlessly and held out her hand toward the corner booth. "As a matter of fact, I do. Obviously not as well as I thought, though." She raised her voice. "Justin? Somebody here to see you."

He looked up, his expression instantly thunderstruck.

Tabby didn't wait around to see any more.

While Gillian gave a little shriek of delighted surprise and clattered on her high heels toward him, Tabby turned on her heel and went through to the kitchen and straight on out the rear door.

Justin looked from the swinging kitchen door to Gillian's face and didn't manage to act fast enough to avoid the arms she threw around his neck as she sat down on the bench seat beside him.

He wanted to curse.

Instead, he looked into Gillian's deceitful green eyes and pulled on her arms. "What are you doing here?"

She pouted a little but let go of the neck lock. "You've always wanted me to come with you to Weaver." She looked at his nearly empty plate and gave a shudder of horror. "Pancakes? Honey, all those carbs—"

"We broke up," he interrupted her. "Remember?"

She waved her hand dismissively. "I know you didn't

really mean it." She snuggled close to his side. "That's what passionate couples like us do. We break up. We make up."

He would have scooted farther away if he weren't already wedged in the corner of the booth thanks to the way she'd launched herself at him. "Not this time." Since he couldn't move one direction, he moved the other, shoving her along the edge of the booth. "Get up."

She didn't have any choice but to scramble somewhat inelegantly to her feet. It was either that or get pushed off onto the butt of her expensive suede pants. "Justin, honey, don't be difficult now. You had to know I'd come. That's what you wanted, isn't it? For me to run after you for once?"

As busy as Ruby's was, her words were still plainly audible to those around them, and Justin felt an urge to wrap his hands around her throat to stop them. Since he wasn't inclined to be convicted of strangling a lying woman, he grabbed her arm instead and pulled her toward the front door. "Bubba," he yelled toward the kitchen, "put Tabby's laptop and files away for her."

Then he marched Gillian out the front door and onto the sidewalk. "You know why I'm not working in Boston," he said through his teeth. "Because you weren't giving me an hour's rest getting through Harmon's project!"

She had to know he was livid, but that had never stopped Gillian. She walked her fingertips up his chest, tilting her head back so her thick blond hair streamed down to the small of her back and she could look coyly at him through her long lashes. "You used to like my little visits to your lab," she said. "Remember?"

He grabbed her hand and deliberately set it away from him. "That look might have worked on me once, but it's lost its appeal. I damn sure didn't come here so you could chase after me!" He wanted to groan when he noticed the couple just rounding the corner on the sidewalk as they headed toward Ruby's. Pam and Rob Rasmussen.

"Justin!" Pam waved merrily at him as she and her husband reached the café's glass door. "I heard you were still in town. We missed you last night at the tree lighting." Her inquisitive gaze lingered on Gillian. "How have you been?"

"Fine, Pam." He wished she'd just go inside. But naturally, that would be too simple for the hell his life had suddenly become.

"I'm Pam Rasmussen." She stuck out her hand toward Gillian. "Justin and I go way back. And you're…" She raised her brows, waiting.

"Gillian Jennings," Justin said at the same time Gillian did.

Only Gillian went even further. She laughed lightly, as if such a thing happened all the time, and bumped her gilded head against Justin's sleeve. "Justin's fiancée," she added.

Pam's jaw dropped, and Justin grabbed Gillian's arm again, tightening his hand warningly.

"Not my fiancée," he said to Pam. But he knew the damage was already done. No matter what he said to her, she'd have him walking down the aisle with Gillian by the time she finished spreading the latest news. "Excuse us," he said before pulling Gillian farther down the street. He didn't stop until he reached the borrowed pickup truck and pulled open the door. "Get in."

She gave the ancient truck a wary look but climbed up gingerly onto the seat.

All the annoyance he felt came out in the slam of the truck door when he shut it.

Then he rounded the truck, momentarily distracted by the sight of a Rolls-Royce driving down the middle of the street before he got behind the wheel. He didn't start the engine. "Are you insane?"

She gave a huffy sniff. "There's no need to be mean."

"And there's damn sure no need for you to be here in Weaver. Much less announcing you're my fiancée!" God only knew what his folks would think when they heard the gossip.

And they would.

To think otherwise would be as insane as Gillian still thinking they had any sort of future together.

And then there was Tabby.

He wasn't going to forget the look on her face in a lifetime of Saturday pancakes, and that was a certainty.

"You know we never agreed on getting married even when we were together." His voice was flat.

"That's just because we were both so wrapped up in our careers. In the success of CNJ. We're meant to be together. You're going to be Daddy's successor. Everyone knows it. We're the perfect couple!"

He was getting a pain in his head. He felt as if she was actually going to cause him a nosebleed. "You've got to be kidding me. What was so perfect that it landed you in bed with another guy? *Again?*"

"I told you that was a mistake. I told you I wanted to start fresh. That I needed a…a real sign from you that you wanted to be with me."

She was exhausting. She might be brilliant when it

came to developing CNJ's line of consumer products, but when it came to the usual logic of surviving every day with other human beings—much less the personal relationships with them—she completely missed the boat. Her reasoning defied explanation.

That fact might have charmed him when they'd been college students, but it had entirely lost its luster.

"What I told you over a *year* ago," he said bluntly, "was that I needed a sign from you that you were done playing games. Which is all you've done in the time since. I told you six months ago we were through. Over. Done. Not together. Not ever going to be together again. And I've repeated it just about every damn week since. How much clearer do I have to be?"

She put on her pouty face again. "But my coming here *is* a sign, honey. I even brought you a surprise."

Beyond the unwelcome surprise of her presence? "I don't want surprises, Gillian."

"You'll want this one." She pushed open the truck door and trotted down the sidewalk, disappearing around the corner.

It would be too much to hope that she wouldn't return. And if he drove away, she'd just come after him again. He knew from experience that she could be relentless when she set her mind to something.

She reappeared around the corner, her blond hair rippling around her shoulders and the unidentifiable bundle she held in her arms.

Then she reached his truck and pulled open the door.

"See?" She smiled brilliantly, ever confident in her own appeal and manipulations as she set the bundle on the truck seat beside him. "Here's proof."

The bundle wriggled, looking up at him with big

brown eyes and a wagging tail. Then the puppy woofed and hopped onto Justin's lap.

He automatically caught the small beagle pup and moved his hand away from the sharp little teeth. "My hand's not a chew toy, little girl," he murmured and looked again at Gillian.

"I knew you couldn't resist a puppy. You've talked about wanting a dog for years," she said. "That's why he's the perfect peacemaking gift." She ran her hands down her slender hips. "We'll raise him and he'll be the perfect dog when we start our family."

Horror engulfed him. "You didn't cook all this up because you're pregnant, did you?"

She looked insulted. "Do I look fat and pregnant to you?"

She looked the same as always. Very thin. Very blonde. Impressively spoiled and inherently selfish.

There was no way any baby she carried could be his. The last time they'd slept together was more than six months ago. She'd have to be showing a decent-size baby bump by now if she were going to claim it was his.

That didn't mean there were no other possible sources of paternity. With Gillian, there were probably more than a few.

But no matter how much Charles Jennings had spoiled his daughter, he wouldn't take kindly to the idea of her having a baby outside of marriage. So at least if she were pregnant, it would explain her unexpected appearance in Weaver. She'd need a husband and right quick.

"Yes or no, Gillian. Are you pregnant?"

She huffed. "No, I am not pregnant."

The puppy squirmed in his lap and started chewing on the ridged steering wheel.

Justin scooped his hand beneath the warm fat belly and held the puppy out to her. "Take the pup—who is a *she*—back to wherever you got her and go home, Gillian."

"But—"

"Take. The. Dog."

She made a face and took the puppy, who whined and scratched her paws against Gillian's leather jacket. "It's not going to be that easy to get rid of me, Justin," she warned, though she had the good sense to back out of the way when he reached across the cab of the truck and yanked the door closed. "I'm not giving up on us!"

He cranked the engine and drove off. When he glanced in his rearview mirror, he saw her standing in the belch of smoke the truck had let out.

He hoped it would be the last he saw of her.

When he got to the triplex, there was no sign of Tabby. He even checked with Mrs. Wachowski but the old woman just shook her white-haired head.

He drove back through town hoping to spot Tabby but steered clear of the restaurant on the off chance that Gillian was still hanging around like an infection. When he reached Shop-World at the other end of town without spotting Tabby, though, he admitted the futility of the exercise. Particularly when he didn't even know whether she drove the same car she used to.

He stopped in a parking lot next to a park that hadn't existed a year ago and pulled out his cell phone. The signal strength was a little better there than it was at the triplex.

He called Tabby's folks' number, but all he got was

the sound of her dad's voice on the answering machine. He knew she had friends, but the notion of calling all over town trying to hunt her down had no appeal, since it would just add fuel to the perpetually turning gossip wheel.

Instead, he dialed Charles at his home and asked the man to rein in his daughter before Justin lost his temper entirely. It was obvious that Charles had no idea what Gillian had done, and the older man assured Justin he'd take care of the matter.

He'd better. Right now, Charles needed Justin to finish the infertility project more than he needed his spoiled little girl to get back the toy she wanted to toss around.

Then, out of ideas, he drove back through town to the hospital.

He couldn't do anything about Tabby until he found her. But at least he could do what he was in town in the first place to do.

Work.

He just wished it held as much satisfaction as it used to.

Chapter Eight

"Tabby, dear." Mrs. Wachowski's voice came through the front door, accompanied by knocking. "Are you home?"

Sighing, Tabby threw off the blanket she'd been huddling beneath since she'd left her brother's vet practice, where she'd gone after walking out of Ruby's that morning, and padded to the front door. She unlocked it and peeked around the edge at her elderly neighbor.

From the scarf tied over her white hair to the low-heeled black pumps she wore on her feet, the short, round woman was clearly dressed for an outing. "You look nice, Mrs. Wachowski. Bingo night in Braden with Mr. Rowe again?"

The woman's head bobbed. "I thought young Justin would be here by now, and I just don't know what to do with her."

Tabby's jaw tightened. "Do with who?"

Mrs. Wachowski shifted, and Tabby spotted the leash she was holding. "The puppy, of course. That pretty fiancée of his left the puppy with me around three because he wasn't home when she came by, but it's six now and I thought he'd certainly be back."

The knot in the pit of her stomach tightened, but she opened the door wider. Sure enough, there was a small brown-and-white puppy at the end of the leash. A puppy who was trying to attack the brick edging of the flower bed lining the front of the triplex.

If Justin wasn't with his *fiancée*, he was probably working. She crouched down and clapped her hands together, drawing the puppy's attention. "Did she say anything else?" Like when the wedding would be? The thought was bitter.

"His fiancée?" Mrs. Wachowski adjusted her scarf slightly and checked her wristwatch. She'd been a stickler for punctuality when she taught high school history and hadn't changed since then. "I was surprised to hear he was engaged, of course. He never mentioned it, even when he was helping me this morning with my furnace."

Justin hadn't mentioned anything to Tabby about helping Mrs. Wachowski, either. Seemed not mentioning things had become his new normal. "What's wrong with your furnace?" The puppy sniffed her way around Mrs. Wachowski's shoes, making her way toward Tabby's fingers.

"Nothing now. The pilot light was out, but he got it going again."

"That's good."

"So what do you think I should do about the puppy?" Mrs. Wachowski looked concerned. "If I leave her alone in my unit, I'm afraid she'll have an accident or two. She's not house-trained in the least. And she wants to chew on everything."

"She's a puppy," Tabby murmured. "Puppies chew."

As evidenced by the way the dog pounced on her fingers. "What's her name?"

"His fiancée never said, actually." Mrs. Wachowski carefully lifted one foot then her other out from the loop in the leash the dog had made around her. "I did think that was odd, but—" She made a worried sound. "There's Mr. Rowe now, ready to drive us to bingo. I don't suppose I could impose on you to—"

"I'll watch the puppy," Tabby said wearily. She scooped up the dog and stood. "Did she—" she couldn't bring herself to say Gillian's name "—leave food or anything else for the dog?"

Mrs. Wachowski handed over the leather leash handle. "Not a single thing. I fed the little beastie some bread that I crumbled up with chicken stock. I didn't know what else to do."

"That's more than a lot would do," Tabby assured her. "Go and enjoy your bingo, Mrs. Wachowski. The puppy will be fine until Justin gets back."

The woman was clearly relieved. "You're such a sweet girl, Tabby."

The puppy switched her attention to Tabby's face, enthusiastically swiping her tongue over every part she could reach. "That's me," Tabby muttered as she watched Mrs. Wachowski scurry to the curb and Mr. Rowe in his waiting car. "Sweet, foolish Tabby."

She watched them drive around the corner and then set the dog on the brown grass. "Don't suppose you know how to potty on command, do you?"

The puppy scampered toward the sidewalk, squatted and peed on the cement.

"Well. It's better than my living room rug." She

tugged gently on the leash. "Come, little beastie. Let's go inside."

Which were words the dog seemed to recognize, because she bounded up the porch step and darted inside, yanking the leash handle right out of Tabby's relaxed grip. A second later, she heard a crash and a yelp, and she vaulted after the pup.

Inside, the lamp that usually sat on Tabby's narrow entryway table was lying on its side on the floor. The white shade was split, but the lightbulb was still intact. "No harm." Tabby set the lamp where it belonged and rubbed the puppy's head.

It wasn't the dog's fault her owner was engaged to an idiot male who didn't know better than to trust a faithless woman.

"Come on." She unclipped the leash from the puppy's too-large blue collar, picked her up and returned to the protective cocoon she'd made for herself on the couch.

The dog immediately burrowed into Tabby's fluffy blanket and tucked her wet nose against Tabby's neck.

She stroked the warm, smooth coat. "I should get myself one of you," she said on a sigh. "My brother takes care of beasties like you. From tiny puppies all the way up to huge horses and most everything in between. If I tell him I want a dog, he'll find one of his many strays and be on my doorstep in two shakes." She looked into the dog's inquisitive brown eyes. "He wanted me to take a cat last year. But I'm afraid of turning into the spinster cat lady." She rested her cheek on the top of the dog's head.

The phone sitting on her end table rang, and she reached blindly to pick it up. "This is your friendly neighborhood dog-sitting service," she said robotically. "Please leave your message after the tone."

"Dog sitting, huh?" Sam Dawson's voice held laughter.

"Hey, Sam." Tabby grabbed the television remote and muted the black-and-white movie she'd been watching. "Diner's closed tomorrow if you're needing more cinnamon rolls."

"Not this time. I wanted to see if you were interested in going to Colbys tonight. Hayley and I are going. Girls' night."

"Why isn't Hayley home romancing her new handsome husband?"

"He's working security out at Cee-Vid tonight."

Covering for another one of the security guards, Tabby guessed, since Seth usually worked days. "I'd go, but I'm puppy sitting," she said, and the sittee in question gave a little woof and started chewing on the point of Tabby's chin. She winced and covered the pooch's muzzle. "No biting."

"If you hadn't just said you were puppy sitting, I'd wonder what was going on over there," Sam said on a chuckle. "You've really got a puppy there?"

"Well, I don't have a man," Tabby returned darkly.

"You would if you ever said yes to the guys who ask you out."

"Is this a lecture on my love life or an invitation to girls' night?"

"You don't have a love life."

"Don't remind me." Tabby redirected the puppy's interest away from chewing on her face again. "*No biting.* And I don't recall you being in the company of any eligible males lately."

"I work with a few dozen every day."

"Socially."

"Ah, well, that's a different story. Sure you don't want to come? Get one of your neighbors to watch the pooch?"

It would serve Justin right if she closed Beastie in his apartment, unsupervised. Let the little girl go crazy, chewing and knocking things over. Maybe give him a nice puddle to slip in when he got home.

"He deserves it, but you don't," she murmured to the dog.

"Talking Greek there, girlfriend."

Tabby tucked the phone against her shoulder and leaned over to set the puppy on the floor. "Sorry, Sam. I would come if I could. A girls' night sounds like just the ticket right now, but I can't."

"This have anything to do with your hunky renter's marital plans?"

Ugh. "Where'd you hear?"

Sam snorted softly. "In the line at Shop-World while I was buying kale and green tea. In the salon when I stopped in to get my hair trimmed. At the Gas 'n' Go when I was filling up. Plus, Hayley and Seth were at the diner this morning. Shall I go on?"

Tabby closed her eyes. "That's what this sudden girls' night is about?" Yes, she was friends with Sam, but they'd only met up the way she was suggesting a few times before.

"Nope. Seth's honestly working. I haven't had sex in six months, and I'm looking for a likely prospect at Colbys. But a girl always needs her wingmen."

Despite herself, Tabby chuckled. It was hard not to,

when it came to Sam. "Fine. But I still have a puppy here who shouldn't be left to her own devices."

"Bring her along, then," Sam said. "Put her in a purse and carry her on your arm like some rich girl from Beverly Hills."

"I don't have a dog-friendly purse," Tabby said drily. But she did have a veterinarian brother. "Fine." She pushed out of her blanket cocoon again and stood. "What time will you be there?"

"Sevenish."

Allowing her enough time to shower, dress and drop off Beastie at Evan's. "All right. But if I end up not showing, don't worry about me. It just means my brother couldn't watch the dog after all."

"Fair enough." Sam rang off, and Tabby looked down at the puppy. She'd sprawled beneath the glass-topped coffee table and was trying to wrap her jaws around one of the wooden legs.

"Sure," Tabby said, tugging the dog free and propping her against her shoulder. "Leave scars. It's only fitting."

The puppy shivered with delight and slathered Tabby's neck with her tongue.

An hour later, freshly showered and dressed in the most presentable pair of jeans she possessed and a thick oat-colored knit turtleneck, she left her house with Beastie on the leash and headed toward her 1979 Buick parked in the triple-wide driveway.

She had just spread a towel on the backseat for Beastie to sit on when Justin's truck pulled up.

She wanted to ignore him. To settle Beastie on the backseat, get in her car and drive away.

But Beastie was *his* dog.

His and Gillian's.

So she crossed her arms and leaned back against the open door and waited.

She didn't have to wait long. The truck's headlights had barely gone out before he climbed out and his long stride carried him rapidly across the lawn.

"That's *your* car?"

She stiffened. "You're not exactly driving the newest model off the production floor." And she happened to know that he didn't even own a vehicle in Boston. "I bought it from Mrs. Wachowski when she had to give up driving. It was her husband's."

He stopped a foot away. "I only meant—" He shook his head, looking impatient. "Where have you been all day?"

"I'm sorry. I wasn't aware that I had to account to you for my personal time. I guess I missed that clause in my employment contract at Ruby's."

"Dammit, Tab—"

"Here." She pushed Beastie into his arms.

"What the hell?"

"Don't drop her. She's just a baby."

"I know what she is!"

The puppy whined, and Tabby snatched her back, cuddling her against her chin. "If you're going to yell, then maybe I should wait until Gillian gets here!"

He shoved his fingers through his hair, and even though the three porch lights on the front of the triplex weren't very bright, she could see he'd left the thick, dark blond strands standing on end. "Gillian was here," he said, sounding like he was talking through his teeth.

"Obviously." Tabby stroked the puppy's back. "She

dumped off your puppy on Mrs. Wachowski. So where is she?"

"Mrs. Wachowski?"

Tabby very nearly stomped her boot. "Gillian!"

The puppy woofed shrilly and Tabby patted her shaking back. "Sorry, Beastie."

"Beastie?"

"Well, your *fiancée* didn't see fit to tell Mrs. Wachowski what this little girl's name was, much less leave any food or toys. So what is her name?"

"I have no idea," he shouted.

Tabby cuddled the puppy. "I warned you about yelling." She pushed the car door closed and headed toward her front door.

Justin grabbed her elbow from behind. "Not so fast."

She yanked free. "Don't touch me!" Beastie whined again, and she tucked her against her other shoulder, patting her again to calm her. "All the years I've known you, I've *never* thought you were a liar, Justin Clay. But to lie about Gillian? What good did that do you? Is your ego so monumental that you needed your childhood friend to swallow your story, hook, line and sinker? What was the point, when you *had* to know I'd learn the truth sooner or later? For God's sake. Why couldn't you have just admitted you were marrying her?"

"I am *not* marrying Gillian." He was talking through his teeth again. "I did not lie about her. I did not *lie* about one damn thing. You're more than a childhood friend. You're my best friend. And she was supposed to take that bloody puppy with her this morning when I told her to leave me the hell alone."

Tabby gave a disbelieving sniff. "The entire town has heard about your engagement."

"Yeah, and the Weaver grapevine proves itself to be as inaccurate as it always is. Something I spent an hour reminding my *mother* about when she called me on the carpet for not telling her the supposed news."

"If you told Gillian to leave, what was she doing coming here and leaving Beastie with Mrs. Wachowski?"

He threw his arms out to his sides. "It'd take more brilliance than I possess to ever explain why Gillian does what she does!" He let his arms drop. "She's bat-crap crazy. You going to believe the word of a crazy person or the guy you've known your whole damn life? I told you Gillian and I were through."

Tabby set Beastie on the ground between them, and the puppy immediately squatted, leaving another puddle on the cement driveway. Then she stood, looking up at them and wagging her curving tail so enthusiastically her butt swayed back and forth, too.

"And I warned you that you weren't," Tabby said and handed him the leash.

Then she got in the ancient car, started up the engine and drove away.

She'd never felt more in need of a girls' night.

"He really said she was bat-crap crazy?" Sam Dawson propped her elbow on the round high-top table they were occupying at Colbys and leaned closer.

Tabby had already gone through the story once. "The point is—" she drained her wineglass and reached for the bottle sitting between her and Sam and Hayley "—Gillian left him with a *dog*. They're not through. They'll never be through."

Hayley's eyes were compassionate. She was the town

psychologist, so Tabby figured that expression was simply ingrained. "And that is upsetting to you because…"

"Because he's my friend," Tabby muttered. "She's yanked him around on the 'Gillian chain—'" she air quoted the term with her fingers "—for years now."

"But if she is his choice, then as his *friend*, shouldn't you be happy for him?"

Tabby glared at Sam. "Whose side are you on?"

Sam grinned and lifted her hands peaceably. "Just playing devil's advocate here."

"Well, don't." Tabby took another sip of wine. Okay, perhaps more than a sip. Her adrenaline was pumping so strongly, she felt as though she was going to vibrate off the bar stool. "He's got terrible taste in women. He always has."

"Sure, 'cause those women aren't you," Sam returned.

Tabby's lips parted. "I don't know what you mean," she lied. But it was a half beat too late, and she saw the look Sam and Hayley exchanged.

She exhaled noisily. "You have a service weapon, Sam. Just shoot me."

"Ha-ha." Sam rolled her eyes. "What you need—" she leaned forward again "—is a man. Someone to get horizontal with and make you forget the unattainable one."

Hayley tsked. "Sam. Honestly."

"What? She's single and well past the age of consent. So—" Sam gestured at the bar, where a half dozen men in jeans and boots were hanging out, drinking beer and watching the television hanging on the wall at the end of the glossy wooden bar top "—take a gander."

"I've known every one of them since I was in diapers," Tabby objected. "I couldn't have a romantic thought about them if I had *three* bottles of wine." She poured more into her glass and frowned a little when she got only a few drops.

"What about one you haven't known all your life?" Sam nudged her boot under the table when the front door of Colbys opened and two tall men—both wearing green hospital scrubs beneath their coats—walked in. "That's Scott Brown with Wyatt Mead. He just started working at the hospital last year. And he comes from Braden."

"How do you know that?"

"Because I had to write Mr. Brown a speeding ticket this summer. He tried talking his way out of it by saying how he was new here and stuff."

Hayley chuckled and shook her head. "I guess that's *one* way of eliciting information."

"Have you known *him* all of your life?" Sam's voice was challenging.

The thought of going out with someone held no appeal. But she couldn't spend her days pining after Justin, either. She'd never move out of the perpetual friend category with him. He'd made that abundantly clear.

But Justin was going to be in Weaver until January. She couldn't escape that fact. So if she didn't want to spend her spare time cleaning kennel cages at her brother's practice to avoid running into him at the triplex, or cocooned in her blankets, or drowning herself in a bottle of wine, she'd better come up with an alternative.

Buoyed by adrenaline and wine and hurt she had no business feeling, anyway, she slapped her hand lightly on the top of their table. "You're right," she told Sam, and hopped off the high bar stool.

Scott and Wyatt had reached the bar and were waiting to give their orders to Merilee, who was bartending that night. Tabby stopped next to them. "Hey, Wyatt." She didn't give herself a chance to stop and get all girlie and stupid. "How're you doing? Haven't seen you in Ruby's in a few weeks." The tall, lanky nurse usually stopped by for coffee several times a week.

Wyatt looked chagrined. "Yeah, I've been—"

"Getting his morning coffee fix from his new squeeze," his companion said easily and stuck out his hand toward Tabby. "I'm Scott."

She set her hand in his. He had a good grip. "Tabby."

"Buy you a drink, Tabby?"

Despite her intention of introducing herself to *him*, Tabby was a little nonplussed at the way the tables had turned so quickly.

So easily.

"Um…sure. Red wine. Jane's got a nice house red." Scott had a nice smile, she decided while he ordered drinks. Not too friendly. Not too wicked. And his eyes were a very ordinary brown. Not an otherworldly shade of purplish blue.

She slid onto the empty bar stool between the two men when Scott pulled it out for her. "So are you an RN like Wyatt?"

Scott shook his head. "I work in the lab."

"He usually works nights," Wyatt told her. He pulled a folded clip of cash out of his pocket and paid Merilee when she delivered their drinks. "Next round's on you, bud," he told Scott.

"I took a shift today for one of the guys on days," Scott said. "Now I'm particularly glad I did." He smiled at her and tapped the edge of his wineglass—also red—against the edge of hers.

Tabby smiled and sipped her wine.

He worked in the lab. *Where Justin is temporarily working.* She gave the voice in her head a mental shove.

"So you own Ruby's?"

She shook her head, letting out a rueful laugh. "I only manage it." *For Justin.*

She shoved harder.

"Haven't made it over there," Scott said. "But everyone around the hospital says it's the best place for breakfast."

"I like to think so. We have a great crew working there." She looked at Wyatt. "But I guess our coffee is taking second place to someone else's. Who is she?"

Wyatt flushed a little. "She's new in town. Works out at Cee-Vid designing computer games."

"Well, I think that's great," she said sincerely. Wyatt was a genuinely nice guy. He deserved to find a genuinely nice girl. "I hope it works out for you."

"She'll be with me at the hospital fund-raiser next weekend," he said. "You're going to be there, right?"

She'd forgotten about the fund-raiser again. "I am." She looked at Scott. "My brother has the vet practice in town. He bought a table and needs people to fill the chairs so it won't be empty. What about you?"

"Dr. Clay wants to trot out the lab rats at the event," he said humorously. "So, yeah. I'll be there."

"You two should go together," Wyatt suggested, looking enthusiastic. "And double with me and Kristen."

Scott lifted his eyebrows. "What d'ya say? You won't

have to sit at your brother's table *all* evening long, will you?"

Tabby hesitated. She glanced over her shoulder at Sam and Hayley. Sam was giving her a none-too-subtle thumbs-up. But it was the sight of Justin walking through the front door of Colbys that made the decision for her.

She looked back at Scott.

"I think it sounds perfect," she said. "I'd love to go with you to the fund-raiser."

Chapter Nine

"Hey, Justin. Heard congratulations are in order."
Sally Gunderson smiled up from the table where she sat
outside the large white tent that had been set up behind
the hospital to house the fund-raiser. He remembered
her easily from high school, pretty much because she
hadn't changed a lick. "Here are your drink tickets."
She handed over two red tickets that she peeled off a
big roll. "Is your fiancée with you?"

After a week of explaining to everyone who mentioned it that he was *not* engaged, Justin was heartily
sick of it. "No." He tucked the tickets in the pocket of
the suit coat he'd borrowed from Jake. JD's husband
was one of the few guys in town to actually own a suit
that wasn't twenty years old. Justin's dad had plenty,
but he'd have looked like a kid playing dress-up if he'd
tried to wear one of Tristan's jackets. Justin was tall. But
he wasn't a freaking Paul Bunyan the way his dad was.

He focused on Sally. There were several racks standing behind her tables that were loaded down with coats.
"I'm supposed to sit at one of the tables the Double-C
purchased. Are they marked, or what?"

"Yup." She handed over a small tented place card. "Double-C" had been printed on one side and a number on the other. "Number four," she said, needlessly, since he could read well enough. "You're the last one to get here." She waved her hand over the table where only a few place cards remained. "But you're still here in plenty of time for dinner. They haven't even finished the speeches yet."

"Thanks." He wanted to attend the fund-raiser the way he wanted to have a hole drilled in his head. He knew that his dad had bought two tables on Cee-Vid's behalf, but the seats were already divvied up among various members of his staff. Which left the seats at the tables his grandfather had gotten on behalf of the family ranch.

Squire had called Justin personally to command his attendance. Just because they hadn't expected him to still be in town when the tickets had been purchased months ago didn't mean that Justin wasn't expected to attend now. He was a Clay. And Clays had always shown their support for the hospital.

So Justin had borrowed the suit coat, bought a tie at Classic Charms on his lunch break that afternoon and here he was.

He stepped through the heavy plastic sheeting that served as the doorway for the party tent just as the attendees—at least two hundred, he was guessing—started clapping.

His aunt Rebecca was standing at the podium on the raised dais. She'd obviously just finished her speech, and he made his way past the empty dance floor area and around the perimeter of the tent to the table in the front row bearing a number four on the stand in the center of it. There was only one empty seat. It faced away from the dais and would have him looking back across the rest of the tables. Feeling self-conscious, he quickly crossed in front of the dais, yanked out the chair and sat.

"You're late," his cousin Casey said out the side of his mouth. "How'd you rate?"

Justin smiled across the table at his grandfather and grandmother, who were seated directly opposite him and Casey. Squire's gaze was steely; Gloria's smile was much more forgiving. "Lost track of time working."

It was partly true. The other part was having to clean up puppy poop, because the puppy had managed to get herself out of the temporary pen he'd fashioned in the living room of his apartment.

"Must be nice," Casey muttered and started clapping again when Jane elbowed him in the side.

Justin couldn't count the number of similar events he'd attended in Boston on behalf of CNJ. The company was always sponsoring one thing or another, and Charles wanted those he considered his key people to be familiar faces at them. Justin even had several custom-made suits hanging in his closet back in Boston. But he was happier wearing his borrowed suit coat from Jake.

It didn't hold a speck of Gillian's influence.

Finally, the applause died down. Rebecca thanked everyone for their support—which spurred another round of applause—and announced that the main course was being served.

That's when Justin noticed the catering crew positioned around the tent. At Rebecca's signal, they began pulling china plates from big metal carts. Salads and rolls were already on the tables.

"Where'd the catering come from?" The fancy carts

made the thing Tabby had used for the tree lighting seem like a toy.

"Cheyenne." His cousin Courtney was sitting on his other side. She was an RN at the hospital. "They came up with a ton of equipment and used the hospital kitchen to finish up. I heard it was a huge task to coordinate."

"Impressive." There was at least one server per table, so delivering the meals was accomplished with remarkable efficiency. Justin hoped the rest of the evening went with similar speed.

Mostly because he'd just spotted Tabby sitting one row over. She wasn't facing him. All he got was the fine line of her profile. But that was enough.

It had been a week since Gillian had come to town, just long enough to rain her particular brand of chaos all over his life. He had a no-name puppy that howled at night unless he let her sleep on his bed. No matter how often he corrected them, he still had people all over town thinking he was engaged to be married. And he had a landlord named Tabby who treated him like a stranger.

No, he corrected himself, as he watched her smile and converse with the other people seated around her. She treated strangers with more warmth than she offered him.

It was even worse than it had been four years ago, when he'd betrayed their entire friendship by getting her into bed.

Then, he'd felt like the biggest crumb on the planet.

Now, he was just pissed. Plain and simple.

She believed he'd lied. She'd rather believe the baloney that Gillian had spewed than the guy she'd known her whole life.

What the hell kind of friendship was that?

Courtney kicked him lightly beneath the table. "You're scowling," she said under her breath.

He wiped the frown off his face and realized everyone at his table had nearly finished their meal while he'd been sitting there fuming. He stabbed his fork into the salmon like it still needed killing and ate enough to avoid a questioning look from the server when she picked up his plate along with the others. It was replaced in short order with dessert—an assortment of crème brûlée, chocolate mousse and some little fruit tart—that he had no interest in, either. But before he could push it away, Courtney stole the entire lot, smiling innocently.

People were starting to move around the room, anyway, making visits to the bars spaced along one side of the heated tent, and he excused himself and went to the nearest one. He handed over one of the red tickets in exchange for a neat shot of whiskey that he tossed back in one gulp. Then he traded his second ticket for a bottle of beer.

When he looked around again, Tabby was no longer sitting at the table with her brother and his cousin Leandra, but he spotted her quickly enough in the center of the dance floor, where she stood out like a white beacon among a sea of little black dresses.

There was a DJ spinning music. It had been pretty much in the background through dinner, but now that the meal was over, the volume and pace had picked up, and Justin watched her dance. It took him a minute to realize the guy she was dancing with was Scott Brown from the hospital lab.

It was the lack of pale green scrubs, he decided.

Someone clapped him on the shoulder. "Yo, Justin. Heard you got hitched. Congratulations, man."

He just shook his head and shook off the hand. "Not married," he said. "Not getting married, either." He waded his way to the center of the dance floor, stopping next to Scott and Tabby. "Mind if I cut in?"

Scott looked surprised, but he started to move aside.

Tabby, on the other hand, gave Justin a searing look. "I mind," she said and quickly linked her hands behind Scott's neck.

Justin watched the other man's hands slide down the shimmering white fabric covering her back and took a long pull on his beer. Tabby's dress reached her thighs, leaving a whole lot of long, shapely leg uncovered.

She definitely didn't have skinned knees anymore.

The fact that people were having to dance around him didn't faze him in the least. "Guess I'll just wait, then," he said, meeting Tabby's fuming eyes with his own.

It was obvious as hell that Scott recognized he was caught in the middle of some sort of skirmish. And equally obvious to Justin that the other man wasn't particularly bothered by that fact.

Not if the guy's hands wrapped around Tabby's waist were anything to go by.

Fortunately, the song ended fairly quickly. During the commotion of people moving on and off the dance floor as the next song cranked up, Scott murmured something close to Tabby's ear that Justin couldn't hear and moved away from them.

Justin grabbed Tabby's hand before she could follow and yanked her close. "Whispering sweet nothings to you already?"

Her body was as stiff as a board, and the grimace of a smile she gave him was just as bad. "Whether he is or isn't, it's none of *your* business. You're bruising my wrist."

"I'm not holding you that tight," he retorted. But he lightened his grip all the same. Not enough to let her weasel out of it—a tactic she immediately tried. When she failed, she planted her sharp, high heel on the toe of his shoe. "Play nice," he warned. "At least for the benefit of the people watching."

She turned up her nose and looked away.

He wasn't able to shake some feeling back into his foot, though he wanted to. She clearly didn't care if *she* left bruises. "I'm the one who has a right to be mad."

She let out a disgusted sound, then turned on a brilliant smile as another dancing couple brushed by them. "Dee Crowder. Honest to Pete, you're the prettiest woman here tonight. I've never seen you look better."

The short, curly-headed blonde beamed back at Tabby. She taught elementary school along with one of Justin's cousins. But she was dancing with a balding man Justin didn't recognize. "The wonders of an engagement ring." Dee waggled her finger on which a diamond ring sparkled.

Tabby seemed to forget the need to mimic a wooden plank at the sight of the ring. "Oh, my goodness! You two are engaged?"

Dee nodded and her curls bounced. "Joe proposed on Thanksgiving Day."

Tabby laughed and gave the balding guy a pointed look. "It's about *time* y'all got your act together."

"Joe felt he needed to go to the school board first."

Justin's curiosity got the better of him. His mom was head of the school board. "School board? What for?"

Tabby blinked. "Oh. Sorry. I guess if you spent more time in Weaver, you'd have met." She delivered the jab along with the introduction. "Joe Gage. Principal at the elementary school. Justin Clay."

The balding guy stretched out a hand, which meant Justin had to release his grip on Tabby so he could reciprocate. "Nice to meet you. My mom used to teach at the elementary school. Hope Clay."

"Hope is your mom? She's a good lady." Joe dropped his arm over Dee's shoulder. She was nodding enthusiastically.

"Hope's one of the only voices of reason on the board," Dee said. "She thought it was ridiculous that Joe needed their permission before he proposed to me. Just because I teach at his school."

"It wasn't permission so much as hoping to avoid a gossip scandal," Joe said wryly. "You know what this town is like."

"Well, I for one couldn't be happier for the two of you," Tabby said. "Have you set a date?"

"It won't be until summer," Dee said. "After the school year is finished."

"Guess you'll have to find a new name for your poker group," Tabby said with a laugh.

Dee laughed, too, and swung back into Joe's arms. The couple two-stepped off to the latest song the DJ was playing.

Which left Tabby and Justin standing, again, in the middle of the dance floor.

"*You're* the prettiest woman here tonight," he said abruptly. "And for the record, I've never once lied to you. Not about Gillian. Not about anything. Not in our entire lives." Then, before she could respond, he turned and walked off the dance floor.

Scott was there waiting, two drinks in his hands.

"You hurt her, you'll answer to me," Justin said softly as he passed him, and he didn't stop until he'd left the tent altogether.

Tabby's cheeks felt as though they were on fire as she watched Justin walk away, leaving her standing there by herself in the middle of the dance floor.

The last time she'd felt remotely like this had been four years ago. At least then there had been no one to witness it.

She saw Scott on the periphery of the dance floor. A perfectly nice guy who deserved a girl equally as nice. Equally as interested.

Someone entirely different from Tabby.

She sighed and headed toward him. "Scott, I'm sorry, but I—" She stopped when he pushed two drinks into her hands.

"Dr. Clay's calling out her lab rats," he said, making her realize that Rebecca had taken the podium again and was calling up various members of the hospital staff. "Shouldn't take long."

Tabby smiled weakly and gave a last glance toward the tent's entrance. She wasn't going to walk out on Scott without at least explaining first. Which meant she was stuck there, at least for now.

"It's so exciting, isn't it?" Wyatt's girlfriend, Kristen, came up to stand next to Tabby.

Tabby shook herself a little and looked at the young woman. "I'm sorry. What's exciting?"

Kristen gave her an odd look. "Vivian Templeton's donation." She raised her eyebrows a little. "For the lab? It puts them over the top of what they needed to raise."

"Oh, right." Tabby smiled, even though she didn't have a clue. "It's very exciting."

"I wonder why she didn't come tonight," Kristen went on, apparently satisfied with Tabby's level of excitement. "If *I* were going to donate a couple million dollars to something, I sure would want to show my face." She giggled. "If I ever even had a couple million dollars. Talk about a fantasy, right?"

"Right."

Kristen soon went off in search of Wyatt, and since Scott was still standing on the dais along with the other lab staff, Tabby found an abandoned table and set down the drinks. Then she went out to the table where Sally was still sitting and retrieved her coat. "If Scott asks, tell him I went to powder my nose, will you?"

"Sure."

It was just an excuse. She made her way around the tent, hoping for some sign of Justin.

She didn't see him. Nor did she see that old truck he was using in the hospital parking lot.

Finally, she gave up and went back into the tent, where the DJ had started up again. The music was even louder, and Tabby wasn't surprised to see some people starting to make their exit. She stepped aside to wait while they retrieved coats and scarves from the racks behind Sally's table.

"Tabby, honey." Hope stopped in surprise at the sight of her. "Are you leaving, too?"

She glanced down at her coat that she hadn't yet removed. "Uh, no. Not just yet." She'd never felt awkward around Justin's mother in the past, and she hated feeling that way now. She pushed her fists into the side pockets. "That was quite some news about Mrs. Templeton's donation."

"Wasn't it?" Hope smiled slightly and held out her arms when Tristan came back with her long wool coat. She smiled up at him as he helped her on with it. "I thought Squire was going to choke on the news, though. Evidently, he was already up in arms because of the Christmas party Vivian's invited all of the family to. Courtney told me the only reason he didn't get up and leave tonight after the donation announcement was because Gloria hissed at him to sit back down."

"Want me to go warm up the car?"

Hope shook her head at Tristan. "No need. I'm too anxious to get out of these high heels." She stuck out her elegantly shod foot from beneath the hem of her long, swinging coat. "I love an excuse to get all dressed up, but there's always a cost."

"Yeah. To my wallet," Tristan drawled. He gave a quick a wink and the two of them headed off.

Sighing faintly, Tabby pulled aside the heavy plastic doorway and went back into the tent. She didn't have to feign a headache when she finally found Scott where he was standing with a bunch of folks from the hospital. Her head was pounding for real.

He took one look at the coat she was still wearing and peeled himself away from the others. "I wondered where you'd gotten to. You all right?"

"Just too much wine and music. Would you mind if I called it a night?"

He shook his head. "Of course not. Let me tell Wyatt we're leaving."

"You don't have to go. I'm practically around the corner."

"You're not walking home."

She could tell from his expression there was no point in arguing. And again, she knew he deserved better company than he'd gotten from her.

Which was exactly what she told him when they pulled up in front of her triplex a short while later. "I'm sorry. You should go back to the fund-raiser," she told him. "You have a lot to celebrate tonight."

"Definitely was a surprise about that Templeton lady's donation." He smiled slightly, obviously noticing her hand on the door handle. "Mind if I ask you a question?"

"Of course not."

"What's going on between you and Justin?"

"Nothing." She quickly looked away from the sight of his old truck parked on the street ahead of them. "Nothing good, anyway."

"So you cutting the night short doesn't have anything to do with him?"

She opened her mouth to say it didn't. But the words wouldn't come. "I'm sorry," she said again. "We just, um, Justin and I used to be friends."

Scott shifted, stretching his hand over the back of her seat. "Sure about that? Because it felt to me like there wasn't a lot of *used to be* going on between the two of you. What it felt like was that there was a whole lot going on right now."

Her cheeks heated. "It's not like that."

He waited a beat. Then he shrugged. "Okay. It's not like it's in my best interest to convince you otherwise." His fingertips toyed with the ends of her hair. "But I figure if we're going to try this again sometime—without Wyatt and his sweet nitwit of a girlfriend—I'd just as soon know what kind of odds I'm looking at."

"Why would you even want to go out with me again?"

"Beautiful. *Not* a nitwit." He chuckled. "Two positives right there."

"You're hard not to like," she admitted ruefully. "But—"

"But you're hung up on the guy who *used* to be your friend."

She exhaled. "Scott—"

"I know. I'm a nice guy. But." He suddenly leaned forward and kissed her.

She was so surprised, all she did was sit there, and then he sat back again.

"That wasn't too bad, was it?"

It hadn't set rockets off inside her, but it hadn't exactly been like kissing a toad, either. "No."

"So, if you decide what used to be really is a used to be, give me a call."

She smiled and pushed open the car door. "G'night, Scott."

"Night, Tabby."

He didn't drive away until she unlocked her front door and went inside. Not bothering to turn on a light, she dropped her keys on the table by the door and discarded her coat on the couch before going to stand in front of the window. There was a streetlight on the corner that cast its glow wide enough to encompass Justin's truck sitting in front of the triplex.

Before she could talk herself out of it, she dashed

back outside, trotted past Mrs. Wachowski's dark windows and knocked on his door.

The second she did, the puppy started barking.

Then she heard Justin telling the dog to be quiet, and he yanked open the door. "What?"

She looked from the squirming puppy he was holding to his annoyed face.

Then she stepped close, pulled his head down and pressed her mouth to his.

He yanked back, staring at her like she'd lost her mind. "What the hell was that for?"

"Rockets," she snapped, and turning on her heel, raced back to her apartment.

She slammed the door behind her and flipped the lock.

Even through the walls, she could hear the puppy still barking.

"Damn rockets," she said thickly.

She stomped into her studio, snatched up the blizzard painting that she'd never been able to part with and added it to the pile waiting to be shipped off to Bolieux.

Then she sat down on the floor and cried.

Chapter Ten

"Tabby," Bubba barked from the kitchen, drawing her attention away from the coffee brewer she was cleaning. "Phone."

She set down the scrub brush, peeled off her rubber gloves and went into the kitchen. It was Monday afternoon, past closing time, but she and Bubba were taking care of some of the heavy-duty cleaning chores. She grabbed the receiver where it was hanging loose by the twisting, coiled cord. "Hello?"

"Tabby, dear. I'm so sorry to bother you at work."

She recognized the voice immediately. "Mrs. Wachowski. What's wrong?"

"It's Justin's puppy, I'm afraid. She's just howling so miserably. Has been all afternoon. I'm afraid she's going to make herself ill. I tried calling Justin at the hospital, but I couldn't reach him. I don't know what else to do."

Tabby held back a sigh. Since she'd kissed him the other night, she hadn't seen or heard from him.

As if she'd needed *more* proof of his romantic disinterest.

"I'll take care of it, Mrs. Wachowski."

"You're such a sweet girl. I knew you would, dear."

After she hung up, she let the sigh loose. She looked at Bubba, whose upper body was nearly engulfed by the oven he was repairing. "I have to run home for a few minutes," she told him and got only a few metallic bangs in response.

She had her car with her because she'd planned to ship the paintings after she was finished at the diner, so running back to the triplex took even less time than usual. As soon as she parked in the driveway, she could hear the puppy's sharp, frantic yipping.

She found the spare keys she kept for the other two units in her bedroom dresser and let herself in through Justin's door.

He'd attempted to make a temporary cardboard pen for the puppy in the living room. That was immediately obvious. Equally obvious, though, was the fact that the creative little dog had managed to eat her way through it. There were scraps of half-eaten cardboard everywhere, as well as what looked like pillow stuffing and a shredded leash.

"Oh, Beastie," Tabby murmured and caught the puppy before she could dash out the open door. She picked up the dog, who was no longer barking shrilly but lavishing her chin with wet licks, and turned her back on the mess. She relocked the door behind her and set the puppy on the brown grass, hoping that she'd tinkle.

Instead, the animal started to take off after a blowing leaf, and Tabby caught her up again just in time to keep her from running into the street. "You need a new leash. A chain one this time."

With the dog standing on her passenger seat, front

paws propped on the dashboard, Tabby drove to her brother's vet practice. His office manager told Tabby he was out on a call, but she was still able to buy a leash there, a tie chain and a few chew toys. Then she drove back to the diner and fixed Beastie up with the chain outside the rear door.

"It's not perfect," she said, crouching down beside the little dog to scratch her ears. "But you've been cooped up inside long enough. Now you can chase all the leaves you want while I finish up here, and the chain will keep you from running out where you're not supposed to be." The puppy yapped and bounced up to lick Tabby's face again, then snatched the squeaky chew toy when Tabby tossed it.

With the dog happily occupied, she went inside.

Bubba had finished the oven repair and had taken up where Tabby had left off on the coffee brewer.

"I can finish that if you want to take off."

"Nah. Nearly done, anyway." He picked up a jug of water and poured it in the brewer. "Run a few gallons of water through it, she's good as new."

Tabby sat on a stool. "And the oven? You think the new heating element will keep it going for a while, or is it time to start thinking replacement?" The oven had been ancient even when Tabby began working at the diner so many years ago. "With the space it takes up, we could have something newer and a lot more efficient."

He grunted in agreement. "Yeah. But newer ain't always better. 'N' you've been baking cinnamon rolls in there for more years than I remember."

"Ruby told me she bought that oven secondhand the very first year she turned a profit on this place. Back then she used it for everything. Not just the rolls." Tabby propped her chin on her hand, staring blindly at the diner around her. "Maybe the reason the rolls are so popular is because I'm still using her old oven."

Bubba snorted and poured another jug of water through the brewer. "Maybe the reason is 'cause you make great rolls and any old oven would do."

She chewed the inside of her lip. "So, you think it might be time to give up on old...habits?"

He gave her a strange look. "I'm saying any working oven'll do." He finished draining the brewer one last time and dumped the water down the sink. "And the brewer's done, so I'm outta here, unless you got somethin' else you need me to do."

She shook her head. You go on, Bubba." She knew he was cooking for Vivian Templeton that evening. "Thanks."

He lifted his hand in a wave and disappeared through the swinging doors to the kitchen. A moment later, she heard the back door slam shut. It opened a second later, though. "You know you got a pooch chained up out here," he yelled.

"Yes, I do, Bubba. See you in the morning."

Her answer was the slam of the metal door again.

She pushed off the stool and finished tidying up, then went to check on the dog. Beastie had managed to wind her chain around the base of the picnic table, limiting her range. "You're making things hard on yourself, little girl. Trust me. I recognize the tendency." She unclipped the puppy from the chain and carried her to the car, setting her on the passenger seat again. "Now you've got to behave," she warned. "Just because my car is old doesn't mean I want you chewing or peeing on the seats."

The puppy cocked her head then yipped and jumped onto Tabby's lap.

"Wish everyone were as agreeable as you." Tabby kissed the dog's silky head and set her aside again before driving all the way to the shipping office in Braden. With the leashed dog by her side, she went inside and mailed off her paintings. Then she picked up some Chinese takeout for her supper and drove back to Weaver, though she had to stop halfway there to put the takeout containers in the trunk, because Beastie kept trying to nuzzle her way into them.

The sun was nearly down by the time she got home. Justin's truck was parked in front of the triplex.

She blew out a breath as she pushed open the car door and gathered the puppy in her arms. "Come on, little girl. Time for you to go home." She nudged the car door closed with her hip, walked reluctantly to the Justin's apartment and knocked.

He answered immediately, reminding her much too vividly of the last time she'd knocked on his door. "Here." She held the puppy out to him. "Mrs. Wachowski called me about the barking."

"She told me."

"Get a kennel cage," she advised. "Before she chews her way through everything you own. She also needs toys. And her shots if she hasn't had them yet."

"How would I know if she's had her shots?"

She smiled tightly. "Ask Gillian." She started to walk away. Then swore under her breath and looked back at him. "I can watch the dog for you in the afternoon after I close up the diner. She's a baby. She's lonely. And I don't particularly want to have to replace the furniture for the next renter." She continued on her way.

"Tabby—"

Even though she'd been determined not to react to him, she felt her nerves tighten. "Don't have time to talk," she lied. "I'm on my way over to my parents'."

"You didn't used to be a coward."

Her jaw tightened. If she were a coward, she never would have kissed him the way she had the other night. She was, however, an idiot for having done so. Even now, her skin felt as though it was burning with humiliation beneath her clothes. But she turned and faced him again, propping her hand on her hip impatiently. "What?"

"Erik added you to the bank account for the diner."

It was the very last thing she expected him to say. "What?"

"All you need to do is sign a card at the bank tomorrow."

She dropped her hand from her hip. "What are you talking about?"

"The diner."

"I know you mean the diner! Why would he do that? Everything worked perfectly well the way it was."

"Because I told him it was stupid when you ran everything else there, and he agreed. Why are you looking all pissed off?" He closed the puppy inside and headed toward her on the sidewalk. "I thought you'd be happy. You don't have to wait on Erik every time you need to pay a bill."

"How many times do I have to say that our system worked just fine? And why are you suddenly acting interested in the way the diner is run?"

"I thought you'd be happy," he repeated. "Dammit, Tabby, what do you want from me? You act like you still hate me. Then you think I lied about Gillian. Then you plant that…that kiss—"

"It was a mistake," she said quickly, before he could go any further. "A stupid mistake."

"But—"

"I've really got to go. You know how mom hates dinner to be late." A ridiculous statement, considering her mother's easygoing personality. Tabby continued backing away. "Evan can get you a kennel. Maybe even loan you one while you're here."

"Tabby—"

She turned on her heel and jogged the short distance to her car, proving she really was a coward after all. "I'll talk to Erik about the bank account," she said and quickly got in, cranking the engine so hard a belch of smoke came out the tailpipe.

She backed out onto the street and drove away.

She saw the red glow of his cigarette before she made out the shape of him sitting in the dark on her front porch.

She'd killed as much time at her folks' house as she could without drawing suspicion. As it was, while she helped her mother wrap Christmas gifts, she'd had to derail Jolie's none-too-subtle remarks about "things" she'd been hearing around town concerning Tabby and Justin. Hiding out there any longer than she had would only have made it worse. It was nearly ten and her parents knew she was the poster child for early to bed, early to rise.

And, evidently, Tabby could only be a coward for so long before even she found herself intolerable.

She closed the car door and clasped the sides of her

coat together in front of her, walking slowly toward him. "You don't seem to be giving them up."

The red glow moved upward and flared briefly as he took a drag. "Don't seem to be," he agreed. "You going to talk to me now, or what?"

It was annoying how quickly her throat went tight.

She reached the porch step and sat down beside him. The second she did, she felt a wet canine nose nudge at her hand. "Hi, Beastie." The puppy climbed onto her lap, and Tabby rubbed her fingertips against her smooth coat.

"It's a fitting name," he said. "She ate one of my shoes this afternoon."

"Get a proper kennel cage."

"I did. She figured out how to unfasten the latch."

"Admittedly brilliant on her part." The dog started crawling up her chest. "But more likely that you didn't fasten the latch properly."

"You want to tell me what that was about the other night?"

She shook her head, which, given the darkness and the fact that her porch light wasn't on, was pretty useless as a form of communication. "Not really." Then she sighed and pushed to her feet, still holding the pup. "I don't know how long you've been sitting there, but my butt is already freezing." She stepped around him and unlocked her front door. "If you're coming in, leave the cigarette outside."

A moment later, he followed her inside, squinting a little at the light she turned on. She set the dog on the floor. "Be nice."

"That a warning for the dog or for me?"

She pulled off her coat and dropped it over one of the

couch arms, and then toed off her tennis shoes. "Maybe for all three of us. You want something to drink?"

"What're you offering?" He removed his leather jacket and left it on top of her coat.

"Arsenic?" She smiled thinly and went into the kitchen. "I have water and—" she pulled open the refrigerator door "—diet soda and one beer." She reached for the beer before he even answered.

"Beer."

She closed the refrigerator and twisted off the cap, handing him the bottle. Then she filled a cereal bowl with some water and set it on the floor for Beastie. "I'm sorry about the other night," she said abruptly. She made a face. "Kissing you like that. It was—" Dumb? Foolish? Fruitless? "Was, um, wildly inappropriate."

He straddled one of her bar stools. His violet eyes studied her while he took a drink from the bottle. "Why?" he asked when he lowered it.

"Why what?"

"Why inappropriate?"

She pressed her tongue against her teeth, searching for an answer. "Because."

He raised his eyebrows. "Because…why?"

She let out a breath and left the kitchen, restlessly going down the hall into her studio.

He followed, scooping up Beastie when she tried to go between his feet. Holding the dog, he leaned his shoulder against the doorjamb. She didn't know if he did it to block her exit or not, but the result was the same either way. She plucked several brushes out of the empty can where she'd left them to dry and began organizing them.

"Tabby."

She abruptly swept all of the brushes into a drawer and slammed it shut. "It's inappropriate because we're not—" She didn't look at him as she waved her hand. "You know. Not that kind of friends. Kissing kind of friends."

He remained silent, which only added to the embarrassment burning through her.

She switched her restless attention to the closest stack of paintings against the wall. Her throat felt tighter than ever as she moved them needlessly from one wall to another.

Justin watched the overhead light shining on her dark hair as she worked. Until he'd messed things up with her four years ago, she'd been a staple in his life. But he wasn't a complete idiot. She was beautiful. He'd always been aware of that. But as she'd said, they weren't that kind of friends. So, aside from his enormous onetime transgression, he'd always done his best to ignore her appeal. Because that's the way she wanted it.

Or so he'd thought.

She'd moved the paintings back to their original places. There were only half the number he'd seen last time. As she crouched down and fussed with them, he could tell that the blizzard painting was gone.

"Maybe that's what our problem is," he said quietly.

She went still.

He set the dog on the floor and reached down to grab Tabby's hands, pulling her to her feet.

Her eyes were wide. Dark. And full of wariness.

"Pretending we weren't the kissing kind of friends," he added, just to be clear. Something in her gaze flickered, and he felt the resistance in her hands. "Don't pull away."

She didn't, though she spread her fingers, almost experimentally, as if she were still planning to. "Justin, this isn't a good idea."

"What isn't a good idea?"

Her fingers curled. "What, uh, whatever it is you're thinking about doing."

He could read her thoughts as clearly as his own.

And damn straight she knew what he was thinking.

He released one of her hands and slid his palm along her jaw. Felt her jerk a little, but not away from him. He pushed her chin up with his thumb and leaned closer. "I think it's one of the best ideas I've had in a really—" he leaned even closer "—really long time." Four years, at least.

He closed the last few inches of distance between them and pressed his mouth against hers.

He didn't close his eyes.

Nor did she.

So he saw in her eyes what he felt in the kiss.

The kick start of blood.

The sudden blast of heat.

The urgent desire for more.

He moved his hand, sliding it behind her neck, threading his fingers through her thick, silky hair, angling her head. Her eyes fluttered closed, and her hands roved over his shoulders, fingertips kneading. Then she made a soft sound, and her lips parted against his.

Whatever he'd planned—an experiment, a test, a challenge—went up in smoke. Any thought beyond getting more of Tabby Taggart was impossible.

More warm flesh beneath the sweater he dragged over her head.

More of the pulse beating like a wild thing below her ear lobe.

More of the sweeter-than-sweet taste of her tight nipple through the lace covering it. She inhaled deeply and yanked at his shirt so forcefully that he heard it rip and buttons pop. He dragged down the zipper on her jeans and pushed his hands inside.

She twined herself around him, gasping against his neck as he lifted her onto her messy worktable and buried himself inside her. She cried out, arching against him sharply as her sweet, hot spasms gloved him, luring him into oblivion.

Justin wasn't sure how long it was after that before his good sense started to return.

He was sure, however, that Tabby wasn't as slow in that regard as he was.

His heart was still pounding and the sweat on their bodies hadn't cooled before she was unwinding her legs and pushing away from him, reaching for her clothes that somehow had spread out from corner to corner of her studio.

"Tabby—"

She shook her head, throwing out her palm. "Whatever you're going to say, don't." She picked up her bra, took one look at the lace that had been torn in two and tossed it aside before yanking her sweater over her head, pulling it down past her bare thighs. "If I hear another apology from you after—" She broke off and waved the jeans she plucked off the floor. "I won't be responsible for what I do."

She might have ended up gloriously naked, but he hadn't gotten that far. He hitched up his jeans. "Well, then relax, because I'm *not* apologizing." He wasn't sure where the stamina came from after the sex storm that had just flattened him, but he was abruptly and wholly pissed. "You were more than willing, Tabbers. And neither one of us has the excuse of being drunk this time." Not that there really was any comparison to the last time.

Hell, after he'd unintentionally, drunkenly mumbled another woman's name to her four years ago, that particular party had screeched to a dead-as-a-doornail stop. There'd been no spectacular finish. No daunting fear that he might actually be in over his head where she was concerned. And damn sure no haunting suspicion that no woman was ever going to fit him as perfectly as Tabitha Taggart did.

Which was a suspicion that freaked him out more than anything else.

"Yes, well, I don't need pity sex from you, either," she said thickly as she left the room.

"What?" He followed her, stepping over his shirt on the floor as she headed down the short hall and into her bedroom. "Where the hell did you get *that* stupid idea?"

She didn't look at him. Just dumped her jeans on the bed and yanked open one of her dresser drawers to pull out a folded shirt. Then she went into the bathroom and slammed the door shut in his face.

His head started to pound. He matched it beat for beat with the palm of his hand against the wooden door. "Dammit, Tabby!"

"Go home, Justin." Maybe it was the door between them that made her voice sound thick. "Take Beastie with you."

He didn't want to go home. Didn't want to leave her.

The fact that she didn't want him, though, was too obvious to ignore.

"This isn't over," he warned through the door.

"There isn't anything *to* be over," she yelled back at him. "Do you want me to watch your dog in the afternoons or not?"

His head pounded even more. "Yes!"

Then he scooped up Beastie, who'd been chewing on his ankle, and looked the puppy in the eye. "God save me from freaking crazy females," he said through his teeth. "And that includes you, too."

Then he walked out.

Chapter Eleven

"Justin's here. He's asking to see you."

When Paulette made her announcement, Tabby didn't pull her hands out of the bread dough she was kneading. After the insanity in her studio the night before, she had been clinging to every shred of normalcy she could find.

Which, to her, meant baking rolls at Ruby's.

She was on her fifth batch even though it was the lunch rush and she should have been working the front along with the other servers.

"Just tell him to chain the dog up out back until I'm finished here," she told Paulette.

"He doesn't have a dog with him."

"Then tell him I'll pick her up at his place when I'm through. So I hope he's got her contained in her kennel."

Paulette shrugged, adjusting her apron around her waist and disappearing through the swinging doors.

"You punishing that bread dough for something?"

Tabby didn't look up. "Not now, Bubba."

"Just sayin'." He slapped a burger on the grill and reached up to the pass-through to grab the next order. "You get one of Miz Templeton's party invitations?"

She shook her head. "Nope." Which was fine with her. The last fancy-dress event she'd attended had been the hospital fund-raiser. Her emotions had been spiraling since.

The swinging door pushed open again. "Paulette—"

"I am not Paulette."

Tabby's fingertips dug into the dough. She glanced at Justin standing in the doorway and looked away just as quickly. He was wearing jeans and a leather jacket. A CNJ-logoed ball cap covered his head, the bill pulled low over his eyes. But the memory of his thick blond hair standing in spikes because of her fingers twisting through it was just as vivid in her mind as the reality of him now. "I told you last night I'd take care of Beastie."

"That's about the *only* thing you told me last night," he countered. He took another step farther into the kitchen, allowing the door to swing shut behind him.

She dashed more flour over the sticky dough. She was excruciatingly aware that Bubba was watching the two of them. "It was the only thing that needed to be said."

He snorted and moved next to the rolling cart where she was working. "What happened was unexpected, but not the end of the world," he said under his breath. "You're acting like an outraged virgin or something."

Her face caught fire. She looked from him to Bubba, who was adding more burgers to the one already sizzling on the grill, and back to Justin again. "This is neither the time nor the place," she hissed.

"Then when *is* the time and place? You were gone before dawn this morning. You had the diner locked up tight when I came by before I went to work."

She faltered for half a moment. She hadn't heard him

come by this morning. "You're the one who wants me to keep the door here locked until opening. Or have you already forgotten?"

"I haven't forgotten anything."

She scooped up the heavy mound of dough, flipped it over and slapped it back down hard against the floury board. A cloud of white exploded over the front of Justin's clothes. "Give it time," she advised.

"You used to say exactly what was on your mind," he said, swiping his hand over his jeans. "What happened?"

You. She turned away from the dough that she was going to have to throw away because of the punishment she'd been giving it and tossed a clean towel at him. "When you finish slumming it here in Weaver, you'll go back to Boston and everything'll return to normal. You won't give a thought to this place until you come back for the next holiday. Is that clear enough now?"

His expression darkened. "This is my hometown, too, Tab. I've never once considered it *slumming*. If that's the word in your head, maybe that's how *you* feel!"

Her jaw loosened. "I love Weaver. I'm not the one who is always leaving it!"

"And why is that? Maybe you're really just afraid to go out and see what else the world has to offer. Instead you stay here, comfortable ruling your Ruby's roost, dabbling with your painting and playing *spinster* poker!"

The music coming from Bubba's ancient radio suddenly shot up in volume, startling them both. Tabby gave her cook a look.

Bubba gave her a look back. "Folks around town are

already talking about the two of you. You want to give 'em even more fuel?"

Her shoulders drooped. She went over to the sink and washed away the dough clinging to her fingers. She could feel Justin watching from behind her; it was like the point of a firebrand pressing between her shoulder blades.

Then she heard the scrape of his shoe, and a moment later the door was swinging hard after him.

She blinked against the burning behind her eyes, turned off the water and blindly reached for the paper towels.

Bubba handed the roll to her.

She avoided his concerned look and tore off a few sheets to dry her hands.

"Wanna tell ol' Bubba what that was about?"

She shook her head and went over to the worktable, where she scraped the dough into the trash barrel.

"Ever consider just telling the guy how you feel?"

She frowned, continuing to scrape the wooden board with the edge of her metal spatula. "I don't know what you mean."

"Yes, you do. You got it bad for the boss. Looks like he's got it bad for you, too."

Her jaw ached from clenching it. "I can tell you that he definitely does not."

"Then what happened last night between the two of you? 'Cause something sure as shootin' did."

"Nothing happened," she lied. Because as much as she loved Bubba Bumble, she wasn't about to tell him what had happened the night before. "Your burgers are starting to burn."

They weren't.

But Bubba mercifully turned his attention back to his grill, anyway. "So, about that party of Miz Templeton's," he said, sounding faintly diffident—which was so entirely out of character for Bubba that it succeeded in penetrating Tabby's misery.

"What about it?"

"She invited me. Sent me one of her fancy invitations and everything." He pulled something from his pocket and tossed it toward her.

She wasn't quick enough to catch it. Kneeling down, she picked up the ivory square from the floor and unfolded it. "Fancier than a wedding invitation," she murmured, waving the engraved card between her fingers.

He made a face, deftly assembling the hamburgers and plating them alongside steaming-hot French fries before setting them on the pass-through. "Order up," he yelled, then looked back at Tabby. "I didn't expect her to invite me."

"Why wouldn't she? You've been cooking for her for a while now. Do you *want* to go?"

He glanced at the orders lined up in front of him and dumped more thin-sliced potatoes into the fryer. "If I don't, she might not ask me to cook for her anymore when Montrose is off. And the money's good."

"I doubt she'd do that."

He looked skeptical. "I don't know, Tabby. She's kind of a crazy old lady."

"So go, if you're worried about it. You can rent a tux in Braden, I'm sure. What's the problem?"

He cracked two eggs with one hand over the grill and pitched the shells in the trash without having to look. "Invitation says me and a guest."

For the first time all day, Tabby felt faintly amused.

"So you get to take a date. That's hardly a problem, Bubba. People all over this town are curious to see inside that mansion she's built."

He let out a disgusted grunt. "I don't wanna find a date. Some girl who'll want a *second* date."

"God forbid," she murmured drily.

"I was thinking maybe you'd go with me."

She raised her eyebrows. "Me?"

"Well, you wouldn't be expecting anything dumb from me, like flowers 'n' stuff. And you'd fit in there better than the ladies I know down at Jojo's."

Jojo's was a dive bar on the other end of town. "Thanks, I think."

"So? Party's Saturday night."

Even though she'd just been counting her blessings that she hadn't received an invitation, she smiled at him. "Sure, Bubba. Why not? I'm curious to see inside her mansion, too." At least there was no need to worry about any romantic complications. The man was like a rough-edged, well-meaning uncle.

And maybe, just maybe, it would give her an opportunity to think about something *other* than Justin.

When the lunch rush abated, she walked home, leaving Paulette to close up the restaurant. It started snowing before she got there, and by the time she'd changed into warmer clothes and liberated Beastie from the kennel cage Justin had procured, the ground was covered in a solid layer of white. This was a source of curiosity to Beastie, who approached the whole matter with obvious wariness before she found a squatworthy corner of the yard. But once she'd done her business, the mystery of the white stuff became a sudden playground, and it took Tabby quite some time before she was able to corral the mischievous pup and go inside.

She called her mom for wardrobe guidance for the Templeton party while she stood guard over the dog wolfing down puppy kibble and water. "Bubba's invitation said black tie. That's fancier than the fund-raiser was, and I had a heck of a time finding a dress for *that*. What's Mrs. Templeton thinking, anyway? This is Weaver. We don't do black tie."

Jolie laughed. "My encounters with Vivian Templeton make me believe that she expects Weaver to adjust to her rather than the other way around. I'm just glad that your father and I had an honest reason to decline the invitation we received, since he needs to be in Cheyenne this weekend. I know she only sent the invitation because I did her gown. From what I've heard, it's mostly family members she's inviting."

The Clays and the Templetons. That included Justin.

Tabby pushed aside the troublesome thought. "Bubba figures he needs to go in order to stay in her good graces," she told her mother. "I wonder if I could just rent a gown somewhere."

"Tabby! You're not going to rent a gown."

"What? Anything else seems silly when I'll only be wearing it a few hours. Bubba only needs me as his plus one. I'm hardly out to impress anyone." Especially Justin. *If* he was going to be there. Which he probably wouldn't be, anyway.

She pinched the bridge of her nose in a vain attempt to stanch her mental nonsense.

"And I've heard there are places that rent gowns," she continued. "Same as guys rent tuxedos. You don't think anything about that."

"There's nothing wrong with renting a gown if you need to," Jolie said. "But I'm a seamstress, for heaven's sake. With a daughter who has never needed a formal gown. Not even for her high school prom."

"I didn't go to prom." She'd stayed home, hiding her misery beneath an I-don't-care-about-stupid-dances attitude because Justin had taken Collette.

"My point exactly," Jolie said. "Come to the house this afternoon. We'll work up a design before dinner."

"What about Vivian's gown?"

"Already finished. See you soon." Without waiting for Tabby to offer another argument, her mother ended the call.

Tabby hung up her phone and looked down at Beastie. The puppy was lying across the toes of her boots, evidently tuckered after romping in the snow and filling her stomach. "You're lucky," Tabby said to the dog. "You never need to worry about this sort of thing."

The dog's ears didn't even twitch. She just continued snoring softly.

"Well, at least you're not chewing up anything," Tabby said.

It wasn't much. But it was something.

Justin stared at the nearly indecipherable note taped to his front door. Obviously Tabby's handwriting. Aside from the word *Beastie*, there was little that he could make out in the rest of the sentence.

He crumpled the note and went inside. He knew she wasn't home. He didn't put it past her not to answer the door if he knocked, but her car was gone.

He stepped around the empty kennel cage and threw himself down on the couch, not bothering to remove his jacket, and closed his eyes. He had less than a month left before he needed to present the finished report to Charles, but he still had twice that many days' worth of materials to get through.

Didn't help that every time he tried to concentrate on the work, he kept thinking about Tabby.

At this rate, he should have just stayed in Boston.

He'd have been equally unproductive, but at least he wouldn't have gotten tangled up with her like he had.

His cell phone vibrated, and he pulled it out of his pocket, wearily focusing on the display. It was his mother.

He hesitated for a moment, then swore softly and answered. "Hey, Mom."

"*What* is going on with you and Tabby?"

He sat up straighter. "What? Nothing."

"Then why have I been hearing all day about some fight the two of you had at Ruby's?"

God help him. "It wasn't a fight."

"I don't know what to make of all this, honey. First that business about being engaged to Gillian. Now all this with Tabby."

"There's no *all this*!" He pushed to his feet and paced around the kennel cage, because evidently he couldn't lie to his mother when he was seated.

"She's like a daughter to me, Justin. I won't tolerate any dissension between the two of you, any more than I would between you and your brother."

If only it were that easy. "There's no dissension."

"See that there isn't," she said crisply. "I don't want to be countering gossip about you long after you've returned to Boston, and you know that's what I'll be doing if people around town don't find something more interesting to speculate about."

"There's no dissension," he repeated.

"Fine." Her tone warmed a little. "Why don't you come out for dinner tonight?"

"I can't." That, at least, was the truth. "I've got too much work to do." He'd only come home long enough to see to the dog.

Who wasn't even there.

He heard his mother sigh. "Well, make sure you eat something," she said. "I know how you can get when you're involved in a project. And make sure you carve out at least a few hours Saturday evening."

"What's going on Saturday evening?"

"Vivian Templeton's Christmas party. I told you about it the last time we talked."

"Right." He'd gotten the invitation. Tossed it somewhere. "I don't even know the lady. Why is it you want me to go?"

"Because, regardless of what your grandfather wants us to think, it's the polite thing to do. She's just dropped a ton of money on the hospital. The woman is family whether Squire wants to admit it or not, and we're going to act like it."

Justin still didn't think his presence would matter to Vivian Templeton one way or another. But it obviously mattered to his mother. And he didn't need to be at cross-purposes with yet another female. "I can spare a few hours."

"You'll need a tux."

He managed not to swear out loud. Tuxedos in Weaver were about the most outlandish thing that he could imagine. "Fine."

"Justin—"

"I'll have a tux," he assured her, containing his impatience with an effort. "You get the same promise from Erik?"

"Erik is Izzy's problem," Hope said. "But I'm sure she'll succeed."

No doubt. His brother would turn cartwheels in a tutu for his wife, particularly now that she was pregnant with their child.

Justin's phone vibrated in his hand, alerting him to another call. "Got another call, Mom. If I don't see you before then, I'll see you Saturday."

"All right. I love you, honey."

"You, too." More interested in getting off the hook with her while he was still in her good graces than anything else, he switched calls. "Yes?"

"Justin, my boy! Charles here. How is the report coming?"

Justin grimaced. Sometimes you were the bug. Sometimes you were the windshield. These days, he was feeling like he was both. "It's coming, Charles."

"I don't have to remind you what it'll mean to the company if you get it completed on time."

"I know." He opened the door and looked out at the falling snow. He'd forgotten that it could actually be a pretty sight. But what really caught his attention was the car pulling into the driveway.

Tabby's car.

"Can I ask you a favor, Charles?"

"As long as it doesn't cost me a few more million dollars."

"Can you send someone over to my apartment?

Someone other than Gillian. Strangely enough, I need to have a tux shipped here by Saturday."

"My secretary can take care of it."

"Thanks. If there's nothing else you needed, I've got a report to get back to."

"That's what I like to hear, my boy. Exactly what I like to hear."

Justin ended the call, pocketing the phone as he stepped off the porch and headed toward Tabby's vehicle. The moment she opened the car door, the puppy escaped, racing toward him so fast she practically tripped over her own long ears.

He scooped her up, and she licked his face a few times before scrabbling at him to be let back down again. The second he did so, she was off like a bolt toward Tabby, who was already on her porch, unlocking the door.

He followed the dog, hoping to make it before Tabby could close the door in his face.

And he would have, too. If his shoe hadn't landed in a pile of dog poop, sending him sliding in the slick snow.

He landed flat on his back, the breath slamming out of him as he stared up at the flecks of white coming down at him from the solid gray sky.

Perfect. Just perfect.

"Oh, my goodness." Mrs. Wachowski opened her door and peered out at him lying half in and half out of the bushes lining the front of her unit. "I saw you through my window. Are you hurt?"

He coughed. "Besides my pride?" He winced when Beastie pounced on his chest. "I'll survive." He sat up and eyed Tabby's door. Which was now closed.

Probably locked again. At least against him.

"Ever have one of those days, Mrs. Wachowski?"

"Sure." She left her porch and bent over beside him, tucking her frail hand beneath his arm. He didn't need her assistance as he got to his feet, but he couldn't help appreciating her effort. "Then I finally retired from teaching history to hooligans like you and that Rasmussen boy, and they stopped." She dashed her hands over his shoulders, brushing away the clinging snow. "There you are. Right as rain. You're certain you're not hurt anywhere?"

He glanced at Tabby's closed door again. "Once I deal with the mess I'm in, I'll be fine."

She wrinkled her nose, obviously thinking he meant the dark smear on his shoe. "Fortunately, messes clean up." She patted his shoulder and returned to her door, going inside.

Justin exhaled and scraped his sole against the edge of the sidewalk as well as he could. Then he continued to Tabby's door and knocked.

The porch light flicked on, and she answered so immediately he wondered if she'd seen his ignominious tumble. "We need to talk."

"Not really." She brushed past him, pulling the door closed again. "I'm on my way out."

"You just got back."

"So?"

"Where are you going now?"

She lifted her eyebrows and headed toward her car. "I don't believe that's any of your business, actually."

"Got a call from my mother because she heard we'd been fighting at the diner. She's concerned about... dissension."

She stopped and looked back at him. "There's no dissension."

He rubbed the puppy's silky head where she'd tucked it under his chin. "That's what I told her."

"So we're both liars," he heard her mutter. "I knew this would happen."

He closed the distance between them. It was getting darker by the second. "There's an easy solution."

She gave him a disbelieving look. "Easy."

He continued, speaking over her. "Have an adult conversation with me for once about what's going on."

"We had sex," she said tightly. "And it was a mistake. That's what's going on."

"I don't think sex was a mistake. I think most everything that's happened since we had sex has been a mistake."

She looked away, dashing a snowflake off her face. "I feel like we're in the middle of a fishbowl," she muttered. "Mrs. Wachowski's watching us through her front window."

"And Mr. Rowe's pretending to sweep snow off his front porch while he looks this way. We are in a fishbowl. That doesn't change anything. We had sex, Tabby. I wasn't doing you some damn sort of favor. We kissed, and that's all she wrote. I thought you were right there with me, but I guess I was wrong."

Her gaze flicked up to his. She moistened her lips. "You weren't wrong," she said almost inaudibly.

Only the knowledge that they were being watched kept him from reaching for her. "Then what's the problem?"

"Besides not wanting to upset either one of our families? I don't want to get used to something that's not going to last."

He opened his mouth to argue the point but couldn't.

And her expression said she knew it. "You're going to finish your work soon and go back to Boston. And I'm going to be here."

"Come with me."

He didn't know where the words had come from, but they were out there now. And she was staring at him as if he'd suggested she move to Mars. "Go *with* you! What are you—"

"You can paint there," he said over her words. "Just as easily as you can paint here."

She blinked, going quiet for a moment. "Painting is my hobby," she finally said.

"One you're earning money doing."

"Yes. But I still enjoy it because it *is* a hobby. If I *had* to paint for my living?" She shook her head.

"Then don't paint!" Something was slipping through his fingers, and he wasn't even sure what it was. "Do something else. Anything else that you want to do. You can live with me. Or…or find a place of your own." That wasn't at all what he wanted, but if he just got her out there, he could sway her.

His gut tightened. He was pretty sure he could.

Her head tilted slightly, and her dark hair slid over her shoulder. She reached out and brushed her fingertips over Beastie's sleeping head. "I am doing what I want to do, Justin. I don't stay in Weaver because I'm afraid to go out into the big bad world. I stay because this is my home. Because every…everything I love is here. You used to understand that. I thought you did, anyway."

"If this is still about what happened four years ago—"

"It's not. What you want out of life has always been different than what I want out of life. When we were kids it didn't matter. But we're not kids anymore. I'm not the kind of girl who can do the friends-with-benefits thing. That might be fine for someone else, but it's just not in my genetic makeup, I guess. I still believe sex should mean more than that. And now that we've gone *there*—" she waved her hand "—I don't know how to get back to just being friends again. Either I get mad. Or you get mad. And someone inevitably notices. You're going to be here for another few weeks, so if only for the sake of a little sanity and keeping our families from getting needlessly upset, I think it would be best if we keep our distance from each other. At least when we have a choice about it."

"What if I don't agree?"

She lifted her shoulder. "Give me a better solution."

He stared at her. Unfortunately, he didn't have one.

So when she broke the tense silence between them by getting in her car, he didn't stop her.

Instead, he watched the taillights of her old car until they were no longer in sight.

Chapter Twelve

"Tabby!" Hayley Banyon, looking elegantly beautiful in a royal blue gown, caught Tabby's hands and leaned forward to kiss her cheek. "I'm so glad to see you." Then she looked up at Bubba. "My goodness, Bubba. Look at you."

Tabby's cook grimaced. He was clean shaven—something she wasn't sure she'd ever seen before. He looked as though he already wanted to rip off his black bow tie, even though they'd just arrived at the party. "Feel like a trussed-up penguin," he said, tugging at his black tuxedo jacket.

"You don't look like a penguin," Hayley assured him. "You're downright handsome."

Which was a compliment that only made Bubba look even more uncomfortable. He muttered a gruff "thank you" that made Hayley's smile widen. She squeezed Tabby's hands once again before excusing herself to greet more people as they entered the high-ceilinged, marble-floored foyer.

Come with me.

Tabby shook the memory of Justin's words out of her

head and slid her hand around Bubba's arm, urging him past the beautifully decorated Christmas tree situated in the center of the spacious entry. She wanted to be there about as much as she wanted holes drilled in her head.

But she wasn't going to let Bubba down just because Justin Clay once again had her twisted in knots. *Come with me.* Just like that. Drop everything that mattered in her life to go with him simply because he'd discovered having sex with her wasn't so bad, after all.

"The sooner Vivian sees you here, the sooner you can leave," she said under her breath.

Bubba made a face. "I never wore stuff like this before."

"I've never worn an evening gown, either," Tabby said, brushing her hand down the heavy red fabric of her dress. "I'll be lucky if I don't trip over the thing and fall on my face. The only floor-length thing I've ever worn was a flannel nightgown when I was little."

As she'd hoped, Bubba's expression lightened up a little. "You don't have on your cowboy boots underneath there, do you?"

"I wish." She lifted the hem a few inches off the floor to reveal the high-heeled pumps her mother had loaned her to go with the dress. "It's going to take alcohol to make me forget the way these shoes are pinching my toes." Though why it might work for her aching toes when it didn't work to help her forget those three little words—*come with me*—she couldn't imagine.

"Pretty sure there'll be plenty of alcohol," Bubba said as they entered a living area that made even Hope and Tristan Clay's great room look small. "I've seen the boxes of stuff Montrose has been getting."

Despite herself, she realized she was gaping at the sight of the room around them, and she made herself stop.

She'd never seen so many pieces of gold furniture in one place before. But then, she'd also never seen people she'd known all of her life dressed in this much formal wear before, either. Not even at the hospital fund-raiser.

She blinked a little at the sight of Tristan Clay, decked out in a tux just as black as Bubba's. But Justin's dad wore his with enviable ease. Probably because he owned and operated the hugely successful Cee-Vid and was more accustomed to such ostentatious displays. Hope, who was standing beside her husband, looked positively radiant in a deep purple gown. They seemed deep in conversation with a couple Tabby didn't know who were similarly attired.

Even though she knew her mom had been glad for a legitimate excuse to miss the party, she was sorry that Jolie wasn't there to see all the glamour.

Right here in Weaver.

For the first time in days, the matter of Justin Clay edged slightly to one side in her mind.

"Bubba," she murmured. "I don't think we're in Kansas anymore."

He responded by turning her slightly so she could see the hostess where she was standing by a tall window, talking with a stern-looking man.

Tabby had only seen Vivian in person a few times. She figured Hayley's grandmother was probably in her eighties. But there was nothing exactly elderly about the white-haired woman. Even though Tabby's mother had described the gown she'd made for Vivian, she still blinked a little at the sight of it. Yards of white satin ought to have overwhelmed the diminutive woman, but they didn't. The shining gold fabric tied around her waist in an oversize bow ought to have seemed silly, but it didn't. Plus it matched the fancy little bolero jacket she wore.

"Do you think she planned it so she'd match the gold flecks in the upholstery?"

Fortunately, Bubba's guffaw was drowned out by Christmas music and conversation. "Knowing her, she might have." Evidently losing interest, he gestured toward a table that was set up as a bar. "Alcohol's over there."

Tabby gratefully headed over with him. This whole thing was feeling decidedly surreal, and fortification would be necessary if and when Justin got there. She'd been praying for two solid days that he'd get so involved with his work that he'd forget all about the party.

But if her prayers of the cowardly variety were answered on a regular basis, he would've gone back to Boston after Thanksgiving the way he usually did.

Gathering her wits about her, she glanced at the elaborate display spread out on the white-and-gold cloth covering the table. There was nothing as simple as beer on offer, which was one more indication that Hayley's grandmother expected those around her to adjust to her style, rather than the other way around.

What else could explain a woman who drove a Rolls-Royce around Weaver when a pickup or SUV would have been far more sensible?

Bubba seemed to take it more in stride, but then he had more personal experience with their hostess than Tabby. He simply poured himself a healthy measure of whiskey and muttered something about needing some fresh air. Tabby let him go. He was more familiar with the big new house than she was, after all.

She studied the collection of wine bottles for a moment, then chose a pinot noir. She took one sip and groaned a little.

"Something wrong with the wine?"

Startled, she glanced up at the tall man who'd stepped behind the table. "Not at all." She smiled ruefully. "It's too good. I'm afraid the usual stuff I drink is never going to satisfy me now."

"My grandmother has good taste in liquor and wine. But—" he angled his blond head and smiled "—I wish she didn't think beer was beneath her." His eyes glinted. "I might survive the evening, though, if you'll tell me that you and I aren't related."

"Mrs. Templeton is your grandmother?"

He glanced over at their hostess, who now seemed to be in heated discussion with her companion. "Yes. And that guy she's arguing with is my old man." He looked back at Tabby and stuck his hand over the bottles. "Archer Templeton."

Tabby's smile widened as she shook his hand. "You're Hayley's brother. The lawyer, right?"

"Guilty."

"She's mentioned you a few times. I'm Tabby Taggart. And I'll admit to knowing quite a few of the people here, but I'm definitely not related to any of them." Never would be.

Come with me. As what?

Archer didn't immediately release her hand. "The evening is looking up."

She flushed a little. It was hard not to. The man was crazy handsome and possessed a devilish smile. If she didn't already know the futility of it, she might have wondered if he was rocket worthy.

She slipped her hand away from his and tucked her hair behind one ear. "Do you live in Braden, Archer?"

"Sort of. I have a house there." He dropped a few ice cubes into a glass and splashed vodka over them before tossing in a few olives. "I spend more of my time in Cheyenne. Sometimes Denver." He lifted his drink. "My dad's idea of a martini." He squinted a little as he took a sip. "So if you're not one of our newfound kin, are you here with one? Hayley says our granny was choosy with her invites."

"I'm here with Bub—er, Robert Bumble." The name obviously meant nothing to him. "He cooks for your grandmother when Montrose is off."

"Ah." Archer nodded his head. "And is it serious between you and 'Bub—er, Robert'?"

She couldn't help but smile. "I would be lost without him," she said seriously, then chuckled when Archer frowned. "We actually work together," she admitted. "I run a diner here in Weaver. He's our regular cook. And I honestly couldn't do it without him."

"Well, then." His frown disappeared, and he held up his highball glass between them. "To new friends."

She narrowed her eyes at him. "Something tells me you already have a lot of *friends*, Archer."

His smile deepened. "I'll plead the Fifth on that."

She laughed and tapped the side of her wineglass against his. "To new friends."

Entering the room on Erik and Izzy's heels, Justin immediately spotted Tabby. It was hard not to. Just as she had at the hospital fund-raiser, she stood out like a shining beacon. Only tonight, instead of a shimmery white dress that stopped midthigh, she was wrapped in red from neck to toe. The only things left bare were her sleekly muscled shoulders and arms. She'd done something to her hair, too. It was as shiny as ever, but it was straight and smooth as glass, streaming behind her back.

She was Tabby. Yet she wasn't.

He was vaguely aware of Erik saying something, and then his brother and sister-in-law were crossing the fancy room, leaving him behind.

He watched Tabby and a strange man share a toast and a smile that looked way too friendly and felt his fists curl.

Without conscious thought, he moved over to them and put his arm around her. When she jumped, he merely cupped his palm around her shoulder, holding her still. "How's the wine?"

The look she gave him spoke volumes.

It didn't stop him from sliding the glass right out of her fingers. He absently did the ritual wine-tasting bit he'd perfected because of CNJ. Swirl. Sniff. Sip. He'd done it with heads of corporations and medical institutions. But he didn't take his eyes off the other man, who was giving him an assessing look in return.

"Not bad," he said, taking a longer sip. "Who's your new friend, Tab?"

She was rigid beside him. "Your cousin, actually," she said through her teeth. "Dr. Justin Clay, meet Archer Templeton." She turned away from him with a sharp little jerk that dislodged his hand. "It's been very nice meeting you, Archer. But if you'll excuse me, I'm going to go find my date." She walked away.

Both men watched her, though Archer was the one

to break his stare first. "Doctor," he drawled. "Hayley gave me the rundown, but I didn't pay her much attention. My uncle is a pediatrician."

"Not that kind of doctor. Tabby just likes jerking my chain."

"Hmm." Archer looked amused and belatedly stuck out his hand. "Which one of Squire Clay's sons do you belong to?"

Justin was supposed to be a civilized man. He crushed the appealing notion of dragging Tabby away where she'd be out of reach of guys like Archer and reluctantly shook the other man's hand. "Tristan is my father. I'm his youngest. He's Squire's youngest. And you? Where do you fit?"

Archer jerked his chin toward a white-haired lady wearing a set expression. "That gray-haired guy arguing with Granny Vivian? He's my father, Carter. Also her youngest."

Erik had reiterated the history for Justin before they'd entered the palatial house. "Your grandfather and my grandfather's first wife were brother and sister."

"Half brother and sister. But, yeah. My grandfather never knew about her, though, until they were adults."

"Your grandfather died when he was still a young man." Erik had told him that, too.

Archer nodded. "And your grandmother died while she was still a young woman." He glanced again at his grandmother. "Viv managed to piss off a lot of people in her day, including your grandfather. Otherwise, we might have learned about each other long before now. But she's trying to make up for it."

"Someone should tell her that dropping a pile of money on the hospital isn't going to sway my grandfather. Squire makes up his mind about something, it's not likely to change. Before my dad was even born, your grandmother disrespected Squire's wife because she was illegitimate. Obviously she didn't have a problem with your grandfather—she named my uncle after him. But my grandfather won't ever forget."

Archer shrugged. "I only met her earlier this year myself, but I already know that Vivian doesn't change her mind, either. Even if she has to build a brand-new fence around the obstacle of your grandfather, she's going to keep mending the rest of them. Trying to, at least. I can give her credit for that, even though my father won't."

"Seems our families have even more in common," Justin said. "Stubborn-as-hell grandparents."

"And similar taste in women." Archer's gaze traveled past Justin, obviously watching Tabby again.

Forget civilized. "She's off the market," he said flatly.

The other man's eyebrows rose. "She didn't give me that impression."

"Regardless. Look somewhere else."

Archer eyed him for a moment. Then he shrugged and topped off his glass with a shot of vodka. "Glad to meet you, Doc. I think we all might be in for an interesting evening," he added as he walked away.

Justin doubted it. If he hadn't heard from three different people that week that Tabby was going to be there with Bubba, he would have excused himself from going altogether, no matter what he'd promised his mother. He still had work to do, and the deadline was looming larger with every passing day.

But he was glad he was there. Archer Templeton was a player. Justin recognized the type.

And there was no way the guy was going to play with Tabby.

Since she'd scraped away his suggestion about Boston the way he'd scraped dog crap from his shoe, he hadn't seen or spoken with her. Until tonight.

From the corner of his eye, he saw her hugging Izzy. Physically, the two women couldn't have been more different. Izzy was short and curvaceous with white-blond hair. Tabby was tall and lean with brown hair so dark it was almost black.

But for a moment—a moment that had his hair standing on end—he imagined Tabby with a baby bump like the one Izzy sported.

He abruptly set down the whiskey he'd been about to pour into a glass and reached instead for one of the fancy-looking bottles of water. It was the same brand that Gillian used to request whenever they'd gone out. He removed the pretentious cork top and took a long drink. As it always had before, the stupidly expensive stuff tasted no better than the tap water he'd grown up with.

His parents waylaid him before he could head Tabby's way again, and he found himself enduring more Templeton introductions. So many, in fact, that he started regretting the water-over-whiskey choice. Then his aunt Rebecca and uncle Sawyer arrived, and she wanted to know how his space was working at the lab. He was in the middle of that conversation when a streak of red entered his line of sight.

"How *dare* you," Tabby said, shoving his shoulder hard. "I'm *off the market*?" Her voice rose above the music and conversation, which dwindled to nothing in the wake of her furious words.

"Calm down. You're overreacting."

Her expression grew even angrier. "*You* are the biggest jerk I have ever known. Why I ever thought I—" She pressed her lips together, breathing hard. "You know what?" She waved her hand. "I'm done. I'm just done. Weaver obviously isn't large enough for the two of us. I thought I could stick it out until you go back to Boston, but I was wrong." She turned away so sharply that her hair spun out from her shoulders.

Not caring about the shocked attention they were getting, he grabbed her arm, halting her progress. "What do you mean, you're *done*?"

She yanked out of his grip. Tears glittered in her eyes. "I mean I don't want anything to do with you! I want you out of my triplex and out of my life."

Panic slid through his gut. "That's never gonna happen. Ruby's—"

She pushed her shaking hands through her hair, raking it back from her face. "Forget Ruby's! I want no part of it as long as you're part of that equation. I *quit*!"

Chapter Thirteen

"I warned everyone that no good would come outta that woman's Christmas party last night." Justin's grandfather sat down across from him at the big round table in the Double-C's kitchen. "But nobody wants to listen to an old man anymore."

Gloria snorted softly. "Don't try the poor-me tack, Squire. Nobody buys it." She set a pitcher of syrup on the table next to the waffle she'd already given Justin. A waffle he didn't want, but one he didn't have the heart to deny.

Not when his grandmother and grandfather were the only ones who hadn't basically slammed a door in his face.

His parents were furious.

His brother was livid.

The rest of the family had pretty much been disgusted. His uncle Matt—who ran the ranch and along with his wife lived in the big house with Squire and Gloria—had blandly suggested Justin bed down in the barn. He hadn't been joking.

The howling puppy Justin had been trying to contain had received a better welcome. Jaimie had grabbed Beastie and disappeared upstairs with her, crooning softly.

Gloria had intervened on Justin's behalf, though, ushering him personally down to the basement and one of the guest rooms there.

"Vivian didn't do a thing," his grandmother went on, taking the seat next to Justin.

"How do you know?" Squire demanded testily. "You weren't there."

"Only because I didn't want you to work yourself into a heart attack if I went," she countered mildly. "I've gotten enough accounts from everyone to feel like I was. Get off your high horse, dear. This isn't about Vivian. It's about Justin."

"And Tabby." His grandfather's gaze pierced through him. "I've always had a soft spot for that little filly. What the hell did you do to her?"

Justin pushed aside his untouched plate. He didn't even want to have breakfast with himself. Was it any wonder Matt and Jaimie had avoided him, too? Not even Beastie had found her way to his lap.

"Squire," Gloria chided softly. "Barking won't solve anything." She covered Justin's clenched fist with her cool palm. "I'm sure everything will work out."

"Yeah," Justin muttered. "Once I haul my ass back to Boston. Sorry, Grandma."

She looked vaguely amused. "I've certainly heard worse. And from all accounts, you behaved like an ass last night. Fortunately, I have plenty of practice loving people who do that." She slid her gaze to her husband as she squeezed Justin's fist with one hand and moved the plate back in front of him with her other. "But not eating won't help, either."

"Only you have the gift of making me feel chastised and cherished all at the same time."

Squire thumped the end of his walking stick against the wood floor. "That's why I married her, boy." He grinned at his own humor and actually winked at Gloria.

Justin scrubbed his hands down his face. "None of this would've happened if she'd have just come to Boston with me," he muttered. He dropped his hands and stabbed his fork into the waffle, then realized that his grandparents were staring at him.

Gloria leaned toward him. "You asked Tabby to go to Boston?"

He set down the fork again. "For all the good it did. She turned me down. Flat. Cares more about the diner and Weaver than she does anything else." He caught the look the two of them exchanged. "She was pretty clear," he said in self-defense.

"But she quit managing the diner." Gloria sat back. "In front of close to fifty people, it sounds like."

"She doesn't mean it."

Neither Gloria nor Squire looked convinced.

"She doesn't." Justin's tone was confident, but only because it stemmed from something that felt uncomfortably like desperation churning inside him. "Tomorrow morning comes around, she'll be serving up those cinnamon rolls of hers at Ruby's just like usual."

She wasn't.

The diner *did* open.

Bubba had seen to that, according to Erik, who came

by the hospital Monday afternoon to lay into Justin again about the whole thing.

But Tabby had never shown. Bubba had assured Erik that she wasn't going to, either, and had grimly produced the keys to the restaurant that Tabby's brother had dropped off.

"What the hell went on between you, anyway?" Justin's brother filled the doorway of the office he was using.

He shut the laptop and the damned report he was trying and failing to write. "Nothing that's anyone else's business."

Erik gave him a look. "This is Weaver. You don't want other people in your business, you shouldn't be having scenes like you did the other night at that party."

"Did you come here to offer any helpful advice or just to bust my chops some more?"

His brother's expression darkened. "Dammit, Justin. This isn't a joke."

He stood so fast that the rolling stool he'd been using bounced off the wall and tipped onto its side. "You think I don't know that?" He got into his brother's face, staring him straight in the eye. "This is my *life*, Erik. When have you ever known me not to take that pretty freaking seriously?"

They were the same height, but his brother outweighed him by a good thirty pounds. Erik had always been patient. Peaceful. It was Justin who'd been an instigator, always trying to take down his older, brawnier brother. There'd been few times in their childhood when Erik hadn't been able to flatten Justin just from his sheer strength. Until Justin had gotten smarter. Wilier. Used his brains against his brother's brawn. Stopped trying to measure up in an area where he never could and started focusing on his own strengths. His own dreams.

Tabby had been the one to help him realize that.

His anger oozed out of him.

What was left was weariness.

He turned away from Erik, righted the stool and sat down on it. "She hates me."

Erik glanced behind him at the hospital lab, then stepped into the office and closed the door. There wasn't another seat, and he leaned back against the door, folding his arms over his chest and the visitor ID tag he was wearing. "Despite the somewhat overwhelming evidence, I kind of doubt it."

"I never should've slept with her."

Erik's eyes sharpened. "So that's it." Then he smiled faintly and shook his head. "I always wondered. The two of you were as close as Frick and Frack when we were kids. Even when you left for college and took up with Nosebleed. So what's the problem?"

"She won't come to Boston."

Erik's eyebrows shot up. "You asked Tabby to marry you?"

"*What?* No!" Justin shoved off the stool again. The office was suddenly too claustrophobic with the door closed, but he didn't want to open it and chance even more people overhearing his business.

"Well, what *did* you say?"

"I asked her to come! I got a 'thanks, but no thanks' in return."

Erik rubbed his hand over his face, looking as though he was trying not to laugh.

It annoyed Justin as much now as it had when they were kids. "Glad I'm entertaining you, bro."

Erik dropped his hand. "For a guy who runs circles around me in the brains department, you are an idiot."

"Once again. Helpful."

"Jesus, Justin. This isn't rocket science or the cure to cancer. Are you in love with Tabby or not?"

"What good does it do me if I am?"

His brother's eyes were laughing. "You've got fifty square feet in here, genius. Don't need to yell."

"I should've poisoned you with my chemistry set when we were kids."

"I'd have seen you coming and just dumped you in the water trough." Erik shook his head again and wrapped his arm around Justin's neck in a hug disguised as a choke hold. "You're a damn idiot, but you're my brother and I love you. So I'm gonna help you even though I came here to kick your butt."

He released the choke hold and pushed Justin toward the stool. "When you asked Tabby—and when I say *asked*, I'm playing fast and loose with the term— did you happen to mention the way you feel about her? I might not have a bunch of university diplomas on my walls, but I have learned a thing or two about women. And one is that you have to say the words!"

The spot between Justin's shoulder blades itched. "Tabby knows me better than anybody."

"Really?" Erik leaned back against the door again. "And I'll bet you think you know her just as well." He spread his arms. "How's that working out for you?"

Justin pushed open his laptop again. "I'll get her back to the diner."

Erik swore. "If you think this is about the diner, you

are even more dimwitted than I thought. And maybe you do deserve Nosebleed." He yanked open the office door. "Fix it, Justin. Not for me. Not for Mom and Dad. Fix it for you. And for her." Then he stepped out of the office and slammed the door.

"Tabby." Jolie followed her from the bedroom back out to the living room. She'd shown up as soon as she heard Evan had dropped off Tabby's keys with Bubba. "I know you're upset. But that diner means everything to you. Are you sure you don't want to reconsider quitting?"

Tabby set the cellophane tape she'd just retrieved on the coffee table and sat down on the floor. The only Christmas gifts she'd managed to get so far were for her nieces and nephew. At least she'd bought them before she'd quit her job. "I'm sure." She unrolled the wrapping paper.

Her mom sat on the couch beside her, setting her hand on Tabby's shoulder. "Honey."

Tabby blinked away the moisture that glazed her vision. "I'm fine."

Jolie sighed and moved her hand away. "I should have seen what was going on between you and Justin."

"Why?" She sniffed and tore off a piece of tape, securing the festive red-and-green paper in place. "Not even Justin can see it." She snapped off another piece. "Of course he's an impossible male," she added darkly.

"They all are at one time or another," Jolie replied. "Even your father. It's in their genetic code, I think. Just as being an impossible female at one time or another is in ours."

Tabby's lips twisted. "Fair-minded as always."

"Have you, ah, spoken with him since—"

"Nope. No reason to. We've said more than enough."

"Hope told me he's staying at the Double-C."

Her hands faltered for a moment. "Good place for Beastie," she said. And Justin had always had a soft spot for his grandmother. And Gloria for him.

Tabby folded the ends of the paper, taped them down and finally pushed aside the wrapped box. "I'm not going to stay at your house on Christmas Eve this year. I'll, uh, I'll come over on Christmas Day instead."

"I'm not losing your company on Christmas Eve because you're afraid of running into Justin."

"I'm not afraid," she muttered. "But I embarrassed myself in front of everyone at Vivian Templeton's party. I'd rather just—"

"Hide."

She wasn't going to deny it. "If that's how you want to put it."

"You're my daughter. If it's a choice between you and the Clays—"

"Don't." She pushed off the floor and paced around the couch. "You and Hope are like sisters. You're not going to change a tradition I've known my entire life because of this. That's exactly what I wanted to avoid!"

Her mom sighed. "Well. Christmas Eve is still five days away. We'll figure it out."

Jolie could do all the figuring she wanted. But it wouldn't change Tabby's mind.

"I'm just glad you've got income coming in from your paintings. But if you need money—"

"I'm not going to ask you for money," Tabby cut her off before she could go any further. "I'm an adult. I have savings. And I'll find another job." She pushed her fingers into her pockets so her mom couldn't see them shaking. "In fact, I have enough savings that maybe I should just open my own restaurant! It would have to be smaller than Ruby's. But with the right space, the right staff?"

Instead of looking comforted, her mother just seemed even more alarmed. "Opening a restaurant is a huge undertaking."

"Yeah, well, maybe it's time I did something huge." Besides sleeping with Justin or causing a scene in front of darn near the entire Clay family.

Jolie glanced at her watch and pushed off the couch. "I don't want to go, but I'm doing a fitting with the mayor's wife. She's throwing a New Year's Eve party for the town council." She caught Tabby's shoulders and gave her a steady look. "Don't do anything rash."

"Anything more rash than I already have, you mean?"

"Yes." She kissed Tabby's cheek. "Call me if you need me."

"I'm fine, Mom."

"Mmm." She tucked her finger under Tabby's chin. "I remember what it feels like when your heart is breaking. So you call your mother if you need her."

Tabby's eyes flooded, and she caught her mom in a fast, tight hug. "I'll always need you," she promised thickly. Then she let her go and sniffed hard. "Now go on for your appointment before we start bawling."

"Tell me what you're doing for the rest of the day."

"I'm not going to throw myself off a cliff, if that's what you're worried about." She gestured at the toys sitting on her coffee table. "I still have to finish wrapping these. And I never got around to putting up a Christmas tree here." Her throat tightened again. She hadn't needed to, because she'd already put up the tree at Ruby's. "There's a tree lot in Braden. I might drive over and get one."

"For heaven's sake. We always cut ours fresh from behind—"

"Rebecca and Sawyer's house." She shrugged. "I'd just rather buy one." She wished she hadn't even brought up the subject, which she'd only done in order to emphasize just how fine she supposedly was. "We'll see."

"If you're going to go, don't go too late. They're calling for a winter storm by tonight." Jolie looked at her watch again and muttered a soft oath.

Tabby opened the door and nudged her mom through the doorway, getting a gust of icy-cold wind in exchange. "Go. I am—ugh. I *will* be fine." She'd been getting over Justin for years now. She ought to be used to the process by now.

She waited until her mother reached her SUV parked on the street before she closed the door and leaned back against it.

Who was she kidding?

She was never going to be used to anything when it came to Justin.

She sat back down at her coffee table and finished wrapping the presents, only to realize she was missing one for Hannah. The custom storybook was still in her locker at Ruby's.

Swearing under her breath, she looked at the clock. If she hurried, she could get to the diner before it closed up for the day.

She grabbed her coat and keys and headed out. Once she was done there, she'd keep driving on to Braden.

Get that Christmas tree.

She'd be back before dark, and tonight, anyone driving by her place would see a festively lit Christmas tree through her front window.

She was going to act like everything was fine, even if it killed her.

When he started out that morning, Justin had intended on finishing at least the first rough draft of his paper before calling it quits for the day. Getting raked over the coals by Erik had been only one of his interruptions. But even if he'd had none at all, he still wouldn't have gotten anything more accomplished than the few pages of crap he'd managed to eke out.

The hospital had been issuing announcements all day about the coming storm. Nonessential personnel were sent home. Medical teams were put on alert.

After hearing the same announcement for about the tenth time and staring at the same nonsensical paragraph in his paper for just as long, he finally packed it in. He shoved his materials into his messenger bag, locked up the office and signed out of the lab.

Outside, the weather had turned to crap. The sky couldn't seem to decide if it wanted to spit out ice or rain or snow. It wasn't dark yet, but it might as well have been with the solid sky and miserable visibility.

He flipped up his collar and bent his head against the driving cold as he ran across the lot to his truck. He saw at least a half dozen other people doing the same thing and hoped they didn't have far to drive.

He cranked the engine and mentally blessed his uncle Matt, whose attention to everything on the Double-C—equipment, vehicles, stock—was as reliable as always. The cold engine started without a hitch. He let it run for several minutes until the heater kicked in. By the time it did, he was shivering from the cold.

"Couldn't wait until I go back to Boston to throw down the weather, I guess," he said to the universe at large and finally put the truck in gear. He didn't even realize he was heading toward the triplex until he turned the corner of Tabby's street, and he cursed his distraction. He noticed her gunboat of a car wasn't parked in the driveway when he used it to turn around and reverse course.

His tires slid as he turned the corner again, and he swore once more. Getting out to the Double-C in this frozen soup wasn't going to be a picnic. Trying at this point wasn't particularly anything he wanted to do, either.

Waiting out the storm somewhere was an option. Except the weather report said they were in for hours of it. Sleeping in his own bed at the triplex was out, but some of his cousins had places in town. The entire family was pissed with him, but not everyone would turn him out in a storm like this.

And if they did, he'd rent a bloody room at the Cozy Motel if he had to.

There were only a few other cars on Main Street as he stopped in front of Ruby's and pulled out his cell phone. He wasn't surprised that the service was out. The lights were still on in the diner, though. Leaving his truck running so he wouldn't lose the heat, he darted across the sidewalk to pull on the glass door. It was locked, and he banged his hand on it hard enough to raise the attention of Bubba back in the kitchen.

Only it wasn't Bubba who appeared and quickly crossed the diner to let him in. It was that one waitress whose name he kept forgetting. "Hey," he greeted, glancing at her name tag. "Paulette. Just need to use the phone." He started toward the counter and the kitchen door. "Weather's getting really bad. Do you have far to go to get home?"

"No." She shook her head, following on his heels. "I'm just over by the community church. Uh—"

He pushed through the swinging door and came to a dead stop at the sight of Tabby, stuck half inside the oven. "Have you decided to play Gretel now?"

She jerked her head out so fast she banged it on the edge of the oven. She rubbed her head, giving him a foul look, and closed the door. "I think it'll be okay for tomorrow, Paulette. But someone needs to tell the *owners* of this place that they should start planning on purchasing a new oven."

Paulette's worried gaze bounced from Tabby's face to Justin's and back again. "Um, I—"

"Paulette, you should go." He gave her a second look. "You do have a vehicle, don't you?"

The waitress nodded frantically. Eagerness oozed from her pores as she opened one of the lockers and pulled out a coat and scarf. She hadn't finished winding the scarf around her neck before she said a quick "G'bye" and left out the rear door.

The sound of the metal door slamming shut seemed to spur Tabby into action. She headed for the lockers, too, reaching into one that was already open. "I only came to get my personal belongings." She pulled out a pair of shoes and dropped them in a half-filled box sitting on the floor. A thick book and a hairbrush followed, then a ratty-looking sweater that she bunched up and shoved on top.

"You don't want to quit."

She kicked the locker door closed and picked up the box, only to set it on the stainless steel rolling table where she made her cinnamon rolls. "Au contraire." She brushed past him through the swinging door and checked the front lock while she doused the lights. Then she hit the power switch on the enormous coffee brewer and nudged on the cash register drawer to be sure it was latched.

She didn't look at him as she came back through the door he was holding for her. "I've decided to open a restaurant of my own." She sent him an insincere smile as she reached for the coat tossed over a box of paper goods.

He grunted impatiently. "You don't need to do that. Ruby's is—"

"Yours." She shoved her arms into the sleeves and flipped her hair out of the collar. It was back to normal again, full and wavy. And he knew it would feel silky and vibrant between his fingers.

"Maybe I'll even poach Bubba from you," she went on. "My rolls and his barbecue? We just might be able to put Ruby's out of business. Not that you'd mind. You never cared all that much about the place to begin with. Had bigger, better things in mind with the fancy degrees and the—"

"Shut up."

She gave him a dark look. "Don't like hearing the truth anymore?" She tsked. "You were a better man when you were ten than you are now."

"The truth?" He advanced on her. "The truth is I've got a job where I feel like the only people I'm helping are shareholders. Which means everything I've done for the past ten years has been a freaking waste of time."

Her expression didn't soften. "If you don't like what you're doing, then change it! I didn't even have to earn a doctorate to figure that one out, much less my plain-Jane online college degree. I knew being an artist wasn't for me. But running this place was."

He stopped short. "You finished your bachelor's degree? When? Why didn't you tell me?"

"A couple years ago. It wasn't that big a deal."

"You've been working here full-time since you graduated from high school. Of course it's a big deal. I know how much that mattered to you."

"Yeah, well, we weren't exactly sharing life news then." She reached for the metal door but didn't push it open. "How long have you been unhappy in your job?"

"A few years now. But like you said. We haven't been big on the whole sharing thing for a while now."

She rubbed her hand against the door latch. "Is it because of Gillian? Your job dissatisfaction, I mean."

"No. That, at least, is one thing I am certain about. Gillian and the job. No matter what anyone thought, they never went hand in hand. Not to me."

Tabby chewed her lip for a moment, then shook her head slightly. "I thought you came in to use the phone."

"I did."

"Well." She gestured at the phone hanging on the wall. "Have at it. Door here will lock automatically after you leave." She flipped up her hood and grabbed her box before pushing the door open. Sleet drove in around her.

"Tabby, wait." He crossed the kitchen in long strides and grabbed her arm, pulling her back inside and dragging the door closed again. In just those few seconds, the floor inside the doorway had gotten covered with the icy stuff. "It's not safe. Let that die down some first."

She clearly wanted to argue. But she also knew he was right. "I don't want to be here with you."

He swallowed that blow. "I know. I'm sorry."

She exhaled and pushed off her hood. Set down the box and pulled off her coat again.

Then she crossed the kitchen, giving him a wide berth, and turned on Bubba's radio. The music stuttered with static, and she twisted the dial a few times until it cleared. Without saying a word, she went through the swinging door. "You're gonna have a dead battery in that truck before long," she called back to him. "Headlights are still on."

He exhaled. He'd left the truck running. But it couldn't run forever. And if it stalled, she was right. He strode through the dim diner, unlocked the front door again and went outside. It only took a few seconds to shut off the engine and lights and return to the diner, but he still felt soaked.

She silently handed him a dry towel and then went to sit on one of the counter stools, dropping her head on her folded arms.

"You didn't use this thing to wipe the floors or toilets, did you?" As an attempt to lighten the situation, it fell pretty flat.

"Have no idea," she said, her voice muffled. "I don't work here anymore."

He ran the towel over his head, then went into the bathroom and held his hands under warm water until they didn't feel like frozen chunks.

Then he looked at himself in the ancient mirror over the plain white sink.

"Fix it," he muttered.

He dried his hands and left the bathroom. He pulled off the wet leather coat that wasn't giving him much warmth, anyway, and hung it on the coat tree by the door to dry. He checked the thermostat to make sure the heat was still running.

She hadn't moved but was still sitting there, hunched over the counter, her head on her arms, dark hair spreading over her slender shoulders.

"You were right," he said.

Chapter Fourteen

Tabby wished she could block out the sound of Justin's voice. She wished she hadn't stopped at the diner to pick up Hannah's gift. If she hadn't, she wouldn't have gotten hung up balancing the till for Paulette and then fiddling with the finicky oven. She would have been long gone before Justin came in.

Of course, she might have stupidly forged on to Braden with her prove-she-was-fine Christmas tree quest and gotten stuck out in the middle of nowhere in the storm, too.

She exhaled and straightened. "Right about what?"

"Sex should mean more than that."

She froze. Inside, though, her nerves began lashing around as violently as the sleet pounding against the windows.

"It just never did. Before."

She stared blindly at the stacks of white china on the shelves opposite her.

"Not with Gillian," he said. "Not with anyone. Even Collette, I guess, if I go back that far. It just…never did. Until you."

She clenched her teeth, feeling something hollow out inside her chest.

"You were a virgin."

She closed her eyes.

"That first time."

"It doesn't matter what I was four years ago. I said I… I forgave you." She surreptitiously swiped her cheek and cleared her throat. "And I didn't think you even noticed that."

"I noticed. I thought talking about it would've just made it worse."

She swallowed a choked laugh that held no amusement. "That logic still applies."

"I don't know why her name came out. I knew exactly who I was with. I wasn't thinking about anyone but you. I couldn't think about anyone but you. The way you felt. The way you tasted—"

"Justin, please. I can't do this."

"Why?"

Her throat felt like a vise. "Because it hurts too much," she whispered.

She heard his footsteps as he moved closer. "Why does it hurt?"

She shook her head without answering.

He stepped closer again. She couldn't see him. Didn't want to turn around and see him.

But her storming nerves imagined him standing only inches away.

"I know why I hurt." His already deep voice dropped a few more notches. "Do you want to know? Do you care? Erik—" He let out an impatient sound. "He says the words matter. God knows I've always gone out of

my way to justify how different I am from him, but he's
got the life he wants and I—"

She clenched the edge of the counter and pushed the
revolving stool around.

He wasn't standing inches behind her.

He was still halfway across the room. But even in
the dwindling, storm-drenched light from outside the
windows, she could see the tight set of his face.

"And I don't," he finished.

"You don't have to justify the person you are. You're
the only one who's ever believed that. Do you have
any idea at all how *proud* they are of you?" She gestured toward the windows. "That whole town out there
is proud of you." Tears clogged her nose. Choked her
voice. "You're our...our very...own genius."

"If I was a genius, why did I take Collette to our high
school prom?" He closed the distance between them
and slid his hands around her face, making her look up
at him, even though she tried to avoid it. "Why didn't
I take *you*? Then it would have been you and me on a
blanket spread out by the swimming hole making love
under the stars, and it *would* have meant something."
He brushed his thumbs over her wet cheeks. "It would
have meant a hell of a lot of something."

"Justin—"

"I have loved you for more years than I can remember," he said gruffly. "And I've been *in* love with you
for most of them."

She caught her lip in her teeth to keep in the sob. She
shook her head. "No."

"Yes." He brushed his mouth over hers.

She trembled. Even though she was determined not
to give in, her arms went around his neck. Her fingers

slid through his thick, damp hair. "Don't tell me you didn't like having sex with Collette after prom. You crowed about it to Caleb for days."

"That's what high school guys do." He pulled her off the stool and up against him. "And high school was a long time ago." He closed his mouth over hers again. "Kiss me back, Tabitha."

She shuddered.

And kissed him back.

His hands tightened on the small of her back, dragging her even closer, and she drew away, hauling in a desperate breath. "Justin, we can't just—"

He lifted her right off her feet and pushed through the swinging door to the kitchen, where he set her down again. "No windows here."

Before she could protest—as if she had even a whispering thought of protest—he whipped her flannel shirt over her head and dropped it on the floor. "Someone could come in."

"Ruby's closes at two." He pushed aside her thin bra strap and kissed her bare shoulder. "It's well past that. And even if it weren't—" he slid her hair away and kissed the side of her neck, then her earlobe "—just listen," he whispered.

Shivers danced down her spine. The furnace was still running, but the air in the kitchen would have been cool if not for the heat of him against her. "Listen to what?" The sound of her heartbeat thudding in her head? The sound of his breath against her ear?

"The storm. Nobody is out in that."

She closed her eyes and pulled his mouth back to hers while blindly feeling down his chest for buttons to liberate. The only storm she knew was the one collecting inside her.

Justin seemed to know it, too. His kiss deepened, and his arms hardened around her for a moment before he pulled back long enough to yank off his shirt and spread it over the stainless steel rolling table. Then he was lifting her again until she was sitting on it. Bubba's radio was spewing soft static instead of music, and rain was driving against the roof.

Justin's hand slid under her thigh, running slowly down the back of her calf as he straightened her leg and finally reached her cowboy boot, tugging it off. After removing the other one, too, he pulled her gently off the table and unfastened her jeans. Peeled them away.

Then he hauled in a deep breath that roused her out of her seduced stupor.

She ran her hands over his bare, sinewy shoulders. Trailed them over the swirl of dark hair covering his hard chest, following downward as it narrowed to a fine line, beyond the round divot that was his navel, and disappeared beneath his jeans.

As many nights as she'd spent tormented by fantasies of this very thing, her fingers shook as she fumbled with his belt. His fly.

And he just smiled faintly and brushed her hands away, finishing the job himself while he settled his lips on hers again. So slowly and sweetly that she would have fallen in love with him right then and there if she hadn't already done so half a lifetime ago. And when the rest of his clothes had gone the way of hers, he set her on the table once more and pulled her thighs around his. "Tell me, Tabby," he murmured, pressing against her, so close but not close enough. "Tell me the words."

Even though Tabby knew it wouldn't last—it couldn't possibly last when Justin had always been meant for so much more than her and the small-town life that she loved—she twined her legs around him and arched, taking him in with a gasp. "I love you, Justin. I love you, I love—" His mouth swallowed the rest.

And neither one of them said any more.

There was just the hum of static. The beat of rain.

And their bodies moving in perfection.

When they finally left the diner the next morning, they emerged into a frozen world. Ice dripped from the tree branches and the picnic table behind the diner. It had collected on the doors of her car and his truck so thickly that they couldn't get either one open.

She put up a sign that Ruby's was closed because of the weather and they walked back to the triplex, she bundled in her hooded coat and Justin in a sweatshirt of Bubba's they'd purloined from his locker layered underneath the leather jacket. It wasn't perfect, but for the three blocks, it was enough to keep both of them from frostbite.

When they got inside, she immediately went to the fireplace and set a match to the wood already there while Justin turned up the furnace and started the shower. She watched until she was sure the small flame was going to take and then pulled off her boots and went down the hall to the bathroom. The sight of steam beginning to curl around the shower curtain was welcome.

The sight of Justin without a stitch on was a revelation. The man was so physically beautiful it seemed a shock each time she witnessed it.

"Guess I don't have to worry about hot water," she said faintly.

"Nope." He tugged her close and started pulling at her clothes. "Get nekkid."

She laughed softly. "Nekkid?"

His violet eyes were wicked. "It's more fun than naked." He kissed her nose and lightly slapped her butt, then stepped into the shower. "Oh, yeah."

She pressed her hand to her chest and felt her uneven heartbeat. *Oh, yeah.*

Then she blew out a breath and quickly finished shedding her clothes. "You never called the Double-C last night."

"They'll have figured out I was at the diner. Truck's still parked in plain sight right in front of it. Sheriff's department had cruisers out. Word will have gotten back."

"I hope Beastie's okay."

He laughed. "That dog is getting better treatment than I am." He snaked an arm out from the shower curtain and yanked her under the water with him.

She laughed, too, then sputtered when she got a mouthful of hot water. "I still have on my socks!"

"Makes you all the more nekkid," he assured her and pulled her close.

Later, when the water was running cold and the bathroom floor was drenched from the splashing, she had to admit it.

Nekkid was more fun than naked.

The sun came out of the clouds that afternoon and the frozen world turned into a constantly dripping one.

Justin called the Double-C to let them know he was back at the triplex. His grandmother wryly told him that she already knew. Mrs. Wachowski had said as much to the church deacon who'd called to check in on her after the storm, and the deacon had passed it on to her daughter who housecleaned a few times a month for Hope Clay.

"And so on and so forth," Justin said after he hung up. "Life in Weaver, where everyone knows what everyone else is doing."

Tabby chewed the inside of her cheek and finished adding the dishes from their lunch to the dishwasher. "I suppose we should go back to the diner. See if the vehicles have thawed out, too."

He nodded and prowled to the front window, looking out. "At the very least I need to get my research stuff."

"For the paper you're writing." She looked away from the long line of his back, sharply outlined by the white shirt he'd been wearing since the afternoon before. "Are you close to being finished?"

His snort said it all.

She slowly shut the dishwasher door and dried her hands on a towel. "Did you decide the data was accurate at least?"

"It's accurate." He turned away from the window. "I think Mrs. Wachowski and Mr. Rowe are getting busy."

She blinked. "I...what? He's fifteen years younger than her!"

"Yeah, well." His lips tilted in a smile. "The heart wants what it wants and all that."

How well she knew it.

"You're imagining things."

"He just left her place wearing a pink flannel robe over his boxers."

She clapped her hand over her eyes as if she could

rid the image from her mind. "Oh, good grief. Don't tell me that."

Justin chuckled as he went down the hall. She thought he was going into her bedroom, but when she followed, she found him in her studio, looking through the paintings that she hadn't yet decided were good enough to give to Bolieux.

"You sent off that blizzardy-looking one, didn't you."

"Yes."

"I liked it."

"So did I. I think it was one of my better efforts." She didn't want to think about the painting or the sentiment that had inspired it. But she did know she was going to do everything she could to get it back. "I'll grab my coat and we can head out. If you're ready."

He straightened. "I am."

Less than a half hour later, they were back at the diner. It was as quiet as it had been when they left it.

"I think I'm going to stay," she said after Justin had successfully gotten into his truck and pulled out his bulging bag. "If I know you, you'll be working on that stuff the rest of the day, anyway. I might as well be useful here. Get a jump on things for tomorrow."

"Unquitting?"

She pressed her teeth together in a crooked smile. Apparently, she could no more stick to her resolution about Ruby's than get over Justin. "So it would seem."

"Good." He kissed her thoroughly, then hitched the bag over his shoulder. "I'll walk over to the hospital," he told her. "Easier than driving on ice. Call me when you're finished."

She nodded and watched until he disappeared around the corner. Then she sighed a little and went back inside the diner. No matter what had occurred between her and Justin over the past twenty-four hours, they were still the same people they'd always been.

She turned on Bubba's radio, found a station playing Christmas music without too much static and pulled on an apron.

She was crazy in love with a man who would probably never stay. Which meant there was only one thing to do.

Start another batch of dough. Same as she'd done day in and day out for years.

The lull lasted five days.

Five perfect days of Justin working at the hospital lab, and filling her nights with passion and laughter, and more than a few arguments when it came to the television remote control and whose turn it was to take Beastie out to do her business.

Five perfect days that came to a screeching halt the day before Christmas when Tabby got home from a quick run to Classic Charms only to find a painfully familiar blonde woman hanging around outside the triplex.

Even though the desire to keep driving was strong, Tabby pulled into the driveway and parked. She clipped Beastie's leash on the puppy's collar. "Come on, sweetie." She slowly pushed open the car door and climbed out of the car.

The ice from the winter storm had all melted. So had most of the snow. After Beastie hopped down from the car, she trotted over to a corner of dead grass and squatted, staring up at Tabby for approval. "Good girl," she murmured and pushed her car door closed.

She didn't speak as Gillian headed toward her, the

high heels of her tall black boots clicking on the sidewalk. She had on camel-colored pants tucked into her boots and a clinging ivory turtleneck beneath a long black leather coat that looked expensive as hell. She made Tabby, dressed in checked flannel and jeans, feel like a bumpkin.

"I remember you," the other woman greeted. "You were at that quaint little diner when I came looking for my fiancé. It appeared to be out of business when I drove by there today."

Tabby's neck stiffened. "Not out of business at all," she said. "Just closed for the holiday. What are you doing here, Gillian?"

Gillian pushed her blond hair behind her shoulder, looking pleased. "I guess Justin told you all about me."

Bat-crap crazy, Tabby thought. She didn't voice it.

"He's working at the hospital." He was finally making headway with his research paper and expected to finish it today. Then in the evening, they were heading to her parents' place to spend Christmas Eve with their families.

But Gillian shook her head. "I've been to the hospital. He wasn't there. They told me he'd left several hours ago."

Tabby ignored the uneasy surprise that niggled at her belly. There could be a dozen reasons to explain Justin's whereabouts. Just because he'd very specifically told her he'd be busy there the entire day was no cause for concern. "I can leave him a message if you like."

Gillian rolled her eyes, dismissing the offer. "I'll wait." She smiled confidently. "He'll want to see me. I came all this way, after all." She gestured toward Mrs.

Wachowski's window. "The old woman told me you own the building."

Tabby knew her neighbor was watching behind the twitching curtains. "Yes."

"Perfect. You can let me into his apartment."

"Is Justin expecting you?"

Gillian laughed lightly. "No. But he loves my little surprises. He's going to be so glad I made it for Christmas Eve. We always spend that together, no matter what's going on in our lives. It's kind of our own special time. I'm sure you understand." She held out her hand. "And I'll take our dog. Nice of you to watch her for us while Justin's busy. I hope he's paying you for it."

The niggling gained little claws that scratched from the inside. Justin hadn't been home to Weaver for Christmas in years. Before Tabby's imagination could start running riot, she handed over Beastie's leash. If nothing else, she found satisfaction in the puppy's total lack of interest in Gillian.

"So, the key?" Gillian rubbed her bare hands together. "I don't want to be an ice cube when Justin arrives."

"Sure," Tabby said, abruptly deciding that letting Gillian into the end unit was better than inviting her into her own. The other woman couldn't do any harm. There weren't even very many pieces of Justin's clothing left over there. "I'll get the key."

She unlocked her door and went inside, closing it after her, just in case Gillian got the idea of following her. She knew it was probably rude leaving her outside on the sidewalk, but she didn't care.

She called Justin's cell phone as she retrieved the spare key. Not only did he not answer, but the call went straight to his voice mail. That was typical when he was working.

But if he wasn't at the hospital, he wasn't exactly working.

"Call me when you can," she said after the beep, and hung up.

She looked at herself in the dresser mirror and abruptly grabbed her hairbrush, yanking it through her disorderly hair. Then, annoyed with herself, she tossed the brush down again, grabbed the spare key and stomped outside.

The sight of Gillian in Justin's arms punched the breath out of her.

She must have made some noise, some animal sound of distress, because Beastie bolted toward her, yanking the chain out of Gillian's grasp. The puppy shot across the sidewalk, chain dragging behind her, and vaulted into Tabby's arms.

"I knew it," she told Justin over the dog's head. "She's not out of your life."

At the sound of Tabby's wounded voice, Justin finished impatiently yanking Gillian's arms from around his neck and pushed her away. She'd launched herself at him so fast he hadn't been able to evade her. "Yes, she is," he told Tabby firmly.

Then he looked back at Gillian. "What the hell are you doing here?"

She huffed. "We spend Christmas together. We always spend Christmas together."

"*We* aren't a *we*."

"Of course we are," Gillian returned. In her typically self-involved way, she wasn't fazed at all by his cold welcome. "You're getting the promotion, by the way. Daddy told me just yesterday."

"I know I am." He looked toward Tabby where she was standing like a statue on her porch. "He called me this morning." Charles had said he wasn't waiting on the research paper. He'd made up his mind and wanted to make the announcement official before the end of the year.

And Justin had spent the rest of the morning deciding what to do about it.

"Congratulations," Tabby said. Her eyes were dark as she studied him over Beastie's silky head.

"I got a promotion, too," Gillian added.

"Your father told me." He was aware of the look she was sliding between him and Tabby.

"So you know that if I say so, *your* promotion turns to dust. Just like that." She snapped her fingers.

"I already turned it down."

He was sure the only time in the history of the world when Tabby and Gillian would think alike was that moment, when they said, *"What?"* in unison.

He ignored Gillian and focused on Tabby.

"I turned down the promotion," he said, slowly heading toward her. "In fact, I turned everything down." Aside from admitting to Tabby that he loved her, it had been one of the most freeing moments he'd ever known. "I told him I'd finish the paper. But I'm not going back."

Gillian grabbed him from behind. "Have you lost your mind?"

He shook her off. "Gillian, you don't really want me. You just don't like losing."

Her eyebrows skyrocketed. "Losing." She looked from him to Tabby. "I suppose you mean to *her*?"

He gained a visceral, abrupt understanding of Squire's continued hatred of Vivian Templeton for once snubbing his wife.

"I can be polite," he warned softly, "but wipe that sneer off your face when you look at the woman I love, or I'll do it for you."

She gaped. "You wouldn't dare."

"He wouldn't," Tabby said suddenly. She stepped off the porch and let Beastie down as she approached. Color rode her cheeks, and her dark eyes snapped. She looked like a dark-haired Valkyrie set on attack. "But I would."

"My father's never going to stand for this," Gillian warned Justin, even though she took a wary step back from Tabby.

He almost smiled at the sight of it.

"Get off my property," Tabby told her.

Gillian rolled her eyes. "People like you don't tell people like me what to do."

He saw Tabby's fist clench and caught it midair. She shot him a look, and his smile did break free. "You don't know what kind of damage I just saved you from," he told Gillian. He kissed Tabby's knuckles. "She packs a punch. Always has."

"Don't talk about me like I'm not here," Tabby said, looking as if she still wanted to break Gillian's plastic surgery–perfect nose.

He firmly peeled open her fist. Turned her palm upward and kissed it. "There's a better use for your hand," he said. He pulled the small ring box out of his pocket and set it on her palm. He'd searched all three jewelry stores in Braden that day before finding the perfect one.

Her eyes widened. Her lips parted. "What, uh, what is that?"

"You know what it is." He opened the box. The diamond ring nestled on the velvet inside sparkled in the winter sunlight. "It's our future."

She moistened her lips. Her eyes suddenly shimmered.

"Marry me, Tabby." He offered a crooked smile. "You might have to give me a job down at the diner for a while until I find gainful employment here in Weaver, but—"

"Yes," she said thickly.

Gillian made a disgusted sound. "You're an idiot, Justin Clay. You have no idea what you're turning down."

He didn't even glance at her. He was too busy sliding his ring on Tabby's trembling finger. "I'm not an idiot anymore," he said and leaned down to press his lips to hers. "I love you, Tabbers."

"I love you, too," she whispered, sliding her arms around his neck.

"I'm taking my dog," Gillian snapped and snatched up the puppy, who immediately started whining.

Tabby slid her fingers through Justin's hair and smiled into his violet eyes. Violet eyes that she'd be looking into for the rest of their lives. "She probably deserves Beastie," she murmured. "She'd love making a meal out of that leather coat Gillian's wearing."

His eyes crinkled. "Yeah. But Beastie doesn't deserve her." He snapped his fingers, and the puppy launched herself out of Gillian's arms. He scooped her up and put his other arm around Tabby again. They turned to go back into the house. "Did you finish your Christmas shopping?"

"I did." Her arm came around his waist and her head

found his shoulder. "Still in the car. I'll need to wrap it before we go to my parents. Did you really quit your job?"

"I really did." He pressed his lips against her forehead. "What time do we have to be at your folks'?"

"Little later this afternoon."

"Good." He handed Beastie to her and swept her off her feet.

She gasped, catching his shoulder with her free hand. "Justin! What are you doing?"

He laughed. "Carrying my family inside," he said and did exactly that.

Tabby glanced over his shoulder as she reached behind him to push the door closed. The only thing she saw of Gillian was the exhaust from her car as she roared away.

Tabby pushed and the door closed with a soft click. She expected him to put her down. Instead he just carried her down the hall toward the bedroom. "You're really sure about this?"

"Yup." He lowered her onto the bed and started pulling off her shirt. "Plenty of time."

She unclipped Beastie's leash and let the dog loose on the bed. The diamond ring felt strange and unfamiliar on her finger. "I mean about marrying me. About staying."

"Yup." He suddenly knelt on the floor in front of her and kissed her finger where the ring sat. "I *had* planned to wait until tonight to ask you, but when the moment strikes and all that." His eyes met hers. "Are *you* sure?"

She pressed her lips to his forehead. His cheeks. "I've been sure about you since I was fifteen years old," she whispered and brushed her lips over his.

Behind them, Beastie pawed experimentally at one of the pillows, then sank her teeth into the fabric, giving a sharp little pull. It tore, and she discovered a fantasy world of feathers that puffed out around her when she pounced. She gave a blissful yip.

Neither Tabby nor Justin even glanced her way.

Epilogue

"Happy New Year, Mrs. Clay."

Tabby wrinkled her nose against a tickle and opened her eyes to find Justin wielding a little white feather. Even after a week, they were still finding them all over the house.

She rolled toward him. "I'm not Mrs. Clay yet."

"You are in my mind." Beneath the quilt covering her bed, he swept his hand down her bare hip. "Only thing holding it up is a marriage license."

"And a wedding," she said on a chuckle that ended with a little gasp when his hand slid between her thighs. "Both—ah—both of our mothers will revolt if we don't give them that."

"So pick a date and I can stop avoiding the question when my mom calls every day asking. I think she's afraid I'll mess it up or something."

Tabby pushed his wide shoulders until he was flat on his back and slid over him. "No, she's not." She grasped his hard length and watched his eyes roll. She loved the fact that she could make him just as crazy as he made her. She balanced herself with one hand on the wall behind his head, accidentally knocking into the painting she'd recalled from Bolieux. It had arrived by messenger on Christmas Day. It had cost her a small fortune, but it was the only gift she wanted to give him. Justin had flattened her in return by giving her *his* gift—ownership of Ruby's. He and Erik had both signed the deed. She still couldn't believe they'd done it. Or that they'd refused to take it back when she argued with them that it was too much.

She moved her hand away from the wall and the painting slid back in place. "February twenty-eighth," she said, suddenly guiding him into her.

"What about it?"

"Wedding."

"Right." His fingers tightened around her hips. "Wedding. Perfect."

She exhaled shakily. "Have you decided about Rebecca's offer? The lab directorship?"

"Probably take it." He inhaled on a hiss.

"What about Charles?" His former boss hadn't taken Justin's resignation lying down. He'd come back with an offer that Justin could work wherever he wanted. As long as it was for CNJ. He'd even promised reassigning his daughter to a position in Europe—something Gillian had leaped on with glee.

"It's good to have options," Justin said and suddenly reversed their positions. "Wanna make a baby?"

She stared into his eyes, easily forgetting everything else in the world but him. "How do you know we haven't already?"

He went still. Deep inside her, she could feel the heat of him reaching to her very soul. "Trying to tell me something, Tabbers?"

She smiled slightly. "No. But we haven't exactly been careful." In fact, they'd been downright uncareful, if she wanted to put a fine point to it.

"Do you want to have a baby?"

"I want to have your babies," she whispered. She'd just never dreamed they'd ever come to be. "Beastie can't be an only child."

His smile was slow. "Well, then." He gently thumbed away the tear slipping down her cheek and lowered his mouth to hers. "Guess we'd better get to work…"

* * * * *

Don't miss these other stories in New York Times *and* USA TODAY *bestselling author Allison Leigh's long-running* RETURN TO THE DOUBLE-C *series:*

THE RANCHER'S DANCE
COURTNEY'S BABY PLAN
A WEAVER PROPOSAL
A WEAVER VOW
A WEAVER BEGINNING
A WEAVER CHRISTMAS GIFT
ONE NIGHT IN WEAVER…

Available from Mills & Boon.

MILLS & BOON®

Cherish™

EXPERIENCE THE ULTIMATE RUSH OF FALLING IN LOVE

0716/23

MILLS & BOON®

Mills & Boon have been at the heart of romance since 1908… and while the fashions may have changed, one thing remains the same: from pulse-pounding passion to the gentlest caress, we're always known how to bring romance alive.

Now, we're delighted to present you with these irresistible illustrations, inspired by the vintage glamour of our covers. So indulge your wildest dreams and unleash your imagination as we present the most iconic Mills & Boon moments of the last century.

Visit **www.millsandboon.co.uk/ArtofRomance** to order yours!

MILLS & BOON®

Why not subscribe?

Never miss a title and save money too!

Here is what's available to you if you join the exclusive **Mills & Boon® Book Club** today:

* *Titles up to a month ahead of the shops*
* *Amazing discounts*
* *Free P&P*
* *Earn Bonus Book points that can be redeemed against other titles and gifts*
* *Choose from monthly or pre-paid plans*

Still want more?

Well, if you join today we'll even give you
50% OFF your first parcel!

So visit **www.millsandboon.co.uk/subscriptions**
or call **Customer Relations on 0844 844 1351***
to be a part of this exclusive Book Club!

*This call will cost you 7 pence per minute plus your
phone company's price per minute access charge.